John Frederick Rowbotham

The Troubadours and Courts of Love

John Frederick Rowbotham

The Troubadours and Courts of Love

ISBN/EAN: 9783337412081

Printed in Europe, USA, Canada, Australia, Japan

Cover: Foto ©Andreas Hilbeck / pixelio.de

More available books at **www.hansebooks.com**

Social England Series

EDITED BY KENELM D. COTES M.A.*OXON.

THE TROUBADOURS AND COURTS OF LOVE.

BY

JOHN FREDERICK ROWBOTHAM

M.A. OXON.

*Author of " The History of Music," " The Great Composers,"
" Roland and Oliver : an Epic Poem," etc., etc.*

WITH 13 ILLUSTRATIONS AND 2 MAPS

London

SWAN SONNENSCHEIN & CO.
NEW YORK: MACMILLAN & CO.
1895

EDITORIAL PREFACE.

A New Subject. In introducing an old subject with some variety of form, it is easy to be brief and at the same time clear, because the reader supplies from previous knowledge so much that is left unsaid; but in stepping quite out of the beaten track nothing perhaps but actually treading the new path can make the goal that it is intended to reach plainly visible. It is not desirable that the whole object of a new series of books written on a new plan should be capable of being condensed into a few pages; this can be done only for subjects whose scope is already well defined, where there are and have been many previous books written on the same lines, though perhaps from slightly different points of view, and in which the only novelty to be looked for is in the style of writing and in the arrangement and amount of matter.

Personality. Undoubted as is the influence of personality upon history, the attention directed to it has hitherto been rather one-sided; the entire course of national life cannot be summed up in a few great names, and the attempt to do so is to confuse biography with history. This narrow view, besides ignoring other causes, leads to the overrating of details, and since a cause must be found somewhere, personal character becomes everything. The stability of law that is seen in a large number of instances cannot be discovered by watching single lives, however exalted ; and history with no intention of discovering the condition of events becomes the sport of accident, resting in great measure for its interest on anecdote and rhetoric.

Politics. The case is not much bettered by long accounts of acts of parliament, with summaries of debates, and numbering of divisions, and more lives of statesmen, eminent and mediocre. The details of parliament no more than the details of biographies afford sufficient data for scientific observation, if the forces of the society that surround them are omitted. Neither does the addition of military detail help much in the comprehension of the course of events; one battle is much like another except when treated by the professional soldier or sailor, or at all events in the light of professional books; and victories or defeats depend upon something else besides the position of the ground or the plans of the moment. It has been reserved for a naval expert of another power to point this out to the multitudinous writers of the history of the great naval power of the world.

Social Questions. Social questions are to-day taking the foremost place in public interest; the power behind the statesman is seen to be greater in controlling contemporary history than the eloquence or experience of any single man. We see this to be so now, and our knowledge of the present suggests the question whether it has not always been so; and whether the life of society, though it has not had the same comparative weight, has not always been a more important factor than the life of the individual.

The "Social England" Series. The "Social England" series rests upon the conviction that it is possible to make a successful attempt to give an account, not merely of politics and wars, but also of religion, commerce, art, literature, law, science, agriculture, and all that follows from their inclusion, and that without a due knowledge of the last we have no real explanation of any of the number.

Not as an Appendix. But the causes that direct the course of events will become no clearer if to one third politics and one third wars we add another third consisting of small portions of other subjects, side by side, but yet apart from one another.

The Central Idea. The central idea is that the greatness or weakness of a nation does not depend on the greatness or weakness of any one man or body of men, and that the odd millions have always had their part to play. To understand how great that was and is, we must understand the way in which they spent their lives, what they really cared for, what they fought for, and in a word what they lived for. To leave out nine-tenths of the national life, and to call the rest a history of the nation, is misleading; it is so misleading that, treated in this mutilated manner, history has no pretension to be a science: it becomes a ponderous chronicle, full of details which, in the absence of any other guiding principle, are held together by chronology. Writers of great name and power escape from this limitation, which, however, holds sway for the most part in the books that reach the great majority of readers, that is those who have not time to read an epoch in several volumes.

The Carrying Out of the Idea. It is not necessary in seeing a famous town to visit every public building and private house, and so for the carrying out of this plan it has been determined that adequate treatment can be secured of certain subjects in a series of books that should be popular, not only in style, but also in the demands they make upon the reader's time.

Specialists. It would be useless for any one writer to pretend to accomplish this task, though when the way is cleared a social history connecting more closely and summarising the work of all the contributors will be possible; but at present it is intended to ask each of them to bring his special knowledge to bear upon the explanation of social life and in treating his portion of the work to look at original authorities to see not merely what light they throw on his own branch separately, but how they affect its conception considered in relation to the whole, that is to the development of the life of the English people.

The Possible Limits of the Series. To bring the series to its completion will need the services of many writers. A few of the number of books which might be suggested may be mentioned. The influence upon thought of geographical discovery, of commerce, and of science would form three volumes. The part inventions have played, the main changes in political theories and, perhaps less commonplace, the main changes in English thought upon great topics, such as the social position of women, of children, and of the church, the treatment of the indigent poor and of the criminal, need all to be studied. The soldier, the sailor, the lawyer, the physician, have still to be written of; the conception of the duties of the noble or the statesman, not in the story of one man's life, but in a general theory illustrated from the lives of many men, has still to be formulated; the wide range of subjects connected with law—the story of crime, laws made in class interest, laws for the protection of trade and for the regulation of industry—are all to be found in the statutes at large. A more comprehensive sketch of the scope of the series should be found in an introductory volume.

Works already Arranged for. But, apart from the probable extension of the series, sufficient works have already been arranged for to describe some leading features of English social life, and to point out some of the numerous highways which lead to a great centre, passing through different provinces, which all have their local colour, but the lives of whose inhabitants need also to be known if we are to understand the country as a whole, and not merely the court and parliament of the capital.

The King's Place. The king is the centre of this life when war and justice form the chief reason for the loose federation of communities; not merely does he give protection on the frontiers, but among his own subjects it is more and more his duty to enforce peace, and we have to see how step by step the local court or franchise is merged in the strengthening of sovereign justice.

Chivalry. What exactly was the ideal of knighthood? How far did it imply an acquaintance with the learning of the day and with foreign countries? Did it strengthen the feeling of pity for the weak, or purify the love for women? In what are wrongly called the dark ages, was there a vast society of men **The Trouba-dours.** of culture, who spread over large parts of Northern Europe, to whom we owe the first-fruits of modern literature, the troubadours, who first came from Provence?

The Manor. In the manor is to be found the story of early village life, of domestic manufactures, of the system of agriculture and of the simplest administration of justice, a system the remains of which last till to-day; while a sketch of the history of **The Working-man.** the working-classes helps to complete the picture, and at the same time to place a wider one beside it, to show especially how wages have been regulated, the condition under which the poor have lived, and to see what on the whole is the part they have played in history.

The Rise of the Merchants. Turning from the working-man, we naturally ask when arose the great class of merchants, how their gradual rise affected the condition of the population, whether their appearance synchronised with any other political and social events, and in fact we prepare for the question as to the influence of commerce on politics and society.

The Univer-sities. Those who know the part that commerce plays in civilization are aware that the growth of intercourse will naturally bring larger culture, and the learning of the old world and of the Saracens

The Travelled Englishman and the Traveller in England. will be taught in the schools of the West. It will be impossible to rigidly confine the currents of thought to the four seas, or even only

to break the barrier here and there by such stories as that of the Roman missionaries. England must be looked on as belonging to the circle of a great civilization. How far Englishmen went abroad, and how far the men of other nations came to England, requires to be set forth.

The Fine Arts. Again, to those who believe in the organic connection of all branches of the national life it will be of interest to learn in what way the character of art partook of the nature of life around it, how far its methods or motives can be borrowed, why the fifteenth century gave pause to our art, why at a certain period cathedrals ceased to be built, and when it was we added great names in our turn to the list of painters.

Music. The music of Anglo-Saxon and of Dane will to some make clearer the influence of skald and gleeman; the effect of poetry will be noted, the growth of instruments, and the increasing complexity of music.

Scenery. Possibly the change in the landscape might be described : the alteration in the face of the country with the draining of fens, the making of roads, and the clearing of forests; the introduction of fresh trees and plants.

The Influence of Geography on Social Life. We must recognise that the position of Great Britain, as the known world grew wider, altered for the better; the effect of rivers, mountains, and seas in fixing the boundaries of kingdoms and sub-kingdoms, in altering or preserving languages, in determining politics and the opinions of districts, and, the chief point of all, in deciding the character of what bids fair to be the language of commerce, and probably of all international communication.

The Homes and Household Implements.

As it is important to know where men lived in relation to the world at large in order to understand how they lived, so we should be acquainted with their dwelling-places, whether in town or country, at any period; we should observe the changing styles of building, distinguish the international influence, the part that the facility of obtaining material played, and notice the gradual evolution of the rooms, the way that they were adorned and furnished, to see how far in beds and baths, in the provision for study and privacy, civilization was advancing.

Social England Classics.

From their literature we can gather most, for here, with not much thought of history, contemporary spoke to contemporary of what each knew well. In the pre-Elizabethan drama we can see the natural touches that show it was not elaborated as an exercise, but with the intention of possessing a living interest, and in what interested them we discover their attitude, not merely to religion, but to much else besides. By recognizing this fact we learn that masterpieces of literature lose their full meaning unless we find in them, besides creative power and command of the technique of art, " the very age and body of the time." Shakespeare's England and Chaucer's England are what Shakespeare and Chaucer knew of life; the outer gallery of pictures the unknown artists drew, from which we pass into the inner rooms whose walls are covered by the groups and figures that the masters painted.

Biography and History. In this widening of history, biography is no longer cramped by being cut off from social life; the great men are not isolated, but take their proper places among their fellow-countrymen, their lives forming fit landmarks, because they are akin to the people among whom they live, their characters not adapted to the century of the commentator, but bearing the impress of the forces round them, whose constant pressure is part of their life. They and those who are lesser than themselves, and the changing conditions that create them and are modified by them, form the great and continuous whole, which constantly alters, as all life alters, coming from the past and linked to the future. It no longer becomes necessary to make all times alike, except for constitutional changes, or improvement in weapons, and the crowning or death of a king, pleading the half-truth that human nature is the same in every age.

CONTENTS

CHAPTER III

How the Troubadours came to England

CHAPTER IV

The Troubadour Queen

CHAPTER V

The Troubadour King

CHAPTER VI

The Poetry of the Troubadours

CHAPTER VII

The Social Life of the Troubadours

CHAPTER VIII

The English Troubadours and Trouvères

CHAPTER IX

The English Troubadours and Trouvères (*continued*)

CHAPTER X

The Gleemen, Jongleurs, Wandering Minstrels, and Glee-maidens

CHAPTER XI

The Gleemen, Jongleurs, Wandering Minstrels, and Glee-maidens (*continued*)

CHAPTER XII

The Troubadours as Musicians

CHAPTER XIII

The Courts of Love

CHAPTER XIV

THE COURTS OF LOVE (*continued*)

CHAPTER XV

STORIES OF THE TROUBADOURS

CHAPTER XVI

STORIES OF THE TROUBADOURS (*continued*)

CHAPTER XVII

THE FALL OF THE TROUBADOURS

—Practical Results of the Adoption of Albigensian Opinions by the Troubadours, 299.—Religious Antagonism among the Troubadours, 301.—A Musical War, 303.—Crusade against the Troubadours and Albigenses, 305.—Incidents of the Crusade, 306.—Continuance of the Crusade and Extinction of the Troubadours, 309.

APPENDICES

ILLUSTRATIONS

MAPS

TROUVÈRE ACCOMPANYING HIMSELF ON THE VIOLIN.

(*Sculptured on the portico of the Abbey of St. Denis, 14th Century.*)

THE TROUBADOURS AND COURTS OF LOVE.

CHAPTER I.

ORIENTAL INFLUENCES.

The Influence of Byzantium—The Byzantine Ideal—The English Ideal—The Character of Beowulf—Estimate of Byzantine Influence before the Crusades—Byzantine Influence Received at the First Crusade—The Saracen Influences of the First Crusade—The Oriental Influence through Spain—The Wealth of its Caliphs—The Romantic Character of the Land and the People—The Saracen Minstrels—The Subject of their Songs —Their Connection with the Seraglio—The Liberal Patronage Bestowed on Them—Not only by the Great, but by all Oriental Moslems—The Attitude of Mahometanism to Minstrelsy—The Character which Oriental Minstrelsy acquired in Consequence—Musical Instruments in Use among Oriental Minstrels—General Characteristics of Arabian Minstrelsy— The Arabian Minstrelsy in Spain—The Native Spaniards and the Arabian Minstrelsy.

THE INFLUENCE OF BYZANTIUM.—Punctilious etiquette, a great attention to the small, if often essential, details of life, marvellous respect, almost veneration, for elaborate ceremony—such were the characteristics of a nation and a court which, while the mass of Europe and of the world was plunged in the profoundest darkness, held a glittering, if isolated, existence on the shores of the

B

Bosphorus.[1] The fame of that nation and its wondrous capital penetrated the gloom of barbarism or semi-barbarism which wrapped the wilderness of the world, and while it aroused the astonishment, and often the incredulity, of the uncultivated Europeans of that date, served as a suggestor of ideas and ideals to minds utterly rude and incapable of high efforts of imagination.

During the seventh and at the beginning of the eighth century of the Christian era, Constantinople, illuminated with the halo of Greek culture and oppressed with the fastidiousness of an overstrained and effete civilization,[2] was, so far as Europe was concerned, the one bright spot in a world of cloud; and the slight glimpses of its distant glory which came from time to time to the eyes of men were regarded as gleams of a higher existence, unattainable, unapproachable, and as certainly unparalleled in the world at large.

On the other hand, the dim wonder and incredulity with which semi-barbarous Europe looked up to distant Byzantium was equalled and exceeded by the contemptuous scorn with which the refined and luxurious

---

[1] The expression " isolated " must, of course, be understood not only in reference to the relations between Byzantium and Europe, but to the isolation of that ancient and Christian empire amid the young and Mahometan powers of the East, more especially after the conquest of Persia.

[2] Yet we must beware of disparaging too far the vigour of the Byzantine civilization, otherwise it may well be asked, How would it have been possible for Byzantium to have retained for centuries her dignity and position in the midst of hostile neighbours ?

Byzantines looked down upon Europe.[1] Their views of life were so different and so superior to those of the nations whom they emphatically termed barbarians, that we may excuse the haughty vanity which refused to allow merit to anybody but themselves.

THE BYZANTINE IDEAL.—The ideal Byzantine, the typical hero whom the denizens of that world of light elected to honour, was a paragon of his species, a chevalier of true antique gallantry, a second Achilles, a master of all arts, an adept in all sciences. " He is pre-eminent in eloquence," writes the panegyrist of such an hero, " wise in counsel; he is endowed with all the good qualities which God and nature can bestow; in war he is most skilful; agility, strength, beauty, are his portion; and he is a finished scholar in all the books that have ever been written."[2]

---

[1] See Anna Comnena's *Alexias, passim.* At the same time we must not forget the curious fact that Anna Comnena described her husband, as a term of praise, as having the appearance of a Norman.

[2] The portrait of Nicephorus Bryennius given by Anna Comnena as a picture of an ideal hero, though belonging to a somewhat later period, is yet amply true of the earlier date we are mentioning in that stereotyped and stationary civilization:—
πάντα γὰρ καὶ ῥωμὴ καὶ τάχος καὶ κάλλος σώματος καὶ ἁπλῶς ἐς ταὐτὸν συνελθόντα ὅσα ψυχῆς καὶ σώματος ἀγαθὰ τὸν ἄνδρα ἐκεῖνον ἐκόσμησεν. ἕνα γὰρ αὐτὸν ἐν τοῖς ἅπασιν ἐξοχώτατον καὶ ἡ φύσις ἀνεβλάστησε καὶ ὁ θεὸς ἐδημιούργησε. καὶ οἷον τὸν Ἀχιλλέα ὕμνησεν Ὅμηρος κ.τ.λ. σοφὸς μὲν τὴν γνώμην ἦν οὗτος ὁ ἀνὴρ καὶ τὸν λόγον σοφώτατος. καὶ τὰ στρατιωτικὰ γεγονὼς ἄριστος, οὐκ ἀμελετήτως ἔσχε πρὸς λόγους, πᾶσαν βίβλον ἀναπτυξάμενος καὶ εἰς πᾶσαν ἐπιστήμην ἐγκεκυφώς κ.τ.λ. (Anna Comnena, *Alexias*, vii. 2). Cf. her contemptuous remarks on the mere personal and bodily endowments of Basilacius (*Alexias*, i. 7).

THE ENGLISH IDEAL.—As a contrast to this, and to see the extreme difference between Byzantium and England, let us take an ideal of our own making at that epoch, and we shall be able to judge the capacities of our national character, which was to become the recipient ere long of vastly advanced, if somewhat artificial, impressions.

The poem of Beowulf was written in the eighth century,[1] and is therefore identical in point of time with the epoch of which we are speaking. The writer of this poem undoubtedly infused into his hero's mind the thoughts and feelings of his age, and in the temper which governs Beowulf and his actions and thoughts we may see the character of the Anglo-Saxons themselves at that date.

THE CHARACTER OF BEOWULF.—The hero is a man of true nobility, doubtless, but ignorant of arts, innocent of letters, a rough warrior and little more, destitute of courtly polish and artistic refinement, and by no means that pink of perfection and gallantry which the Byzantines upheld as their ideal exponent of heroism. The joy of Beowulf is when his band, refreshed with abundant beer, boast over the ale-can their past exploits and vaunt their future prowess.[2] He himself is a man of audacious speech, often brimming over into exaggerations,[3] eulogistic chiefly of bold and boisterous behaviour. He

---

[1] To speak with greater strictness, it was re-edited in the eighth century, whatever the date of its original production may be.

[2] *The Deeds of Beowulf*, ed. Earle, i. 7.

[3] "We twain kept swimming in the sea for five days and five nights. My shirt gave me protection against the fish of the sea. . . . But a spotty monster dragged me to the bottom of the ocean. I got at the vermin, however, with a bill-hook that I

admits little merit to anybody but himself. His fights
are " the hardest fights that ever man fought"; his adventures are, according to his own account, the most
remarkable adventures that man had ever engaged in.
Such was the type of the heroic character in those days
in its national and indigenous form, a type indicative of a
primitive condition of the human mind, inexperienced in
the great world beyond its own immediate circle, and
with none of those angles rubbed off which are so effectually worn away by the intercourse and culture of varied
society.[1]

ESTIMATE OF BYZANTINE INFLUENCE BEFORE THE
CRUSADES.—The stray gleams of Byzantine courtesy and
refinement which fell upon such a world as this must
have struck that world with wonder. But their effect
most likely ended here. Their effect might have been to
make that world think a little, but not to make it act.
Something in the way of personal contact is nearly always
necessary as the preliminary to action; and centuries
passed away before that direct personal contact took
place. The news and information respecting Byzantium
which came to England or to France through the advent

---

had in my hand, and after a long combat under water I despatched him " (*Deeds of Beowulf*, ed. Earle, i. 8).

[1] At the same time we must remember that at a time when
nature is untamed, and personal prowess is vital to free existence,
a warrior necessarily vaunts his own deeds, and promises to do
others—cf. the Vikings—not as an empty boast, but as a vow. We
must remember also the heroism that faces unknown dangers
and the powers of evil, and the conception of duty, v. III. xxxvii.
2730.

of embassies or the reports of travellers produced little effect beyond additional curiosity.

A curious example of the influence of embassies may be mentioned in the effect of Byzantium on the music of England. The introduction of the organ and of organ-playing into our land was directly due to the influence of a Byzantine embassy which Constantine Copronymus sent to Charlemagne. Byzantium was always the home of the organ, and organs had continued in that great treasure-house of art from the early years of the Christian era. When the ambassadors came to Charlemagne they brought an organ with them, and the workmen in the palace of Aix-la-Chapelle were bidden construct another like it. On this model the great organ at Winchester was erected, which was pumped by twenty-six sets of bellows,[1] with two bellows-blowers to each, and the keys of which were so large and clumsy that the organist had to strike them with his fist instead of his fingers.[2]

BYZANTINE INFLUENCE RECEIVED AT THE FIRST CRUSADE. — From another quarter and from another set of feelings came the impulse which gave the momentum to the First Crusade (1096–1099), but the First Crusade was in its consequences of the utmost importance to the development of character which we are speaking of. The vast majority of the Norman and the Anglo-Norman noblesse, together with many Saxon thanes and swarms of the lower orders, found themselves precipitated on the

---

[1] Volstanus Diaconus says, "Bisseni supra sociantur ordine folles, Inferiusque jacent quatuor atque decem."

[2] Prætorius, *Syntagma Musicum.*

East; and before they could realize the marvellous adventure to which they were committed, they were at Constantinople itself, in the shadow of that punctilious court, in the thick of those elaborate ceremonies, and amid those exquisite and refined Greeks whose life and doings they had known by hearsay only, and had regarded with incredulity and amazement.

The brawny warriors of our remote climes beheld openeyed the refinements of luxury which met them on all sides in this capital of the East. They witnessed, no doubt, with a secret contempt the laboured science of etiquette,[1] which rendered every interview an irksome toil; they transgressed with good humour or with mortification the countless rules of good behaviour, which no memory could retain and no reason could fathom; and they witnessed with astonishment, and it may be with envy, the imposing pageants and ceremonies, in the arrangement and devising of which no city ever excelled the glittering mistress of the Bosphorus.

THE SARACEN INFLUENCES OF THE FIRST CRUSADE.— But their education was not to end here. From Constantinople they proceeded on their way, and in their foes the

---

[1] Cf. *Les Croniques et Excellentz Faits des Ducs de Normandie*, folio 41: " Il estoit lors ordonnancé que quiconques parloit à l'Empereur, il ostoit son mantel et le faisoit cheoir à terre. Si ordonna le Duc que quiconques de ses gens parleroit à l'Empereur quant il auroit osté son mantel, qu'il le laissast et qu'il ne le redressast pas; et ainsi fu fait. Et quant le Duc eut parlé à l'Empereur, il ne dressa pas son mantel. Ung des chevaliers de l'Empereur luy voulut bailler, et luy dist, puis qu'il avoit touché à terre, qu'il ne le vestiroit jamais."

Saracens, whom they were sworn to oppose, but with whom in the varied course of campaigns they frequently came into social contact, they became aware of the existence of a race almost as highly cultivated as the Greeks themselves.

It was in the seventh century of the Christian era that the Arabians, then a raw race of warriors fighting under the immediate followers of Mahomet, attacked and subdued the great empire of Persia—an empire and a civilization contiguous to that of Constantinople, and in many important respects not unlike it ; effete, luxurious, a treasury of arts,[1] of culture, and of riches.   All the spoils of this wealthy empire fell into the hands of its conquerors.   The conquest of Persia civilized the Arabians, transforming them almost suddenly from rude warriors into haughty and chivalrous soldiers; and when, proceeding on the wings of conquest, they swept into Egypt, Syria, Assyria, and India, and united all these countries into one vast empire, with its centre at Bagdad, they did little more than extend the civilization of Persia throughout this vast area, and assimilate to it the various elements they already found existing.

It was with this nation of foemen, who are called by the generic name of Saracens, a nation of chevaliers, whose history and adventures in the loveliest parts of the earth had been of the most brilliant description—it

---

[1] That the Arabian minstrelsy was specially derived from Persia is noted with great completeness and elaborately alluded to by Ibn Chaldun, the Montesquieu of the East, in *Fundgraben des Orients*, ii.

was with these enemies that the warriors of England and Normandy came into collision; and starting to deliver the Holy Sepulchre from, as they supposed, the maltreatment of savages, they found themselves in conflict with one of the most cultivated and romantic nations of the earth.

THE ORIENTAL INFLUENCE THROUGH SPAIN.—The culture of the East had, however, been coming steadily nearer to our land through yet another channel; and through Spain England and Europe alike were destined to receive the gleams of a brightness whose influence pointed still more strongly in the same direction. Spain at that time, very different from what it afterwards became, was a Saracen province, or rather a Saracen empire. At the beginning of the eighth century, a great wing of the Mahometan conquerors, who were fast laying the whole earth at their feet, flushed with triumph and secure of victory, passed over into Spain under Tarik and Musa, and with little trouble subjugated that fertile land, imprinting on it the image and the culture of the East.[1] Palaces, mosques, minarets, rose like an exhalation in vanquished Spain. Arabian cities were founded; Arabian universities were opened; and the luxury which was the wonder of barbarous Europe in the case of Constantinople was soon

---

[1] There thus became two rival empires or caliphates among the Mahometans: one ruled by the caliphs of Spain, and the other by the caliphs of Bagdad. The caliphs of the East, it may be mentioned, swayed the power which was afterwards engrossed or usurped by the Turkish sultans. The Caliph to a greater degree than the Sultan was a religious as well as a political sovereign.

surpassed by the stupendous luxury of the Spanish Arabians.

THE WEALTH OF ITS CALIPHS.—In reading of the wealth of the Spanish caliphs, we seem to be transported to the region of legend. We hear with amazement of the mines of gold and silver;[1] of the iron, loadstone, and crystal that were quarried from the rocks; of the amber and sulphur that could be picked up in profusion from the soil. Silks, oils, sugar, and saffron were the easy produce of the fields; coral was collected on the shores of Andalusia; pearl fisheries of immense value existed off the coast of Catalonia; and there were two mines of rubies, one at Malaga, the other at Baja.[2]

THE ROMANTIC CHARACTER OF THE LAND AND THE PEOPLE.—The land was a land of romance, and romance was the life of the people. On the banks of the Guadalquivir, a stately stream, whose enormous basin was lined in those days of opulence with twelve thousand towns and villages, lights in never-ending myriads twinkled the whole length of the stream. And as the boatman glided past village after village on his way, from the populous and twinkling banks came the perpetual sounds of instru-

---

[1] According to Del Mar, who is a good authority, the production of the precious metals failed from the time of the barbarian invasion of the Roman empire in Europe, and indeed all over the world. But recent discoveries of disused and abandoned mines in Provence, which had once been worked by the Saracens (Lenthéric, *La Provence Maritime*), prove incontestably that the preceding statement is of far too sweeping a character, and that to deny the Saracens the knowledge of mining is an error.

[2] Cardonne's *Histoire de l'Afrique et de l'Espagne*, i.

ments and voices which mingled with the breeze and floated over the surface of the stream.

In Cordova, the capital of this wonderful land, from every balcony in the evening-time swelled the tinkling of lutes and the melody of voices, so that the city seemed wreathed in musical airs after the bazaars were closed, and the evening's recreation had begun.[1]

The Caliph himself, secluded from public curiosity in his voluptuous retreat of Zehra, passed his hours of recreation and repose amid scenes that may well recall the descriptions of fable. The " pavilion of his pleasures " was constructed of gold and polished steel, the walls of which were encrusted with precious stones. In the midst of the splendour produced by lights reflected from a hundred crystal lustres, a sheaf of living quicksilver jetted up in a basin of alabaster, and made a brightness too dazzling for the eye to look upon. Amid other decorations of rare and stupendous luxury was a musical tree—a similar construction is said to have existed at Constantinople, and one at Bagdad—the branches of which were made of gold and silver. On eighteen large branches and a number of twigs beneath them sat a multitude of birds shaped out of the same precious metals. By an ingenious mechanism inside the golden tree, the birds were made to sing in most melodious chorus, to the delight and amazement of the listeners.[2]

---

[1] Rowbotham's *History of Music*, iii. 562; Fétis, *Histoire de la Musique*, ii.

[2] Cardonne's *Histoire de l'Afrique et de l'Espagne* i.; Power's *History of the Mussulmans in Spain*.

THE SARACEN MINSTRELS.—Characteristic figures in their culture which the Arabians brought with them from the East, and who received a new access of importance in the vanquished world of Spain, where they, no less than their patrons, were masters and the dominant class, were the raouis, or minstrels, a race of interesting itinerants whose performances are often mentioned with approbation in the *Arabian Nights*, and whose biographies, to the number of some score or two, have been written by a learned Arabian, Ali of Ispahan, and are still to be read in his *Liber Cantilenarum* either in the Arabic or in a Latin translation.[1]

THE SUBJECT OF THEIR SONGS.—These raouis, unlike the bards and minstrels of our more Northern and sterner climes, were indisposed by their race and by their surroundings to sing of such themes as fortitude, heroism, and war. We never hear of them, for instance, placing themselves at the head of armies, in the manner of the Celtic bards, and hurling themselves against the enemy, whom they disconcerted by their personal boldness and by the marvellous excitement which they communicated to the soldiers who followed behind them; we never hear of them selecting for continuous and usual laudation the hero, the lawgiver, and the seer. But their main theme was love[2] in all its glancing variety, love in its countless

---

[1] Ali of Ispahan, *Liber Cantilenarum*. The most typical life given by Ali of Ispahan is the life of Mabed, which may well be studied as a curious illustration of the manners of the time.

[2] This devotion to the theme of love on the part of the minstrels must not be understood as assuming that love was the exclusive

manifestations, its million shades of feeling—love, its nature, its objects, its history, its vicissitudes, its entire scope and associations.

THEIR CONNECTION WITH THE SERAGLIO.—This theme in the warm East, from whence they had sprung, found a market impossible and undesirable in the colder climes of the West. The seraglios of the caliphs, princes, and viziers in Bagdad, Grand Cairo, Damascus, and elsewhere, crowded with creatures of exquisite and often peerless beauty, destined throughout their existence for the gratification of passion from the most modest attachment to the extreme of profligacy, required as their natural complement a clan of minstrels or orators who could celebrate the charms of these earthly houries, praise the favourite, vilify the fallen, and generally act as mouthpieces and auxiliaries to all the intrigues of the seraglio.[1] At the court of the Caliph, and ready to take the cue of their minstrelsy from his smiles, were scores of bards, whose spontaneous and well-timed efforts were liberally rewarded by a generous and sensitive prince, prepared to bestow on the panegyrist of his newest lover at least a tithe of the bounty which he scattered on herself.

THE LIBERAL PATRONAGE BESTOWED ON THEM.—At the court of the Caliph Haroun-al-Raschid, Zobeir Ibn Dahman

---

subject they sang of. They treated of other subjects, of subjects, too, of wide range, as wide as the culture of their numerous universities.

[1] Ali of Ispahan gives at considerable length the various intrigues in which the famous Ibrahim of Mossoul, the patriarch of Arabian minstrelsy, competed with and distanced all his rivals (*Liber Cantilenarum*).

was one of the most successful and dexterous among a very
bevy of court minstrels, who all contended with varying
success for the smiles and largess of their lord. The Caliph
having recently purchased a Georgian slave, to whom his
fickle heart became inordinately devoted, proposed that
the minstrels of the court should enter into competition
for composing a song in her honour. More than twenty
such songs were immediately produced by the versatile
and eager competitors; but the song of Zobeir's was
esteemed by the best judges and likewise by the Caliph
himself to be far in advance of all the others in point of
refinement and sentiment. The first place in the competition was accordingly adjudged to this lucky bard, and
a reward of twenty thousand dirhems was paid him for
this solitary composition, which praised as she only
deserved to be praised the sylph and houri of the Caliph's
latest dreams.[1]   On another occasion the same Zobeir
received as much as fifty thousand dirhems for one song;
and being told to demand whatever further reward
he wished, he asked for a country house, but the Caliph
gave him two villages.[2]

The palaces of princes and viziers observed a similar
munificence, though on a smaller scale, and were thronged
in like manner by minstrels equally assiduous, though
of less esteem.

NOT ONLY BY THE GREAT, BUT BY ALL ORIENTAL MOS-
LEMS.—But not the palaces of the great alone were
responsible for this abundance of the race of minstrels in

---

[1] *Anecdotes Arabes* (Paris, 1752).   [2] *Ibid.*

the East. The houses of the average citizens, of the merchants, of the shopkeepers, and even of the poor, were all open to the bard, were ready in their entertainment, lavish in their rewards, and keen in their appreciation.[1] Among these latter classes, obviously, in Grand Cairo and Bagdad, there was no question of supporting minstrels as part and parcel of the staff of the establishment. But, to meet their demands, a class of wandering minstrels arose, who perambulated the cities and country districts from house to house, and, at the invitation of the hosts, regaled the company with a song, or series of songs, generally after the midday meal, when the family was seated round the fountain or sheet of water which played on the lawn in the courts of their houses in the afternoon.

The houses of Bagdad and generally throughout the East were built much in the manner of the houses in Paris at the present day, with a porter's lodge at the door and a passage leading into an interior court or square. At the porter's lodge a stock of musical instruments was generally kept for the express use of any minstrels who might arrive. After the midday meal, the afternoon sun would beat down upon the house and the grassy and emerald court in its interior. The family and the guests would sit in a circle round the basin of water, in the midst of which was the fountain, throwing up its spray. Most welcome was the news to the little party,

---

[1] The appreciation of minstrels among the Arabians is well illustrated in Power's *History of the Mussulman Empire*, and in Jorsen's notes to the Arabic version of the *Thousand and One Nights*.

when intelligence was brought that a minstrel was at the gate.

He was conducted, having first selected what instrument he would prefer from the stock at the porter's lodge, into the lawn, and bidden sit down and commence his delightful minstrelsy. Around him were the ladies and their families of the small seraglio, and no fitter subject could ever suggest itself than the fabrication of compliments and adulatory verses in praise of those who sat before him. At the request of the master of the house, or urged thereto by the contending beauties, he addressed in high-flown flattery one lady after another, extemporising his verse to meet the requirements of the case, and commencing each song with the stock formula, " Shut your eyelids, ye eyes of the gazelle! " [1]

THE ATTITUDE OF MAHOMETANISM TO MINSTRELSY.—If the requirements of life in the East gave rise to such a class of minstrels as these, the precise character of their minstrelsy was determined in a further and quite as pronounced a measure by Mahometanism itself. We might imagine, surely, that in a nation and a civilization that had reached such heights of stupendous luxury as the Arabians, when arts and sciences had attained such a pitch of development, when architecture, embroidery, carving, and numerous other sister arts had reached a point of intricate beauty which has never since been equalled [2]—we might imagine that the music of those

---

[1] Fétis, *Histoire de la Musique*, ii. 107.

[2] " The great palace of the caliphs at Bagdad had thirty-eight thousand pieces of tapestry hanging on its walls, twelve thousand

times would surely be remarkable for majestic bands, for complex and expensive instruments, for orchestras, choruses, and all the other results of profusion which were observable in the arts of the day, instead of being depressed and limited to the often extemporised performances of individual minstrels. But Mahomet had frowned on music from the very first; he had decried it; he had condemned it. His practical spirit had set itself in strong opposition to all such gay and pleasant unbending and relaxing of the soul; and music, so far as its mechanical development was concerned—that is, in the growth of instruments, and orchestras, and bands—languished under the frown of the Prophet. "Music," said Mahomet, "must be kept in check." "Your prayers," he said to the people of Mecca, "if music form a part of them, will end but in piping and hand-clapping." And elsewhere he denounces it in these terms: "Music and singing cause hypocrisy to grow in the heart, as water makes the corn to grow." So there was no music in the Mahometan heaven, and the black-eyed houries of that paradise, though made of pure musk and dwelling in houses of hollow pearls, were constrained to waste their dalliance in an eternal silence.

On earth, in the same way, there was no music in the mosques. Even bells were disallowed to call the faithful to prayers; and the muezzin must needs mount the minaret to do that duty with his voice, which other na-

---

five hundred of which were of silk, embroidered with gold. The carpets on the floor were twenty-two thousand in number" (Abulfeda, *Annal. Moslem.*, p. 185).

tions, less rigid in their rulings, have assigned unsus-
piciously to instruments of harmony.

THE CHARACTER WHICH ORIENTAL MINSTRELSY AC-
QUIRED IN CONSEQUENCE.—Thus banished from its natural
and ennobling liaison with religion, music became to
the Moslems an illicit pleasure, like wine was; and it
grew up amid myrtle blossoms and the laughter of women,
and became most like to its companions. Frowned at and
execrated by the earliest followers of Mahomet, it was next
connived at, and at last could appear in public places, and
even before the Caliph himself. For in the days of the
earlier caliphs we read how, agreeably to the law of
Mahomet which forbade the practice of music, a young
man was apprehended with a lute in his possession.
Brought before the judgment-seat, the Caliph asked him
what that thing was. The young man replied, "Commander of the faithful, it is called a lute. It is made by
taking some of the wood of the pistachio tree, and cutting
it into thin pieces, and gluing them together, and then
attaching over them some cords. And when a beautiful
girl touches these cords, they give forth sounds more
lovely than the sound of rain falling on a desert land." [1]

MUSICAL INSTRUMENTS IN USE AMONG ORIENTAL MIN-
STRELS.—The Persian lute, the Arabian lyre, the Tartar
pipe, and the Egyptian dulcimer were the instruments
which were generally kept in the porter's lodge for the
convenience of the minstrels who might visit the house
in the afternoon; but of these it is obvious that the

---

[1] Lane's *Arabians of the Middle Ages.*

stringed instruments would have greatly the preference, because they would admit of the performer singing while he played, and would not necessitate a special accompanist being engaged, as the pipe or flute would. Of stringed instruments, indeed, the Arabians, doubtless on this account especially, had an amazing number. While we at the present day can count up on our fingers the stringed instruments which are in common use among us, the Arabians had in constant employment sixty-one varieties of stringed instruments, on many or most of which a skilled musician would deem it entirely essential to be proficient.[1] The largest variety of string was of the lute species, that is to say of the species of stringed instrument which has a long neck and a curved sounding-board, is plucked by the fingers, and is held in the hands in the same way in which we hold a guitar. It is the favourite and the supreme species of stringed instrument among the Arabians.

It had thirty-two varieties of shape and structure, these being differentiated from one another by some slight and often inappreciable distinctions, such as the number of pegs, the bend of the neck, the character of the wood. The Great Lute which gave the character and type to the form was made of twenty-one pieces of maple wood, glued together and separated from each other by twenty filaments of St. Lucie wood. The face was flat, with three rosettes in it, and the back was full and round. The strings were of catgut, and the nut, where they turn down be-

---

[1] Rowbotham's *History of Music*, iii. 501; Kiesewetter's *La Musique des Arabes*.

tween the pegs and the neck, was of ivory.[1]   It was kept in a bag of damask silk in the Arabian houses, though sometimes it was hung up to make a show by a piece of ribbon tied round the head which sloped at almost a right-angle with the neck.

GENERAL CHARACTERISTICS OF ARABIAN MINSTRELSY. —The remaining twenty-nine varieties of stringed instruments consisted of fourteen varieties of the violin form and fifteen of the lyre and dulcimer species.   And it was with these instruments, and particularly with the lute forms, that the minstrels accompanied their delightful songs and extemporisations.

Naturally enough, in such a music the main centre of gravity rested on the words and the voice, rather than on the instrument and the tune.   Not only does the character of the instruments point in this way, but the genius of the art, agreeably to the inculcations of Mahomet, the practice of the minstrels themselves, and last, not least, the total Arabic theory of music.   The mere jingling of tunes was ever decried by the learned theorists of the Mussul-mans as inducing degeneracy in an art which is among the most beautiful expositors of human sentiment.   "To be a good musician," says Ibn Chaldun,[2] "it is neces-sary not to play pretty tunes and jingle nice melodies, but to utter clever words and make your hearers understand every word as you chant it."   "A good musician," says Ali of Ispahan, "will have at his fingers' ends a hun-

---

[1] Ali of Ispahan, *Liber Cantilenarum*, folio 52.
[2] Ibn Chaldun in *Fundgraben des Orients*, ii.

dred pieces of poetry, and countless songs, both humorous and melancholy ; he will have a fluent tongue and a copious command of speech ; he will be a good grammarian, and know how to form his sentences properly and elegantly."[1] Another theorist praises as the great essential in music "an abundant wit," which comprises all that is desirable in the art, and is equally strong on the necessity of "a refined sentiment," which is entirely indispensable to the existence of music; "without it there is no music: it is all music, and nothing but music."[2] To these definitions of the art of music another theorist adds the prime qualification of "a clear pronunciation," which brings home to the hearer the words that are uttered.

THE ARABIAN MINSTRELSY IN SPAIN.—From the above we may judge very clearly what the Arabians' conception of the art of music really was. We have seen what instruments they employed ; we have learnt what was the unfailing theme of their lays ; and we have gathered who the minstrels were and under what circumstances they came forward as the expositors of that theme. Now that the most flourishing and prosperous wing of the caliphate was transferred from the East to Spain, and that Spain had become orientalized, they transferred the scene of their energies from the glowing East to the new home of their adoption, where a sky almost as blue and a sun almost as warm invited to a repetition of that life of love and song of which they were the prime expositors and in some measure the supporters. Spain was covered with a network of Moslem cities ; gilded minarets and cupolas

---

[1] Ali of Ispahan, *Liber Cantilenarum.*   [2] *Ibid.*

glittered in an unending chain well-nigh from shore to shore ; and through this forest of Arabian civilization the minstrels wandered incessantly to and fro,[1] expounding for evermore their favourite, their single theme, and expatiating with the learning of profound and experienced scholars upon the countless varieties of the universal passion.

THE NATIVE SPANIARDS AND THE ARABIAN MINSTRELSY.—The influence of the Arabian minstrelsy was not confined to the purely Mahometan regions of the Peninsula ; but even the native Spaniards in the north, in Leon, Castile, and Catalonia, were not insensible to the charms of the Arabic song, and learnt to offer it a ready welcome.[2]

But at the beginning of the twelfth century, contemporaneously almost with the First Crusade, the court of Barcelona, to whom the greater part of Catalonia belonged, obtained by marriage the crown of Provence, a land of roses and of everlasting summer ; and the intercourse between Provence and Spain, which even before now had not been slight,[3] became close and permanent. The lore of Arabian minstrelsy, the traditions of Arabian music, were thus enabled to pass in a steady stream into a land eminently calculated to give them welcome, a land where the climate invited to love, where the air wooed to song, and where the nightingales sang sweeter, it is said, than in all the world beside.

---

[1] Fauriel, *Histoire de la Poésie Provençale*, iii. 338.

[2] Balaguer's *Historia de los Trovadores* (Madrid, 1888), Discurso Preliminare, i. 177 sq.; *Ib.* 216 sq.

[3] Diago, *Historia de los Victorissimos Condes.*

CHAPTER II.

THE CRADLE OF THE TROUBADOURS.

Provence: its Boundaries and Natural Features—Susceptibility
of Provence to Oriental Influences—Adaptation of Provence
to be the Cradle of Minstrelsy—Theory of an Indigenous
Minstrelsy in Provence—Greater Probability of the Derivation of the Provençal Minstrelsy from the Arabians—
Peculiar Forms of the Arabian and Semitic Minstrelsy—
Rhyme: Two Theories as to its Origin—The *Langue d'Oc*
and the *Langue d'Oïl*—Geographical Extent of the *Langue
d'Oc* and the Term " Provençal."

Provence: its Boundaries and Natural Features.—
In the eleventh century of the Christian era the kingdom
of Provence embraced a large, compact, and fertile terri-
tory lying along the shores of the Mediterranean. It was
bounded on the north by that range of mountains of
which Mount Ventoux is the highest and most important;
on the east by the Maritime Alps and Italy; on the

23

south by the Mediterranean ; while on the west the rapid
current of the Rhone and its branching mouths offered a
natural boundary unequalled in distinctness and defence.[1]
Its natural features were a combination of beauty and
fertility rarely equalled in the earth, certainly never
surpassed in Europe; and the same delicious climate
which tempts travellers in search of health or pleasure to
the Riviera to-day smiled with larger lustre on a land
which included not only the Riviera, but the fertile districts of the inland, in its limits.

The wines of Provence were hardly more celebrated
than its oil and wheat, than the almonds, melons, figs,
citrons, chestnuts, and mulberries which were the easy
produce of its soil. Nor must we forget in estimating the
natural wealth of the country the busy cities of Arles,
Avignon, Aix, and Marseilles—Arles a mart for the oil
and wine of the country, Avignon a centre of its manufactures, Aix an emporium for its fruits and wool, and Marseilles the busy focus of its commerce and shipping, in
whose spacious harbour argosies from all parts of the
Mediterranean unloaded their stores.[2]

SUSCEPTIBILITY OF PROVENCE TO ORIENTAL INFLU-
ENCES.—The dazzling sun and glowing climate of Provence
gave it from the first a striking similitude to the countries
of the East, and that similarity has been extended to its
inhabitants by repeated colonizations of the country at the
hands of Oriental explorers or emigrants. It lay in

---

[1] Fournier, *Le Royaume d'Arles et de Vienne* (Paris, 1891), Introduction.

[2] *Ibid.*

the old trade route between the East and Gaul and
Britain. The Phœnicians first brought the elements of
Eastern luxury to this most Oriental of European lands;
and Ionian Greeks from Asia Minor introduced the softest
of the Hellenic forms of culture, together with those
Oriental tastes which they had learnt in their Asiatic
home. The existence of Byzantine governors at Marseilles speaks of a communion between Provence and Constantinople.[1] Coming down nearer to the times we
write of, no less than five times had Saracen emirs guided
their hosts into the heart of Provence, and not content
with the influence of arms, had endeavoured to subjugate
and mahometanize the land by the more peaceful and surer
influence of arts and industries.[2] Unexpected discoveries
of late of disused mines and subterranean engineering
works,[3] the obvious outcome of a Saracen occupation, bear
witness only too clearly to the exceeding intimacy of communication which united the inhabitants of the garden
of Europe with the most polished nation of the Eastern
world. The Provençals were therefore prepared for that
still more copious infusion of Eastern elements which
began to pour in a more continuous channel on the acquisition of their crown by Raymond Bérenger, Count of
Barcelona, who in 1112 married the heiress of the Provençal kings.

"The Arabian songs and Arabian melodies," we

---

[1] Fabre's *Histoire de Marseille*, i. 217.
[2] Barche, *Essai sur l'Histoire de Provins* (Marseilles).
[3] Lenthéric, *La Provence Maritime.*

read in Casiri,[1] "were wonderful favourites with the people of Catalonia, not only when delivered by apt singers, but even when carelessly sung by rough sailors at the ports." But they had long ago been provided with far more intelligent expositors than these latter in the persons of trained and cultivated singers of the upper classes in Catalonia, Arragon, and Leon,[2] who "imbibed the traditions of Arabian minstrelsy, and added to it by original creations of their own."

ADAPTATION OF PROVENCE TO BE THE CRADLE OF MINSTRELSY.—But Provence, shielded from the clash of arms which hurtled so incessantly over the northern portions of Spain, and by her luxurious and fertile climate contributing that ease and affluence which the rugged mountains of Arragon denied, was far better calculated for rearing a race of singers who could in ease and freedom develop the elements of poetry and song into a national and indigenous art. The seigneurs of Provence inhabited *châteaux* at a convenient distance from one another, to make intercourse easy and agreeable. They had little to distract their attention from the arts of peace beyond the management of their démesnes and the practice of military exercises, which was often destined to end in practice alone. Under these circumstances they developed a blithe and comely life compared to that lived by the baronage in most parts of Europe, and with the development of this life came as a necessary consequence the predominance of those softer phases of energy which appear as culture and

---

[1] *Historia Arabe estractada por Casiri.*
[2] *Ibid.*

song. Their growing excellence in these caused the more gifted of the Provençal seigneurs to be known as *troubadours*, a word which in Provençal means "inventors " or "makers," from *trobar*, "to invent," just as in Greek from ποιέω, " to make," was derived ποιήτης, " a maker " or " poet."

THEORY OF AN INDIGENOUS MINSTRELSY IN PROVENCE. —That from very remote times, indeed from the days of the Roman empire, whose *provincia Gallica*, or " Gallic province," the country was—deriving from Rome both its name and its civilization—a species of homely, artless poetry may have survived and lived on among all the changes of masters and surroundings which succeeded the dissolution of the empire, is a supposition which would be rendered all the more probable if any remains of that poetry, even one line of it, had escaped the ravages of time. It may be justly argued, however, perhaps, that the homely and unsophisticated effusions of the peasantry are not as a rule committed to writing, but are bequeathed from one generation to another by a species of oral tradition, which as effectually preserves the songs for the enjoyment and interpretation of their expositors, though not for the curious inquisition of a remote posterity.

GREATER PROBABILITY OF THE DERIVATION OF THE PROVENÇAL MINSTRELSY FROM THE ARABIANS.—If such a corpus of homely and oral poetry were in existence, it had, however, little or no influence on the inspirations of the cultivated seigneurs of Provence, whose choice of subjects was singularly unlike the familiar themes of homely and rustic song, being rare, fastidious, often extravagant and far-fetched, and recalling in its style and method of expression the artificial and highly coloured mannerisms of Byzantine literature, not the plain and unsophisticated spirit which would have sprung from the sons of the soil; while from its form and the constant preponderance given to one chosen theme, that of love, the influence of the Arabian minstrelsy is so emphatically evident as to leave no doubt that here, and here alone, the origin of this latter aspect of Provençal song must be sought and found. To go no further than give a few of the more palpable and striking points of influence. "In the days of ignorance," says the Arabian grammarian, "before Mahomet came, the shepherds watching sheep in the desert were wont to while away the night by answering one another on their flutes, with which they poured out alternate melodies, one flute responding to the other."[1]   And later on, though still in the days of ignorance before Mahomet, we hear of the supplanting of the two flutes by the voices of two singers, who answered one another in precisely the same manner as the instruments had done, singing each a part of a verse alternately.[2]

Peculiar Forms of the Arabian and Semitic Minstrelsy.—We quote these words, "in the days of ignorance before Mahomet," with special purpose to show the earliness of the date, and to prove that this peculiar fancy of song was indigenous to the Arabians; nay more, it was pre-eminently Semitic. We have but to turn to the Bible

---

[1] Schott's *Proverbia Græca*, p. 87.
[2] Fauriel, *Histoire de la Poésie Provençale*, iii. 387.

for an illustration and a proof of this. Let us consider when "Miriam the prophetess took a timbrel in her hand, and all the women went out after her with timbrels and dances, and Miriam *answered* them, Sing ye to the Lord," etc., and when Moses and the children of Israel went forth, and Moses *answered* them. In Hebrew, in fact, "to answer" meant "to sing," so common was the habit in song, so entirely identical was "answering" in public declamation to "singing."

But if we go back still further to the oldest Semitic poem in the world—viz., the Song of Lamech in Genesis, Lamech, the father of Jubal the minstrel—we shall find that this poem is constructed in such a manner that one half of the verse *answers* the other half. This is what is meant by Hebrew parallelism; and through all the Psalms of David the verses, even as we read them to-day, bear witness to that structure of parallel or "answering" clauses [1] which we say is essentially Semitic, and which early imprinted its influence on Arabian minstrelsy; so that the unsophisticated shepherds, whiling away the watches of the night, "answered" one another with their flutes, and subsequently as culture advanced with their voices, extemporising words as they formerly had done tones.

In course of time this favourite practice grew into an artistic form of song among the Arabians, known as the "contention"—a form of song in which two singers took

---

[1] *E.g.*, "Praise the Lord, O my soul: and, all that is within me, praise His holy name," the division of the verse being marked in the English Psalms by a colon.

part instead of one, both being as essential to the exposition of the song as the second line of a couplet to the completion of the metre.[1] Now, when we turn to the minstrelsy of the troubadours, what do we find as one of its prominent and predominant forms? The *tenson*,[2] which is Provençal for "con-*tention*," and which was performed in like manner by two troubadours "contending" with one another in the same sort of poetical duel which the Arabian singers engaged in, and in which either performer was as necessary to the other as the lines in a couplet are to the metre. "I have searched," says M. Fauriel,[3] "through the poetical literature of all nations; and the Arabians are the only people with whom I find such a form current." And although this assertion must be qualified by reference to the amœbæan "contentions" of the ancient pastoral poets of Sicily and Italy, and to some other forms in use among the Greeks,[4] yet the manifest derivation of the form in the present in-

---

[1] Fauriel, *Histoire de la Poésie Provençale*, iii.

[2] In Provençal, *tenso*.

[3] Fauriel, *Histoire de la Poésie Provençale*, iii. 337.

[4] "But he went a step further: his rhapsode of actor did not confine his speech to mere narration; he addressed it to the chorus, who by means of its coryphæi carried on a sort of dialogue" (Donaldson's *Theatre of the Greeks*, p. 60).

"The first of these steps may be taken to be the splitting up of the chorus into two semi-choruses, for the purpose of emphasizing by brief and rapid dialogue some critical point in the ode. The leader of the chorus holds conversation with the rest of the chorus. Meaning of 'actor,' ὑποκροτης, 'answering reciter'" (*Ancient Classical Drama*, Moulton).

"The answerer because he told his tale in answer to the questions of the coryphæus" (Lewis's *Greek Tragedy*).

stance from the Arabians by the troubadours is too obvious to need further allusion. In their compositions for solo singers, the Arabians were in the habit of employing dual verses, each matching with the other. In the poetry of the troubadours we find exactly the same poetical form, the verses so constructed being called *coblas*,[1] or "couplets." One most favourite style of versification among the Arabians was the *casida*, which was a long poem so ingeniously constructed that from beginning to end there was only one rhyme throughout it. With equal wealth of verbal melody at their disposal in the beautiful and harmonious Provençal tongue, which had now attained its full maturity, the troubadours spent in like manner their ingenuity and pains in constructing poems on one rhyme—so successfully and copiously that sometimes the composition was extended to one hundred lines, and the original rhyme never departed from. In the manufacture of these ditties they beat their masters, whose tongue was less supple and more prolific in harsh-sounding consonants; for we do not recollect an instance of an Arabic *casida* which exceeds fifty lines and fifty identical rhymes. Another favourite form of Arabic verse was the *maouchah*—a short lyric song, so bestuck and bespangled with rhymes of motley and heterogeneous character as well to merit the name by which it was called—*maouchah*—which, being translated, means "embroidery." Most admirably reflected

---

[1] In its original sense. But the word comes to mean generally "a stanza."

was the spirit of the *maouchah* in the short lyric poems of the troubadours, whose dainty jinglings and artful ambushings of rhymes might well compare with the best Arabian embroidery. But a still closer connection and relationship is apparent when we turn to the names by which the various orders of songs were known. The Arabians had a well-marked order of songs which they called their "complaints" (we translate in this and the following instances the original Arabic names into English)—a species of song in which the poet mourned the death of his lady-love, or a friend, or a monarch. This form appears among the troubadours as the *Planh*—a well-marked species of dirge devoted to the same subjects. The Arabian minstrels and gallants were accustomed to sing a certain form of song outside the windows of their lady-loves in the evening, and this they called the "evening song." The troubadours likewise cultivated the same order of ditty, calling it the "serenade," from *sera*, "the evening." Not content with regaling the object of their affections with poetical effusions at nightfall, the Saracen cavaliers and minstrels awoke early in the morning, and repeated a similar soft application to her ears and heart when the dawn began to whiten the sky. This they called their "morning song." In precisely the same way the troubadours wrote what they called their *alba*, or "morning song" (from *alba*, "the morning"), destined for the same purposes and composed in the same style.

RHYME: TWO THEORIES AS TO ITS ORIGIN.—We might go on enumerating. But it seems right to pass from the

minuteness of detail to consider the general question of
the Arabian influence in its relation to rhyme. Rhyme
certainly flowered into roses among the Provençals, and
in Provence was first heard in any living tongue but the
Arabic. Among the Arabians it had been developed and
employed at a very early period in their literature. There
seems every likelihood that the troubadours derived likewise their adornment of rhyme from Arabic influence.[1]
But this assertion, it may be remarked, has been denied.
Two main contrary opinions have been upheld, both with
some shadow of probability and both warmly championed
by their respective partisans. The first is that the introduction of rhyme into European literature was due to the
natural springing up of rhymes in the learned Latin versification of the age, the composition of which was principally
in the hands of the monks. Indeed, it seems certain that
the practice of rhyming syllables, which was studiously
avoided by the classical poets as an adventitious and
even unhealthy decoration of their metre, gradually crept
into the Latin versification of the monks, whose taste was
not so pure nor whose literary self-control so great.
Accordingly rhyming spondees with the two syllables
rhyming, and rhyming dactyls with the three syllables
in accord, found occasional but increasing introduction
into Latin verses, until towards the end of the twelfth century Leo Parisius, an eminent scholar of the age, set the
fashion, and gave the name to rhyming Latin verses,

---

[1] Uezio in Andres, i. 307 : " Ex Arabibus meo quidem judicio
versuum simili sono concludendorum artem accepimus." Cf.
L'Abbé Massieu, *Storia della Poesia Francese.*

D

which were called after him "Leonine verses." But
nearly a century before, the first troubadour had written
scores of simpler and more unstudied rhymes in the
tongue of his country, and towards the close of the
twelfth century the art of rhyme was a brilliant decoration in the hands of all the Provençal minstrels. Preceding the time of the Leonine verses, nothing but a few occasional and often clumsy attempts at rhyme in monastic
manuscripts, a few inscriptions, a few epitaphs on grave-
stones, gave indication of the existence, or rather of the
tentative existence, of such an adornment of literature in
the classical atmosphere of Europe ; and it has been well
said, Were the troubadours likely to have gone to manuscripts and epitaphs for the discovery of that sparkling
polish to their songs ?[1] The second view which we have
alluded to is that rhyme was a natural growth in Northern
poetry, and that from the earliest times the barbarians
who invaded the Roman empire were partial to or were
acquainted with the delightful art of ending measured
lines with syllables of similar sound. Examples of this
theory have not been forthcoming in such plenty as might
have been desired. At the same time, while among the
most ancient specimens of Anglo-Saxon poetry we do not
find traces of rhymes, in a collection of verses referred to
by Muratori, and called "semi-Saxon," we have numerous
examples of, if not rhyme, at least assonance. The
rhymed Teutonic poems of the monk Otfried are known

---

[1] Andres, *Dell' Origine e Stato Attuale d'Ogni Letteratura*, i.
809.

to most students; and the theory has been put forward that these Anglo-Saxon and Teutonic approaches to rhyme were spread and promulgated through Europe by the Normans. On the other hand, the skalds of Scandinavia were ignorant of rhyme throughout all the earlier ages of their poetry, and we are expressly told that Einar Scowluson introduced this adornment of metre into Swedish poetry about the middle of the twelfth century. But even if Sweden and Norway had tallied with the greatly unsupported theory of a plenitude of rhyme among the barbarians, we must conclude in the words of Olaus Verelius in his *Runografia*, "The barbarians who supplanted the culture of Rome did not force their literature upon the conquered, but themselves learned letters from them." How much easier, instead of going so far afield, to assume what is well-nigh so transparent as to scarcely need assumption : that the art of rhyme came from the Arabians through Spain to the troubadours, and was by them disseminated and made popular through Europe ! The Arabian language, as we have said before, lent itself marvellously to that melodizing of the syllables which we call rhyme, though not so much even as its younger imitator the *langue d'Oc*, or the Provençal. In the library of the Escurial, there are numerous Arabic dictionaries, the arrangement of which is not on the plan pursued among us of tabulating the words by their initial letters, but by their rhymes. It has been well observed in relation to this that the Arabians' delight in rhyme was obviously and naturally so great that they had a far more vivid apprehension of the endings of words than we have of their beginnings. We may add to these facts the further remark that all the Arabian poetry was in rhyme from time immemorial, not merely stray sections of it, and those sections at specially favoured periods; while the channels through which its influence flowed into Europe are not wrapped in the darkness of theory or diminished to attenuated threads, but broad, voluminous, and apparent, and, as we said before, the most easy to dilate upon and to account for.

THE "LANGUE D'OC" AND THE "LANGUE D'OÏL."—The language of Provence, which, from whatever quarter it received, gave earliest utterance to this delight of modern literature, may best be characterized and comprehended by having reference to the original classification of Dante's,[1] as ingenious as it is lasting, which divides the Romance languages into three groups, distinguished from one another by the difference of the word expressing "yes." In one set of dialects and one large language "yes" was *Oc*, in another it was *Oïl*, and in another it was *Sì*. The three languages were accordingly described as the *langue d'Oc*, the *langue d'Oïl*, and the *lingua di Sì*. The *langue d'Oc* was the Provençal, the *langue d'Oïl* Northern French, and the *lingua di Sì* the Italian.

GEOGRAPHICAL EXTENT OF THE "LANGUE D'OC" AND THE TERM "PROVENÇAL."—The *langue d'Oc*, independently of geographical limits, although described generally as Provençal, was practically the language of the whole of

---

[1] *De Vulgari Eloquio*, i. 8: "Nam alii *Oc*, alii *Oïl*, alii *Sì*, affirmando loquuntur."

the south of France ; and the area of its prevalence might
very clearly be indicated by drawing a line from the mouth
of the Garonne to the Alps, which would include within
its limits the provinces of Guienne, Gascony, Béarn, Foix,
Roussillon, Languedoc, Dauphiny, Auvergne, part of
Lyonnais, Limousin, part of Marche, Angoulême,
Saintonge, and Poitou, with Provence itself. The phy-
sical and social characteristics of the people inhabiting
these regions have always been remarkably similar ; and
these inalienable features, impressed by nature, have led
over and over again to their grouping in an exclusive category, irrespectively of the chance and temporary requirements and changes of political domination. The Romans
were keen in apprehending this racial similarity, and in
constituting their *provincia*, or " province," in which the
name of the more favoured quarter originated, embraced
the inhabitants of the whole of the south of France from
the Alps to the Pyrenees in its natural limits, including
most of those whose affinity we have just now called
attention to. In the same way, the mediæval geo-
graphers, long after the demarcation of this astute and
profound division of France had passed away, were accustomed to style by the term *provinciales*, or Provençals,
not only the inhabitants of Provence proper, but those of
Languedoc, Aquitaine, and all the others which we
recently enumerated,[1] though governed by other rulers
and holding allegiance to other crowns.

Throughout all this large district the *langue d'Oc* ex-

---

[1] Even including Arragon, Catalonia, and Navarre in the list.

tended, and the community of language implied, as it always does, community of thought and community of custom. The doings and the manners in the glowing centre of Provençal vitality, in Provence itself, awoke sympathy and produced imitation in the whole of that vast region which palpitated in harmony with it, and acknowledged, if not identity of political association, that more complete and intimate union of feeling and nature which one language and one spirit alone can give. The seigneurs of Provence in their lordly castles, giving ear to all the strange influences of the times and seeking in fastidious refinement that isolation from the common vulgar which from first to last it was the aim of the old noblesse to secure, were faithfully imitated by their companion Provençal nobles of Aquitaine, Limousin, Auvergne, Saintonge, Foix, Roussillon, and the other affiliated domains, whose sole ambition was to equal them in refinement and to deserve the character for superior excellence and eminence of aristocratic taste which they so signally possessed.

CHAPTER III.

The English and Normans in the Crusade—Ostentation and Formality of the Byzantines—Gallantry of the Turks and Saracens—The First Troubadour and his Connection with England—William of Poitou's Poetical Skill—His Antagonism to the Church—Anecdotes of William of Poitou—William and Eleanor, the Patrons of Troubadours.

THE ENGLISH AND NORMANS IN THE CRUSADE.—It was at this moment that the call to the First Crusade resounded through Europe, and there was a general awakening into vivid vitality of latent energies and unsuspected powers throughout all the countries which engaged prominently in that enterprise. The Normans and the English formed no inconsiderable contingent of the forces, the former being led by Robert surnamed Courte-heuse, Duke of Normandy, the eldest son of William the Conqueror, and the latter by Edgar Atheling, comprising a stalwart band of Saxon thanes and yeomen. We read that the latter took an honourable part in the siege of Jerusalem, being placed near to the Normans towards the north of the city from the gate of Herod to the gate of Cedar or St. Stephen. But still more important than the contact of war to these unsophisticated soldiers of the West must have been the associations into which they were brought with friends or foes in those far-distant regions in the way of entertainment, intercourse, or parley. Their march towards Palestine led them through the gorgeous capital of the East, Constantinople, in whose environs for a short period the Crusaders took up their abode, pouring in their thousands, according to Anna Comnena, "like the sands of the sea or the stars of heaven in multitude, or like the innumerable torrents which unite to form a river." An Armenian historian, with still more convincing eloquence, compares the approach of the Crusaders towards Constantinople to that of "a flight of locusts swarming from the gates of the West."

OSTENTATION AND FORMALITY OF THE BYZANTINES.— The Emperor Alexius redoubled the pomp and magnificence of his court before the eyes of the simple and unlettered strangers. He sought to disguise his own weakness by an increased elaboration of ceremonial and ostentation of wealth.[1] " Ceremonial indeed was at Constantinople," says Michaud, " the most serious and the most important business of life."[2] The multiplication of minute and trifling details of etiquette was made a regular business at the Byzantine court, and he required to be a learned and experienced courtier who could go through the entire routine of punctilious observances without committing a mistake. Alexius entirely succeeded by his ostentation and display[3] in creating the profound

---

[1] Michaud, *Histoire des Croisades*, ii. 193.

[2] " La cérémonial était d'ailleurs à la cour de Constantinople la chose la plus sérieuse et la plus importante " (*Ibid.*, ii. 197).

[3] At the same time we must not overlook the words of Finlay, " When Europe poured into his dominions innumerable hosts of

Troubadour in Banqueting-hall.

impression he desired. He extorted homage from the unwilling lips of the Norman chieftains, and made knees bend before the aspect of his vain magnificence which would never have sunk in submission save to the God of battles Himself. When they departed from the Byzantine shores, the Christian knights were never weary of extolling the palaces, the splendid edifices, the riches, and the lovely Greek women that had been presented to their contemplation and silent worship. " What a city," says Fulcher the chronicler of Robert, Duke of Normandy—" What a city is Constantinople! how large! how beautiful! How many monasteries, how many palaces, are there! What wonders are to be seen in the streets and in the squares! Indeed, it would take me too long to recite everything which this city contains in the way of riches in gold, silver, stuffs, and holy relics ! " [1] with much more to the same effect. The writer, who was present with his patron Duke Robert of Normandy at various functions of the court, proceeds to extol the Emperor Alexius as the mentor and indispensable auxiliary of the Western princes. Indeed, so beclouded does his brain become with the pageantry and ceremony which he must have witnessed, that he does not hesitate to give Alexius the credit of supplying the Crusaders with all the money, horses, and arms which they required

Crusaders, whose militant force set all direct opposition at defiance, his prudence and administrative knowledge carried the empire through that difficult crisis in safety " (Finlay's *History of Greece*, iii. 55).

[1] *Fulcherii Carnotensis Gesta Peregrinantium Francorum*, i.

for their expedition. In a word, having allusion to the
new spirit which was entering Europe at this critical
epoch in its social life, and which was destined to find
such signal and pronounced expositors in the troubadours,
we do not hesitate to attribute the new science of refined
manners, the art of ceremony, the rules of etiquette, to
the influence of Constantinople on the plain and un-
varnished character of our forefathers which was thus
presented so suddenly to the sphere of its operation.[1]

GALLANTRY OF THE TURKS AND SARACENS.—But the
Crusades brought the untutored warriors likewise into connection with the polished and courtly Saracens, and to the
influence of the latter we should attribute the new spirit
of gallantry, which was likewise to find its first and most
pronounced exponents in the persons of the troubadours.
The First Crusade indeed acted, if we may so say, as a
sort of edict for the emancipation of women. Women who
till now had been trained after the domestic and learned
ideal of the Anglo-Saxons,[2] or who under the Normans,
or in France generally, lived in constant terror, as weak
and unprotected beings, of ill-usage and violent treatment,[3] now ventured forth in crowds to far-distant coun.

---

[1] In addition the Crusaders brought back the industrial arts,
such as the manufacture of cloth, glass, silk, etc. (Blanqui's *History
of Political Economy*; Michaud's *Histoire des Croisades*, vi. 346).
"The movement of the Crusades was facilitated by the circumstance that Europe began to adopt habits of order just at the
time when Asia was thrown into a state of anarchy" (Finlay,
iii. 95).

[2] Child, *History of Women*, ii. 117.

[3] Cf. the terrors of Matilda, wife of Henry I., at the insults

tries, sometimes accompanying their husbands or lovers, sometimes setting forth alone. Arrayed in squadrons, they at times took up arms in defence of the Holy Cross. A new world opened a new life to them, and the ideas of men with respect to them changed accordingly. They were brought, as were the knights and soldiers of the Cross, into contact with the most gallant race upon earth,[1] a race whose passionate adoration of women was, in fact, the main motive of their social existence. Numerous are the romantic episodes of love between the Turkish warriors and the fair Christian pilgrims; and we need only allude to the story of the lady of Treves and her Saracen lover before the walls of Nicæa in the history of Albert of Aix,[2] to the romantic history of the lady of Fulke in the environs of Antioch, to the frequent tales of the same nature which decorate and relieve the accounts of Fulcher, to the remarks of Gauthier on the Christian ladies in his *Wars of Antioch*,[3] to the romantic stories in Guibert,[4] and to the accounts of William of Tyre, to illustrate this remark by interesting examples.[5] We should probably not do wrong

which were likely to be offered her, to escape which she entered a convent.

[1] Perron, *Femmes Arabes.*

[2] *Historia Hierosolymitanæ Expeditionis, edita ab Alberto Canonico, Aquensis Ecclesiæ.*

[3] *Gauterii Bella Antiochena*, folio 4.

[4] Guibert, *Gesta Dei per Francos.* fin.

[5] For the passionate and complete devotion of the Saracens to female charms, see the Arabic poets *passim,* and M. Perron's interesting work, *Femmes Arabes avant et depuis l'Islamisme* (Algiers, 1858).

to attribute to this source the rise of that new spirit of studious and refined gallantry which we shall have such frequent cause to allude to in the succeeding pages.

THE FIRST TROUBADOUR AND HIS CONNECTION WITH ENGLAND.—Among the Crusaders who returned from the East was one who, though not himself a native of our land, has a curious and abiding connection with England in many ways. This was the grandfather of Queen Eleanor, the wife of Henry II.: William IX., Count of Poitou and Duke of Aquitaine, who likewise enjoys the distinction of being the first of the troubadours.[1] To him and to his retainers has been very ingeniously traced the English war-cry, which, after having afforded a problem to the students of minute research for a considerable period, was at last by one most acutely ascribed to this origin. The French herald Gilles de Bonnier expressly states that the war-cry of Duke William of Aquitaine—before it was heard in England—was "St. George for the puissant Duke!" To substitute for " puissant Duke " " merry England " was but a natural change of terminology, agreeably to the altered conditions of the duchy, to which we shall immediately refer. In the same way that the English war-cry has been derived with every probability from this famous troubadour, the armorial bearings of the English kings are justly supposed to come from the same quarter.

---

[1] By this term we must understand the first troubadour of world-wide celebrity, for, as we have seen, other troubadours of small note had preceded him.

The kings of England bore leopards on their shields until after the time of Edward I. King Edward III. is called " the Valiant Pard " in his epitaph ; and when the Emperor of Germany would make an acceptable present to King Henry III., he could think of nothing more appropriate or more suitable than a leash of three leopards, which he transmitted to the English monarch with the remark that they were in compliment and allusion to his armorial bearings. Now the crest of William the Troubadour was a leopard ; and, as we shall presently see, he was the ancestor of the royal line of England. But yet more close is his relationship to us owing to his being, through his grandchild Eleanor, the progenitor of our line of English kings. For her he abdicated his immense dominions, and Eleanor by this abdication became the heiress of Gascony, Guienne, Poitou, Saintonge, and Toulouse. On reference to the map it will be found that these domains unite nearly the whole of Southern France, and include the greater part of those countries which are designated by the adjective Provençal.

William of Poitou's Poetical Skill.—This first of the troubadour seven before his departure for the Holy Land had written a number of poems, which, however, are more remarkable for their coarseness than their interest; and on his return from the wars against the infidels he devoted his genius to singing the fatigues, the adventures, and the dangers of the expedition. He touched the subject with a light and graceful hand, and studded his recital of disasters with pleasantries, of perils with wit, and of toils with vivacity of sentiment[1]; and the verses of this illustrious troubadour, the first coryphée of his race, are remarkable for a facility of versification, a copious flow of language, an elegance of style, and a harmony of numbers, of which the first essays in an art would scarcely seem capable. Yet they are found to be eminently so in the case of William of Poitou. Such consummate ease of diction, such freedom of style and perfect conception of literary effect, are not often found at the beginning of any genealogy of literature, but come as a rule after at least a generation of effort.[2] But if William of Poitou's poetical art is ripened and refined, his choice of subject exhibits immaturity and rawness. In almost each instance in those specimens of his art which remain to us, the subject is flagrantly and vulgarly immodest. The coarse and brutal terms in which he invariably alludes to women recall rather the bluff spirit of the pre-crusading baronage than speak of that delicate and over-refined timorousness of amorous sentiment which was to be the marked character of the troubadours. William of Poitou had not yet mastered the new spirit of refined Europe, although he was a consummate master of the form in which that new spirit was to be expressed.

His Antagonism to the Church.—The accounts which have reached us of his life have suffered in many respects from his unfortunate attitude towards the Church, which

---

[1] *La Curne de Sainte-Palaie*; *Histoire Littéraire des Trouba-dours*, i. 16 (Paris, 1774).

[2] Balaguer, *Historia de los Trovadores* ii.

in those days was almost the sole conservator of history and chronicle. From a spirit of intellectual contempt or moral bravado, he constantly opposed the Church and churchmen throughout his dominions, turned the customs of the former into mockery and flouted openly the latter. We must bear in mind in studying the history of the troubadours that this spirit, which was so strongly pronounced in the first of their race, was in a manner common more or less to all.[1] Whether it were a secret unbelief or a spirit of social rebellion against the moral constraints of religion engendered by luxury and looseness of life, certain it is that the troubadours throughout their history will generally be found to constitute the anti-clerical party—a natural position, some will say, for a race of men and poets who represented so strikingly the blithe, unfettered, and pagan conceptions of life.

ANECDOTES OF WILLIAM OF POITOU.—Such was eminently the case with William of Poitou. We have said that he turned the customs of religion into mockery. Regarding nunneries with no very favourable eye, in which young and often beautiful girls buried themselves at ecclesiastical bidding from the eyes of the world and the intercourse of society, and often sunk fortunes of large value in what appeared to him worthless endowments, he opened a mock nunnery at Niort, which was governed, according to due monastic custom, by an abbess and a prioress, and

---

[1] Opposition to the Church seems to have been more or less a prevalent feeling at this time, though the learning of the troubadours might put it in a more lasting literary form.

for which an elaborate scheme of rules was drawn up for the use of the nuns and novices in their various cells. The spirit, not only the letter, of conventual regulations was parodied in these arrangements; and the avowed object of the abbess and her assistants was to train up pupils in profligacy.[1] We have said that William of Poitou flouted churchmen to their face. The following instance may suffice of that:—The Count, in defiance of ecclesiastical law, had taken to wife Malberge, who had formerly been the spouse of the Vicomte de Châtelleraud. This audacious and impious marriage excited the animosity of the episcopate,[2] and the Bishop of Poitiers was commissioned by the prelates his brethren to excommunicate the offending Troubadour. He proceeded to his castle, and, with commendable boldness in the presence of so fiery a spirit as William of Poitou, denounced him for his impiety and commenced to read the formula of excommunication. William clapped his hand to his sword, and swore that he would run the Bishop through unless he ceased immediately. The prelate feigned to be greatly alarmed, and under that pretence demanded a few moments for the purpose of reflection. During these

---

[1] William of Malmesbury, *De Gest. Reg. Angl.*

[2] "A certain looseness in the marriage tie was long observable in Northern Europe." "Queen after queen must have been set aside by Charlemagne, unless he is credited with a plurality of wives; and when the beauty and illustrious descent of Matilda first attracted the notice of Henry, the Fowler repudiated his wife Stallbury without further ceremony" (Robertson's *Historical Essays*, p. 172). "With equal alacrity Malcolm seems to have set aside Ingebiorge in order to marry the high-born Margaret of England" (*Ibid.*, p. 172).

E

moments of respite, he secretly finished the formula of excommunication. "Now," he said, "Sir Count, I have done my duty to God, and I am ready. Strike!" "No," exclaimed the Troubadour, sheathing his sword. "You have done your duty, and you are at your prayers. I do not love you well enough to send your soul to paradise; but I will send your body into exile."

The latter threat he accordingly carried out, and the courageous Bishop was banished from the domains of William to another district, where less haughty subjects awaited his ecclesiastical censures.[1]

WILLIAM AND ELEANOR, THE PATRONS OF TROUBADOURS.—From these two instances—and more might be quoted—it will be plain what was the attitude of William of Poitou towards the Church. The Church has amply revenged itself on him by holding him up to all posterity as a monster of impiety and guilt, comparable only to King John or William Rufus, or worse than either. The capital of William and afterwards of Eleanor was Bordeaux, the centre and meeting-place of all the wealth and luxury of their vast dominions. Hither to the court of the great troubadour and his granddaughter flocked the troubadours and poets of all the Provençal countries, secure of finding in Eleanor a friend, a protectress, and a genial critic,[2] chief among the brilliant coterie who paid their court to her being the celebrated troubadour Bernard de Ventadour. To Bordeaux Eleanor constantly repaired

---

[1] *La Curne de Sainte-Palaye*, i. 5.
[2] Raynouard, *Choix des Poésies*, ii. 89.

even after her marriage with the Dauphin of France which was soon to make her queen of that country; and when, after her divorce from the French king, she was united to Henry II., King of England, her cultivated tastes still continued, and her patronage of literature and song was unabated as ever. It was under the latter circumstances—after her marriage at Bordeaux, on the 1st of May, 1152, with Henry II., at that time not yet King of England, but only Duke of Normandy—that when he shortly afterwards succeeded to the English throne she was crowned with him at Westminster and proceeded to take up her abode in the palace of Bermondsey. Strange example of the mutation of human affairs, that this district, which is now associated in one's mind with tanners' yards and the squalor of East London poverty, should have once been the home of the great Provençal queen and her court of glittering troubadours!

CHAPTER IV.

THE TROUBADOUR QUEEN.

London in the Days of Henry II.—The Extent of the English
Dominions—Provençal Influence on England—Eleanor as a
Crusader—Bernard de Ventadour—Bernard's Love for Queen
Eleanor.

LONDON IN THE DAYS OF HENRY II.—In those days
Bermondsey was a pastoral village of a somewhat Flemish
character in general appearance. It was diversified
with private gardens, carefully and beautifully cultivated,
and with meadows rich in green and velvet grass, on
which herds of cattle fed and strayed. Beside the Palace,
there was also a priory there, whose newness and trim-
ness contrasted strangely with the hoary age of the royal
pile.[1] Looking from the palace windows upon the London of that date, the eye of Eleanor would behold a large
and fortified city, surrounded with castellated towers and
massive walls, washed at their base by the river Thames.
On the east rose, in all its massive and *recent* grandeur,
the Tower of London, frowning over the prospect with new
stones, and with bastions not a century old. On the west,
the great cathedral rose into the air and towered aloft,
hard by the gateway of Ludgate.[2] Such was the prospect
which would have met the gaze of Eleanor of Guienne at

---

[1] *London Restituta.*   [2] *Ibid.*

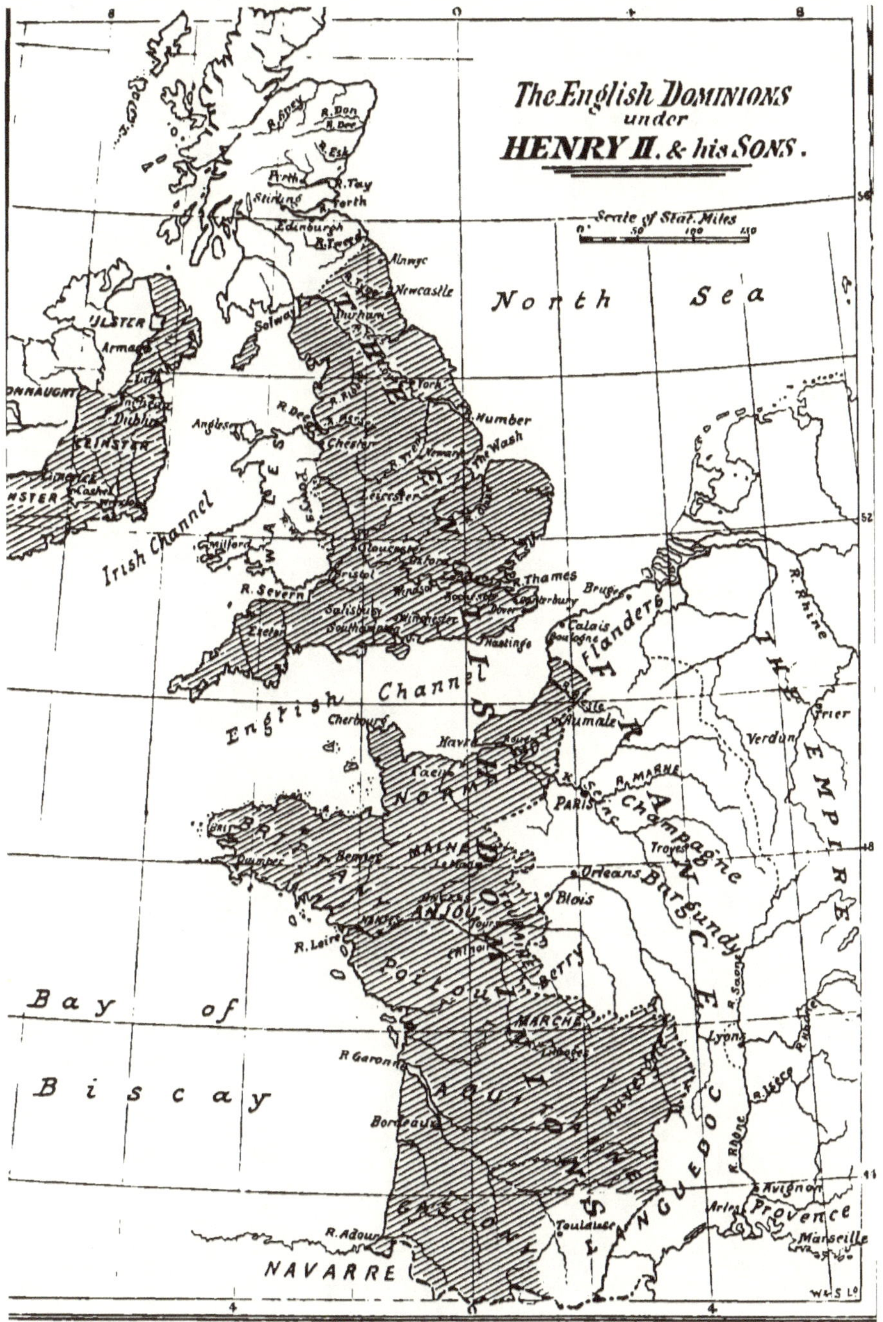

The English DOMINIONS
under
HENRY II. & his SONS.
Scale of Stat. Miles
North Sea
ULSTER
Armagh
CONNAUGHT
Dublin
LEINSTER
MUNSTER
Cashel
Limerick
R. Spey
R. Don
R. Dee
R. Esk
Forth
Stirling
Edinburgh
R. Tweed
R. Tay
Forth
Alnwic
Newcastle
Durham
Solway
York
R. Dee
R. Ouse
Humber
Chester
The Wash
WALES
Newark
Leicester
Anglesea
Milford
Gloucester
Stafford
Bristol
Windsor
London
R. Thames
R. Severn
Salisbury
Winchester
Canterbury
Dover
Exeter
Southampton
Hastings
Irish Channel
English Channel
Cherbourg
Havre
Calais
Boulogne
Flanders
Rouen
Aumale
Lille
Trier
Verdun
R. Rhine
NORMANDY
Caen
Paris
R. Seine
R. MARNE
Troyes
Champagne
THE EMPIRE
BRITTANY
Brest
Quimper
R. Benier
MAINE
Le Mans
Orleans
Blois
Burgundy
R. Saone
ANJOU
Nantes
Tours
Chinon
Berry
R. Loire
POITOU
MARCHE
Limoges
Lyons
R. Rhone
Bay of Biscay
AQUITAINE
R. Garonne
Bordeaux
GASCONY
LANGUEDOC
Avignon
Arles
Provence
Marseille
R. Adour
Toulouse
NAVARRE
W. & S. Lº
[Face p. 54.

the time of her coronation as Queen of England, after her marriage with Henry II.

THE EXTENT OF THE ENGLISH DOMINIONS.—By that marriage and that coronation, the power of the English crown was extended over an enormous area, and the kingdom of England might be said generally to have embraced all England and more than half of France. Not only did Normandy, Anjou, Maine, Touraine, and Brittany acknowledge the sceptre of Henry, but the wealthy and fertile Provençal lands of southern France constituted essential portions of his monarchy, and were as completely recognised as such as were Leinster, Munster, and the other annexed portions of Ireland at a later date. These Provençal districts, the dowry of Eleanor, included the fertile regions of Poitou, Marche, the Limousin, Auvergne, Gascony, and Guienne. In fact, speaking roughly, a line drawn from Boulogne due south, and thus dividing France into two unequal halves, would embrace in the larger and western half the general configuration of the English dominion.

PROVENÇAL INFLUENCE ON ENGLAND.— Throughout this immense monarchy intercourse was comparatively unhindered, and the communication between Leicester and Bordeaux, or York and Poitiers, might be compared to that existing a century ago between two such towns as Dover and Aberdeen.[1] It is easy to see then how this

---

[1] In illustration of this, it may be remarked that immediately after the marriage of Eleanor and Henry, the land was flooded with importations of Gascon wine. This, and the rapid fortunes

opened a door for the influence of Provençal manners and customs, and with them Provençal literature, to insinuate itself most potently into English life, and how the various streams which we have shown gathering from various tributaries, were enabled to converge in a strong river pouring into England. But before we consider the question from this point of view, let us pause for a moment over the great Provençal queen, and see how she was eminently and in every way a type of the chivalry, romance, and sentiment of the troubadours.

ELEANOR AS A CRUSADER.—Before her marriage with Henry II. she had gone to the crusades along with her first husband, Louis VII. of France. Not content with accompanying her chivalrous husband to the war, she conceived the idea of appearing in a more prominent *rôle* than merely the wife of a warrior; she determined to assume the character of a warrior, an Amazon, herself. The first thing with a lady, in the middle ages as to-day, when she enters upon any public and conspicuous function, is to consider the dress she shall appear in. Eleanor, whose millinery and dress-making orders were the wonder of her contemporaries, having settled this important item to her complete satisfaction, attired herself in a graceful combination of spangles, surcoat, breastplate,

made by some of the London merchants of this date, who dealt in that commodity, point to a closeness of intercourse.

"An English merchant sojourned at Marseilles in the eighth century" . . . "and a year in which the usual communication with Rome did not take place seemed to deserve special mention from the chronicler."—Cunningham, *Growth of English Industry and Commerce*, p. 81.

and helmet, in the guise of an Amazon, and gathering a troop of ladies around her silken standard, all similarly accoutred, rode off with the hosts of the Second Crusade to the holy war, the cynosure of every eye, and, in the opinion of the vulgar, the most important personage of the expedition.[1] The distaffs which the band of lady crusaders had flung away in zeal to don their Amazonian attire, were sent as a present to any stay-at-home knights who happened to have shirked the invitations to the crusade, much in the same way that presents of white feathers are made to officers of the army to-day, and shamed many into joining the expedition. Eleanor, who began the crusade in the spirit of a woman of fashion, conducted it on the same terms. Her over-indulgent husband, having foolishly committed to her care the van of the army during the march through Asia Minor, the queen made her strategic movements depend on the beauty of the landscape, not upon the military considerations of the ground, and brought herself and the army into jeopardy more than once by her manœuvres. She diversified the fatigues of war by romantic episodes of love with the Saracen warriors, and particularly with a youthful emir in the service of the Sultan Noureddin.[2] In short, she conducted her wars in the same spirit in which the armour-clad ladies of the stage, in some extravaganza at the present day, clash their harmless arms with becoming gestures, interrupt the campaign at any moment to sing a song

[1] William of Tyre describes her Amazonian exploits.
[2] Suger, in Duchesne.

or pursue an amour, and delight to feel the limelight or the coloured electric lamp play upon their magnificent and silver suits of mail. Such was the romantic and extraordinary life of Queen Eleanor—a life hard to understand and sympathise with at the present hour, because so utterly removed from any possibility of imitation or experience.

Bernard de Ventadour.—We mentioned that her court was the home and in more senses than one the paradise of contemporary troubadours, of whom her grandfather had been so conspicuous and distinguished a member. Chief among those who thus sang her praises was Bernard de Ventadour, a troubadour of such fame and such literary taste, that Petrarch has not scrupled to eulogise him and to extol those beauties of style which the Italian poet seems to think are unequalled in Bernard's special domain. Very different in his origin and lineage from Eleanor's grandfather, one of the greatest princes in Christendom, was the second troubadour on the long and illustrious *rôle* of Provençal poets. Bernard de Ventadour was the son of a servant belonging to the Château de Ventadour, in Limousin. The functions performed by Bernard's father are believed to have been connected with the bakehouse of the castle, and the young boy from the first seems to have been keenly conscious of his inferior station. But the Seigneur de Ventadour took a fancy to the lad and had him taught the elements of a good education. When we ask what the elements of a good education were in those days, the answer may be given in the words of the old French chronicler, from whom we draw the above particulars. They were, to be courteous and well-behaved, to learn how to compose a song and to sing it. In the midst of the babel of subjects which constitute a good education nowadays, we should not do wrong sometimes if we were to lay stress on the acquisition of these now almost forgotten essentials of culture. The Seigneur of Ventadour, by name Ebles, had the common good fortune in those days to possess a charming wife, as beautiful as she was clever, and considerably younger, it appears, than himself. Young Bernard, having put into practice his knowledge of composition and song, by chanting of spring, which gives back their leaves to the trees, of the meadows, which in spring and summer-time become enamelled with a wealth of flowers, and of the nightingale, which acquires its lovely voice in summer-time, as surely as the trees their leaves, or the meadows their flowers, began to employ his more matured power in singing the praises of the young Viscountess of Ventadour, who seemed to her youthful dependant and servitor the most wondrous object in nature. We are given to understand that he suffered his muse to evaporate in generalities and vague compliments, until one day when he was sitting near her, probably singing one of his songs—they were both under the shade of a pine-tree—the viscountess, in a fit of sudden rapture, kissed the young minstrel, who thereupon, to use his own words, " was lost in a trance of ecstasy. He saw nothing, he heard nothing, he knew not what he did or what he said. It happened to be winter-time, but his dizzy head imagined it the month of

May. The meadows seemed covered with lovely verdure. The snow was transfigured into a tapestry of flowers, and universal summer rejoiced over nature." The effect of this kiss was to encourage the young troubadour to more direct forms of eulogy and compliment. Not only did he point all his allusions in a direct and unmistakable manner to the young viscountess, but he abandoned the fictitious name under which he had formerly sung her praises, and did not scruple to compose songs in her honour which let all the world know in whose honour they were composed. This audacity in a dependant was too much for the hot blood of the Vicomte de Ventadour, who, in order best to put a stop to the too familiar intercourse of the twain, shut up the viscountess in a secluded chamber in the castle, and drove the troubadour with threats and objurgations from the district.[1]

BERNARD'S LOVE FOR QUEEN ELEANOR.—An ever open asylum for those unfortunate in love and fortunate in war, was the court of Eleanor, at that time Duchess of Normandy—for Henry II. had not yet succeeded to the English throne—and thither Bernard de Ventadour repaired. His impressionable heart soon began to sigh for the new mistress of its fortunes, and to aspire with the same audacity to her favour and her love. If we may judge from the poems in which this passion is chronicled, we should certainly be inclined to describe this second *affaire de cœur* of the ambitious troubadour

---

[1] For the preceding particulars, see *La Curne de Ste. Palaye, Histoire Littéraire ;* Victor Balaguer, *Historia de los Trovadores ;* Diez, *Leben und Werke,* etc.

as a more serious one than the former. Both Eleanor and Bernard appear to have been deeply enamoured, and King Henry was an indulgent or indifferent husband, whose affections or attention were often engaged elsewhere than on his romantic and volatile queen. In a beautiful poem Bernard has celebrated Eleanor's departure for England. He declares, in what is the commonplace of poetry now, but then was its perfect and most original vein of thought, that " though absent from his beloved lady, her image will always be engraved on his heart." He speaks further on in the same song of the nightingale, which awakes him in the morning by chanting of its love, and thus recalls to him the lovely Eleanor. The sweet thought of her is far sweeter than the pleasures of sleep, and he lies awake in the morning hours dreaming of her alone.[1]

This song he sends across the sea to the Queen of England and Normandy, and promises that ere long he will follow his song across the channel. " Across the sea before the coming winter will I come," he says, " from Normandy to England; for I am both a Norman and an Englishman now."

---

[1] *Le Parnasse Occitanien.*

CHAPTER V.

THE TROUBADOUR KING.

Richard Cœur de Lion, the Troubadour King—The Poetry of
King Richard—Richard and Blondel—Bertrand de Born—
The Dauphin of Auvergne—Pons de Capdeuil—Arnaud
Daniel—Arnaud Daniel and the Jongleur.

RICHARD CŒUR DE LION, THE TROUBADOUR KING.—
After Eleanor, the patroness of troubadours, had been its
queen, England was to have a troubadour king. Richard
Cœur de Lion was esteemed the most accomplished prince
of the time, in an age when troubadour instead of scholar
was the synonym for an accomplished man. He too, like
Bernard de Ventadour, had learnt at an early age the
rules of courtesy and good breeding, and how to compose
verses and to sing them.

Richard was born at Beaumont Palace, Oxford. His
mother Eleanor was attached to her palace at Beaumont,
and the subsequent romantic events in her life which
have connected her name with Woodstock and Fair
Rosamond, and those in turn with Godstow and Godstow
Nunnery, will be too familiar to readers to need repetition. We read that Richard owed his taste and qualifications for the *rôle* of troubadour to a sort of hereditary
function which was devolved on him when managing his
mother's dominions in Aquitaine, to show himself the

patron of troubadours, and to keep open court for them.[1] In addition to this, he had been from childhood the intimate friend of Prince Sancho of Navarre, himself a troubadour, and the son of one of their greatest patrons outside Provence and the Provençal districts of France. Of these extra-Provençal troubadours the two Sanchos may be mentioned as examples, also Alphonso II., King of Arragon.[2] In such company, and amid the naturally cultivated surroundings of his court, young Richard early learnt not only the practical accomplishments of the troubadour's art, but acquired also a wide sympathy and interest in the achievements of the courtly minstrels. No tie was more likely to consummate this than his union with Berengaria of Navarre, the sister of his friend Sancho. She, like her brother, was an expert in the art of poetry, or, at least, in the appreciation of it, and her gentle character acted as a corrective to the natural sternness of Richard.

THE POETRY OF KING RICHARD.—The poetical remains of King Richard, however, are not devoted to celebrating the usual theme of love, but to the same martial subjects which made up the chief interest of his life. We have only two pieces left which can be regarded as the undoubted offspring of his muse. The first is a sirvente, said to have been composed while he was in prison after his return from the Holy Land. The second is an exhortation to his two friends, the Dauphin of Auvergne,

---

[1] *La Curnede Ste. Palaye, Histoire Littéraire des Troubadours : Vie de Richard ;* Diez, *Leben und Werke.*

[2] *Ib.*

and Count Guy, his cousin, to join Richard's alliance
against Philip Augustus of France, and was composed
after he had been set at liberty from his German prison.
We give the first of these as a specimen of his style :—

> Ah ! woe betide the wight in prison bound !
> Nought can he ponder but his woe profound.
> Yet, but for comfort's sake, let song resound ;
> Sing of his friends all false and faithless found,
> Who see him languish, valiant and renowned,
>   Three years in dungeon vile.
>
> Ye barons all in merry England mine,
> Ye knights of Normandy of ancient line,
> Hear me declare, that ne'er would I resign
> My poorest soldier thus in ward to pine.
> I mean not to reproach you, courtiers fine,
>   Yet here my hours I wile.
>
> Dead men can injure not, so saws declare ;
> But should no ransom come to bless my prayer,
> Not for myself do I so fondly care
> As for my people's honour, once so fair,
> If I perchance incline to dire despair
>   And die in dungeon vile.
>
> What marvel that my heart is full of woe ?
> Full well I wot how things in England go ;
> How France, despising oaths sworn long ago,
> O'erwhelms my dear domains with cruel blow.
> Ah, God ! I will not languish evermoe,
>   Nor die in dungeon vile.[1]

RICHARD AND BLONDEL.—The story of Blondel and
King Richard, although much has been done to discredit
it, is so thoroughly in keeping with the manners of the
time, that whether it be true or false we shall not scruple

---

[1] *Le Parnasse Occitanien.*

to repeat it here. [1]   Blondel, who is said to have owed his fortune to Richard, the liberal patron of minstrelsy, resolved to go over the whole of Europe but he would find in what prison his lord and master was incarcerated. He had traversed the greater part of the continent, and was returning through Germany, when one day at Linz, in Austria, he heard of the existence of a strong and ancient castle at the entrance of a forest near the city, in which was a prisoner who was guarded with the greatest possible care.   A secret impulse persuaded Blondel that this prisoner was Richard, and he went immediately to the castle.   The sight of its hoary and massive walls made him tremble.   He endeavoured, by hanging round the place some days, to corrupt the fidelity of the domestics, or to glean from the peasantry what prisoner of state had the misfortune to be confined in so impregnable a dungeon.   But nothing came of his efforts in that direction, except to discover, and to have pointed out to him, a small grated window, through which, as his solitary amusement, the prisoner was in the habit of gazing over the adjacent country.

Blondel found, from the height and narrowness of this window, that he could not gain a sight of the famous recluse, whom he fully believed to be his dear master. Accordingly he bethought himself of a song, which, as

---

[1] The anecdote of Blondel is only attested by Fauchet, who follows an ancient French chronicle.   But the Chronicle of Normandy attests the same fact, and their testimonies united are of considerable value.   See Abbé de la Rue, *Essais Historiques*, II. 327.

was sometimes the way in those days, had been the off-spring of a musical collaboration on the part of Richard and himself. He sang part of this song, and waited for the answer. To his ineffable joy the answer came in the loud clear voice of the king, who from his cell sang the conclusion of the air.

BERTRAND DE BORN.—One of Richard's most intimate troubadour friends was the warlike troubadour Bertrand de Born. The character of Bertrand was as violent and martial as that of Richard himself. It is strange to find this bellicose baron employing his undoubted gifts of verse for a somewhat similar purpose as Tyrtæus or Archilochus, that is to say, to stir up and stimulate his military friends to arms. He did not limit himself, however, to martial lays entirely, but indulged in amorous verses at times. Being on terms of the closest intimacy with Richard, so much so that all appellations of royalty and dignity were dropped between them, and they called one another by the nickname "Oc" ("Yes") and "No"—Bertrand cemented this fraternal union by marked attention to Richard's sister, the Princess Helena,[1] and in her honour softened the natural sternness of his muse, which does indeed seem to be Minerva in mail, so entirely is it penetrated with the spirit of war. Rightly or wrongly, to Bertrand's turbulent influence over Richard are attributed the revolt of Richard and his brothers against their

---

[1] For the account of this troubadour see Villedat, *Sur la position historique de Bertrand de Born*, and Albert Stimmung's *Bertrand de Born.*

father, Henry II., and their frequent quarrels between themselves.

But the martial baron and his princely opponents or friends united, in deference to their profession of troubadours, in paying court to one and the same beauty. We have spoken of Bertrand's attachment to the Princess Helena, Richard's sister, but we have now to mention a lady in troubadour annals of even more celebrity. This was Maenz of Martagnac, whose dazzling loveliness completely captured the hearts of all these turbulent barons. In her train of admirers she reckoned the following distinguished troubadours, besides others doubtless of lesser note whose affection history has not recorded: Richard I. of England; Geoffrey Plantagenet, his brother; Alphonso, King of Arragon; Raymond, Count of Toulouse; and Bertrand de Born. The latter, being a plain baron among this coterie of princes, was tormented with ungovernable uneasiness lest the Lady Maenz should prefer any of them before him. But her heart was actuated by motives of affection alone, and despising the rank of the others, she gave to Bertrand her acknowledged love.[1] In the sunshine of her eyes and in the effulgence of her smile he basked for a considerable while contented, in the intervals of his martial exploits. But a lady named Guiscarde de Camborn having composed some verses in his honour, he did not hesitate to transfer the appearance at least of his affections to this new deity, and to compose in his turn several *chansons* in the praise of

---

[1] Albert Stimmung, *Bertrand de Born.*

Guiscarde. Maenz, deeming him unworthy of her favour, dismissed him from her presence, and the martial troubadour endeavoured to right himself in her eyes in vigorous and forcible strains. With the exception of these streaks of sunshine and threads of sentiment which run through the martial baron's life, the main portion of his poetry and his life breathes bellicosity and battle. In that lay his engrossing interest, and the joy of turbulence and commotion seems to have been completely necessary for his existence. Military intriguing and counter-intriguing, alliances and counter-alliances, either with Richard and his brothers or with others of the nobility of the English dominions, in an endless succession, constitute the record of Bertrand's career; and Dante has placed him in his *Inferno* not so much for his violence, however, as for his impiety in exciting the children of Henry II. to rebel against their father.

THE DAUPHIN OF AUVERGNE.—Of a softer and more refined character was another troubadour friend of Richard's—the Dauphin of Auvergne. Although accomplished in all the practice of arms, the Dauphin has earned the praises of his contemporaries as being eminent in arms and eminent in love, the most courteous of men, the most full of genial life; while his poetry itself fully attests his graceful style of expression and his discretion of judgment and taste. Himself a troubadour, he was likewise an encourager and patron of troubadours; and Hugues Brunet, Pierre d'Auvergne, Perdigon, and others, had the privilege of participating in his favours. Despite these excellencies and accomplishments, however, the

Dauphin's career both in minstrelsy and in life was the reverse of peaceful, and most important in interest of the remains of this troubadour are his passionate invectives against the follies and the ways of others of the courtly race. The chief victim of his philippics is a troubadour bishop; and here the reader may very likely pause in amazement at the collocation of two such opposite functions in the person of one man. But the Bishop of Clermont, who was a cultivated and courtly ecclesiastic, united these two *rôles* with complete success, and celebrated the praises of his chosen lady-love with no less earnestness and extravagance than the other troubadours of his time. His thus distinguishing himself in the paths of love seems to be no demerit in the eyes of the Dauphin, and if the bishop had stopped short of assassinating the husband of the lady of his choice, doubtless posterity would never have been informed of the amour. The Bishop of Clermont was the Dauphin's cousin, and had espoused different sides in politics. Perhaps these two facts may account in some measure for the passion and acrimony which was introduced into the dispute between the two relatives, and the monstrous charges which the Dauphin brings against the prelate. But the latter doubtless laid himself open to attack in many ways, and his attempt to reconcile the professions of bishop and troubadour erred, as was most likely to be the case, in giving undue predominance to the latter function.[1]

---

[1] For the preceding particulars of the Dauphin's life see Diez, *Leben und Werke;* Balaguer, *Historia de los Trovadores;* and La Curne de Ste. Palaye, *Histoire.*

Pons de Capdeuil.—Another troubadour who came within the circle of Richard's influence, and followed him to the Holy Land, was Pons de Capdeuil, a wealthy and courtly baron in Puy, who, it is said, with approbation, " possessed in every way the true manners of chivalry, and rendered his passionate attachment to the fair to be famous and celebrated, without overstepping the bounds of virtuous modesty." Azalaïs de Mercœur was the name of the lady, ever illustrious in troubadour annals, who was the object of Pons de Capdeuil's chivalrous devotion. The *fêtes* and feasts he held in honour of her were celebrated above all others in troubadour history. The tournaments in which he tilted in her favour, with her for the queen of the tourney, were the most splendid yet known, except those given by kings ; and to his festivals in honour of Azalaïs the nobility of the Angevin provinces resorted in crowds. Such romantic love, however, being full of delicate and sensitive suspicions, must ever be subject to whim and caprice. And thus it happened to Pons de Capdeuil. After having long possessed the good graces of Azalaïs, and having cultivated her favour and pleased her fancy with such extravagancies of expense, he began to conceive the idea that her love resulted only from the diversions he procured her. Tormented by this secret idea, he became unjust and insensible to every proof of kindness from the lady ; and in order to try her affection, he retired into the south of Provence, and paid assiduous court to the Viscountess of Marseilles. When Azalaïs de Mercœur—who, in fact, was the sweetest of women—heard of this new attachment, and believed herself unjustly despised, she resolved to forget, if possible, her old lover entirely, and forbade her maidens so much as to pronounce his name. Pons de Capdeuil, in affected retirement at Marseilles, made himself acquainted by constant inquiries of the apparent state of Azalaïs' heart, and believing that she was really on the point of forgetting him, his state of mind became pitiable indeed. At once he proceeded to the other extreme, and sent poem after poem to the apparently obdurate fair, pleading, beseeching, imploring, that she would receive him once more into favour. To his complete and appalling surprise, Azalaïs affected to pay no attention to these appeals; which, in fact, racked her gentle heart till it almost broke. Pons de Capdeuil then felt himself compelled to descend to the last extremity possible for a lover who has lost favour with his lady, and he invoked the aid of three noble ladies of the neighbourhood, near friends of Azalaïs and confidantes of all her secrets, to bring him back to favour with her again. With difficulty he succeeded in enlisting their good offices, and by this means he was reunited to the affections of the sweet mistress, whom he should never for a moment have doubted nor departed from, for she was as true to him as the sun in the heavens, and she loved him as much as her own life. Foolish troubadour! was the comment of the time, to have shattered for the sake of a silly experiment that period of bliss which in poor human life is all too short already. A little while after he had returned to the loved society of Azalaïs, she died of a grievous sickness, and Pons de Capdeuil was left to deplore the loss of his beautiful love, whom he so unkindly had mistrusted, but whom he had proved so faithful and true. What remained for him but to fling away his life in battle with the Turk? He accordingly took the cross with Richard, and passing over the seas with him, died gallantly fighting in the Holy Land.[1]

ARNAUD DANIEL.—Among the troubadours who brightened for a while the court of Henry II., we must not forget the celebrated Arnaud Daniel, who, according to Petrarch, whose opinion is entitled to some credit, was the most popular of all the troubadours. The Italian poet designates him as " the great master of love." Petrarch's estimate of the troubadour may, however, be exaggerated by the natural sympathy which one master of metre would have for another. Arnaud, whatever his poetical spirit be—concerning which we ourselves are not inclined to form so high a judgment—was admittedly one of the most elegant of the troubadour versifiers, his pretensions in that particular being attested by his invention of the Sestino or Sixtine, of which we give an illustration in the ensuing chapter. More candid or impartial critics of this troubadour's poetry will be apt rather to arraign him of a fondness for conceits, and of cloaking his thoughts in ambiguous and fantastic terms. Thus, on one occasion, he makes an elaborate comparison of his mistress to a castle. This castle has been presented to him as a freehold. He himself wishes heartily that it had been a

---

[1] The life of Pons de Capdeuil occurs with some variations in Balaguer, Diez, and Ste. Palaye.

copyhold or a leasehold, in order that he might have had
to pay the revenue of a few kisses as an acknowledg-
ment of his ownership—where it will be seen, not only
that the similitude is unreal and artificial, but likewise
that it is mixed and indistinct.

ARNAUD DANIEL AND THE JONGLEUR.—At the court of
the King of England, Arnaud met an English jongleur, who
was celebrated for his skill in constructing difficult
rhymes. As this was the very excellence on which the
troubadour prided himself, he was naturally piqued at
hearing the praises of an inferior who, according to the
common talk of Winchester and London, was considered
as good a minstrel as he.[1] A match was therefore proposed between these two doughty champions of the art
of rhyming, the object of which was to decide who could
produce in the most artistic form the hardest rhymes.
Stakes were laid on this most peculiar match by the
English and Norman nobles, and the king himself, who
took a great interest in the encounter, arranged the terms
of this poetical duel. He ordered the competitors to be
shut up in different chambers, and to be allowed fifteen
days for their preparation of the *tenson*,—ten days for its
composition, and five days for committing to memory the
words and music. At the end of this time the *tenson* was
to be sung in his presence. The two disputants at once
fell to work on their respective parts; but as ill-luck
would have it, on this most momentous occasion the muse

---

[1] The whole account of this contest may be found in La Curne
de Ste. Palaye, *Histoire Littéraire: Vie de A. Daniel.*

of Arnaud, as a rule so prolific and versatile, became quite
dumb, and not a line or a rhyme could he compose. The
chambers of the two antagonists happened to be adjoining
ones, and one evening, shortly before the expiration of the
allotted time, the troubadour, while wrestling in despair
with an unwilling inspiration, which seemed determined
not to come, suddenly heard in the adjoining apartment
the voice of the more successful jongleur declaiming in
loud and jubilant tones the admirable lines of skilful
verse which he had with great facility composed, and
with which he intended to triumph over his antagonist in
a few days' time. The troubadour was favoured by nature
with a most retentive memory, and after hearing the
jongleur repeat time after time his verses and rhymes, he
was not long before he committed them to heart, and
could repeat them word for word and note by note as well
as the unsuspecting author himself. The time came on
for the public exhibition of the *tenson* in presence of the
king, and when the monarch and his court were assembled
the two antagonists were brought into the lists. It fell
to the troubadour's lot to sing first. He touched his lute,
and to the surprise and confusion of the jongleur, poured
forth the very song with its artful rhymes and laboured
structure which the unfortunate minstrel had spent so
much time in composing, and on which he relied for
the victory. The jongleur with a loud voice and great
indignation claimed the song as his own, but the king
would by no means admit the claim. The stratagem of
the troubadour brought complete confusion on the head of
his rival, who was so thunderstruck at the audacity of his

antagonist that he could scarce utter a word of further
protest. We learn in the sequel to this strange story
that the troubadour very generously confessed the
innocent imposition later on, and that the king was so
pleased with the piece of merriment that he divided the
stakes between them.

CHAPTER VI.

THE POETRY OF THE TROUBADOURS.

General Character of the Poetry of the Troubadours—The Verse —The Chanson—The Sonnet—The Couplet or Stanza—The Plainte or Dirge—The Tenson or Contention—The Sirvente (War Song or Pasquinade)—The Sixtine—The Discord—The Pastorelle or Pastoral Piece—The Aubade and the Serenade —The Ballad—The Novel—The Romance.

GENERAL CHARACTER OF THE POETRY OF THE TROU-BADOURS.—The poetry of the troubadours was partly lyrical, partly epic. The lyrical poems were always intended to be sung, with the exception of a certain class of them, called Epitres, or " Letters," which were destined to be read or recited. The epic poems were designed to be recited with occasional music.[1] In some MSS. of the latter we have the musical notes interspersed every now and then in the epic poems, with directions to the minstrel, be he troubadour or glee-man, when the singing is to commence and the recitation to end. For instance, in the

---

[1] "Aye d'Avignon," line 1403. Bourdillon, *Introduction to Aucassin et Nicolette.*

epic poem by an unknown troubadour, entitled " Aucassin et Nicolette," very popular in England at the time of its composition, the musical notes ever and anon interrupt the text of the MS., and directions " This is read," or " This is sung," are given to the minstrel who recited the epic poem, very much in the way of stage directions to a player.[1] The style of verse affected by the troubadours had many varieties, and we will begin by considering the simplest form of all.

THE VERSE.—This term was exceedingly general in its application. There was no particular length of line or collocation of syllables to which it was applied. The verse was sometimes divided into couplets, but sometimes not. In the former case it generally consisted of seven couplets, though eight and six are also found. But the division into couplets does not seem to have been by any means a necessity, as the following example will prove:—

> " Of lies can cunning men
> Oft make a truthful show;
> But God hath made me know
> My course in life will be
> To sing eternally."[2]

This is the commencement of a verse by Giraud Riquier, and it will be observed that the first line is unpaired.

THE CHANSON.—Like the term " verse," chanson is very general in its application. The main difference, so far as we can judge, between the chanson and the verse, is

---

[1] See the MS. of *Aucassin et Nicolette* in the Bibliothèque Nationale, Paris, No. 2168, formerly No. 7989b.

[2] Giraud Riquier, " Car de grans."

that the chanson was necessarily divided into stanzas. It was composed generally in five or six stanzas.

THE SONNET.—This title with the troubadours had no reference to any definite number of lines or to recurrence of rhymes, such as it afterwards acquired. It was quite general in its meaning, being applied to any species of song.

THE COUPLET OR STANZA.—This term likewise was very general in its application, being used by the troubadours to designate their love songs in opposition to their martial ditties, and thus having reference rather to the subject of the song than to the metre.

Sometimes, however, we find it applied in the modern sense of " stanza," as in the following example, which we translate from William de St. Didier[1]:—

> " Since she is fair, the dame I celebrate,
>> Fair her great name, and fair her broad domain,
> Fair her sweet words, and fair her stately gait,
>> My couplets eke to be as fair are fain." [1]

THE " PLANH " OR DIRGE.—The name Planh was applied by the troubadours to those pieces in which they celebrated the memory of a lady-love, a friend, or a benefactor, snatched away by death. Sometimes, but more rarely, public calamities were the subjects of the planh. The metre was nearly always ten or twelve syllables, and the following example, which is a planh of Bertrand de Born's on the death of the young prince of England, the son of Henry II., will show the form and the manner of treatment employed in this celebrated order of composition.[2]

---

[1] Guillaume de St. Didier, " Aissi cum."
[2] Bertrand de Born, " Si tut le dol."

If all the dolour and the weary woe,
The grief, the pity, and the misery
Which through this age in copious current flow,
Could in a swell of grief united be,
Ne'er could they wail our lovely English prince
With a sufficiency of wild lament;
His death hath all the fane of honour rent,
And left the world a prey to dire despair.

Weeping and sorrowful, and full of woe
Be Europe's paragons of chivalry!
The mourning troubadours and jongleurs know
How death is now their fiercest enemy—
Death which has pierced our lovely English prince,
For generous heart so proudly eminent.
Ne'er will there be again for dire event
Such grief, such sorrow, such profound despair.

Death, cruel death, so plenteous of woe,
Now canst thou boast t' have won the victory
O'er the best prince whom chivalry can show ;
For nought on earth could offer rivalry
To our renowned and lovely English prince.
Ah! if but God by reason could be bent,
How better far that life to him be lent
Than to men rude, the workers of despair.

If from this age so plenteous in woe,
Love perisheth, alack! then, joy, good-bye!
Things will to worse proceed for evermoe,
Each day will see a new calamity;
For in our vanished lovely English prince
Each man doth see his own prefigurement—
Our prince, for every virtue excellent,
Who now hath died and left to us despair.

Now then to Him, who for our primal woe
Came to the world in sweet nativity,
And suffered death and dolour here below,
To Him, our Lord and Monarch, let us cry,
That to our young and lovely English prince
He may vouchsafe full pardon permanent,

> And take him to His heavenly tenement,
> Where is no woe, nor suffering, nor despair.

In this we may notice the exceeding art with which the rhyming is arranged, so that the three words, " woe," " prince," and " despair," being unrhymed and repeated in the same place in every stanza, may strike the ear full and emphatically, and may keep up, so to speak, a refrain of " woe for the prince, and despair ! " throughout the poem. No doubt this would be doubly emphasized by the music.

THE TENSON OR CONTENTION.—This species of composition, as its name implies, was in the form of a dialogue, in the course of which two combatants maintained in turn, by couplets of the same measure, and terminated with similar rhymes, contradictory opinions on questions of love, chivalry, morality, etc.

We may take as an example of this most celebrated species of troubadour poetry the following tenson, between the Countess of Die and Rambaud of Orange, by the mention of which combatants it will be seen that the poetical duel was not necessarily confined to persons of the sterner sex.

In this tenson it will be noticed that each of three principal rhymes is employed sixteen times.

THE COUNTESS.

> " Friend, with what a weight of woe
> Day by day I sit repining !
> 'Tis from you that comes the blow ;
> Yet you scarce suspect my pain.
> Why do you my love remain,
> When we so unfairly share
> You the joy, and I the care ? "

RAMBAUD.

" Lady, love is measured so,
When two lovers 'tis entwining,
Each must in their manner know
Joy and care, its constant train.
But, my lady, I maintain
Thy contention is unfair ;
For 'tis I the sorrows bear."

THE COUNTESS.

" Friend, if half the cares, I trow,
That are mine, o'er thee were twining,
Soon thou'dst feel thy spirit low.
But thou reckest not, 'tis plain,
How I ne'er can respite gain.
'Tis the same to thee, howe'er
I thy hapless lover fare."

RAMBAUD.

" Lady mine, since slanders grow,
Me to sorrow sad confining,
And each slanderer is thy foe ;
I of them my leave have ta'en ;
For through them it is in vain
That we seek for sunshine e'er,
Or one day of pleasure rare."

THE COUNTESS.

" Friend, I falter to bestow
Favours I would be designing,
For thy very actions show
Thee regardless of my bane.
If thou wert of other strain,
Then unto a saint I'd dare
Thee for virtue to compare."

RAMBAUD.

" Lady, lady, long ago,
Fear has been my bliss maligning,
Lest that slander, foul and slow,

O'er our love might weave its skein.
Hence it is that I complain ;
Hence it is that I declare
Thou alone canst bless my prayer."

THE COUNTESS.

" Friend, so soft thy flatteries flow,
So to love thou art inclining,
Thou from chivalry wilt go
And descend to poor chicane.
I thy interest would explain,
For thou lookest otherwhere,
And of me thou reckest ne'er."

RAMBAUD.

" Lady mine, may I forego
Hawking when the sun is shining,
If my eyes elsewhere I throw,
Since thou first in tender vein
Didst to look upon me deign.
But my rivals do not spare
To malign me everywhere. "

THE COUNTESS.

" Friend, I will believe in thee
And thy spotless loyalty."

RAMBAUD.[1]

" Think me so, and thou wilt see
Thy most loyal knight in me."

When more than two interlocutors took part in a
tenson, it was called a Tournament. Of this species of
composition the following example is a good illustration
(it will be noticed that the three principal rhymes are

---

[1] Rambaud d'Orange, " Amicx als gran."

played upon respectively twelve, eighteen, and twenty-
seven times):—

SAVARI DE MAULÉON.[1]

"Gaucelm and Hugh, I give to you,
Three amorous questions to contest:
Accept the one you like the best,
And leave to me the one you fear.
A lady, kind as she was fair,
Had lovers three who made their prayer.
She, at one moment, gave to all
Encouragement equivocal.
At one she glanced most amorously,
The other's hand she pressed with glee,
The other's foot touched furtively.
To whom of all, good Gaucelm, say
Did she the greatest favour pay."

GAUCELM FAIDIT.

" I'll give thee my opinion clear,
Since thou dost put me to the test.
With him, I say, the palm must rest
Who got the glance.   My reasons hear.
A glance, which in its lustre rare,
Is shot from eyes, a peerless pair,
Comes from the heart our sense t' enthrall,
The heart, love's seat angelical.
And hence the love in priceless fee
Lies in the glance assuredly.
The hand—the hand—why that may be
Mere greeting.   While the foot—it may
By accident thus go astray."

HUGUES DE LA BACHÉLERIE.

"Gaucelm, thou makest sorry cheer
With reasons such as that hast pressed.

---

[1] Savari de Mauléon, "Gaucelms, tres jocx."

I see but little love expressed
In any glance or silly leer.
The eyes may wander anywhere,
And scanty meaning can declare.
But when a hand symmetrical,
White as the snow celestial,
Ungloved, and ravishing to see,
Presses one's fingers amorously,
There—there is love's true augury.
Prove, if thou can'st, Savari, pray,
The foot can better love display."

SAVARI DE MAULÉON.

" Good Hugh, thy choice has cost thee dear,
For thou hast left the easiest
To me, as 'twill be soon confessed.
The foot's soft signal must appear,
From its mere secrecy and care,
To earn the palm beyond compare.
Its pressure timorous did fall,
Concealed from eyes inimical,
And spoke of love convincingly,
Love without trick or treachery.
What is a shaken hand? To me
A common thing done every day.
While glances flutter, and away!"

GAUCELM FAIDIT.

" Savari, thou who art severe
On eyes, of things the loveliest,
Surely thou not rememberest
That glances carry far and near
The heart's deep secrets which we dare
Never by other means declare.
Glances the messengers I call,
Sent by the heart imperial.
As to the foot—why commonly
A foot meets foot when none's to spy,
Yet 'tis but accidentally.
While for the hand—'tis wrong to lay
Such stress upon mere idle play."

HUGUES DE LA BACHÉLERIE.

" Right in the teeth thou drivest sheer
Of love and all the signs confessed,
Which it for ages hath possessed.
Talk not to me of glances clear.
Have not the eyes, so oft unfair,
Betrayed whole legions to despair ?
Talk not of foot fantastical.
Prevail on me it never shall.
For if my lady's foot touched me—
Pshaw ! 'twere a trifling vanity.
But if her hand did lovingly
Cling on to mine—ah, God ! I pray,
Grant I may live to see that day ! "

THE SIRVENTE (WAR SONG OR PASQUINADE).—The sirvente was one of the commonest forms of poetry cultivated
among the troubadours.   They expressed in it their feuds
with one another, and their animosities against enemies
who had offended them.   They employed the sirvente to
censure political and social disorders, and to be the medium
of bringing grievances before the attention of the public.
The sirvente was also, and perhaps primarily, a veritable
war song, with which the troubadour cheered his soldiers
to battle and nerved himself to prowess against the foe.
No special form of verse was peculiar to the sirvente,
which adopted the greatest freedom in its metre.   As an
example of the best form of sirvente we may cite the following from the compositions of Bertrand de Born (the
entire composition being constructed, as will be noticed,
on four rhymes alone) : [1]—

---

[1] Bertrand de Born, " Be m play."

Well do I love the lusty spring,
When leaves and flow'rets peep to light!
I love to hear the song birds sing
Among the leafage in delight
  Which forms their airy dwelling.
And when on tented fields I spy
Tall tents and proud pavilions high,
  My breast with joy is swelling;
Or when I see in legions lie
Squadrons of armoured chivalry.

What joy when scouts are skirmishing,
And scatter craven knaves in flight!
What joy to hear the fighters fling
High words and cries about the fight!
  What bliss is in me welling,
When castle walls that flout the sky
Stagger to their foundations nigh!
  What joys are me impelling,
When gallant troops a city try,
With trenches fenced impreguably!

And equal pleasure does it bring
When some gay gallant is in sight,
On lordly charger galloping,
Who cheers his men from base affright,
  Of rich rewards them telling.
And when the camp he cometh nigh,
Then must his men their prowess ply,
  Their very lifeblood selling.
For not a man is rated high
Until to blows he can reply.

Swords, spears, and helmets glittering,
Shields shivered, and in sorry plight—
Such sights and sounds does battle bring;
With crowds of vassals left and right
  Their master's foemen felling,
And horses mad, with rolling eye,
Who frenzied through the battle fly.
  The man of race excelling

> Thinks but of blood and butchery,
> And yearns for death or victory.

THE SIXTINE.—The Sixtine was composed of six stanzas. Each stanza consisted of six verses, which were not rhymed with one another; but the rhyme-words which came at the ends of the lines were repeated in the following stanzas in inverted orders. Only six rhyme-words were allowed through the whole poem, which words had to appear in every stanza consecutively, according to the following scheme :—At the end of the stanza of six verses, the sixth rhyme-word was taken for the first one of the next stanza, the first rhyme-word being the second, the fifth the third, the second the fourth, the fourth the fifth, and the third the last.

The curious inversion thus produced was rendered still more intricate in the third stanza, which applied the same principle to the second stanza which the second had to the first, and entangled the rhyme-words still more intricately. Yet more complex was the entanglement in the fourth stanza which entangled the third, and so on. In the Envoi, or address to the jongleur at the end, all the six rhyme-words must appear. As it consisted of only three lines, the three last rhyme-words of the sixth stanza, in the order in which they came in that stanza, were employed as the rhyme-words, while the three first of the same stanza, likewise in the order in which they came, were placed immediately before them. We give the following example of a Sixtine from the compositions of Arnaud Daniel :—

Endings : "comes," "nail," "soul," "rod," "kin," "room."

The doughty will which to my spirit comes
Is no defence 'gainst slanderer's claw and nail—
The slanderer who for slander damns his soul.
Since him I cannot lash with whip or rod,
At least will I, freed from censorious kin,
Taste sweet delights in meadow or in room.

Ah, when I think of that celestial room,
Where man of flesh ne'er by commandment comes,
Then my thoughts soar above my kith and kin,
I quail, I thrill down to my very nail,
And like a silly child before the rod
I fear I may be banished from her soul.

Fain would I love her body, not her soul,
If she would but conceal me in her room.
Her sternness wounds me more than any rod,
For where she is, her loving slave ne'er comes.
Near should we be as to the flesh the nail,
And then good-bye to protests from my kin!

Ah, never have I so adored my kin
As I do her—I swear it by my soul.
As near as is the finger to the nail,
So would I be unto her secret room.
From her sweet love new vigour o'er me comes,
As waxes stout and strong a feeble rod.

Since into flower oft bursts the withered rod,
And from old Adam come all kith and kin,
So the pure love which o'er my spirit comes
Waxes, and deeper could not have its soul.
Where'er she be, in meadow or in room,
My heart clings to her, as to flesh the nail.

For oh! my heart, as fastened by a nail,
Cleaves unto her, as bark to growing rod.
She is joy's tower, its palace, and its room.
I love her more than all my kith and kin,
And doubly paradise will bless my soul,
If for love's sake a lover thither comes.

> Arnaud's fair song of nail and kith and kin ;
> And by her grace who whips with rod his soul,
> 'Twill be his joy if to her room he comes.[1]

THE DISCORD.—The name of this species of min-strelsy, which may perhaps be likened to the free fantasia in music, sufficiently indicates its character. The "discord" was not divided into stanzas, and it was written in verse of different measures. The troubadour who has the credit of inventing this peculiar species of versification was Garins d'Apchier. If the "discord" is ever found in stanzas, such an arrangement has been adopted by the poet for exceptional purposes, and an examination of the stanzas will generally reveal the fact that each stanza—in order to keep up in the language the "discord" which has been dropped in the metre—is couched in a different idiom. Thus we have a "discord" of Rambaud de Vaqueiras, of which the first stanza is in the Romance dialect, the second in Tuscan, the third in French, the fourth in Gascon, the fifth in Spanish, and the sixth in a farrago of several dialects blended to-gether.

THE PASTORELLE OR PASTORAL PIECE.—The Pastorelle or Pastoral might be expressed in any measure, but generally short lines were preferred to long ones. The subject of the pastoral was usually a dialogue between the troubadour and a shepherdess. Sometimes, instead of the shepherdess, a shepherd was the second personage of the dialogue, as in the following pastoral by Cadenet, which we quote.

---

[1] Arnaud Daniel, "Lo ferm voler."

The pastoral generally commenced with a little descriptive piece delineating the locality of the scene, and serving as an introduction to the dialogue which is to follow. This form of composition is remarkable for the charming simplicity of style and thought, which the troubadour generally succeeds in infusing into the verse.

> By a lone and leafy brake
>   I did on my way
> A sad shepherd overtake,
>   Who in grief did say—
> "Love, alack for me
> And the shafts of calumny!
>   For my ladye
>   Sorrows evermoe,
> Which doth give me woe."
>
> "Shepherd, slanderers are awake
>   Round me every day,
> Saying that I pleasure take
>   Of a lady gay,
>   Who increasingly
> Loves me in sweet modesty.
>   I in verity
> Fain would have it so
> As these slanderers show.
>
> "Seigneur, since the lies they make
>   Lightly on thee lay,
> Thou canst love not, or 'twould break
>   Thy fond heart for aye.
>   See what misery
> Such foul slanderers bring me, see,
>   Most recklessly!
> Foolish he, I trow,
> Who defies their blow." [1]

---

[1] Cadenet, "L'autr' ier."

THE AUBADE AND THE SERENADE.—In these two forms of poetry, the sentiment and manner of expression were of greater consequence than any peculiarity of metre, which we do not find necessarily attached to either variety. They gain their separate characteristics however from the almost perpetual appendage of a refrain to each stanza. In the aubade the word Alba or " dawn " was incorporated in every refrain ; in the serenade the word Sers or " evening " had a like position.

THE BALLAD.—This form of poetry was greatly cultivated among the troubadours, and more especially among their northern brethren of the Langue d'Oïl, popularly known as Trouvères, but whom we may perhaps more conveniently term Northern troubadours. The ballad is specially valuable as being the foundation of all the metres of the epics, which are in some cases palpable accretions of ballads. The ballads are generally written among the Northern troubadours in eight syllable or seven syllable measure.

THE NOVEL.—Principally confined to the troubadours of the south, who delighted rather in the subtle refinement of amorous expression, while their brethren of the north were more disposed to a broader choice of subject and to singing themes of war and heroism—the novel was a short and sparkling poem, containing as a rule some gallant anecdote, in well-turned phrase. The novel, like the romance which we shall next consider, is not divided into stanzas ; and like the romance also it was not supplied with an envoi. The envoi we must explain was a few lines of address to the glee-man or jongleur, which the troubadour or trouvère placed at the end of his poem, in order that the jongleur might know to whom the poem was to be sung, or, on the principle of Hamlet's address to the players, how to sing it. Originating probably in a practical aim such as this, it came to be a regular literary appendix to the songs of the troubadours. But to a long romance, consisting sometimes of thousands of lines, and giving often the entire history of the hero,[1] or indeed the history of several successive heroes, as Robert Wace's Roman de Rou or " Romance of Rollo," which extols the exploits of all the successive Dukes of Normandy and Kings of England, from the time of Rollo to that of Henry I. (Beauclerk)[2]—in a composition of this nature an envoi was obviously out of place and unnecessary. It now remains to speak of the romance.

THE ROMANCE.—This most important of all the forms of composition cultivated by the troubadours and trouvères, or, as we prefer to call them, the Southern and Northern troubadours, gains in importance over the other order of poems owing to its length, and therefore its better state of preservation. Short poems are much more fugitive than long, perishing sooner ; and students of Greek literature will remember that while we have the Iliad of Homer, a composition of some 12,000 lines, in a state of practical integrity, the songs of Sappho, which once filled seven books, survive only in a few fragments.

---

[1] " La fable comprend ordinairement la vie entière ou une grande partie de la vie du heros qui en fait le sujet."—Raynouard, *Choix des Poésies des Troubadours*, II. 290.

[2] *Infra*, Chapter IX.

The same history has attended the romances of the troubadours. The shorter songs have indeed in many cases been preserved from obliteration, but the longer poems have survived in spite of time, and either in their enormous entirety or in large fragments form an immense fund of literature awaiting the interest of an appreciative age. These romances were written by the troubadours of the Langue d'Oc, no less than those of the Langue d'Oïl, but among the latter, who were designated *par excellence* the trouvères, the fecundity of production is far superior, and the tone of heroic thought higher. The romance was generally written in eight or seven syllable measure, sometimes in Alexandrines, sometimes, as in Robert Wace's Roman de Rou, with the metres mixed, one measure being appropriated to one canto, and another to another. That the versification of the trouvères is looser and less symmetrical than that of the troubadours, must not be imputed, as some have done, to the fact that the ear of the English and Anglo-Norman bards of the north was less fine and keen than of those in the Provençal districts in the south of our continental dominions; but merely to the fact that in long poems, to which they had so marked a proclivity, the metre most naturally assumes a more pliable and a freer form than in any gemmed and jewelled trinket of words. This may be easily demonstrated as the reason, by a consideration of a romance or romantic epic (for the latter term is more clearly expressive of them all) by a Southern troubadour entitled Gerard de Rossillon, consisting of eight thousand lines, and containing frequent and recurring violations of

metre and rudeness of style well nigh unparalleled in any
northern romances. [1]   The same remark of a tendency to
laxity in proportion to the length will apply to all the
romantic epics of the Southern troubadours.

Passing from the realm of verse, it may be mentioned
that many of the troubadours' romances were written in
prose.   This form was not freely affected by the troubadours of the south, the only prose romance which exists by
one of them being entitled Philoména, a work belonging
to the Carlovingian cycle of romances. [2]   Among the
northern trouvères, however, the prose romance was held
in much greater favour. [3]   It is interesting to notice
however that the troubadours frequently exhort their
jongleurs to make themselves familiar with prose
romances, [4] presumably in order that the jongleur may
have plenty of materials for improvising a song.

---

[1] MS. Bibliothèque Nationale (Paris), No. 7991.

[2] MS. Bibliothèque Nationale, 10,807.   In the Colbert MSS.,
there is a copy of this romance in modern character, this copy
having been taken from a very old MS. in the archives of the city
of Carcassonne.

[3] Sometimes prose and verse were mixed, as in the romance of
Aucassin et Nicolette, by an unknown troubadour, quoted above
p. 75.

[4] Giraud de Cabreira, "Cabra Juglar."   Giraud de Calanson,
" Fadet Joglar."

CHAPTER VII

THE SOCIAL LIFE OF THE TROUBADOURS.

The Troubadours an Aristocratic Caste—Expenses Attaching to the *Rôle* of Troubadour—Qualifications for being a Troubadour—The Life of a Troubadour—Illustration from the English Romance of King Horn—The Minstrel's Gallery—Amusements during the Day—The Troubadours, the Knight-errants of Literature—Refining Influences of the Troubadours—Pernicious Influences—Dress of the Troubadours—Public and Private Visits and Tournaments.

THE TROUBADOURS AN ARISTOCRATIC CASTE. — The troubadours moved in a very different social sphere from the musicians of to-day, and indeed from all musicians and minstrels before or since them. The history of music discloses on perusal the painful fact, that the majority of the personages whom it records and celebrates have been poor and despised, or at any rate have belonged to the lower order of society almost exclusively. With the troubadours, however, the contrary was the case. The very name of troubadour was, so to speak, a general indication of "nobleman," and the troubadours themselves were courtly gentlemen, who pursued the art of music and song for the love they bore it. Perhaps in this latter sentence an explanation of the difference of social status may be forthcoming. As long as a musician is content to practise his art for the love of it alone, he will be esteemed, even now, on a very different and superior footing from him who pursues the same calling for hire. It was the complete elimination of this latter element from the musical life of the troubadours which caused the stigma, so often attaching to the art, to be entirely absent from them. Not only did they participate in no way in the rewards given to music, but they often employed servants of their own to assist in the apt rendering of their compositions, as a gentleman at the present day might employ a private band or give occupation to two or three instrumentalists for the amusement of himself and his friends. To these servants of the troubadours, denominated glee-men or jongleurs, the same disparagement of class attached as does to the professional musician of modern times, and it is important, in considering the history of the troubadours, to remember this important fact, both with regard to themselves and their attendant jongleurs, if we are to form a due and just appreciation of the character and status of these courtly bards.

EXPENSES ATTACHING TO THE RÔLE OF TROUBADOUR.— The troubadours, as we have said, were all cultivated and accomplished gentlemen, nearly all of them being highly born, although a few owed their distinguished position to supereminent ability, which enabled them to break through the bands of class and lift themselves into a superior rank, just as in the army at the present day the sergeant may sometimes rise to be the commissioned officer, although such advance is rare. Equally rare, equally exceptional, was the advance of the jongleur to be the troubadour. The expenses attaching to the troubadour's life alone would be sufficient to deter most men from

The Troubadour on his Travels.

harbouring even the wish to rise into that superiority of social status. The troubadour was expected to entertain his friends sumptuously—far more so, indeed, than any ordinary feudal lord or seigneur. He was expected to give numerous *fêtes* of originality, and nearly always of extravagance, and his taste in such matters was looked up to as a sort of canon for other men to regulate their own by. He was, in short, a sort of *arbiter elegantiarum* among the nobility of his district, and as troubadour vied with troubadour to outdo one another in matters of expense and prodigality, we may imagine very well to what disastrous results this would sometimes lead.[1] Frequently we read in the annals of the troubadours of these courtly musicians and poets ruining themselves by their reckless and prodigal expenses, and losing for the sake of useless display and extravagant ostentation, castle and lands,[2] the patrimony which they had inherited from generations of ancestors. The usual cure for such ruin was to go to Palestine with the crusaders, and die fighting against the infidel. Some troubadours to whom such an opportunity did not conveniently present itself, or who were of a too pacific turn to take it, were content to sink from the class of troubadour into that of jongleur. Thus we read in the chronicles that the troubadour Peirols could not maintain himself as a troubadour, and became a jongleur,

---

[1] Bernardus Silvester, *De gubernat. rei familiaris*, " Homo joculatoribus intentus cito habebit uxorem cui nomen erit paupertas, ex qua generabitur filius cui nomen erit derisio."

[2] Lambert Ardensis, p. 247. " Arnoldus ita ministrantibus . . . omnibusque ejus nomen invocantibus suffecit, etc."

and of the Seigneur of Marveis the same, with several more.[1] In the same way, in illustration of the interchange of classes, we find it mentioned occasionally that such and such a jongleur had been allowed to become a troubadour, in consideration of the conditions to which we adverted a page or two ago, and on condition likewise that he was able to support the expense of his new position—a fact which seems to have been the subject of a particular, perhaps a formal, inquiry. Instances are to be found in the chronicles.

QUALIFICATIONS FOR BEING A TROUBADOUR.—The troubadours, besides being courtly and cultivated gentlemen, were expected to have passed through all the degrees of knighthood, and to have attained the dignity of the first degree, which entitled them to the designation of Cavalier or Chevalier. So entirely was this understood to be the case, that the terms " troubadour " and " cavalier " were treated as identical,[2] and to a cavalier were ascribed the various qualifications which we have mentioned as being peculiar and necessary to the troubadour. That the troubadours, many of whom were notorious for their pride of position and lineage, were in a manner justified in this assumption of aristocratic hauteur, may be gathered when we remark that among their numbers they could reckon counts and dukes by the dozen—so common, in fact, were the former that the troubadours placed but little honour in

---

[1] " Peirols no se poc mantener per cavallier c venc joglars." " E 'l senher de Marveis si 'l fes cavallier . . . no poc mantener cavalaria, si se fes jotglar."

[2] " No se poc mantener per cavallier, e venc joglars."

H

such an infusion in their ranks—many princes of royal blood, and finally four kings.[1] All these, the kings no less than the princes and the chevaliers of lower degree, were considered on a footing of social equality from the fact of their being troubadours, and fraternised freely with those of their class who were dignified with the same musical and poetical patent of nobility. In what then did the difference of a troubadour consist from, let us say, a musical nobleman of the present day, who, like his prototype the troubadour, not only composes music and poetry and performs it for the amusement of his friends, but likewise holds in pay a private orchestra or band, which plays for the edification of his guests whenever desired? What, and in what respect, was the difference? The leading and characteristic feature in the life of every troubadour was that he was expected to "go through the world,"[2] as the phrase was. Not content with keeping his music and his song for the benefit of himself and his chosen circle of friends, the troubadour was expected to go into the world and give the aristocratic public at large a specimen of his powers, and a means of judging his proficiency. Another phrase likewise applied to this necessary custom among the troubadours may, perhaps, explain it yet more fully—" to go from court to court."[3] Every gentleman's castle was called in its social aspect " a court," and, arguing from the style that was kept up in it, the name was entirely deserved. The

---

[1] Millot, *Les vies des plus célèbres troubadours.*
[2] " Allar par le mon."
[3] " Allar par les cortz."

author of Sir Gawayne finds pleasure in describing the visits which his knight gives and receives, in painting his lady so beautiful, in depicting the possibility of gay adventures on the way, etc.[1]

The troubadour then, if he was to be entitled to the name, must visit the castles of his neighbourhood—or extend his peregrinations as far afield as he pleased—and in these, and for the benefit of their inhabitants, must give various specimens of his powers, partly to delight the dwellers there, and partly to authenticate his claim and his capacity for the much-prized name of "troubadour."[2]

THE LIFE OF A TROUBADOUR.—At the first breath of spring, then, the troubadour, who had passed the winter in his castle varying the exercise of arms with the composition of music, mounted on his steed, and, attended by his jongleurs, sallied out in quest of listeners and prepared to indulge in what adventures might befall him on the way. As the knight-errants of chivalry, so these chevaliers of music, commending themselves to fortune and their lady, gave the reins to their steed, and let it carry them where it chose, abandoning themselves to delightful contemplation, while their jongleurs on foot in the rear, tuning up their instruments, sang out their master's songs, that echoed through the meadows and woods as they passed along.

In no long time they would reach a castle, where the

---

[1] *Sir Gawayne and the Green Knight*, Ed. R. Morris, Early English Text Society, 1864, p. 38.

[2] To quote the words of the chroniclers, the troubadour "anava per cortz, e menava chantadors, que chantavon las soas chansos."

news of their coming had already been announced by a jongleur despatched for the purpose in front. And when they arrived at the castle gate the troubadour dismounted, and was soon the centre of a courtly throng assembled to receive him, who helped to divest him of his armour (for being a knight bachelor he always rode in knightly panoply) and arrayed him in a costly mantle as was usual in the hospitality of the time ;[1] while the jongleurs, ranging themselves in a row before the company, began the preface to their concert, which was often couched in the most fantastic terms :—

"We come," they sang, " bringing a precious balsam which cures all sorts of ills, and heals the troubles both of body and mind. It is contained in a vase of gold, adorned with jewels the most rare. Even to see it is wonderful pleasure, as you will find if you care to try. The balsam is the music of our master, the vase of gold is our courtly company. Would you have the vase open, and disclose its ineffable treasure ?"[2]

ILLUSTRATION FROM THE ENGLISH ROMANCE OF KING HORN.—In a similar way, Horn and his companions disguise themselves as minstrels, and present themselves at the gate of Rymenhild's castle :—

> " Hi yeden bi the grauel
> Toward the castel,
> Hi gunnie murie singie,
> And makede here gleowinge.

---

[1] The above is agreeable to the usual descriptions given by the troubadours themselves.

[2] Such is the preface in Fauriel, *Histoire de la Poésie*, III. 234.

> Rymenhild hit gan ihere
> And axede what hi were :
> Hi sede, hi weren harpurs,
> And sume were gigours.
> He dude Horn inn late
> Right at halle gate.
> He sette him on a benche,
> His harpe for to clenche." [1]

Thus they prattled on in most harmonious music, twanging their instruments and piping the while, for this was the prelude to a long list of songs, that might take days for their apt delivery.[2] For not all their songs were sung in the courtyard at their entry, but only a chosen few, and these the most appropriate. And after this, royal cheer in the banqueting hall, and the jongleurs, sitting below the salt,[3] would ever and anon break out in some harmonious strain at a signal from their master, most *à propos* and pleasant for the occasion.[4]

THE MINSTRELS' GALLERY.—In many baronial halls the architecture was planned with a view to the jongleurs' presence, and facilities were offered by the architect so that a more elaborate display of music might be given than would be possible at table or sitting on benches in the hall. For this reason a gallery was specially built, called the Jongleurs' or Minstrels' Gallery, which had its

[1] *King Horn*, Ed. J. R. Lumby, Early English Text Society, 1866, line 1465.

[2] Fauriel, *Histoire de la Poésie Provençale*, III.

[3] Sitting below the salt or standing in front of the table. "Vor dem Tische staat," runs the old traveller's narrative in Scheid, *Dissertatio de jure in musicos*, p. 18, in allusion to the jongleurs.

[4] Ducange, Art. *Ministelli*.

place, as a rule, above the door of entrance, opposite the daïs, where the table of the lord of the castle was set. A drawing of one of these galleries may be studied in Eccleston's *Introduction to English Antiquities.*[1] One of later date is still to be seen at the Marquis of Salisbury's seat at Hatfield. It is constructed with great fidelity on more ancient models, and, belonging to the early part of the seventeenth century, may lay claim of itself to a respectable antiquity. An excellent specimen of the same style of architecture may be seen in the minstrels' galleries in Exeter Cathedral and at Battle Abbey. In many old baronial halls in England minstrels' galleries may be found, often diverted from their proper use, and unintentionally ignored. Sometimes organs are to be found placed in them, in which case they have reverted in some sort to their original function, though quite without the knowledge of their possessor.

AMUSEMENTS DURING THE DAY.—After evening festivities of such a nature, next morning there would be music on the ramparts overlooking the moat, where the ladies were wont to walk and talk in the early part of the day with the knights and squires; or in the meadows outside the castle, and this more often in the afternoon, where a gallant company of knights and ladies from the surrounding districts were assembled, and carpets of brocade were spread on the grass, and they sat in groups up and down the meadow, while the jongleurs moved about, singing as

---

[1] Eccleston's *Introduction to English Antiquities,* p. 221.

before.[1] Here it was, and on such distinguished occasions, that the troubadour himself would sing—a rare privilege, which he was chary of according. And taking his guitar from the hands of an attendant jongleur, he would strike the strings and commence his excellent refrain; and very soon all that courtly company had gathered round the spot where he was singing, for such singing was no common privilege to hear.

In every castle there was a large book kept, and the lord of the castle had a scrivener on purpose to copy in it whatever song greatly pleased him. And wherever the troubadour and his jongleurs went, they always left many such songs behind.[2] So it continued all the summer time, and when the winter came, Amanieu de Escas, the troubadour, shall tell us how they employed their time then. "When hail and frost cover the earth, and cause man and beast to shelter themselves from the cold, I am sitting in the house with my pages, singing of love, of joy, and of arms. The warm fire burns bright, and the floors are well covered with mats. White wines and red are on the table."[3] And every day a new song written, and the jongleurs rehearsing it under their master's guidance, against bespangled spring, when the round of pleasures began again.

But with the troubadours all is spring and summer, nor do we know any passage but the present one where winter and its occupations intrudes itself into their

---

[1] This picture is common in mediæval romance.

[2] Fauriel, *Histoire de la Poésie*, III. 233.

[3] Amanieu de Escas, in Raynouard's *Reculée*.

thoughts. But all is sunshine, and their month is May. Music is to them the "Gay Science," and they styled one another in jest, the "Doctors of the Gay Science." We might tell of contests that they had together, in which the prize was a golden violet, and of their efforts so untiring to outvie each other in the composition of beautiful music; for in the cultivation of music and in the pursuit of arms was their life entirely passed.

THE TROUBADOURS, THE KNIGHT-ERRANTS OF LITERATURE.—There is a singular similarity between the troubadours and the knight-errants, in respect to these enforced pilgrimages which were incumbent upon both. As the knight-errants themselves, whom chivalrous romance informs us of, roamed the world in quest of adventures, engaging in perilous enterprises, or stationing themselves at passes in forests, or at bridges, and compelling all those that went by to acknowledge the superiority of their lady-love, so the troubadours journeyed from castle to castle and from court to court, singing of the lady, whose beauty attracts all eyes, her skin white as the driven snow, her complexion like the rosebud in spring, and wreaths of flowers woven round her long flaxen hair, which shines like gold.[1] As it was imperative for every knight-errant to have a lady-love, so was it equally incumbent on the troubadour. To spread her name and fame was the avowed object of his pilgrimage, and very often his ardour was whetted by the fact of another troubadour having arrived at the castle shortly before him whose mission was to vaunt

---

[1] The common heroine of the troubadour's poems.

throughout the world the beauty of another peerless dame. This emulation and desire to strike admiration and win attention led the troubadour to much fanciful, high-flown, and fantastic language, and if there be a blemish in their poetry this is the fault most prominent. But it is astonishing how little this blemish interferes with the enjoyment of the reader now-a-days, and how, when we compare them with the Eastern bards, whose amatory poems are as celebrated, how subdued and temperate appears their style on a theme in which there is a natural tendency to exaggerate and overstrain both sentiment and allusion.

REFINING INFLUENCES OF THE TROUBADOURS.—The life that we have just attempted to describe speaks of a singular ease and freedom of social intercourse, and exhibits in a peculiar manner the softening and re-fining influence of poetry and song on the general char-acter of the time. Before the rise of the troubadours, and the humanizing effect of their songs, and the contagious influence of their refined pleasures, these same castles which gave so ready a welcome to them and their courtly train, were often the morose homes of rapine and semi-barbarism. To suppress the excesses of individuals and to effect a change in the general character of an era, the only effectual means is the slow creation of a public opinion favourable to the new ideas. It should seem that nothing is so conducive towards influencing public opinion as the existence of an art such as that of the troubadours, which could infuse itself at every turn into the most unguarded moments of private life, and which was devoted to the encouragement of blitheness and gaiety. It was carried on by those who professed it, not in any spirit of self-seeking, but with the most chivalrous and ideal aims. And when the noblest and wealthiest men in the land go so far that they can consecrate their talents and their possessions to the pursuit of a high ideal, we need not be surprised if the rudeness and ferocity of their neighbours and friends is mitigated and subdued, even if it be not totally extinguished.

PERNICIOUS INFLUENCES.—We have now considered the beneficial effects of the troubadours' life and manners upon the spirit of the times. We must not, however, forget to look at the reverse of the picture. This easy admission to the domestic society of a neighbour's castle, especially when the privilege was accorded to a gallant, the whole aim and object of whose existence was not only to sing of love, but to make it, and who was possessed moreover of the most seductive manners, and was the master of an art which has never failed with women —often led to disastrous consequences in respect of domestic peace. Immorality was fostered, as it has rarely been before or since, by this exceeding freedom of intercourse, which at any time might bring a fascinating and brilliant stranger into the midst of a family circle, and give him the privilege of access and intimate communion with every member of it. The custom, moreover, among the troubadours, that each one should possess an acknowledged lady-love in whose honour, and to spread whose praise, he undertook all his journeys and carried on all his musical and poetical labours—this alone was a potent source of the same evil. In the first place, the lady whom the troubadour chose for his goddess incarnate, was naturally greatly flattered by his preference, and felt a very excusable pride in having her name made so famous as her gallant lover had it in his power to make it. In order to reward him for his services, if she were a vain woman, there was no sacrifice which she could not permit herself to make, and immoral relations were the usual sequel of the troubadour's praises. In the second place, among the female sex at large an incessant ambition began to grow, for each lady to have, so to speak, a troubadour in her employ, who would sing her praises as those of other women were being sung, and by this means render her in no respect inferior to others of her equals. And lastly, when a troubadour visited a family and sang so sweetly the wondrous charms of such and such a lady, there was the very natural emulation among the members of that quiet domestic circle, that their names should be equally celebrated, or that they should even be substituted for that of the lady whose exaltation had just charmed their ear. Hence arose a greed of praise among women, a love of empty compliment, an exhaustless vanity, and, as we said before, the inclination to do all in their power, at whatever price, to capture one of these musical gallants and have him as the spokesman of their fame. That it was so, will be at once apparent from the fact that the lady-loves of the troubadours were nearly all of them married women, whom the gay knights had met and made the acquaintance of when tarrying at their husband's castles, whither they had gone in the usual course of things, while travelling through the world.   Very possibly the troubadour had come in the first instance to the castle, with the name of some maiden beauty on his lips, who might have been a young lady of rank of his neighbourhood, or a relation of his own, whose innocent loveliness had charmed his eye.   But her influence was soon destined to pale before that of the courtly and cultivated women of the world, who in the character of *châtelaines* inhabited the castles which lay in limitless succession over the whole face of the land, from the extreme east of Provence, through the Provençal districts of the English realm, and through England itself up to the northern limits of the English dominions in Northumbria. These ladies,—who were the undisputed leaders of society in their respective neighbourhoods, who set the fashions, and had great influence in their immediate localities, —were the principal encouragers of the troubadours, who if found in greatest profusion throughout Provence and the Provençal districts of the south, were yet known to roam throughout the whole extent of our monarchy, and to spread the benefits of their peculiar calling, and likewise its evils, in greater or less proportion everywhere.

Dress of the Troubadours.—We have mentioned that when the troubadour alighted at the castle gate, he was arrayed in a costly mantle and conducted in that guise into the castle.   This leads us to offer a few remarks on the dress of the troubadours. Strange though it may seem, yet the military relations of these musical errants were always kept up in their costume down to the latest time we hear of them. It was as if they prided themselves as greatly on their martial prowess and capabilities as they did on their music. At any rate, although their errand to every castle was always a peaceful one, and lutes not lances were the weapons with which they fought, they invariably rode from castle to castle in full armour, mounted on a war-horse, with their visor up, and with their lance in bucket at their horse's side, ready to be placed in rest should occasion arise.[1] What *rôle* the jongleurs would have played were their master attacked, we do not know. Such a circumstance is not often recorded in the chronicles of these musical cavaliers, and if it is recorded, no information is given us on that head. Some people might argue that this peregrination in martial habiliments was entirely intended for purposes of safety. But to this we reply, that if such had been the case the jongleurs likewise would most probably have been armed. Since, therefore, the jongleurs formed but a peaceful party in the rear of the cavalier, we can only conclude that the martial accoutrement was a matter of fashion, not of necessity, and that because the troubadours were knight bachelors they were compelled to wear knightly panoply.

The attendants at the castle gate, aided by the members of the family, the ladies of the castle being among

---

[1] Even when going to an amorous rendezvous it was usual to don full armour. See *Flamenca*, p. 224, line 7465–69. See also the *Preface to the Romance of Hugues Capet*, published by the Marquis de la Grange, p. 65 (Paris 1864); and compare likewise *Li Roumans dou Chastelain de Couci*, p. 81, line 2427.

them, helped the troubadour to divest himself of his
heavy breastplate, his helmet, his greaves, and his surcoat of mail.[1] Beneath this brazen panoply he wore a
light tunic, which was not sufficient protection against
the cold, nor was it for purposes of dignity in habiliment
of any consideration whatsoever. Accordingly the custom prevailed of having a costly mantle ready, often
trimmed with rare furs and edged with gold,[2] and itself
the product of the dainty embroidery of the ladies of the
castle themselves. This was thrown over his shoulders as
he entered the castle from the courtyard,[3] and thus arrayed
he was conducted to a chamber which was often kept exclusively for these musical knight-errants in many castles,
and was called the troubadour's chamber. Water was
brought him here, and poured over his hands by a page,
and a towel was provided as a luxury with which he
might complete his toilette. His attendant jongleurs
during dinner gave vent to all sorts of harmonious
strains, each exciting more admiration and astonishment
than the other.

When Sir Gawain takes his repast at the castle of his
host the Green Knight, the meals are seasoned with songs
and music. On the second day the amusement extends
till after supper ; they listen during the meal and after it

---

[1] See Ritson, note to *Ywaine and Gawin*, line 2419—this being
the ordinary method of disarming.

[2] Even the jongleurs were sometimes arrayed in rich fur robes.
Jusserand, *Wayfaring Life*, p. 200.

[3] The above is agreeable to the descriptions given by the troubadours themselves. See also the Preface to the *Roman de
Hugues Capet* (Paris).

to many noble songs, such as Christmas carols and new songs, with all possible mirth.

> " Mony athel songez
> As coundutes of Kryst-masse and carolez newe,
> With all the manerly merthe that mon may of telle." [1]

On the third day.

> " With merthe and mynstralsye, with metez at hor wylle
> Thay maden as mery as any men moghten." [2]

The troubadour himself would often during these ceremonies affect a haughty or indifferent demeanour, and would occupy himself with conversation with the master of the house, or with paying lofty compliments to the ladies, " as not deigning," says an old chronicle, " to concern himself with so ignoble a thing as music, until it pleased his own fancy or the wishes of the sweet ladies round him." [3]

PUBLIC AND PRIVATE VISITS. TOURNAMENTS.—We have given the remainder of this picture in the earlier part of this chapter, and we do not propose to repeat it here. But we must add that these visits of the troubadours who were "going through the world," to the various castles, were sometimes made in comparative privacy, on which occasion the courtly minstrel would be entertained by the baron and his family. More often they were the occasions of princely and profuse pageantry and festivity. It depended on the troubadour himself, whether for instance he were a celebrated one or no, and whether his

---

[1] *Sir Gawayne and the Green Knight*, line 484.
[2] *Ibid.* lines 1652–6 and 1952.
[3] Quoted in La Curne de Ste. Palaye, III.

visit were expected or were made without announcement. On the occasions when the visit was made the subject of special preparation and festivity, the fêtes which took place sometimes lasted two days, and were attended in great throngs by the nobility and gentry of the neighbourhood.[1] The jongleurs on such occasions often passed from the mere recital of their master's songs, and performed a little play or interlude, in which they studied to impersonate by various dresses and appropriate action the characters which were the subject of the poem.[2] The festivities consisted in the main of banquets, of concerts in which the troubadours took part, of musical duels in which two troubadours maintained the superiority of their respective lady-loves, and last, not least, of actual tournaments, not merely musical ones. In these contentions of real gallantry, not merely of artistic competition, the troubadours were eager to evince their prowess, and to prove to the eyes of the surrounding crowd that they were as able to do battle for their lady with their sword as with their lute. Arrayed therefore in full armour, the same knight who the evening before had discoursed to a crowd of admiring dames and seigneurs on his lute of the surpassing beauty of his lady-love, whom he challenged all the world to match, mounted on his war-horse, and made ready to support his words with blows. A difference when a troubadour tilted, from the tilts and tourneys of other knights, was this, that the jongleurs were always stationed in some

---

[1] La Curne de Ste. Palaye, *Vie de Pons Capdeuil.*
[2] La Curne de Ste. Palaye, *Vie de Giraud Calanson.*

conspicuous place[1] outside the barriers of the lists, who, when their master started for the fray, set up a chorus of instruments and voices, singing and playing war music of his composition, to cheer him in the battle, and to excite the attention of all the spectators round the lists to the musical warrior who thus harmoniously and to the tune of music fought.[2]

The words of these warlike compositions were full of high-flown descriptions of the musical warrior's prowess, and of taunts and defiances hurled at his adversary. The songs continued during the fight,[3] and the jongleurs, in order to make the music peal forth above the noise of stamping steeds and the crash of clashing blades, often performed the accompaniment to the words on horns and bells[4] and stranger instruments than these, which they had learnt to use and play when they followed their master to the Holy Land. If the troubadour fell in one of these encounters, it was the jongleur's duty to carry his dead body from the lists after the *mêlée* was over, when the ground was strewn with glittering pieces of armour and sparkling spangles.

---

[1] For two remarkable cases of jongleurs figuring at tournaments, see the *Issue Roll of Thomas Brantingham.*

[2] Justinus Lippiensis.

[3] The account is from Justinus Lippiensis, in Lerberke's *Chronicon Comitum Schaw.*

[4] " Tibia dat varias," it runs in the poem above cited, " per mille foramina voces ; Dant quoque terribilem tympana pulsa sonum."

CHAPTER VIII.

THE ENGLISH TROUBADOURS AND TROUVÈRES.

English Troubadours—Savari de Mauléon and others—Munificent Patronage of Minstrelsy—David the Troubadour and others—Chardry—Thomas de Bailleul—The Genius of the English Troubadours and its Tendencies—Parallel Evolution in Greek Literature—Troubadours and Trouvères—Denis Pyramus—French the Spoken Language of England till Middle of 14th Century—Geoffrey Gaimar and others—Adam de Ros: compared to Dante—Account of His Poem.

ENGLISH TROUBADOURS. — It was made a special point of eulogy in the panegyric passed on a marriage between a certain French king and the daughter of one of the Counts of Provence, that this event (to quote the words of the Provençal historian), " had introduced into France, and particularly into the royal court, the art of the troubadours, the gay science, that is to say, the agreeable manners, the polished behaviour, and the customs of gallantry which had prevailed in the Provençal region of the south."[1] By substituting for France the name of England in the above passage, we might describe with tolerable clearness, though necessarily with some generality, the effect on our own land of the marriage of Henry

---

[1] " Avait introduit chez les Français et surtout à la cour des rois, l'art des troubadours, la gaye science, c'est à dire, les manières agréables," etc.

II. with Queen Eleanor. We say the statement would not be a perfect description of the matter, because England by itself seems to have possessed the power of evolving that artistic life to a certain extent, though marvellously aided by the alliance with the Provençal queen and the lustre of culture which was thereby shed over the court of Henry. But if some authors are right in describing Robert Duke of Normandy, son of the Conqueror, as a troubadour, then to an earlier date than even the reign of Henry II. must we refer the appearance of troubadours in English history—to a date indeed coincident with that of the first celebrated troubadour, William of Poitiers, of whom Robert Duke of Normandy was a contemporary and possibly a friend. The solitary relic of the muse of this crusading son of the Conqueror is said to be an Elegy on an old chestnut tree, which he composed at Cardiff Castle. While immured in that frowning fortress by his brother Henry I., his eye is said have wandered with singular pleasure over a vast prospect of chestnut trees, which were the solitary span of verdure visible from his dungeon window. Selecting one of these as the subject of his song, he composed the elegy before-mentioned.[1] Yet the piece bears a suspicion of spuriousness, from the character of its structure alone, which is identical with that ordinarily in vogue among the Welsh bards. The mere traditional attribution of the song, however, to Duke Robert may be supposed to argue a poetical talent on his part.

---

[1] Abbé de la Rue, *Essais Historiques*, II. 95.

Closely connected with the accounts of Duke Robert of Normandy, is the history of an English or Anglo-Norman troubadour, by name Luc de la Barre, who is described as the son of Simon, Seigneur de la Barre. In the contest between Duke Robert and Henry I. for the crown of England, he attached himself conspicuously to the party of the former, and composed a number of sirventes or pasquinades[1] against Henry, which stung that sensitive monarch to fury. These sirventes proved the cause of his ruin; for Henry, having captured him, caused his eyes to be put out, according to the cruel custom of the time, in consequence of which Luc de la Barre perished miserably in his captivity.[2] "The troubadour," says Lingard, "in a paroxysm of agony, burst from the hands of the officers, and destroyed himself."[3]

SAVARI DE MAULÉON AND OTHERS.—One of the most celebrated troubadours who ever lived, whose fame was by no means confined to England but spread throughout the Provençal possessions of the English crown and the length and breadth of Provence itself, was the English troubadour, Savari de Mauléon.[4] In Chapter VI., when speaking of the poetry of the troubadours, we gave a tenson, of a quaint and humorous nature, in which Savari de Mauléon played a conspicuous part. The whole of this tenson, indeed, as it stands at present, is supposed to be the offspring of his muse. This troubadour was a great

---

[1] See Chapter VI., "The Poetry of the Troubadours."

[2] Duchesne, *Normannorum historia scriptorum*, fol. 880.

[3] Lingard, History of England, II., 148.

[4] " Selon quelques auteurs ce troubadour était d'origine anglaise."—De la Rue, *Essais*, III. 125.

favourite with King John and also with his son, Henry III., both of whom loaded him with favours.[1] The long and elaborate account of his life which remains to us is less interesting than might have been expected, owing to the major part of it being concerned with his intrigues or adventures in connection with the sinister policy of King John.[2] Among English troubadours of less celebrity, we must enumerate Sir William Talbot, who is described to us as " full of gaiety and well skilled in the gests of the ancients ; "[3] Raoul de Ferrières, ancestor of the present Lord Ferrers,[4] whose love songs were spoken of with admiration by his contemporaries, and who seems to have excelled in this species of composition so conspicuously, that he attempted no other; Pierre de Craon, of Burton in Lincolnshire ; and more especially Maurice de Craon, the father of the last named, Baron of Burton in Lincolnshire.[5] In addition to his estates in that county, Maurice de Craon was the owner of extensive domains in Surrey—Ham, Walton, Ewell, and other places belonging to him.[6] His songs, which form a goodly collection, exist in MS. in the Bibliothèque Nationale at Paris, and may be studied with interest and enjoyment by all those who admire fresh and spirited poetry.[7] Roger

---

[1] Abbé de la Rue, *Essais Historiques*, III. 123, 124.

[2] La Curne de Ste. Palaye, *Histoire littéraire des troubadours : Vie de Savari de Mauléon.*

[3] Ritson, *Dissertation on Romance and Minstrelsy*, p. 183.

[4] Domesday Book.

[5] *Ibid.*

[6] *Litt. pat.* 17, *Johann. Reg. M.* 24.

[7] Bibliothèque Nationale, Paris : MSS. de Cangé.

d'Audely, from whose name and family two well-known thoroughfares in London derive their designation—North and South Audley Street—was a well-known troubadour at the court of King John. He wrote many songs, which were deservedly popular in his day. Richard de Semilly was famous for his beautiful pastorals, many of which have been preserved, to delight readers of to-day as much as they did the listeners of six centuries ago.[1] It seems uncertain whether we should place this troubadour in the reign of John or Henry III. If we extend our list so as to include Norman troubadours as well as English, we may add the following names of troubadours who were famous like the preceding, though it may not be in so great a degree, for their chansons or songs, the themes of which sometimes varied, though gallantry and love formed the main subject dilated on:—Pierre de Viesmaisons, who sang of the First Crusade, and likewise composed many love songs; Charles, Count of Anjou; Pierre de Dreux, Duke of Brittany; Jean de Dreux, Count of Braine; Hugues de Lusignan, Count of Marche; the Chastelain de Coucy; the Vicomte de Chartres; the Count of Bar; and the Count of Béthune. Most of these were frequenters of the English court.

MUNIFICENT PATRONAGE OF MINSTRELSY.—Distinction can be gained by sumptuous and liberal patronage as well as by eminence of genius; and if Richard de Semilly deserved the name of troubadour for the beauty of his strains, Peter de Courtenay merited the title no less,

---

[1] Bibliothèque Nationale, MSS. de Cangé.

owing to the magnificence of his musical establishment. His jongleurs were renowned for their large numbers and for their excellent appointments, which made their appearance as brilliant as their music was copious and pleasing. We read that when Peter de Courtenay went to France to fight against Guy de la Trimouille, such was the brilliance of his musical retinue that the French king caused a hundred francs of gold to be given to this troubadour's jongleurs.[1] Hugh, Earl of Chester, was another no less lavish patron of jongleurs and minstrelsy. The court which he kept was magnificent in the extreme, and while he spent part of his time in Normandy and part in England, he was enabled to lend the brilliancy of his surroundings to each country alternately.[2] William Longsword, the son of Henry II. and Fair Rosamond, though we know not whether he was a professed troubadour, was famed for his munificent patronage of minstrelsy,[3] and when we hear that he maintained a special staff of jongleurs, we should probably do right in crediting him with a title to the honoured name of troubadour.[4] Private jongleurs were likewise kept by Baron Stafford, the Duke of Gloucester, Baron Lovell, and Baron L'Estrange.[5]

DAVID THE TROUBADOUR, AND OTHERS.—David the Troubadour, who lived in the reign of Stephen was probably a jongleur rather than a troubadour. He was in high favour, we learn, with Maud the wife

---

[1] Chambre des comptes, dépôt du greffe, No. 1391.
[2] De La Rue, *Essais historiques*, I. 138. [3] *Ib.*, I. 230. [4] *Ib.*
[5] Warton's *History of English Poetry*, I.

of Stephen,[1] but was likewise famed for several
pieces which he wrote in the style of panegyrics on
Henry I. He is also credited with being the composer
of a metrical romance or history of that prince.[2]
Gace le Blount was a courtly troubadour, who was a
blood relation of King Henry II.[3] Guernes de Pont
Ste. Maxence was of earlier date than he, though likewise of the twelfth century, and composed most of his
works at Canterbury, though said to have been born
in France.[4] Samson de Nanteuil devoted himself to
Adelaide de Condé as his lady love, who was the heiress
of Hornecastle in Lincolnshire.[5] Whether her husband
approved of the attachment we cannot say, but certain it
is that the lady was of an exceedingly religious turn of
mind, and at her request Samson applied his talents to a
versified translation of the Proverbs of Solomon. Osbert
de Condé was the name of this lady's husband,[6] and to
her liberality are due many princely benefactions to
the priory of Rufford.[7] Guichard de Beaulieu, like so
many of those we have mentioned, was a monk. In his
youth steeped in all sorts of vices, he repented in his age
and devoted himself to attacking the vices of his time.[8]
The priory of Beaulieu was a dependency on the Abbey
of St. Albans. Luc du Gast was born of a noble family in

---

[1] De La Rue, *Essais*, III. 119.

[2] *Ib.*   [3] *Ib.*, II. 241.   [4] *Ib.*, III. 78.

[5] Camden's *Britan.*, II. 229.

[6] *Monast. Angl.*, II. 645. [7] Thornton's *Nottinghamshire*, p. 370.

[8] De La Rue, *Essais*, II. 136.

England. He was a chevalier, and seigneur of the Castle of Gast. He generally lived in the neighbourhood of Salisbury.[1] Luc du Gast is the author of the romance of Tristram, which treats of the search for the Holy Grail. Two other English poets have written in French verse the Romance of Tristram. One of these is known by the name of Thomas le Trouvère.

CHARDRY.—Chardry was a troubadour born in Gloucestershire, where his family possessed large fiefs and were of high territorial influence.[2] From certain passages in his works the supposition might be hazarded that this troubadour was a jongleur who had taken the Chardrys' name, as he speaks to his audience sometimes as " Seigneurs "—a most unusual method of address from the lips of a troubadour.[3]

THOMAS DE BAILLEUL.—Thomas de Bailleul was an English troubadour of the end of the twelfth century. " His family were renowned in England, illustrious in Scotland, ancient in Normandy," says De La Rue.[4] That he possessed considerable influence at court is plain from the fact that in 1205, King John gave him one of the revenues payable to the Exchequer of London for his maintenance, which must have supported him in affluence as long as he enjoyed it. We have of his a sirvente,[5] which curiously

---

[1] We learn this from his own account.
[2] *Lib. nig. scacar.*, I. 165.
[3] See MS. British Museum, Cotton, Caligula, A. 4.
[4] *Essais Historiques*, III. 41.
[5] British Museum MS., King's Library, 20 B. XVII.

enough is directed against his benefactor. Details of his life are too meagre to allow us to understand why he should have chosen John as the mark of his invective. This sirvente rises into more artistic regions than the majority of pieces of its class. The troubadour begins with a glowing description of spring (we may remember a somewhat similar opening in a sirvente of Bertrand de Born which we translated).[1] This description is unusually elaborate. The troubadour sings the sweetness of the season, the beauty of the country roads, the loveliness of the foliage, the songs of the birds. He expatiates on the elegance of the peasant maidens, and dilates on the joy and mirth of the shepherds. "In this same season," continues the troubadour with marked and significant contrast, "and at the commencement of May, two powerful armies encamped against each other near a village built by the Saracens. They were sworn foes to each other were these hosts, and had come with murderous intent." We are to understand that one of them is the army of King John, as can be easily gathered by the subsequent description in the poem. After a long and minute account of the constituents of each army, the troubadour passes on to the catastrophe of his sirvente, which is the march of the two hosts against each other. With vivid language he depicts the alarm which spreads in the beautiful country, so opposed to its former peaceful tranquillity and silence. Hereafter follows a long and elaborate description of the dress and armour of the

---

[1] Chapter VI.

warriors in the opposing hosts, and the sirvente ends somewhat abruptly, suggesting the obvious reflection that we have not the complete work before us.[1]

THE GENIUS OF THE ENGLISH TROUBADOURS AND ITS TENDENCIES. — From this piece and from others by English troubadours that we have alluded to, it will be obvious that the genius of our own bards was of a sterner and a more epic cast than that of the Provençal minstrels in the southern and continental dominions of the Angevin kings. While the latter sung chiefly of love or plunged occasionally into the equally impassioned frenzy of war, the former applied deliberate care and art rather than the heat of impulse to their compositions, and were thus most naturally led to admit other subjects into the sphere of their treatment. At the same time, from the same reason and also owing to the deep set literary character of the English people, they were inclined to prefer the epic method of treatment to the lyric, and to delight in long and elaborate poems which can be frequently returned to by the composer and offer more labour, but at the same time more abiding interest, than short and impulsive effusions. The natural consequence of such a feeling in our northern minstrels may be readily imagined, in its influence on the character and complexion of their minstrelsy. There was from the first a tendency to discard or depreciate the musical moment in that combination of poetry and music which constituted the troubadour's art; and this tendency which operated as

---

[1] British Museum MS., King's Library, 20 B. XVI.

we say from the very first, at last took actual form in a visible and conspicuous effort on the part of the English bards to shake themselves free from the trammels of music altogether.

PARALLEL EVOLUTION IN GREEK LITERATURE.—Students of Greek literature will remember a similar tendency which can be historically traced, step by step, among the minstrels and rhapsodists of ancient Greece. Such precision of detail is not possible in the imperfect and undigested materials that are at the disposal of the student of English troubadour poetry. In the case of the Greek rhapsodists, the rhapsodes who in the time of Homer invariably accompanied their recitation with a prelude on the lyre, began in course of time either to lose that accomplishment, or to enhance it. From the ancient and ideal rhapsode of the Homeric period, two schools branched off. One, the musical one, which was best typified by Terpander, increased and developed the prelude beyond all bounds of poetical requirement. The poetry fell away, and the school of Terpander became the musicians of Greece. The other group, which found their highest culmination in the poet Hesiod, proceeded on an exactly opposite theory. They discarded the lyre from their recitation, and instead of it used a staff or an olive branch, which they held ceremoniously in their hands as a mere sign of their profession of art. Music fell away from their recitation, and only poetry was left. This school developed naturally into the didactic and historical style of Hesiod.

TROUBADOURS AND TROUVÈRES.—A precisely similar

transformation passed over the poetry of the troubadours. In the north of France and in England a separation between the music and the poetry ultimately occurred in a most pronounced form, and a race of trouvères, as they were called, branched off from the troubadours. Their distinguishing characteristic was to carry to excess the love for long elaborate poems, to prefer the historical style to the amorous, and finally most naturally to discard the employment of music in the recitation of their compositions. The name Trouvère has been applied by writers in the most indiscriminate and undecided manner. It has been employed to designate all the northern troubadours, whose sole distinction from their brethren was a geographical one, and who, because they did not happen to be born in countries which spelt " trouver " with a b, were termed trouvères instead of troubadours owing to this dialectic difference.

It has been applied to a small group of troubadours in Champagne and Lorraine, headed by Thibaut, Count of Champagne, and including in their number Adam de la Hale, and others—a small and select group of courtly poets, who, perhaps, strange to say, were the most essentially " musical " of any troubadours who ever lived. Their songs are more akin to modern sympathies than the songs of any of the Provençal troubadours, and it is principally to their exertions and musical genius that we owe the invaluable contributions of the troubadours to the modern science of harmony.

The name Trouvère has been applied to an inferior class of troubadours which existed in some parts, whose social status was midway between the troubadours and the glee-men or jongleurs. Such minstrels as these, deficient in the wealth which enabled them to support the state of troubadours, and yet of better birth or education than the itinerant jongleurs, seemed to deserve a distinguishing name, and, un-named by their contemporaries, were called Trouvères by succeeding writers on the subject. Finally, the name trouvère has been applied, and we think best limited, to those troubadours who, letting fall the musical moment of their strangely combined art and encouraging the literary, developed a new school of poetical composition, and transformed themselves at last completely from a race of courtly knights into a generation of literary men.

DENIS PYRAMUS.—At the outset of this wave of tendency which swept over the troubadour poetry, we find it hard to distinguish to what particular class the trouvère belongs. But gradually the outlines become clearer, and we are able to refer with certainty each individual to this or that category. One of the most notable of these trouvères, difficult to be distinguished from troubadours, was Denis Pyramus, who lived in the reign of Henry III. Most of his life was passed at the court of Henry III. and at the various castles or courts of the English barons. From the latter information we may conjecture the life of a troubadour, who was accustomed "to go from court to court," that is to say, from mansion to mansion of the nobility; while from some of the works he composed notably "The Life of St. Edmund, King of England,"[1]

---

[1] MS. British Museum, Cotton, Domitian, A. XI.

and "The Miracles of St. Edmund,"[1] we have strong proof of the trouvère tendency. At the same time, he wrote sirventes innumerable, which we may suppose to have been instinct with all the martial energy of the troubadour spirit, since they were "sung by the chevaliers," he tells us; and in addition he was the composer of numerous chansons, serenades, aubades, etc., all more or less popular.[2] A welcome figures in all the parties of pleasure of the time, he seems to have passed his life in unrestrained enjoyment, and still more frequently in abandoned dissipation. " Il usa sa vie," according to his own confession—"he drank the cup of pleasure to the dregs"; and in the opinion of his contemporaries was a libertine and profligate of no common order. He was an epicure, a free liver, a thoughtless, extravagant Don Juan, who, unlike most men, was not at all ashamed of making his offences against social propriety common conversation to the world. Old age alone brought repentance and reformation. To his old age we owe the two works which have survived the oblivion which has overwhelmed the compositions of this brilliant troubadour-trouvère, " La vie de St. Edmond," and "Les Miracles de St. Edmond," to which we have alluded before.

FRENCH, THE SPOKEN LANGUAGE OF ENGLAND TILL THE MIDDLE OF THE 14TH CENTURY.—It will be noticed that the compositions of Denis Pyramus and of others that have been quoted, although the compositions of Englishmen, are yet invariably couched in French, and

---

[1] MS. British Museum, Cotton, Tiberius, B. XI.
[2] De La Rue, *Essais*, III. 102.

this strange fact may strike many a reader as peculiar, who is oblivious or unconscious of the state of our language at the time of which we write. People, in considering the past history of our literature and our social life, are apt to forget that all the cultivated classes in England spoke French as their regular and natural tongue at the times we write of; and this ostracism of Saxon from the common parlance of educated people lasted till the middle of the 14th century. Kings, and probably great officers of state, certainly if they were ecclesiastics, were familiar with Latin, and could make orations or deliver judgments in that language. Most naturally, therefore, did the trouvères couch their inspirations in French rather than English, as by this means alone they could reach the cultivated and appreciative portion of society.

GEOFFREY GAIMAR AND OTHERS.—Geoffrey Gaimar was a celebrated English trouvère of the twelfth century,[1] whose chief composition that has descended to us is a metrical romance of the Anglo-Saxon Kings, which contains among other curious and interesting passages a description of the tricks of the jongleur Taillefer at the battle of Hastings. Benoît de Sainte-More was a famous Anglo Norman trouvère at the court of Henry II.[2] Henry caused him to undertake the composition and translation in verse of the Story of the Dukes of Normandy, and his

---

[1] Pluquet, *Notice sur la vie de Geoffroy Gaimar*, p. 70.

[2] *Ib.*, p. 12. For details of this trouvère's life see the Essay of the Abbé de la Rue, *Archéologia*, vol. XII., and some facts in Ginguené's *Histoire littéraire de France*, vol. III.

long and elaborate poem of that title was the result. It may be found in MS. at the British Museum, among the Harleian MSS., No. 1717. It is written in very good verse and with a consistent infusion of poetical feeling. It contains many interesting details about its various heroes, among other things a number of curious facts relating to the education of Richard I. of Normandy. Hue Archevesque was an Anglo-Norman trouvère of the thirteenth century, who has left some beautiful relics of his muse, entitled *Les Dits*, comprising short poems: De Larguece et de Debonereté, Le Dit de la Dent, La Poissance d'Amors, and De la Mort Larguece. We know little about this trouvère except that, having made a journey to Cherbourg, he was grievously attacked with illness in that city, and made a vow, if he were cured, to go on a pilgrimage to Bauduin és Bours, a priory dependent on the Abbey of Fécamp. When he arrived there he took up his abode for awhile with his friend Richard du Pont,[1] and here our information ceases. "Unfortunately," says the modern editor of this trouvère, M. Heron, making a remark which may apply more or less to all, "we know the troubadours principally by the details which they have been willing to give us themselves, and these details as a rule are meagre and insufficient."[2]

---

[1] *Introduction à Les Dits de Hue Archevesque*, par A. Heron (published by the Société Rouennaise de Bibliophiles. Paris, 1885), p. 14.

[2] "Presque toujours nous ne connaissons les troubadours que par les details qu'eux-mêmes ont bien voulu nous donner sur leur compte, et ces détails sont d'ordinaire bien rares et bien insuffisants."—*Ibid.*, p. 12.

K

ADAM DE ROS: COMPARED TO DANTE.—We now come to one of the most celebrated English trouvères who ever lived, and, we may add, a man of that unique and original genius which nature has vouchsafed only to a few of the most favoured of her children. Adam de Ros came of a distinguished family, which was settled partly in Yorkshire and partly in Kent. He took orders, agreeably to the custom of many of the cultivated men of his time, but his main interests were obviously literary and poetical. His wonderful mind, soaring over nature and history in search of a subject worthy of its vast imagination, lighted on the theme of St. Paul's Visit to Hell as a subject at once epic and sublime.[1] In this marvellous poem the whole of the *Divina Commedia* of Dante is anticipated and displayed. The original idea of the visit by a living man to the regions of the dead, who should be able to treasure and communicate his impressions to his fellows in the upper world—such an idea which we think so wonderful and pregnant of possibilities in the poem of Dante—has been anticipated and admirably developed by the English troubadour.[2] With a far finer sense of con-

---

[1] " Aidez mei a translater
La vision St. Pol," etc.,

says Adam de Ros in his exordium (British Museum, Cotton MSS., Vespasian, A. 7). This is not to be considered, however, as in any sense of the word betokening a translation. Very often the translators announced such a thing as a translation from the Latin, when really it was not so, in order to enhance its value. " Souvent les trouvères, pour donner plus de prix à leurs ouvrages, les annoncèrent comme traduits du latin," says the Abbé De la Rue, *Essais Historiques*, III. 141.

[2] We must go back however to the Apocalypse of St. Peter if we seek the prime original of these visits to the Shades.

gruity than that which prompted Dante to take as his companion in the Christian hell a Pagan poet, devoid of all sympathies and all connection with such a place of post-Augustan torment, Adam de Ros has elected the Archangel Michael to be the companion and cicerone of St. Paul in his curious and extraordinary journey through the Shades. The reason of this or that spectacle, of this or that punishment of a sinner, of which Virgil might naturally be supposed to be entirely ignorant, comes with good grace and admirable aptitude from the lips of an archangel familiar with the mysterious dispensations of the Second Person of the Trinity, to whom the Pagan poet was for ever a regrettable stranger. And St. Paul, the traveller and observer of this world of wonders, is a far more likely person to occupy such a privileged position than a chance Italian burning with the petty animosities of the Bianchi and the Neri.

ACCOUNT OF HIS POEM.—Arrived at the gate of Hell, the first thing which meets the eyes of the apostle is a tree of fire, which rears its awful trunk and branches to immeasurable height, and spreads sparks and eternal conflagration over the infernal portals. Terrible is the aspect of that tree, as depicted by the English troubadour, and its lively terrors are quite as tremendous in their impressiveness as the graphic despair which the Florentine poet has shed over the scene. On the branches of this blazing tree are hung the souls of the avaricious and the slanderers, whom, of all the damned, the troubadour seems to think most worthy of this public spectacle of their torture. Avarice, which is the secret spring of all oppression, and slander, the most festering and foulest of all social sores, are justly condemned to yield up their votaries and supporters to blaze for ever at the doors of hell. After St. Paul and his divine guide have had leisure to look around on the spectacle presented to them, the air is filled with multitudes of demons, who bring a crowd of sinners to the punishments they deserve; while simultaneously companies of angels are seen escorting good spirits to heaven. The number of the latter, the troubadour significantly adds, was considerably inferior to that of the damned. Into the abyss of hell now proceed the apostle and his heavenly guide. The abyss, of increasing depth and increasing torments, is constructed exactly like Dante's abyss, and St. Paul, in all his actions of wonderment, inquiry, and fear, acts precisely as Dante acts in the company of his poetical protector. The archangel, like Virgil, but with superior guarantee of knowledge, points out to his mortal companion the different punishments that are proceeding in hell, expounds to him the causes of them all, and quiets the terrors which they produce. The methods of punishment are in the main identical with those of Dante. Human imagination, when face to face with the problem of hell, evinces a singular tendency to repetition; and entire novelty is, of course, impossible on a theme in regard to whose general features all men are agreed. We cannot, therefore, blame the Italian poet if he has exactly repeated in several instances the tortures invented by the English troubadour, and if, where he has departed from Adam de Ros' poem, he has failed to improve upon that great original. Glowing furnaces, rivers of molten iron with demons swimming in the ruddy waves, sinners who are buried more or less deep according to the gravity of their offences—such are the scenes through which we are conducted and such the characters we observe. The identity of the work, in its method and theme, with that of Dante is apparent in every line. So much so, that after a short perusal of the manuscript the reader is apt to lay it down and to say with an air of profound self-conviction, "Dante must have read this poem. He has read it; he has plagiarised it; and he wears laurels which by rights should belong to an ill-used and unjustly treated genius." What ground there may be for this unavoidable suspicion, we leave critics of the Italian master, too numerous, alas! and too bigoted already, to discover. We have neither the space to make the inquiry, nor does it lie within the scope of this work.

The poem of Adam de Ros may be studied in the Cotton MSS. of the British museum (Vespasian, A. VII.) and is written in the favourite eight-foot measure.

CHAPTER IX.

Origin of Early English Romances—General Taste for Romances
—Le Brut d'Angleterre—The Romance of Rollo and the Dukes
of Normandy—Robert Wace—Translations of the Brut—The
Saxon Trouvère—Walter Map—Thomas of Kent—Three
Cycles of Romances—Minstrelsy, Law, and Religion—Further
Romances—King Horn—The Romance of Guy of Warwick—
Generydes—Sir Percival of Galles—Sir Isumbras—Sir Egla-
mour of Artois—Sir Fierabras—Popularity of Fierabras in
England and Scotland—The Romance of Floriant et Florete
—The Romance of Beuves—Aucassin et Nicolette.

ORIGIN OF EARLY ENGLISH ROMANCES.—We now proceed to an illustrious gallery where names, the most
eminent, though forgotten or ignored, are to be found, and
where the origin and foundation is to be sought of all our
medieval romances, and possibly of all our romantic
literature. The origin of the early English romances has
been made a matter of controversy. But many of them
may be ascribed, with probable exactitude, to one or other
specific trouvère. Various theories, more or less sweeping,
have been advanced about them. According to Tyrwhitt,
all romances before Chaucer were translations or imita-
tions of the French. But, on the contrary, we find Marie
de France[1] acknowledging her obligations to the Welsh

---

[1] *Infra*, Chapter XI.

and Bretons. Wales, Cumberland, Cornwall, and Brittany were probably far more nearly connected with the central life of England than we are apt to imagine in those days, and the Saxon gleemen may have availed themselves of materials and traditions which had been originally, and for a long time, current in those regions. These materials may have ultimately come into the possession of the English and Anglo-Norman trouvères. According to a view, which may be taken as supplementary to that of Tyrwhitt, the first romances recited in England were necessarily French, not because they were composed in France, or drawn from French materials, but because French was the spoken language of England up to the year 1362, and no other means of communication was possible if educated people were to be addressed by the troubadour or jongleur. Whichever view may be held on the subject, certain it is that the bulk of the English romances were originally written in French, and as long as that language was the usual vehicle of communication, and practically the vernacular in this country, they remained in that tongue.[1] When French began to be ousted by English as the ordinary vernacular, then the romances began to be translated into English. Very few were composed in English originally, according to our present state of knowledge; though increasing investigation may add to their numbers.

GENERAL TASTE FOR ROMANCES.—A great taste for

---

[1] All the upper classes were bilingual. The chronicles were written in Latin.

these romances was spread abroad among the people at large.   The jongleurs in *Cursor Mundi* sing :—

> "Men lykyn jestis for to here,
>   And romans rede in diuers manere
>   Of Alexandre the conqueroure,
>   Of Julius Cesar the emperoure,
>   Of Grece and Troy the strong stryf,
>   There many a man lost his lyf ;
>   Of Brute that baron bold of hond,
>   The first conqueroure of Englond,
>   Of King Artour, that was so riche,
>   Was not in his tyme him liche,
>   How Kyng Charlis and Rowlond fawght
>   With sarzyns nold they be cawght,
>   Of Tristrem and of Ysoude the swete,
>   How they with love first gan mete,
>   Of King John and of Isombras,
>   Of Ydoyne and of Amadas,
>   Stories of diuerce thinggis,
>   Of pryncis, prelatis, and of kynggis,
>   Many songgis of diuers ryme,
>   As english, frensh, and latyne."[1]

King Henry II. was marvellously fond, says Gerald of Wales, of hearing these "jestis,"[2] and the taste for them ran through all classes of society, from the king on his throne to the peasant in his cottage.

Le Brut d'Angleterre.—One of these romances, which was held in special honour and achieved the highest popularity in England, was entitled *Le Brut d'Angle-*

---

[1] *Cursor Mundi*, a Northumbrian poem of the 14th century. Edited by G. R. Morris, for the Early English Text Society, vol. V., p. 1651, and vol. I., p. 8.

[2] "Rex autem hoc ex gestis Britonum et eorum cantoribus historicis frequenter audiverat."—Giraldus Cambrensis, in Lelandi *Assert. Arturi.* folio 50, Cf. Malmesb. *Hist.*, ap. Gale, folio 295.

terre,[1] or "Brutus of England." It was publicly recited at the courts of the kings of England. It contains, with full detail, the story of the Round Table, of the fêtes, the tourneys, and the chevaliers connected with the weavings of that legend. It had been composed originally in Lower Breton, then translated into Latin by Geoffrey of Monmouth, and then turned by the trouvère Robert Wace into the above-named poem. The verse is of eight syllables. The era of the composition is 1155, that is to say, in the second year of King Henry II.'s reign.[2]

THE ROMANCE OF ROLLO AND THE DUKE OF NORMANDY. —This is the most important of the compositions of the same celebrated trouvère. It is composed in several parts, obviously destined for separate performance and recitation. The first part, written in verse of eight syllables, apparently intended as an introduction, comprehends the story of the first irruption of the Normans into France and England. The second, in Alexandrines, gives the story of Rou or Rollo. The third, in verse of the same measure, recites the tale of William Long-Sword and of Richard I. his son, Duke of Normandy. The fourth part, written in verse of eight syllables, recounts the story of the Norman dukes and kings of England, from the death of Richard I. Duke of Normandy, till the sixth year of Henry I. King of England.[3] Among other works by this celebrated

---

[1] "On le lisait publiquement à la cour des rois d'Angleterre." Frédéric Pluquet, *Notice sur la vie de Robert Wace.* (Rouen, 1824.)

[2] *Ibid.,* p. 9.   [3] *Ibid.,* p. 9.

trouvère are *Chronique ascendante des Ducs de Normandie*, *L'Etablissement de la Feste de la Conception*, and *La Vie de St. Nicolas*.

ROBERT WACE.—We have spoken of the works of the celebrated trouvère. Let us now add a few details about his life. We have already heard of a troubadour bishop. This celebrated Anglo-Norman trouvère was a prebendary. A brilliant ornament of the learned Court of Henry I. in his early days, he completed his " Roman de Rou," or Romance of Rollo and the Dukes of Normandy, in the reign of Henry II. and dedicated it to that monarch. Henry in return gave him a prebend's stall in the cathedral of Bayeux.[1] He cultivated with success various styles of the troubadour minstrelsy, and speaks of the sirventes and the ballads which he wrote with pardonable pride.[2] But his main laurels were won as a romancer.

TRANSLATIONS OF THE BRUT.—The *Brut d'Angleterre* of Wace was subsequently translated into English by Layamon, a monk of Ernely, and about a century later another monk, Robert of Gloucester, performed the same task. An English trouvère, Robert de Brunne by name, likewise did the same office for Robert Wace ; but Robert de Brunne, beside being a translator of French into English, likewise has the rare merit of composing original verse in the English tongue. He concludes the prologue to a chronicle of his by affirming that he

---

[1] Frédéric Pluquet, *Notice sur la vie de Robert Wace*, p. 6. (Rouen, 1824.)

[2] *Ibid.*, p. 12.

> " Did it write for felawes
>   When thai wild solace make,"

by which we are to understand that he intended his chronicle to be sung to the harp, at least by parts, at public festivals.[1]

THE SAXON TROUVERE.—The " Brut d'Angleterre " was continued by an anonymous trouvère of Saxon parentage, whose date probably falls in the reign of Henry III. Not only is he of Saxon parentage, but every line in his poem seems to be full of burning indignation against the Normans. His work may be studied in manuscript at the British Museum,[2] and the eternity of the hate between the Saxons and the Normans can never be better illustrated than by reference to the verses of the Saxon trouvère. What violent indignation does he hurl at William the Conqueror for his spoliations and rapacity! What eloquence of invective does he employ against the forest laws! The anger of the minstrel, the hatred of the poet, the vengeance of the vanquished—all breathe in the lines of the Saxon trouvère. He pillories the oppression of the king to all eternity. He holds up to everlasting infamy the immorality of the queen Matilda. A curious anecdote is related by the trouvère in illustration of Matilda's sins. While a girl in Flanders, says the Saxon trouvère, Matilda fell in love with a young Anglo-Saxon earl named Brichtrichman. So infatuated did she become with this handsome young nobleman that she offered him her hand, but, to her intense mortification and

---

[1] Warton, *History of English Poetry*, I. 56.
[2] Cotton MSS. British Museum, *Vitellius*, A. X.

shame, he refused the proffered boon, and Matilda, rejected and disdained, waited the time when she could revenge herself on her contemptuous lover. Time wore on, and Matilda, in the course of events, became queen of England. She then had her enemy at her mercy, and acting on the principle of Potiphar's wife, she excited the jealousy of William against the earl. William, boiling with rage, placed troops at her disposal and gave her permission to deal with the Saxon nobleman as she pleased. Accordingly the vindictive queen caused her old lover to be besieged in the castle of Haneley, where he was taken prisoner. He was thence conducted to life-long captivity at Winchester, where he miserably died. In this way did the queen revenge herself for her slighted love. We know not what authority the troubadour may have had for this story,[1] and we leave to others the task of investigating the veracity of his charges of immorality against the Conqueror's queen. But the manuscript of his poetry is well worthy of attention, not only in connection with the history of the troubadours and of the social life of England, but also in relation to the history of England itself. He was born at Amesbury in Wiltshire, and as a versifier is rough but vigorous.

WALTER MAP.—Walter Map, Archdeacon of Oxford, Precentor of Lincoln, Canon of London, and chaplain of Henry II., was nevertheless a chevalier of the first degree of knighthood. It is a mistake, therefore, to suppose that such a chivalrous rank and the ecclesiastical profession

---

[1] The story is certainly told in the Domesday Book.

were incompatible. In addition to these functions he was
a judge,[1] and presided at the Assizes of Gloucestershire.
Walter wrote several Romances of the Round Table, and
dedicated the *Romance of Percival* to Henry II. At
Henry's request he wrote likewise *La Mort d'Artur*,
or "The Death of Arthur," and *Lancelot of the Lake*.[2]

THOMAS OF KENT [3]—Wrote in French verse a trans-
lation of that remarkable poem, *The Romance of King
Horn*. Hugh of Rutland was a contemporary of Walter
Map, and lived in the reign of Henry II. Under this
king appeared nearly all the Romances of the Round Table.
Hugh's principal work is the *Romance of Ypomedon*.

THREE CYCLES OF ROMANCES.—We may notice three
principal cycles in the writings of our trouvères and
romancers — the first the Carlovingian, containing the
stories of Roland and the Twelve Peers, etc. ; the second the
Arturian, with tales of the Round Table ; and the third
the Alexandrian, under which name we may class all the
romances relating to antiquity, dealing especially with
Alexander and his exploits. William of Normandy, a
trouvère, was the author of that most charming romance,
The Romance of Fregus. "After Robert Wace [4] he was
the most copious of the trouvères, and at the same time
the most versatile," says a panegyrist ; and even, on an im-

---

[1] Madox's *History of the Exchequer*, p. 483.

[2] De la Rue, *Essais*, II. 241–2.

[3] For a discussion of the vexed question of Thomas of Kent's
birthplace, see De La Rue, II. 251.

[4] "Après Robert Wace celui qui a le plus écrit et le plus varié
s.s sujets." De La Rue, III. 12.

partial survey, no one can deny him a high degree of talent.

MINSTRELSY, LAW, AND RELIGION.—With Henry d'Audeley, the trouvère, to whom we owe *Le Dictie du chancelier Philippe*, and Richard Annebaut, a trouvère of Somersetshire, we find the troubadour minstrelsy brought into connection with new and unexpected subjects; in the former case with gnomic poetry, in the latter with law. Moral Distiques were a favourite subject for exercising the art of versification on, especially among the trouvères of Normandy. But an essentially English trouvère, Helie de Winchester, translated the " Distiques de Caton," the manuscript of which is in the library of Corpus Christi College, Cambridge, remarking at the same time that he wrote for those of the English who did not understand Latin and only spoke Romance ;[1] while Adam le Clerc did the same office to the same original, and the fruits of his labours may be studied in a manuscript in the Harleian collection at the British Museum.[2] Most curious, however, are the versifications of laws. That lawyers themselves could be very good poets we know from the fact that Philippe de Beaumanoir, the great lawyer, composed two metrical romances, *La Manekine* and *Blonde of Oxford* but to find law itself yielding materials for poetry is another matter. Richard Annebaut, the English trouvère to whom we alluded, versified the Institutes of Justinian, transforming the dry-as-dust legal formularies

---

[1] Helie de Winchester, MS. Corpus Christi College, Cambridge.

[2] Adam le Clerc, Harleian MS., British Museum.

into harmonious French verse.[1] The family of this trouvère had accompanied the Conqueror to England, and had been endowed with large estates in Somersetshire. In like manner William Cauph, another English trouvère versified the Roman and Saxon laws.[2] This versification of such things as laws, this selection of such a prosaic subject as a theme for poetry, might be decried by the hasty or the ignorant, and quoted as a proof of an unpoetic mind or an artificial and unnatural taste in verse, did we not know that primitive barbarian nations, the genuineness of whose poetic impulses there is no possibility of doubting, very commonly set their laws to verse and music, of which ancient method of poetising, the efforts of Annebaut and Cauph were revivals. Thus the laws of the Celts were couched in hymns and were sung to an accompaniment of the lyre.[3] The laws of the Gepidæ, in like manner, were set to music and verse;[4] of the Turdetani[5] and other barbarian nations whom we might quote. In the same way when we find the English trouvère, William de Wadington, composing a religious treatise in harmonious French verse—a Manual of Sins it was, which gave in metrical form all the doctrines and dogmas of morality[6] — or read of the monk-jongleurs who were accustomed to go about singing lives of the saints in

---

[1] Harleian MSS., 447, British Museum.

[2] *Reliquiæ manuscriptorum omnis ævi diplomatum ac monumentorum adhuc ineditorum*, vol. VII.

[3] Pelloutier, *Histoire des Celtes*, II. 186.

[4] Ricobaldus Ferrariensis, III.   [5] Strabo, III.

[6] MSS. British Museum, King's Library, 20 B. XIV., and Harleian 273, 4657 and 4974.

verse or other religious poetry of their own composing,[1] we should allow our fancies to go back, in order to find the archetypes, to those distant and barbarian times when the dogmas of religion among the Celts[2] and other nations[3] were couched in verse and sung by bards and priests to the lyre. That was the glorious manhood of such a theme for poetry, of which this rare specimen that we speak of was the vestige and decay.[4] Wadington lived at the end of the thirteenth century, at which date many of his family were settled in Lincolnshire.[5]

FURTHER ROMANCES.—A meritorious trouvère was Robert Bikez, who wrote *Le Lai du Corn* towards the end of the thirteenth century. Peter Langtoft—to return more closely to the romances—was a trouvère of the fourteenth century, who, like so many of his day, combined the ecclesiastical profession with the poetical. He was canon of the priory of St. Augustin de Bridlington, Yorkshire, and wrote a Metrical History of the British Kings from Brutus to Cadwallader, which was in effect a translation of Geoffrey of Monmouth's *Historia Britonum.*[6] We also owe to him a Metrical History of the Anglo-Saxon kings, in

---

[1] *Statut. Concil. Sarisburens.*, cap. 8. *Statut. Synod. Episc. Leodic.*, cap. 12., 5., etc.

[2] Ammianus Marcellinus, XV. 19.

[3] Prudentius Apotheos., 206.

[4] Though perhaps we ought to modify this expression when we remember *Cursor Mundi*, a metrical version of the Scriptures in old English, several MSS. of which are preserved in our public libraries.

[5] *Cartulaire de Bullington*, Sir Joseph Banks' MSS.

[6] MS. British Museum, King's Library, 20, B. xi.

which he followed chiefly the accounts of Bede and others,[1] and a Life in verse of Edward I.[2] He composed many lays and songs likewise. The Anonymous Troubadour or trouvère, who is the author of the Romance of Haveloc the Dane, deserves attention for the vigour of his style. Pierre Sarrasin, the last of the trouvères who treated the subject of King Arthur and the Knights of the Round Table, lived at the Court of King Henry III., and in return for his poetical services received several sums from the exchequer, probably at the behest of that monarch. His work, the *Roman du Ham* may be studied in manuscript in the Bibliothèque Nationale at Paris, and will afford delight, and often astonishment, in the perusal.[3]

KING HORN.—We have already alluded to the romance of King Horn, when speaking of Thomas the trouvère, who translated it. Thomas himself lived in the reign of Richard I. But with regard to this celebrated romance we have to mention the curious fact, that it was probably written originally in English, and from this the French version was made. King Horn, in its English form, is written in the common short Anglo-Saxon metre. There are three complete versions of King Horn in English: Harl. MS. 2253; MS. Laud. (Bodleian, fol. 219*b*); and the MS. GG. 4, 27, 2, in the Cambridge University Library.

THE ROMANCE OF GUY OF WARWICK and Felice, daughter of the Earl of Buckingham, is the work of the trouvère Walter of Exeter, who wrote it in French verse. It is one of the most ancient and popular of its class. Guy of

---

[1] MS. British Museum, King's Library, 20, B. XI.   [2] *Ibid.*
[3] MS. Bibliothèque Nationale, No. 7603.

Warwick is a noble and pious hero something after the pattern of Æneas,[1] and likely to enlist most strongly the sympathies of a chivalrous age. A translation of Guy of Warwick into English verse was executed in the fourteenth century, and into French prose in the sixteenth century, at which date it was published in Paris.

GENERYDES.—Our knowledge of this romance is derived from a manuscript in the library of Trinity College, Cambridge, the date of which is 1440 A.D. We cannot say who was the author of it, as the manuscript gives no clue whatever. It is written in the Chaucerian stanza, and in English. No French version of this romance has yet been discovered, though probably it is a translation.

SIR PERCEVAL OF GALLES.—This is an Anglo-Norman romance of 20,178 lines,[2] the author of which was the trouvère Chrestien de Troyes, who lived at the end of the twelfth century. The romance was subsequently continued by Gautier de Denet and Manessier, who completed the second part early in the thirteenth century. The tale of Perceval enjoyed the greatest popularity, and was ultimately translated into English. The translation is executed in the same stanza in which Drayton wrote *Queen Mab* and the English version forms one of the Thornton MSS. preserved in Lincoln Cathedral.

SIR ISUMBRAS.—No French original of this romance has been discovered, though probably it is Anglo-Norman in origin. It is written in stanzas, and forms another of the

---

[1] See the *Introduction to the French Romance of Waldef*.
[2] *Hist. Lib. de France*, XV. 196.

Thornton MSS. before alluded to. Sir Isumbras is similar to Robert of Sicily in plot, both romances relating to the reclaiming of their heroes by Divine interposition.

SIR EGLAMOUR OF ARTOIS and Sir Degrevant are two romances in English, which are probably translations. Very possibly the French originals of both may be in existence, but we are not aware of them. The best manuscripts of these two romances are, of Sir Eglamour, the Cambridge MS , Ff. II. 38, and of Sir Degrevant, the Cambridge MS., Ff. I. 6.

SIR FIERABRAS.—A full account of all the Charlemagne Romances will be found in Gaston Paris' exhaustive work, *Histoire poétique de Charlemagne* (Paris, 1865), and in Léon Gautier's *Epopées Françaises* (Paris, 1867). Of all the poems sung by troubadour and trouvère alike, none attained the popularity and enduring fame of the Charlemagne Romances, of which it is said that they were sung by these minstrels, " both in Provençal and in French, both in the south and in the north." [1] The romance of Fierabras is one of the most celebrated. This romance, both in its French and English forms, was most popular in England, as we may know, among other reasons, from the illuminated picture in one of the MSS. of the poem, which represents John Talbot, Earl of Shrewsbury, presenting a copy of the manuscript to Margaret of Anjou, who is seated beside her husband on a kind of bed, in a chamber of which the

---

[1] " Chantée en provençal et en français . . . au midi et au nord."—*Fierabras, Chanson de reste,* Paris, 1860.

tapestry bears everywhere the arms of England quartered.[1]
The poem itself is divided into three books, the second
of which contains the whole of the romance of Sir
Fierabras.   The earliest known mention of this romance
is a deed of gift in the fourteenth century, by which Guy de
Beauchamp, Earl of Warwick, bequeathed his library to
the Abbey of Bordesley, in the county of Warwick, in
the catalogue of which we find a " Volum del romance des
mareschaus et de Fierabras de Alisauudre." [2] This poem
was translated into English verse, tinged largely with
evidence of a southern, probably a Devonshire, dialect.
In this dialect, however, there are many intermixtures of
midland and northern form.   From this it is evident
that the skilful versifier and bard had travelled far and
wide over England, and had not limited his actual resid-
ence to Devonshire, but had remained for long periods,
long enough to become infected with dialectic peculiar-
ities, in counties far distant from his own.

Popularity of Fierabras in England and Scotland.
—These romances were chanted with the accompaniment
of musical instruments,[3] and were the favourite diversions
of lords and ladies, who listened to them with extreme
delight.[4] To testify to the exceeding popularity of this
class of composition, it is recorded that when King Robert

---

[1] Grenville Library, British Museum, MS. 10,531.

[2] *Fierabras*, edited by MM. Kroeber et Servois.   Introduction,
p. 22.

[3] Aye d'Avignon, line 1403.

[4] " Font ces fables dire et escouter chansons," was mentioned
as one of their greatest pleasures. *Ib.* 2685.

the Bruce was on the banks of Loch Lomond, over which his men were slowly ferried, he beguiled the hours and diverted their minds from misfortunes by those tales of the heroes of romance, in which he, like all other medieval chevaliers, took exceeding delight. " The story of Fierabras and the unconquered Oliver, with the adventures of the twelve peers of Charlemagne, when they were besieged in the city of Eglamour and relieved by Richard, Duke of Normandy, were told to an audience of Scottish knights and squires, whose own escapes were scarcely less extraordinary than the marvels to which they listened. Amused and solaced by the interest of the tale and the spirit with which it was recounted, the Scotch knights and warriors returned, with lighter hearts and renewed resolution, from the dream of romance into the bitter reality with which they were surrounded." [1]

THE ROMANCE OF FLORIANT ET FLORETE.—Such is the name of another of these romances, which was versified by a trouvère in the fourteenth century, most probably. King Arthur plays a principal part in this romance, holding his court at Cardigan, while Florete, the heroine of the poem, is the daughter of the Emperor of Constantinople, the place to which the attention of the cultivated world again and again turned as the land of romance. The style of Floriant and Florete is in general elegant, easy, and graceful. The verse of eight syllables, in this, even more than in other French or Provençal poems, flows

---

[1] Tytler, *Lives of Scottish Worthies*, I. 318 (London, 1831).

on with a charming ease and copiousness. The manuscript of this romance in its metrical form, to which we allude, was discovered in the library of Newbattle Abbey, near Dalkeith, Edinburgh. Apropos of this allusion to Arthur, we may remark that such a work dealing with any of the British prince's adventures would be likely to be popular, owing to the firm belief in many parts of England—then not a mere dream, but a creed with many —that Arthur would one day return. "In the time of Henry II.," says William Newbridge, "the belief in the return of Arthur was so widespread, that when it was a question of naming the son of Geoffrey Plantagenet, Duke of Brittany, the Britons opposed the notion of the name Henry being given, and importuned the king to call him Arthur, which he did." [1]

THE ROMANCE OF BEUVES and his lady love, Josiane, daughter of the King of Armenia.—The author of this work was Pierre du Ries, an Anglo-Norman trouvère. Beuves was a veritable historical personage, being Earl of Southampton at the time of the Conquest. He lived at Duneton, in Wiltshire. There is a very old English metrical translation of this romance.[2]

AUCASSIN ET NICOLETTE.—The name of the troubadour who wrote this charming romance is unfortunately lost to us, nor is there the slightest likelihood that we shall discover it, until the treasures of troubadour literature now lying in the Bibliothèque Nationale in Paris have been

---

[1] William Newbridge, III. 7.
[2] See Ellis' *Specimens of Early English Metrical Romances*, II. 95.

thoroughly ransacked and examined. From one solitary MS. in that library, the poem has been recovered. All that we know of the troubadour who composed it is from his own allusion to himself in the poem. He speaks of himself as "viel caitif," from which Du Méril[1] assumes with some justice that the troubadour had been taken prisoner in the crusades, and had come back from captivity among the Saracens. The troubadour may have been "an aged captive" truly, but his poem became popular throughout the length and breadth of England directly it was composed,[2] and since its recovery from a single ill-written manuscript, which only received attention at the beginning of last century, it has awakened growing interest in modern times. The work shows in every part of it the hand of the practised troubadour, who had had plenty of experience in ballad singing, as well as in the weaving of separate ballads together into one long composition.[3] An interesting picture in the poem—a picture teeming with fresh and spontaneous imagery, which seems to have been reflected from fact—is the description of Nicolette disguising herself as a jongleur, going through the country playing on the violin, and improvising before Aucassin and his court.

---

[1] Du Méril's Introduction to *Floire et Blanceflor.*

[2] "At the time when the story was written," says Mr. Bourdillon, the English editor, "it would have been nearly or quite as much at home among the educated classes in England as in its native land." Bourdillon's Introduction to *Aucassin et Nicolette.*

[3] Bourdillon's Introduction to *Aucassin et Nicolette,* pp. 24-5.

CHAPTER X.

THE GLEEMEN, JONGLEURS, WANDERING MINSTRELS, AND GLEEMAIDENS.

The Jongleurs—Their Social Status—The Character of the Jongleurs—The Musical Proficiency of the Jongleurs—Some of the Jongleurs' Instruments in Detail—English Origin of the Violin—Other Instruments played by the Jongleurs—The Regals and other Instruments—Historical Importance of the Jongleurs in Musical History—The Jongleurs as Independent Minstrels—The Wandering Minstrels—Dress and Life of the Wandering Minstrels.

THE JONGLEURS. THEIR SOCIAL STATUS. — The jongleurs or gleemen stood to the troubadours very much in the relation of squire to knight. They were the musical attendants on their courtly masters, the performers who sang their songs, the instrumentalists who accompanied them. They followed them in a retinue, and helped to keep up their ceremony and state ; while we hear of other offices rendered by the jongleurs to the troubadours, irrespective of music and of assistance during musical functions. At tournaments, they attended their master, and carried his body from the lists if he were killed or wounded. They were the constant bearers of messages and letters from the troubadour to his friends—a species of service which often led them into great danger, and was never devoid of a spice of peril. Even if these missives

ANGLO SAXON ILLUMINATION SHOWING VARIOUS MUSICAL
INSTRUMENTS FROM THE COTTON MSS,
153

were merely from the troubadour to his lady-love, there
was peril in the errands; for that lady-love generally had
a husband, and exemplary punishment was meted out to
the unfortunate jongleur, if he were caught carrying on
this clandestine correspondence.   But very frequently the
missives with which the jongleur was entrusted were
destined for delivery to distant countries in time of war,
and his person was exposed to the utmost risk from
capture by the enemy.   The jongleurs likewise, accompanied their master into battle, and the account of the
jongleur Taillefer, who was in attendance on some Norman troubadour at the battle of Hastings, will be familiar
to many.   He asked for the honour of striking the first
blow against the Saxons, and the permission having been
granted, he sprang into the front of the Norman army
and astonished the unsophisticated Saxons by the
clownish tricks he played.   He cast his lance three times
into the air, and caught it by the handle.   Then he
hurled his sword aloft, and on its glittering descent
caught the blade by the same means.   The clumsy foot-
soldiers in Harold's army, who only knew how to cleave
coats of mail by blows from their battle-axes, were
astonished, saying to one another that it was magic which
enabled the mountebank to perform these feats.

THE CHARACTER OF THE JONGLEURS.—There was in
truth a great deal of the mountebank and the charlatan
in the character of the jongleurs.   They were men who
emphatically lived by their wits.   They were employed
by the troubadours very much in the way that kings of a
later age employed jesters and court-fools—purely out of

consideration for their talents to astonish or to amuse. A jongleur's very existence depended on the preservation of his voice, or on the dexterity of his instrumental playing, or on the appropriateness of his action and gestures while singing a song, or taking part in a dialogue. There was every inducement for a jongleur to overdo his *rôle* rather than underdo it, in order that his performance might be striking, and that the lords and ladies who heard him sing or play might speak with admiration or surprise at his graphic delineations of character or incident, and possibly recommend others of their friends to offer him employment—much in the same way that the audiences at private concerts now-a-days will recommend the singers they are struck with to the notice of their acquaintances. But there was this difference. In those times, the jongleur passed into the continuous employment of his new masters, and received a stipulated wage, in return for which he always held himself and his talents at the disposal of the troubadour.

THE MUSICAL PROFICIENCY OF THE JONGLEURS.—The main musical proficiency of the jongleurs was that gained on instruments. We do not hear their vocal excellence praised so highly as their instrumental, while the latter not only merits all the eulogy bestowed on it, but entitles them, on a just estimate, to a very high position in the history of music. It was the natural tendency of men, who had to gain their livelihood by their skill as musicians, to be ambitious to play as many instruments as possible, and to play them well. But, to the credit of the jongleurs be it said, it was a point of honour among them to possess this remarkable proficiency, quite irrespective of any pecuniary profit which might result therefrom. Among themselves, and in their own estimate of one another, they looked upon him as the best minstrel who could play the largest number of instruments, who could exhibit the greatest versatility of style in his musical performances, and who could render himself upon occasions the most amusing and entertaining, when the company were inclined to laugh rather than to sigh, or when the wine cup had driven love and its thoughts for a while out of the clouded brains of the revellers. "I can play," says the minstrel, in the Bodleian manuscript at Oxford, "the lute, the violin, the pipe, the bagpipe, the syrinx, the harp, the gigue, the gittern, the symphony, the psaltery, the organistrum, the regals, the tabor, and the rote. I can sing a song well, and make tales and fables. I can tell a story against any man. I can make love verses to please young ladies, and can play the gallant for them if necessary. Then I can throw knives into the air, and catch them without cutting my fingers. I can do dodges with string, most extraordinary and amusing. I can balance chairs, and make tables dance. I can throw a somersault, and walk on my head."[1] Such were the qualifications for a jongleur's life which he boasts of possessing, and such, as a rule, were the qualifications of them all. In fact, it was owing to these feats of dexterity of theirs, which once learnt, they were rather proud of showing off, perhaps more than

---

[1] *Les deux Menestriers.* Digby MS., Bodleian Library, Oxford.

was necessary, that the gleemen—for so they were originally called—began to get the name of "jugglers," or "jougeleurs," which the corrupt pronunciation of dialects or the mis-spelling of manuscripts transformed into "jongleurs."

Such were the instruments which that jongleur could play, whom we have spoken of. And other jongleurs were not behind him. "I can play," says another, "the flute, the trumpet, the guitar, the harp, the flageolet, the tambourine, the violin, the set of bells, the organistrum, the bagpipe, the psaltery, the tabor, the lute, the sackbut, the rebeck, the trumpet marine, and the gigue." Says a third jongleur, "I play the shalm, the timbrel, the cymbals, the regals, the gittern, the sackbut, the fiddle, and the lute: the Spanish penola that is struck with a quill, the organistrum that a wheel turns round, the wait so delightful, the rebeck so enchanting, the little gigue that chirps up on high, and the great big horn that booms like thunder." Thus do they go on, trying to out-do one another in boasting of the variety and multiplicity of their musical powers. But irrespective of their tendency to self-glorification, the service which they rendered to the art of music at this juncture must never be forgotten by the historian, and deserves the future thanks of a grateful world. In order to please their masters the troubadours, and decorate with as great a skill as they could the compositions of their employers, they ransacked Europe for instruments, and spent endless time in practising them.

SOME OF THE JONGLEURS' INSTRUMENTS IN DETAIL.—To allude to a few only of these instruments that the jongleurs whom we mentioned spoke of playing. The lute, one of the most important instruments in the world of music, was in the present instance an essentially English growth, and, if we may trust to the musical knowledge of a Latin epigrammatist, was developed among us by the ancient Britons. Diodorus Siculus, in speaking of the ancient Britons who were led by their bards and minstrels into the combat, says: "With instruments like lyres in their hands, the British minstrels advanced" at the head of the armies.[1] As to what these lyre-like instruments actually were, and that they constituted a special class. distinct and distinguishable from the instruments of other nations, we may learn from a distich of Fortunatus, who says :—

"Let the Roman delight in his lyre, the barbarian in his harp,
The Greek in the lyre of his heroes, the Briton in his chrotta."[2]

It may be a question among scholars what precisely the chrotta was. The name, so grotesque in its Roman form, obviously points to a native name Latinized. We need not go very far to find what that native name was, for even at the present day among the Welsh we may find an instrument, or at least the well-preserved traditions of an old instrument, entitled the crwth.[3] The crwth was a purely indigenous instrument in England and first played by the Welsh bards. In medieval manuscripts we find it alluded to by the term "chorus," which,

---

[1] Μετ' ὀργάνων ταῖς λύραις ὁμοίων κ.τ.λ.   (Diodorus Siculus).
[2] Fortunatus.
[3] See the crwth figured in Gerbert's *Musica Antiqua*, II. fin.

we may be allowed to imagine, is a more elegant Latin form of the name " crwth," the " s " appearing for the " th " and the " o " helping to facilitate the pronunciation of a word otherwise ungainly for the tongue.

ENGLISH ORIGIN OF THE VIOLIN.—But the next instrument which our minstrel speaks of playing—the violin—had a connection with England quite as close, though by no means universally acknowledged. The violin was bred and born among the Saxon gleemen, for by that name, in the most early Saxon period, the minstrels were described. Numerous have been the attempts to impugn or to ignore the evidence of this fact, and writers on the genesis of musical instruments have conspired to look anywhere else but to England for the origin of this popular favourite. Most of them, indeed all, have agreed hitherto that the violin was introduced somewhere about the ninth or tenth century into Europe, and with regard to its point of origin, some maintain one quarter some another. But we, on the contrary, can point to an immature violin, drawn on a Saxon MS. of the seventh century, and to engravings taken from trustworthy manuscripts, representing the violin in the hands of Saxon kings.[1] According to this view of the origin of the violin which we here propound, the violin was a development of that ancient British instrument, the crwth, which we mentioned a moment ago. The crwth was played exactly in the manner of the Grecian lyre, that is, resting on the left shoulder, with both hands employed on the strings,

---

[1] See the engravings in Strutt's *Horda, Angel Cym*, I.

the left hand naturally at the back of the strings, and the right hand at the front.[1]   Next the art of stopping came in among the Saxons, and a narrow piece of wood was run up the back of the strings, in the empty space where the strings lay, that is, from the belly of the frame to where the ends of the frame were joined in a semi-circular cross-piece.   The strings were brought closer together, so as to allow of their being stopped on this narrow piece of wood: and they, which at first had spread out in their ascent like a fan, were now compact and near together like strings on a guitar to-day.[2]   The arms were then brought closer together, as the strings had been, their great semi-circular expanse being now useless and unmeaning; wherefore they were brought near together, as we have said, till the form of the instrument resembled an oblong, or rather an attenuated oval.   The next step was the introduction of the bow. How was this step taken?   Here, unfortunately, we are left to the source of conjecture.   This link, the most important in the chain of improvements is, unfortunately, entirely wanting.   We find in one period crwths, with the strings twanged with the right hand, and stopped above with the left, being held as we hold a violoncello to-day, but being small, on the lap.[3]   In the next period, we find the same crwths played in the same position and in the same manner, only that the right hand of the

---

[1] In the earlier MS. this is the method of holding.

[2] Fetis (*Histoire de la Musique*) has engraved an example of this form from a Breton abbey.

[3] In all drawings of the crwth this manner holds good.

player is now furnished with a bow,[1] and we are left to seek how the innovation came. The next step after the introduction of the bow, and the crwth held violoncello-wise, was to turn it the other way in the hands of the player, and hold it as we hold our violins to-day. This was an obvious change, and merely a matter of convenience. For some time both ways of holding were in use, though the new one eventually obtained the preference.[2]

OTHER INSTRUMENTS PLAYED BY THE JONGLEURS.—The pipe, the bagpipe and the syrinx—to continue the enumeration—instruments existent but not indigenous to England, were rendered additionally popular by the jongleurs. The bagpipe might seem, perhaps, a novelty of modern times; but the instrument is indeed of extreme antiquity, being known and freely used by the Normans, and even a familiar instrument of music to the Assyrians of Nineveh. Among the jongleurs the bagpipe was not limited to the simple form of the instrument known to us.[3] It was often made with its bag in the shape of a tortoise, the hide sewn into the shape of the body of that animal, while the lower part of the projecting pipe was carved in the figure of its head.[4] Sometimes it was constructed in the shape of a serpent, with a long writhing bag, that writhed and wound round the body of the jongleur like

---

[1] The most pertinent examples are the engravings of Saxon kings in Strutt's *Horda*.

[2] A third method of holding, viz., with the bow in the left hand, is also found.

[3] Digby MS., Bodleian Library.

[4] British Museum, Cotton MSS., Tiberius VI.

M

the long peacock's feather in his hat.[1]   The harp was
an instrument which had never gone out of fashion in
Europe, but its especial home seems to have been with
the Anglo-Saxons in England, to whom it appears to have
been indigenous.   The gigue and the gittern, on the
contrary, owed their introduction entirely to the keen-
sightedness of the jongleur, who foresaw of what utility
they would be to him in the pursuit of his calling.   The
gigue was a small variety of the violin, likely to come
in useful at *fêtes champêtres.*   It was a shrill little instrument, which tinkled most saucily and merrily.   The
gittern was a guitar strung with catgut.[2]   It was introduced, an unknown instrument before, by the zeal of the
jongleurs, and with it the guitar,[3] the most melodious and
dulcet guitar, which had been brought to the West by the
Arabians, whose Kuitra it was, having been received by
them from the Persians, whose Sitar it was; having
travelled all the way from Persia to be the joy of Europe,
and the delight of that courtly world of chivalry which
was then beginning to glitter.   Now the guitar was
strung with wire, but the little gittern with catgut, as
we have said, and this was all the difference between
them.[4]

THE REGALS AND OTHER INSTRUMENTS.—The psaltery
had descended from the later Roman period, while the
regals were dwarf organs which had but six notes to

---

[1] British Museum, Cotton MSS., Tiberius VI.
[2] See the illustration in Strutt's *Horda Angel Cymmon.*
[3] Roman d'Alexandre MS., Bodleian Library, Oxford.
[4] La Borde, *Essai sur la Musique,* I.

them,[1] and were so light, as we have said, that they could be held in the palm of the hand. They had a pair of bellows at the back, which the jongleur could work with his left arm holding them in the fold of his elbow, while he played the keys with his right hand, supporting the instrument on the palm of his left. And they puled and piped so melodiously, that every one was glad to hear them—dainty little mechanisms, artful toys, that yet would make rare harmony.

The organistrum was the strangest instrument we have yet described, for it was a lute or guitar with keys, and it was worked by a wheel, in this way—keys, like those of an organ, were placed on the neck, and they were raised a little to touch the strings by means of handles at the side of the neck. There were two bridges, one for the strings to go over, as in a common bridge, but the other bridge was a wheel, which was turned by a handle at the end of the instrument; this lightly touched the strings and made them vibrate by friction, and the keys, when pressed against them, made them sound. Sometimes two jongleurs played this instrument together,[2] one turning the wheel, the other managing the keys. But yet one player was sufficient, if need be. The tabor was a species of tambourine. The rote was an instrument of many strings, almost indistinguishable from the harp, except that it was squarish rather than triangular, and its sound-board was carried down much below the frame.

---

[1] *Poésies du roi de Navarre*, I. 224. I have seen six and also seven keys in regals in MSS., but never more.

[2] See the bas relief in the Abbey of St. George de Boscherville.

The form of the rote was that of the letter " P."   It
was a light, small, portable instrument.

HISTORICAL IMPORTANCE OF THE JONGLEURS IN MUSICAL
HISTORY.—All these instruments could the jongleurs play.
Many of them they had introduced into the music of
Europe, and by assiduous practice had gained such skill
as to recommend them to the approval of a world which
has since adopted them with joy.   The historical importance of the jongleurs in the history of music must never
be overlooked.   Quite as much as the troubadours they
deserve the thanks of a grateful posterity.   What the
troubadours did for vocal music, for melody, for harmony,
and for the science of sound, that did the jongleurs for
instrumental music.   Beneath the guise of servants and
the carelessness of strollers they often hid the ambition
of virtuosos.   Under their skilful hands this teeming
variety of musical instruments grew up, which otherwise
had never seen a genesis.   Ancient instruments were
revived to satisfy their versatility, new instruments were
invented, strange instruments were imported from abroad
—and all for the jongleurs.   The troubadours scarcely
deigned to concern themselves minutely with instruments,
and the common people could not play them ; and the
monks in their cloisters contented themselves with the
organ alone, as they had done for centuries before—and
all the novelty and advance came from the jongleurs.
Had the introduction of that noble instrument, the violin,
been the sole innovation they effected, even then they
would have merited the thanks of posterity.   But as we
have seen, the violin was but one of a crowd, all new, and

all jongleurs' instruments ; and thus, most important and even transcendent is the historical position of these men.

THE JONGLEURS AS INDEPENDENT MINSTRELS.—The service of the troubadours became too narrow a field to satisfy their ambition. They broke loose from their masters and sought larger and more miscellaneous audiences than the courtly assemblies of lords and ladies, for whose edification alone they were, in the troubadours' service, compelled to play. They aspired for a larger sphere and a complete independence of style. Music and its kindred art, the drama, have always been noticeable for the restlessness and disposition to wandering which they encourage among their votaries, whence the term "stroller" has been applied indiscriminately to the professors of both these arts. The jongleurs, to a certain extent, combined both these professions in their own persons. Even by their masters' instructions there was a considerable dash of the dramatic element required in their composition, and this tendency was naturally greatly increased when they started life independently of the troubadours. In the instructions of the troubadour, Girard Calanson, to his jongleurs, the following list of precepts will illustrate the above remark :—" Learn, my good jongleurs," says the troubadour, " to act well, to speak well, and to extemporise rhymes well. Learn to invent clever and amusing games to please people. Learn to play on the tabor, the cymbals, and the bagpipe. Learn to throw and catch little apples on the point of knives. Learn to imitate the songs of birds with your voices, to pretend to make an attack on a castle as if you were besieging it, to jump through four hoops, to play on the citall and the mandore, to perform on the cloncorde and the guitar, for they are delightful to all. Learn how to string the viol with seventeen chords, to sound the bells, to play the harp, and to compose a jig that shall enliven the sound of the psaltery. A jongleur ought to prepare nine instruments of ten chords, and if he learns to play well on them, they will furnish him with ample melody."[1] If these qualifications were insisted on by their masters as useful and necessary for the purpose of amusement, we may imagine that still greater stress would be laid on them by the jongleurs themselves, when the exigencies of providing their own livelihood in the world at large made them study every source of attraction with which their art could supply them.

THE WANDERING MINSTRELS.—It is impossible to say what cause, beyond the love of a roving life and the general tendencies of the time, induced large numbers of the jongleurs to detach themselves from the service of the troubadours and (if we may employ an expressive colloquialism) "to start business on their own account." But so it was. Jongleurs, as a rule, had no reason to be dissatisfied with the terms of their service. They were liberally treated by their masters, and there are many stories of ardent and even romantic attachments between jongleur and troubadour, which amply attest the good relations between the two classes. Perhaps, as we find so commonly the case in relation to callings in modern days, the supply

---

[1] La Curne de Ste. Palaye, *Histoire littéraire des troubadours*, "Vie de Girard Calanson."

of jongleurs became too large for the demand, and the superfluous aspirants had to turn elsewhere for a livelihood. Perhaps the contagion of restlessness and roving, which was quite a feature of the age, communicated itself irresistibly to the jongleurs, and drew large numbers of them into its vortex. At any rate, when the First Crusade was over and the taste for a wandering life which it had engendered still strong in the minds of men, the country roads began to be crowded with itinerants of all sorts—such wayfarers as Chaucer at a later date so graphically depicts, but who had their origin and commencement at present—travellers anxious to see the country, loiterers idling from town to town, pilgrims *en route* to distant shrines, pedlars, tramps, and among the rest jongleurs starting life on their own account and preparing to see if they could not imitate their masters, the troubadours, in a lower level of society. As the troubadours were accustomed "*allar par le mon*," 'to go through the world,' so the jongleurs were determined to try the experiment likewise, and to turn their peregrinations to the practical account of serving as a means of livelihood.

DRESS AND LIFE OF THE WANDERING MINSTRELS.— Their dress was specially designed to strike the vulgar. With a few varieties of decoration and colour it was the same with all the jongleurs. They wore a hat with a peacock's feather standing to a great height above the crown, and nodding with every motion of its owner's body; a jacket tricked up with streaming ribbons and decorated down the front with rosettes of various colours. This jacket was generally made of some bright-hued material, such as grass-green or peach-coloured cloth; hose and stockings of gaudy colours, and large rosettes on their shoes. At their back was slung a wallet, which served the double purpose of containing provisions for the day and receiving any chance doles in the shape of eatables which the country people might substitute for the more ordinary largess of money. Any present, no matter of what nature it might be, came acceptable to the wandering jongleurs, who now began to be called by the generic title of " Wandering Minstrels," a name which has had the greater longevity of the two.

The wallets of some of them at the end of their day's journey contained such nondescript contents as a pullet, a lace collar, a silver candlestick, and a flask of wine. The articles which were not perishable were disposed of for what they would fetch at the nearest town. Of all presents money was, of course, preferred, not only as being more convenient, but because it could fly sooner—for every hostelry was with them a place of call and entertainment. Round their neck and over their shoulder, fastened to a blue ribbon, was slung their lute. Every moment their fingers were dallying with the strings, and their perambulation along the highways was accompanied by showers of rippling music which was incessantly issuing from the strings. Let us now see a wandering minstrel at his work. He has been travelling along the road all day among a company of good fellows, who have insisted on his turning in with them at every tavern by the wayside to taste their free-handed hospitality. In this way he comes to a village. It is a summer's evening. The quaint medieval houses, with thatched roofs and overhanging gables with old-fashioned windows abutting on, and nearly overspreading, the pavement below, are all gilded with the glow of a summer sunset. The women are knitting at their doors, the men in little knots talking in the street or lounging on rustic benches outside their houses after the labour of the day is over.

Into the midst of this scene of simple and rural tranquillity our friend with the peacock's feather and the gaudy clothes is suddenly precipitated. He scans the people narrowly as he passes, and they as narrowly scan him. At last he makes selection of a happy looking family party near the end of the little village, and without more ado stops in front of them, slings his lute round, and after tempering a string or two with his tuning key, and a little warbling on the strings by way of prelude, he begins. Amid the applause that greets the termination of his song he takes advantage of the opportunity to doff his hat and hand it round for maravedis. Perhaps he may receive enough to pay for his night's lodging at the hostelry; if not, he is fully prepared to sleep under a haystack. Perhaps he may be still more fortunate, and those particular cottagers whom he has chosen as his patrons may be kind enough to accommodate him with a shelter. From the light of their fire and the bustle that is going on within he can judge that supper is preparing, and thither in no long time he is invited.

At taverns, no less than at houses, the wandering minstrels were to be found. Often in abundance they were to be met with at the inns with all their arts ready

to amuse travellers, who by chance might come thither.[1]
In that curious manual, "La manière de langage," written in French by an Englishman of the fourteenth century,
the traveller of distinction listens at an inn thus, and
mingles his voice with theirs :—"Then come forward into
our lord's presence the trumpeters and hornblowers with
their frestele and clarions, and begin to play and blow
very hard ; and the lord with his squires begin to move,
to sway, to dance, to utter and sing fine carols till midnight without ceasing."[2]

---

[1] Jusserand's *Wayfaring Life*, p. 196.
[2] Ed. P. Meyer, in the *Revue Critique*, X. 373.

[Anglo-Saxon Illumination, representing a Dance with Minstrels, from the Cotton MSS.]

CHAPTER XI.

THE GLEEMEN, JONGLEURS, WANDERING MINSTRELS, AND GLEE-MAIDENS (*continued*).

The Minstrels' Shifts for a Livelihood—Disfranchisement of the Wandering Minstrels—The Guild of Minstrels—Guilds of Minstrels at Dutton, Beverly, York, etc.—Guild Day and its Ceremonies—The King of the Minstrels and his Court—Charter to the Minstrels—Further Ceremonies on Guild Day—Plenary Courts—Popularity of the Minstrels—The King's Jongleurs—The Anglo-Saxon Gleemen—Jongleurs in Towns—Town Minstrels at Norwich and elsewhere—The Glee-maidens—Marie de France—Glee-maidens and Gleemen.

THE MINSTRELS' SHIFTS FOR A LIVELIHOOD.—The confraternity of these gay itinerants of music was diffused through the length and breadth of the land. They cast themselves upon the world, and the world, as they

171

held, was responsible for their maintenance. Sometimes the world did not see the matter quite in the same light, and the gay and festive days of the wandering minstrels were interspersed with many gloomy ones, when the trilling of lutes and the warbling of innumerable songs brought not a stiver to their coffers. In such dilemmas they were forced to resort to the most extraordinary devices for raising the wind. It was not uncommon for two or three minstrels, finding themselves at a deadlock in a village, where perhaps they had swept charity clean, had sung their songs dry, and purses would no longer open at the call of music, to rig up a platform and turn quack doctors for the nonce, loudly vaunting the virtues of nostrums and purgatives, that were composed no one knew how, but still were sovereign cures for all diseases; and by these means they would sometimes make a rare harvest from the peasantry.[1]

Highly delighted at their success, two or three of them would club together for the hire of a cart, to the end of which they would attach a great drum, and dressing themselves up in fantastic costumes they would ride about from village to village, signalling their arrival by loud beating of the drum, and he who had the largest share of effrontery, or the greatest practice in the art, would commence vaunting his physics. Meanwhile, the country people would come gaping round, and in no long time their hard earnings were transferred to the pockets of the minstrels.[2]

---

[1] Rowbotham's *History of Music*, III.   [2] *Ibid.*

Others, when reduced to extremity, with similar wishes but different qualifications, would utilise their skill in capering and dancing, which all the minstrels more or less practised, as side issues and decorations to their songs; and laying down their lutes and fiddles till better times should dawn for music, would cut capers many feet high, to the amazement of the rustics, turn somersaults, twine their legs round their necks or their arms under their feet, and having attracted a crowd by their extraordinary performances, send round their hat for contributions. Others of similar bent would find knives thrown into the air and caught dexterously by the handle, a most successful means of extracting money, or even that art of swallowing knives, or eating blazing tow, at which the peasants would stand open-mouthed, and willingly pay I know not what to have the wonderful performance over again.[1] Although the name of "wandering minstrels" was the ordinary appellation of these men in England, as we may learn, among other sources, from the charter of John of Gaunt, Duke of Lancaster, quoted later on, yet perhaps it was not so essentially English as the term "gleemen." This was certainly their favourite designation among the Saxon portion of the population. The Anglo-Saxon gleemen in the camp of King Alfred will at once suggest themselves as examples of the name and the profession in those early days. The name "minstrel" was of Anglo-Norman origin. In the French provinces of the English monarchy, and in France generally, they were

---

[1] Rowbotham's *History of Music*, III.

termed "menetriers." In the Netherlands they were known as "ministrele." In Germany they were called "the wandering folk," "varende lüte," or "fahrende" or "gehrende." In Provence they retained their original designation, "joglares," which was likewise the case in Spain.[1]

Disfranchisement of the Wandering Minstrels.—We enumerate these countries because the gleemen or wandering minstrels passed from place to place, being variously entitled as they set their foot in a new land, and in the course of a year they might hear themselves described by a dozen different designations, not one of which would seem to their ears more nationally appropriate than another. They were the citizens of no country—homeless and friendless, without even the vague claim on a native land for protection. For to become a gleeman or a wandering minstrel was to forfeit citizenship and to forfeit country. The wandering minstrel from the first day he took to the road henceforth ceased to be the countryman of any nation, and became instead a vagabond of Europe, and a common vagrant,[2] for whose protection no laws existed, whose wrongs no court would take cognisance of, and for whose maltreatment, or even for whose death, no punishment could be inflicted.[3] When he started his career as a gleeman or a wandering jongleur, he laid down

---

[1] See Ducange, Art. "Joculatores, Ministelli, Menestriers," etc.

[2] "Heimath- und rechtlos," in the words of Reissmann, *Musikalisches Conversations-Lexikon*. Their children were illegitimate. "Minstrels and harlots" are found coupled together in the same statute. Blount's *Law Dictionary*, Art. "Minstrels."

[3] Grimm's *Rechtsalterthümer*, I. 678.

three distinct privileges : first and foremost, the privilege of protection and support which he enjoyed at the hands of his master the troubadour ; secondly, his privileges as the member of a nation, which we may call his political rights; thirdly, his privileges as a member of human society.   He might be killed, and his murderer could not be brought to justice.[1]   The murder was not of a man, but of a minstrel—a being beyond the pale of any law, less protected by enactment than the swine of the forest, of less value in the eyes of people generally than a sapling by the roadside.   If the minstrel was robbed, he had no defence ; beaten and maltreated, there was no help for it, he had only to suffer and bear.[2]   But woe betide him if he attempted to retaliate an injury !   Then laws which were allowed to rust in his defence, were set in merciless operation against him.   He was treated with unnecessary severity, and since exile was no punishment to a vagrant, branding and maiming were substituted in his case as appropriate legal penalties.[3]

THE GUILD OF MINSTRELS.—In keeping, therefore, with the spirit of the middle ages, which led men to combine in masses, and made leagues among the merchants, guilds among the trades, and in political life those secret societies of which we have heard so much ; so also had the gleemen their guilds or brotherhoods, which enacted rules for their welfare, exacted contributions from the various members, and which indeed it was the interest

---

[1] Grimm's *Rechtsalterthümer*, I. 678.
[2] *Ibid.*   Scheid. *Dissertatio de jure in musicos.*
[3] *Ibid.*

of all gleemen and minstrels by all means to support. The Guild of the Minstrels and its objects were to counteract as far as possible the unkindness of the laws, and to offer by the mutual co-operation of its members that protection which it was impossible for them otherwise to obtain. One of the members being sick, he received a dole of money or necessaries from the common stock, and was not left to die on the road, as it otherwise might have been.[1] A minstrel, being wronged or mal-treated, had proper defenders secured for him by the kindness of the guild, to plead his cause before a court, and, in the absence of justice, at least to awaken com-passion in his behalf.[2] All the gleemen in England were members of respective guilds, which in their turn had their various subdivisions and local branches—to borrow a modern word, we might call them " Lodges,"—to each of which those gleemen belonged who were natives of that particular part of the country, or were accustomed to make it the principal scene of the peregrinations. Once a year, on Guild Day, every minstrel of the lodge would assemble in a great company, sometimes 400 or 500 strong.[3]

GUILDS OF MINSTRELS AT DUTTON, BEVERLY, YORK, ETC.—At Dutton, the Guild Day was always at Midsum-mer Fair, and the minstrels assembled there from all the adjacent counties. At Chester the Guild Day was on the

---

[1] Scheid, *Dissertatio de jure in Musicos;* Mattheson, *Critica Musica;* Grimm's *Rechtsalterthümer.*
[2] *Ibid.*
[3] Mattheson, *Critica Musica,* II. 813.

16th of August annually, and gleemen and minstrels from five adjoining counties assembled to take part in the proceedings. There was a celebrated guild of minstrels at Beverly, which dated from very ancient times. It exercised jurisdiction over all the minstrels between the Trent and the Tweed.[1] Another guild of minstrels had its headquarters at York.[2] Another guild was established at Canterbury.[3] So that there was no lack of these guilds throughout England.

The guilds of Canterbury, York, Chester, etc., would presumably exercise jurisdiction over the surrounding districts in the same manner as the guild of Beverly, though on this point we have no precise information. The minstrels of Chester, we are told, apropos to the mention of their guild, enjoyed singular privileges in that city,[4] possibly of a similar nature to those accorded to the minstrels of Paris, who among other things were exempted from all toll on entering the city, on condition that they sang a song at the city gates before passing through.[5]

GUILD DAY AND ITS CEREMONIES.—Once a year Guild Day was held at the various lodges throughout the country, the day being different in various localities, as we mentioned, and being fixed according to the convenience of the minstrels who frequented the neighbourhood. Having

---

[1] Poulson's *Beverlac*, p. 302.
[2] *York Plays*, Oxford, p. 38, note.
[3] Welfitt's *Extracts from Canterbury Records*, No. 21.
[4] Hawkins' *History of Music*, I. 191.
[5] La Borde, *Essai sur la Musique*, I. 315.

N

all met at some spot agreed upon, their regular rule was to march in procession to church, after which they would hold their court. Then going to the lawn of the castle of the lord of the manor, they would play their instruments and sport awhile, and finally close the day by a feast in the hostelry.[1]

The ceremonies of their court are particularly interesting, for here it was that such barren justice as they might have was administered, and being debarred from courts of law they discussed their wrongs before a Court of Minstrels, which was presided over by their king. Once a year the finest player in the district was elected " King of the Minstrels," and the badges of his office were a white wand and a crown of gold; and he had stewards, and pages, and a retinue, as befitted his mimic state.[2]

THE KING OF THE MINSTRELS AND HIS COURT.—The King of the Minstrels at Beverly was called Alderman of the Minstrels.[3] Elsewhere, the title Marshal of the Minstrels was bestowed on him. But the usual and generic name of the office was " King," which accorded also best with the mimicry of royalty. Among other kings of the minstrels who held rule in England we may mention John Caumz, to whom Richard II. granted a passport when he was setting out for a foreign country, and expressly designated him in it " Rex ministrallorum nostrorum," or "King of our Minstrels." Another famous

---

[1] Mattheson, *Critica Musica*, II. 343.
[2] Ducange, Art. "Rex Ministrallorum."
[3] Poulson's *Beverlac.*

king of the minstrels was Walter Haliday, who was considered so skilful a musician that a pension of ten marks annually was awarded him by the Crown to be paid out of the exchequer. In the formal grant of the pension we notice that the minstrel king was very ceremoniously alluded to by the reigning monarch as, " Our beloved Walter Haliday, King of the Minstrels."[1] It was the king of the minstrels, then, who presided over the court, as we have said.   The court had no legal power ; yet doubtless the publicity with which its proceedings were conducted, acted as a deterrent no less effectual than the penalties of a regular tribunal of justice.

In the following manner the court was held. After having marched in procession to church, with trumpets blowing and drums beating, the minstrels marching six abreast, with their king and his pursuivant-at-arms in their midst, the court was constituted in the castle hall of the lord of the manor. First of all, all minstrels in arrears of payments to the fund of the guild were amerced in the amount, and compelled to pay. Then two juries of minstrels were sworn, twelve in each, and they were sworn on the Holy Evangelists. And the king of the minstrels charged them as follows : that, considering the excellence and antiquity of music, which was an established art in the days of the Greeks and Romans, and, considering the skill in it esteemed so considerable, and that music is even at the present time one of the liberal accomplishments, they should judge and decide as good men and true,

---

[1] Rymer's *Fœdera*, ad a. 1464, XI. p. 512.

and with due regard to the oath they had taken. That although some musicians were counted as rogues and vagabonds, such organised societies as theirs were excepted, to preserve the repute of which should be their greatest concern, nor could they find a better way of doing so than by being upright and righteous in their verdicts. With this, the court proceeded, and the various cases of complaint and injury were brought forward one by one, and decided according to their merits.[1]

CHARTER TO THE MINSTRELS.—This mimic pageantry of justice, so wholesome and necessary did it seem, was in a manner recognised and acknowledged by kings and princes; and actual charters remain to us that give to the Minstrel King full legal rights over his fellows, and the right of free speech and honest complaint against men at large. Such a one is the following from John of Gaunt, Duke of Lancaster, to the king of the minstrels in Tutbury:—"John, Duke of Lancaster, to all them who shall see or hear these our letters, greeting. Know ye, we have ordained, constituted, and assigned to our well-beloved, the King of the Minstrels, who is or for the time shall be, to apprehend and arrest all the minstrels in our honour and franchise that refuse to do the services and minstrelsy, as appertain to them to do from ancient times, yearly on the day of the Assumption of our Lady; giving and granting to the said King of the Minstrels for the

---

[1] Mattheson, *Critica Musica*, II. 348. Reissman, *Musikalisches Conversations-Lexikon*, Art. "Spielleute." Scheid, *Dissertatio de jure in musicos*, p. 47. Burney's *History of Music*, II.

time being, full power and commandment to make them reasonably to justify and to constrain them to do their services and minstrelsies in manner as belongeth to them, and as it hath been and of ancient times accustomed. In witness whereof we have caused these our letters to be made patent."

FURTHER CEREMONIES ON GUILD DAY.—When the court was over, the minstrels adjourned in full force to the hostelry, where a banquet was prepared for them, and sitting at long tables they caroused. At the head of the company sat the minstrel king, on this day above all in the year enjoying the full privileges of his office, crowned with his golden crown, and drinking wine out of a silver cup, which passed from king to king year after year, as one of his official symbols, like the white wand and retinue of pages.[1] He led the revel and proposed the toasts, and held high court in imitation of the mythical king of the minstrels, King Blegabres, who in their creed was the prime originator of the office; who lived many hundred years before Christ in the land of Nowhere, and toped and tippled eternally, to the sound of harps, psalteries, rebecks, and flutes, and could play every instrument under the sun, and first founded the gallant company of minstrels, which since his day had flourished, God be praised![2]

Now as they had a mythical king and pedigree of royalty, whence they deduced the lineage of their monarch, so also had they a patron saint. And let us see how such merry

---

[1] Mattheson, *Critica Musica*, II.
[2] *Ibid.*

fellows had contrived to establish their strange profession in the calendar. They had at first been hard put whom to choose, so opposed was the practice of their craft to saintliness, and so alien were the attributes of the saints, and would lend themselves to no such travestyings. Till at last some merry head hit upon St. Julian as a saint that might well serve their turn, for the following valid reason : St. Julian, having passed a life of pride and haughtiness, repented at last of his arrogance, and resolved to atone for his misdeeds in the past by going to the opposite extreme in the future. He made a vow accordingly to take into his house anybody and everybody ; and presuming that among the rest even poor strollers would not have been denied, the minstrels dubbed him their patron saint accordingly. So it was King Blegabres and St. Julian, as the glass passed round, and St. Julian and King Blegabres. And equipped with two such traditionary heroes, they could at least lay claim to a history. A curious Latin poem exists which gives an account in detail of one of these carnivals, and depicts the minstrels in the full tide of their enjoyment, such as we might have imagined them engaged in at the Tabard at Southwark, or other famous inn of the time, either before the banquet or after it, when they were diverting themselves with all sorts of professional amusements. " Some of them," says the poem, " were playing harps, others blowing bagpipes, others twanging lutes, others playing pipe and lute together, others tuning up their rebecks ; and sets of bells were tinkling, and trumpets braying, and drums roaring ; there were symphonies, psalteries, shalms, monochords, all playing at once ; there were gitterns, regals, violins, cymbals, tabors, dulcimers, flageolets, nabelles, enmoraches, micamons, naquaires, douceines, huissines, mouscordes, —all these were the minstrels playing. And some were telling stories, and others were making verses." [1]

And then the antics that went on ! What frolicking ! What sport ! For they were throwing somersaults, many of them, and walking on their head, and balancing chairs and tables in all sorts of impossible positions, showing off to their brothers-in-arms their latest feats in litheness and dexterity. Language fails the Latin chronicler to describe their doings. He gets bewildered in the attempt. "He folds himself," says he, speaking of an athletic minstrel, " he folds himself, and unfolds himself, and in unfolding himself, he folds himself." [2]

PLENARY COURTS.—These assemblages in which the gleemen and jongleurs played the exclusive part, were very similar in character, and perhaps they were modelled upon, the more brilliant gatherings in which not only jongleurs, but troubadours and their lady-loves, knights, barons, and the principal nobility of the land took part. It was the custom, we are told, of the kings of England to hold what was called a *cour plenière*, or plenary court, at the three principal feasts of the year. On such occasions, which lasted more than a week, they were attended by the nobility. Ladies, troubadours, knights, and damsels, dined together at the royal table in sumptuous style ; gleemen, minstrels, and jongleurs flocked together from

---

[1] Aimericus de Pergrato, in Ducange.
[2] *Ibid.*

all parts; while tilting and tournaments, and other entertainments in use at the time, were performed. There are lengthy descriptions of these splendid feasts in Geoffrey of Monmouth's *Historia Britonum*, book ix., chap. 7, and in Wace's *Roman de Brut*, line 10,609–10,900. They are also noticed by Roger de Hoveden, Matthew Paris, and other chroniclers. But, of course, they occur most frequently in the old romances. See, for instance, *Le Bel Inconnu*, p. 2, l. 11, which gives an admirable imaginative description, drawn for the most part from contemporary manners and customs, of King Arthur's court at Kaerleon, attended by "Li rois Horels et Floriens" (l. 34). Similar accounts are to be found in *Huon of Bordeaux*, pp. 2 and 9, l. 29, and 256; in "Le Lai du Conseil" in *Lais inédits*, p. 85; in *Syr Gawaine*, p. 310; in *Ywaine and Gawin*, l. 15 sq. Treating of the same subject with his usual minuteness of illustration, Ducange has written a dissertation, copious, ample, and masterly, which is to be found at the end of his edition of *Joinville*, pp. 157–165, and in the seventh volume of his *Glossary*.[1]

POPULARITY OF THE MINSTRELS.—Of the immense popularity of the minstrels among all classes of society there can be no manner of doubt. The minstrel Galfrid or Jeffrey even received an annuity from the abbey of Hide, near Winchester, in the time of Henry II., to play and sing to the monks, and to provide others of his class to perform a like function. William, Bishop of Ely, chancellor of Richard I., engaged a number of minstrels to go about

---

[1] Cf. also Le Grand d'Aussy, *Fabliaux et Contes*, t. 1, pp. 25, 292, and *Histoire de la vie privée des Français*, t. 3, p. 337.

England singing of him and his renown. We hear that at the priory of St. Swithun, at Winchester, the defeat of the Danish giant Colbron and the triumph of Queen Emma was sung by a party of minstrels or gleemen, for the delectation of the monks.[1] When a bishop went on his pastoral rounds, he was very often greeted at place after place by bands of minstrels hired for the purpose. When Bishop Swinfield, for instance, was making his episcopal progress through his diocese, we read that on one occasion he gave twelve pence a-piece to the minstrels who played before him. On another occasion he gave a penny a-piece to them.[2] With equal courtesy and liberality it was the custom when a king, or nobleman, or bishop brought his own minstrels with him, for his host to recompense those minstrels for their trouble just as he would have bestowed largess on any strange minstrels that had been hired for the same purpose. Thus, in the Accounts of Winchester College, we read that minstrels belonging to the King, the Earl of Arundel, Lord de la Ware, the Duke of Gloucester, the Earl of Northumberland, and the Bishop of Winchester, received largess and recompense from the college for their music; and in the accounts of the expenses of the entertainment of the Countess of Westmoreland, we read that she brought minstrels with her, who were gratified with largess from the college.

The King's Jongleurs.—This leads us to the interest-

---

[1] Warton's *History of English Poetry*, I.

[2] *Roll of Household Expenses of Richard de Swinfield, Bishop of Hereford.* Camden Society, II. 155, 152.

[3] Warton's *History of English Poetry*, II., 98.

ing question of the king's minstrels, or king's jongleurs. Who and what were they? They seem to have been attached to the king's person sometimes. In the Squire's Tale in Chaucer we may remember that the minstrels of Cambuscan are represented as attached to his person. This is true to history. Even so late as the reign of King Henry V. the custom still remained—eighteen minstrels following Henry to Guienne and elsewhere, agreeably to the following indenture:—

"This indenture made June 5th in the 3rd year of our sovereign lord King Henry the Fifth since the Conquest, witnesseth that John Clyff, minstrel, and 17 other minstrels, have received from our said lord the king, through Thomas Earl of Arundel and Surrey, treasurer of England, £40 as the wages to each of them, at 12*d.* a day for a quarter of a year, for serving our said lord in the parts of Guyenne and elsewhere." [1]

In the Roll of Thomas Brantingham, treasurer to Edward III., we find frequent mention of royal minstrels engaged to play at 7½*d.* a day. Richard II. constantly had minstrels in his company.[2] When he went the last time to Ireland, he was delayed at Milford Haven for ten days, and passed the time mainly with the music and songs of minstrels.

> " Là feumes nous en joie et en depport
>   Dix jours entiers, attendant le vent nort
>   Pour nous partir.
>   Mainte trompette y povoit en oir,
>   De jour, de nuit, menestrelz retentir." [3]

---

[1] Rymer's *Fœdera, ad annum* 1415, Vol. IX., p. 230.

[2] Jusserand, *Wayfaring Life*, 199.

[3] MS. British Museum. Harleian, No. 1319.

Edward II. received four minstrels in his chamber at Westminster, and heard their songs. When they went away he gave them twenty ells of cloth for their reward.[1] At the marriage of Princess Margaret, daughter of Edward I., we read that four hundred and twenty-six minstrels and singers were engaged.[2] Edward III. gave a hundred pounds to those gleemen who were present at the marriage of his daughter Isabella, and were responsible for the chief portion of the musical entertainment.[3] Some of these minstrels, we are told, figured at the tournaments.[4] Henry V. was a musical king, for when he gave to his English subjects the lands of the Norman seigneurs who had refused to recognise him as their sovereign, he stipulated that their fees (*redevances*) should be paid in instruments of music. Thus Thomas Appleton is assessed to pay for the land of Asnières (near Bayeux) one pair of flutes yearly, called recorders.[5] There was for a long time a regular office at court, called "the king's jongleur," which endured down to a comparatively late period. Richard Geoffrey was king's jongleur under Henry V. and Henry VI., and we read that he was presented by one or other of these monarchs with the estate of Vaux-sur-Mer.[6] Richard Hoby was king's jongleur from 1439 to 1450. Berdic was king's jongleur

---

[1] Wardrobe Accounts, *Archæologia*, XXVI. p. 342.

[2] Thomas Wright, *Domestic Manners and Sentiments*, p. 181.

[3] Devon's *Issue Rolls of the Exchequer*, p. 188, 40 Ed. III.

[4] See two examples of like cases in the *Issue Roll of Thomas Brantingham.*

[5] Rot. an. 5 Henry VI.

[6] *Ibid.*

under William the Conqueror. Rahier was king's jongleur under Henry I. With regard to this celebrated jongleur, we are told that he amassed great wealth, and applied his property to founding St. Bartholomew's Hospital—a noble monument of his thrift and liberality. Geoffrey was king's jongleur under Henry II. Guillaume Blondel was king's jongleur under Richard Cœur-de-Lion, the troubadour king.

THE ANGLO-SAXON GLEEMEN.—In allusion to the king's jongleurs, and the antiquity and honour of the office, the Abbé de la Rue calls attention to the fact that, in very early days in our history, the king of England himself disguised his person as a gleeman, and in this novel and unwonted garb penetrated into the camp of the enemy.[1] He alludes to King Alfred; and if the story of Alfred's visit to the Danish camp disguised as a minstrel be a true one, this along with other similar incidents would substantiate the existence of gleemen and minstrels as popular entertainers in England even at a date more remote than that which we assigned to it. Robson, in his *Introduction to Three Metrical Romances*,[2] building upon this fact presumably, supposes that there were a class of Anglo-Saxon gleemen who held their own amid the civilization of the Normans, and that while the troubadours and jongleurs addressed themselves to the cultivated section of the community, they (the Saxon gleemen) had an audience in peasant, burgher, and

---

[1] De la Rue, *Essais*, I. 150.

[2] Robson's *Introduction to Three Metrical Romances*. (Printed for the Camden Society.)

franklin. The talents as well as the status of these gleemen he supposes to have been inferior, and fragments of their poems only to have survived, owing to the accidental admiration of a few monks, who were struck by their beauty or vigour.

JONGLEURS IN TOWNS.—Towards the end of their era—for the jongleurs, like their masters the troubadours, ultimately passed away from history, though their life was of longer duration—they adopted the plan of abandoning to a great extent their wandering life, and settling in large numbers in towns, the quarter they inhabited being generally called St. Julian's Quarter. Like the Jews, who have conferred the title of Jewry or Jerusalem on parts of several great cities, or the Templars, who have left so many a "Temple" in the nomenclature of English places, so the minstrels have here and there left us reminiscences of their existence in streets and localities called after their patron saint, St. Julian. The reason for the clustering of minstrels in towns may be found in the fact that, in the multitude and superabundance of their numbers, some found a better market for their talents by hanging about large towns, at least in the summer time, and catering the music that was wanted there for marriages, festivals, and routs. Whenever the people desired music for their entertainments they used to send a message to St. Julian's Quarter, and a troop of minstrels would in no long time be in attendance.[1] And such crowds of them would

---

[1] Burney's *History of Music*, II.

sometimes come, in a dull time, or in rivalry with one
another, that laws had to be passed in some places pro-
hibiting more than a certain number from attending;
for what with those who were engaged to play, playing
and singing inside the house, and a crowd of others who
had come unbidden, blowing and twanging their instruments outside the doors, the street was in an uproar : and
such was the general occurrence till these disturbances
were prevented by law.[1]   But in their own peculiar
quarter of the town there was no checking their merriment, and, if we may believe report, a noisy place was
St. Julian's Quarter.   From every window came the
sound of music from minstrels practising or minstrels
carousing ; others sat fiddling outside, and girls were
romping and dancing in the street.   To accustom themselves to the staid life of towns was a hard thing for the
wandering minstrels to do, and their sojourn there was
often temporary.   Yet many were led to take up their
abode in towns for good, being principally those who had
married, and, with a wife and children dependent on
them, found it more convenient to have a fixed habitation.

TOWN MINSTRELS AT NORWICH AND ELSEWHERE.—Several towns had their regular staff of minstrels or jongleurs,
to whom they paid a fixed salary, and whose services were
at the disposal of the mayor for the time being.   These
town minstrels were the original of our Waits.   They
were called Waits in some of the old documents which
relate to their functions,[2] the name " Waits " being

---

[1] La Borde, *Essai sur la Musique*, I.
[2] *English Guilds.*

derived from the instrument they chiefly played, the hautboy or oboe, the old English name for which was "the wait." Thus we read that the town of Bristol supported a band of city minstrels, for the maintenance of which an annual sum of money was allowed in the city expenses.[1] The city of Norwich also had its band of minstrels, and paid them a regular salary on condition that their services should always be at the disposal of the mayor and corporation.[2] In a similar way the city of York was provided with a staff of minstrels, whose duty it was to make music for the town at the bidding of the mayor.[3]

THE GLEE-MAIDENS.—Not to all the minstrels, however, did the staid life of the towns offer a strong enough attraction to cause them to settle there. Many still preferred the gay adventures of the road, and such men as these did not scruple to take their wife and children with them, travelling in caravans, as the gipsies to-day ; or strolling about in company with glee-maidens, or minstrel girls, those most romantic figures of the minstrel life, on whom we must now spend a few words.

Sometimes these glee-maidens would wander unaccompanied about the country, passing unprotected through solitary ways, braving all the dangers of the road, and yet escaping harmless. One would have a little goat with her, and another a dog, to bear her company in her wanderings. A glee-maiden was generally dressed

---

[1] *English Guilds*, p. 423.

[2] *Ibid.*, p. 417.

[3] R. Davies' *Extracts from York Records*, p. 14.

in a blue or other bright-coloured jacket embroidered with silver, sitting close to her figure. She had a mock silver chain round her neck, and gaudy jewellery about her, short petticoats, red stockings, and buskins of Spanish leather.

Standing in the middle of a crowd, mounted on a slight elevation, she would play her violin, and sing in time to it. The courts of monasteries were not ignorant of the glee-maiden, and in the courtyards of castles she was a frequent figure. One of the most celebrated glee-maidens whose name has come down to us was the famous Adeline, who received an estate from William the Conqueror.[1] We must not forget as an admirable example of her class, that glee-maiden of romance, the fair Josiane, who sang before Sir Bevis of Southampton;[2] while Melior, another glee-maiden of romance, is introduced in the poem in which she figures, as telling her lover " les fais del ancien tems." [3]

MARIE DE FRANCE.—We have to come down to the reign of Henry III. before we meet with a great and commanding figure in the ranks of the glee-maidens ; and then we find the celebrated Marie de France, who enjoyed the patronage of William Longsword. She was his jongleuse or glee-maiden, and it must ever remain a main merit of this chivalrous son of Henry II. and Fair Rosamond, that he had sufficient penetration to detect and encourage the talent of this remarkable woman. Whether she was

---

[1] Taine, *Histoire littéraire de l'Angleterre*, I., ii.
[2] *Histoire littéraire de la France*, t. 22, p. 264.
[3] *Partenopeus de Blois*, t. 1, p. 64.

English by birth we are not assured. But she lived the greater part of her life in England, composed her poems for the English, and obviously borrowed many ideas in them from thoroughly national sources. She was probably born in Brittany—hence her strong sympathy with Breton themes. At that time the Duke of Richmond was Duke of Brittany. If she was not born in Brittany, she must have learnt Breton in England. She was perfectly acquainted with the English language,[1] and she was likewise familiar with Latin.[2] Her first work was a collection of Lays in French verse.[3] Throughout England these Lays became extremely popular, and gained her the title of the Sappho of her age. The " courts " of the English barons (*les cours des barons anglais*)—by which term we are given to understand that the English nobility kept a similar state, and termed it by the same name as the Provençal nobles—rang with the praises of this celebrated jongleuse. The nobility delighted to have her lays sung. The songs of the great glee-maiden were the chief enjoyment of the ladies of her time, who never wearied of listening to them.[4] Perhaps part of her popularity was due to the fact that she wrote essentially and emphatically for the English, and not for the Normans or the people of Brittany.[5] She is, for instance, at pains to translate the French or

---

[1] De La Rue, *Essais*, III. 49.　　　　[2] *Ibid.*

[3] MS. British Museum, Cotton Library, Domitian, A. XI.

[4] Denis Pyramus, MS. British Museum, Cotton Library, Domitian, XI.

[5] " Marie écrivait pour les Anglais." De La Rue, *Essais*, III. 49.

Low Breton proper names into English words.[1] Thus in the *Lai de Bisclaveret*, she says that the English translation of "Loupgarou" is "Garwaf," in the *Lai du Laustic*, that of "Rossignol" is "Nightingale." In the *Lai du Chevrefeuille* there are examples of the same thing. She says that she formed the idea of translating the Latin authors, because so many people were engaged in the task. It is probably to Henry III. that she dedicated her Lays, of which there are twelve in the collection in the British Museum. The fifth lay, *Lai de Lauval*, is a beautiful one, dealing with King Arthur and the Knights of the Round Table. Her style is charming, and evinces remarkable depth of feeling. She succeeds in spreading an interest over all her thoughts, which are always simple and naïve. Although her style is rapid and vigorous, nothing is forgotten in respect to details. Her second work is a Collection of Æsopian fables set to verse. She did this, she says, at the suggestion, or for the love, of William Longsword.

> " Ki fleurs est de chevalerie
> D'anseignement et curteisie ;[2]
> Pur amur de Cumte Willaume
> Le plus vaillant de cest royaume
> M'entremis de cest livre feire
> Et de l'Angleiz en Roman treire."[3]

The third work of Marie's is a History or story about the Purgatory of St. Patrick in Ireland. It is a translation of the Latin of Henry the monk of Saltry.

---

[1] De La Rue, *Essais*, III. 51.

[2] Prologue de Marie.   [3] Epilogue de Marie.

Her works may be studied in the following MSS., all of which are at the British Museum : — Cotton MSS., Vespasian, B. XIV.; Harleian MSS., 4333; Harleian MSS., 978.

GLEE-MAIDENS AND GLEEMEN.—Not all glee-maidens were so refined and cultivated as Marie, or enjoyed the high position which she did in the opinion of her contemporaries. Many of a lower class would travel about the country, as we have said, sometimes by themselves, often in the company of gleemen or min-strels, who found the glee-maiden an excellent additional attraction to their music, by which the hearts of the audience were led captive, not merely their ears alone. So they played and sang, while their minstrel friends cut capers, and stood on their heads, or performed other antics likely to attract the vulgar.

One ingenious minstrel, to crown the bevy of attractions, and deal a striking blow at the humour of the rustics, conceived the idea of taking about dancing bears, as an unfailing means when all others failed, of filling the hat with money. An old Latin poem describes this apex of grotesqueness which the practice reached in England, and nearly in the following words :—

" A party of gleemen and glee-maidens came to the village, leading a pair of dancing bears with them. As soon as the gleemen touched the strings, the bears reared themselves up to dance, and marked the time with their feet, springing very high at times, and often feinting to come to blows with one another, and doing other antics while the music lasted. Then the bears would dance with the glee-maidens, who sang the song of the dance with most melodious voices ; and the bears would dance with them, putting their great paws in their pretty hands, and footing step by step and quite correctly the measure of the dance, growling contentedly the while."

CHAPTER XII.

THE TROUBADOURS AS MUSICIANS.

Musical Poetry and Literary Poetry—Musical Poetry of the Troubadours — The Troubadours' Knowledge of Music — Character of the Troubadours' Music—Specimen of Song—Remarks on Song—The Troubadours' Use of the Ecclesiastical Modes — Song of the Trouvères — The Troubadours' Achievements in Harmony — Method of Performance when the Troubadours Sang—The Troubadours and Harmony—The State of Harmony at the Time of the Troubadours—Growth of Harmony under the Troubadours — Harmony with the Treble.

MUSICAL POETRY AND LITERARY POETRY.—It will have been noticed in the sixth chapter that some of the poetical forms there described were said expressly to have been delivered by a reciter, not a singer, and to have been deprived of the ornament of a musical instrument to accompany their delivery. Such exceptions, however, were opposed to the general spirit of the troubadours' genius. The wedding of poetry with music, which takes place periodically in the history of literature, seems to have an invigorating effect upon poetic art, and to clear the mind of the poets from too great conscientiousness and from that disposition to labour and overelaborate ideas and versification into which mere literary poetry is always apt to degenerate. Poetry is of two kinds: musical and literary. We have not had a great era of musical poetry in modern English literature yet, unless we reckon as such the poetry of Burns, which was always redolent and linked with tune. Ancient nations, such as the Greeks for instance, had epochs and ages remarkable and brilliant, when musical poetry was the great art of the time. Such was the age of Sappho [1] and the Lesbian school, all of whose compositions were written to be sung, not to be recited, the poet, or rather the poetess, writing the music no less than the words, and the two things being considered to be indissoluble. Another age in Greek literature of a similar marked union of music and poetry was the era of the choral poets, when Pindar,[2] Bacchylides, and others, not content with merely writing the language of their odes and even fitting it with music, arranged that music on an elaborate plan for performance by choruses of youths and men, who danced as they sang, and whose steps, we are told, no less than their declamations, were devised by the poets themselves. The tragedians of Greece belong to a modified school of musical poetry, in which some of the effusions (the choral odes and the monodies) were written to be sung, but others (the dialogues) were recited. Even Homer must not be denied the title of a musical poet, for the recitation of the rhapsodists—of whom probably he was one—was invariably preluded by an introduction of music played on the lyre, while various musical cadences from the same instrument diversified and adorned the gravity of the declamation as the rhapsody proceeded. How eminently

---

[1] Fl. b.c. 604.
[2] Fl. b.c. 473.

this would deserve the name of "musical" as contrasted with such a jejune and soundless poetry as our modern verse, which is written to be *read*, we can best comprehend, if we reflect how curious would seem the poet nowadays who should entertain his friends or an audience by reciting his poetry while playing an occasional musical accompaniment on the piano. A literary poetry, by contrast with a musical poetry, is such a poetry as prevails with us at present, when the poet writes his verses without the slightest intention that music shall ever be wedded to them, is often or nearly always innocent of any musical knowledge himself, and assumes a similar absence of a very essential thing on the part of his readers. Literary poetry must always possess the same sort of tameness which imbues literary drama. Those dramas and laboured plays that are written by philosophic or imaginative poets, without any intention of their ever being put on the stage, possess a dulness and deficiency of dramatic interest as contrasted with those bright and vivacious pieces that are specially written for the boards. And in the same way literary poetry is deprived of much of its adornment and of half its charm owing to the divorce betwixt it and music.

MUSICAL POETRY OF THE TROUBADOURS. — Musical poetry, on the other hand, in the sense in which it was conceived by the troubadours, differs essentially from the poetry set to music which is made familiar to us at the present day in concert-rooms and in the windows of music-publishers. Poetry set to music, in the modern sense of the term, is the extreme antithesis to literary poetry.

In literary poetry there is no music at all; in poetry set to music by a modern song-writer or composer there is too much music. The poetry is completely hidden and lost in the music; and the modern composer shows his indifference to the claims of the poetry upon his attention by contenting himself as a rule with very indifferent words. The troubadours' conception of musical poetry was something quite distinct from these two views. It observed the mean, and the happy mean, between them, and if an age of musical poetry is ever so fortunate as to arise again in England, the theory of the troubadours will no doubt once more rule unconsciously the configuration of the art. The troubadours' poetry differed from the first order of poetry that we mentioned, —the literary poetry—in being commonly allied with music; it differed from the second order—the poetry set to music—in assigning the chief place, not to the music but to the poetry. And though the music of the troubadours was a highly cultivated and elaborate form of the art in comparison with the general music of that day, it was always kept subordinate to the poetry. No troubadour worth the name would have ever studied to exalt and elaborate his music at the expense of the poetry. If he had done so, he would have ceased to be a troubadour, and would have been reckoned a mere minstrel or maker of tunes.

THE TROUBADOURS' KNOWLEDGE OF MUSIC.—Yet despite all this the troubadours, and more particularly the Northern and Anglo-Norman trouvères, possessed an excellent knowledge of music, quite sufficient to prove that they could have made a preponderant use of the music instead of the poetry, if they had so chosen. To sum up the exact extent of their musical knowledge may be a somewhat difficult task, yet we think that the following outline may be accepted as a pretty general indication of the compass of their acquaintance with and practice of the art, which they rendered so illustrious.

They were familiar first and foremost with the principles of singing in a most advanced form. That is to say, they knew and made allowance for the various compasses of voice, and were quite able to calculate the musical effect of such and such a passage as delivered by such and such a voice and to compose their music agreeably thereto. While eminently able to write vocal melodies of an intricate order, which would have taken excessive practice and musical culture to sing, they preferred, on the contrary, to preserve the melody of the voice in comparative simplicity and to endeavour to make it express as far as possible the meaning and the emotion of the words. This latter was their great aim throughout. The words were the chief subject at issue. The meaning and sentiment of the poetry were the themes the expression of which was to tax their musical utterance. What were the use of devoting any special or superfluous attention to the elaboration of the music, when, if it could be made to exactly express and breathe in sweet sound the spirit of the poetry, all its end and aim would be achieved? Accordingly, when composing the music to the poem, they looked only to that prime consideration that it should render in sweet and harmonious declamation the sense of the poetry and allow that poetry to assert itself to the full.

Such a consummation, one of those most devoutly to be desired in vocal music, was comparatively easy for composers who were themselves the authors of the poem which they set to music. Coming fresh from the effusion of the words, and instinct with the same inspiration, it was not likely that they would do anything to prejudice the poetical effect of the former. They merely added the music as an additional adornment to the charm of melody, in which they had already wrapped the thoughts by the harmony of their versification.

CHARACTER OF THE TROUBADOURS' MUSIC.—As was natural, the melodies which they wrote were quite in keeping with the ordinary music of the age, and as such, while comparatively simple in general outline, were full of strange graces and turns of voice, which to our ears would seem affected and overdone. Musical readers familiar with the writings of Handel will remember the countless turns and runs with which that great composer diversifies the majestic march of his melody. It was the taste of the age in which he lived to have an abundance of such florid turns and passages; and, like a wise man, he easily submitted to allowing that taste to impress itself on his writings. In precisely the same manner the troubadours interlarded the march of their tunes, not with lengthy runs, which were not fashionable then, but with grace-notes, appoggiaturas, slurred intervals sung in the manner of the modern *portamento*, and other devices of a trivial character, as they may appear to us, yet at the time important and necessary additions to song. Owing to this constant suggestion of quaintness and peculiarity, complete sympathy with the troubadours' music is not easily attainable in the present state of the art. Should ever such decorations come into fashion again, then men will learn to love and admire a beautiful treasury of melodies, which were said to fall on the ear with all the charm of birds singing on a spring morning or nightingales warbling in the cool of the night.

SPECIMEN OF SONG.—As an instance of the troubadour melody, let us take the following composition of Pons de Capdeuil :— [1]

<hr>

[1] Extracted from Rowbotham's *History of Music*, III. 591.

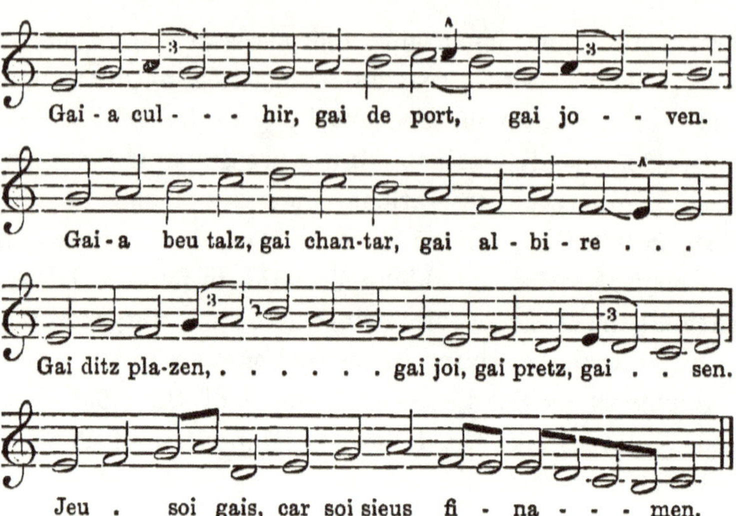

REMARKS ON SONG.—It will be noticed in this piece that at the very points in the melody where the modern ear expects repose and an agreeable cadence the music contains that peculiar grace which we express by a crotchet and a minim, thus:— , of which the first note falls in a very unexpected and jerky manner upon our ear. This unsteadiness of intonation communicates its character to the whole piece, and a style of music which was admired in its own day for its smooth and flowing beauty of utterance becomes to us, owing to a difference of taste, remarkably restless in its general effect. The difference of scales, too, is another bar to any completeness of sympathy which the ordinary musician of to-day could feel for the troubadours' songs. At the present time the whole of musical expression is very unhappily confined to two musical modes, the major and the minor, in which narrow frame the entire aspirations of the art have to be expressed. Although we are popularly supposed to have twenty-four scales, major and minor, and the unhappy schoolgirl spends her miserable mornings in floundering among what she imagines the elaborateness of modern music, in reality there are but two scales in all; and for twenty-two of her laborious tasks she might, if our music were arranged on a more rational basis, spare herself the trouble of her detested drudgery. The two scales, the major and the minor, are repeated on the twelve degrees of the keyboard, but are obviously the same, the identical two, performed over and over again at different pitches. One can quite imagine the mechanism of the piano being so constructed as to render such a superabundance of labour entirely unnecessary. One can imagine and sigh for that state of musical art when, instead of the monotony of merely two scales, on which the changes are rung till the ear is weary, many scales, each entirely different from its neighbour, occupied the attention of musicians and saved the necessity of performing such multitudinous variations on a trivial two.

THE TROUBADOURS' USE OF THE ECCLESIASTICAL MODES. —The troubadours composed their songs in the ecclesiastical scales or modes, which were the lineal musical descendants of the Greek system of music, as that system had become transformed and simplified at Constantinople under the Byzantine theorists. In this later form it had passed into the common use of Europe, though we are not quite certain as yet whether it had been adopted by the peasantry in their simple and unsophisticated ditties. But among those who laid claim to any musical culture—the ecclesiastics, who composed for the churches and monasteries; the troubadours, who did the same office for the courtly and fashionable circles of the age—the Byzantine modes were in full employment, and of these modes eight were in use among the troubadours,—

these eight being practically reduced to seven owing to
the fact of the Dorian and the Hypomixolydian both being
in pitch and tonal configuration identical, although in
point of character and musical treatment they were diverse.
Each of these eight modes had its peculiar character. One
was reckoned blithe, another mournful, one able to utter
best the accents of love, another more attuned to despair.
In this way, and owing to having such a diversity of means
of expression, composers were taught to look more at the
character of the language than they are at present, and
to seriously consider how best they might transfuse the
precise glow and inspiration of the poetry into the music,
a fact to-day too frequently and too unfortunately left out
of sight. The gradual decay and disappearance of these
various scales has been directly owing to the rapid advance made by instrumental music and the consequent
retreat of vocal. Instrumental music, owing to mechanical difficulties connected with the construction of its
mouthpieces of expression—the instruments—delights in
having as few scales as possible and in gaining variety
by countless variations of pitch. With the apt and appropriate expression of poetical sentiment it has little to
do, and prefers to riot in complete self-abandonment to
the joy of sweet sounds, unfettered by any special object
of illustration or by any necessity of specified interpretation. In this way it has been led to neglect and discard
those old scales which came into the world for an object
so alien to its spirit; and since instrumental music is now
at its zenith, our sympathy for these lost scales and for
the music which was expressed by them is naturally at a
low ebb indeed.

Song of the Trouvères. — The sweeter and more popular style of the Northern trouvères may be exemplified in the following song:—

¹ Quoted in Rowbotham's *History of Music*, III. 593.

THE TROUBADOURS' ACHIEVEMENTS IN HARMONY.—More interesting to modern musicians will be the consideration of the work of the troubadours in respect to harmony—a sphere of music in which their improvements and usages have been of untold value to the art, and are of patent and palpable influence on the music of to-day. In this especial relation the services of the trouvères of English, French, or Anglo-Norman origin, must be highly acknowledged, more perhaps than their brethren of the South. The troubadours did not only write the music of their songs for one musician alone. Committing the performance of those songs very often to a company of jongleurs, they were naturally led to arrange the music so as to include more than one performer in an independent part in its exposition. If a party of jongleurs performed a song, it was possible, and indeed often the case, that one jongleur sang the ditty as a vocal solo, and the remainder standing by, accompanied their comrade's voice by the music of their instruments. With these instruments they would double the part that he was singing, or would throw in snatches of extemporised harmony here and there, as they thought best suitable and most likely to improve the effect of the concert. If a pair of jongleurs had been chosen as the exponents of the song, one jongleur commonly sang the melody, while the other on his instrument touched it off with threads of light accompaniment. Sometimes only one jongleur was employed to combine both vocal and instrumental parts in his delivery, in which case his usual instrument was the guitar or lute, and he supported his voice by an accompaniment of its twanging strings, while he breathed into the song all the ardour which his emotional style of delivery was capable of.

METHOD OF PERFORMANCE WHEN THE TROUBADOUR SANG. —Such was usually the method of performance when the troubadour himself sang. Taking his guitar or lute from the hands of an attendant jongleur, he touched a few notes on its chords, and then broke forth into an impassioned strain with finished delivery, while he varied the declamation of the vocal music by accompanying or interposing strains and chords on his instrument. Sometimes, though more rarely, he ordered his jongleurs to accompany him, or one of them on whom he could best rely as the possessor of the most refined taste and most able to illustrate on his instrument the emotion of the song. Such were the general ways of musical performance in vogue among the troubadours, and it is to the first of these that we would turn and pay special attention, for there the art of harmony was enabled to effect an entry and to receive at the hands of the troubadours a careful and tasteful development.

THE TROUBADOURS AND HARMONY.—When a troubadour entrusted the delivery of his song to a jongleur who was to be accompanied by some of his fellows, it was natural that in no long time the desire should arise that more than one jongleur should take part in the delivery of the song. Consequently two were allowed by their master to undertake the execution of the ditty, and while the troubadour still contented himself with composing only one vocal melody, the second jongleur was permitted to add a sort of extempore part to the troubadour's melody, in much the same way that his comrades with their instruments were already doing. Sometimes then the whole body of the jongleurs sang the original melody, and one, the cleverest and best musician of their number, added the extemporised harmony.. This harmony was called descant; and its character, according to the audacity or the sobriety of the jongleur who exhibited it, passed from the most tasteful commentary on the song to the wildest and most surprising excesses of licence.

THE STATE OF HARMONY AT THE TIME OF THE TROUBADOURS.—Let us briefly consider the state of harmony at the time of the troubadours. To find it in its scientific and admittedly correct form, we must look at its conditions in the churches of the day. In church music, in the sequences, hymns, and graduals which made use of harmony, the only permissible progressions were concords of fourths, fifths, and octaves, which proceeded in monotonous succession, varied by nothing but interchange of themselves, from beginning to end of the piece. Fresh variety was considered to be sufficiently consulted if the octave were added to the harmony of fifths or fourths, or if both the parts of a concord, say two-fifths or two-fourths, were doubled in the octave above or below one another. With these extreme licences, the permission to depart from the regular sequence of fifths, fourths, and octaves ceased; and for many centuries this theory of harmony held the vogue in churches and cloisters, and, in fact, all through Europe, as the canon and the norm of consonance. By the time the troubadours began their

singing, a few changes of comparatively little moment
had been introduced into the series of consecutive fourths,
fifths, and octaves.   An invariable octave had begun to
be employed as an opening for every piece, and while the
old form of the harmony would have run

by virtue of this new ornament the opening became [1]

From this principle another had easily flowed.   For if
the melody fell at its second note, instead of rising as
it here does, the octave at the commencement would
necessitate too great a leap for the voice on to the succeed·
ing note.   In place therefore of

the octave was placed at the second note of the piece instead of the first, with the following result :—[2]

Such was the simple innovation which the singers in the
churches ventured to make in the hard and fast regulations of the ancient harmony—and made it, too, with fear

<hr>

[1] Treatise.   MS. Fonds St. Victor.   Bibliothèque Nationale, 813.
[2] Guy de Chalis.   MS. Fonds St. Victor, 813.

and trembling. The influence of tradition and authority was so great, that people universally preferred the prescription of the past to any innovation, however simple, which seemed to them utterly uncalled for and wrong.

GROWTH OF HARMONY UNDER THE TROUBADOURS.—But now to the jongleur, whose ear was his only guide, and who received an encouragement from the applause of those who heard him for any clever and surprising musical combination, the hard and fast regulations of the old science began rapidly to give way. This method of extemporising known as " Descant," at once, and without any laborious development, led to such a result. We must mention as a strange fact that the Descant was always improvised *above* the melody, not below it. Thus to give an example of the improvisation of Descant, let us take the following :— [1]

---

[1] MS. Bibliothèque Nationale, 7451.

From one extempore descanter, who descanted on the
main melody of the troubadour, so successful and
generally appreciated was the style, two began to be
employed. Two jongleurs each prepared to illustrate his
originality of invention and musical combination, and
each extemporising on his own account, became in no
long time the most favourite addition to the song. In
the court-yards of the castles, in the castle halls when
they sat at meat, or on the ramparts, or on the lawn
when the ladies were assembled in the afternoon, the
deft devices of the pair of jongleurs, who added such an
unexpected charm to the music, were always in request,
and no performance of the troubadours' music began to
be considered as complete without them. As the old descant had been sung above the melody, in such a collocation
as we have shown on the preceding page, so was the new
descant sung yet again above the old one, and became the
highest part in the concert. Being the third part that
had now been added to the harmony, it was known as the
triple or treble or third part. The second of these
names is the one that has survived the destructiveness of
time, and in the countless "trebles" of our musical
pieces to-day we may recognise the lineal descendant
of a harmonising part which began first to be used when

a third or treble jongleur was added to the harmony of the troubadours.

HARMONY WITH THE TREBLE. — The condition of the harmony then, as it stood, with the new addition of the triple or treble performer was as follows : the main body of the singers sang the melody, which was the lowest part in the concord. This part, being the leading part in the song, and giving the deliberately arranged air or melody, to which the other two chosen singers did but add their momentary inspirations from time to time, all of which had to be shaped according to the tenor of the melody below, was called the *tenor*, that is, the leading, the steady part of the concord. This, as we say, was declaimed by the main body of the singers, and if any of the guests or the audience chose to join in a verse of a well-known song, they joined in this part of the harmony, which rolled on steady and substantial through all. Above the tenor came the first of the descanters, who was the second person in the harmony. As he sang immediately above the tenor, he was called the counter-tenor, or the part opposed to the tenor. Above him came the third part in the concord, the treble, or triple, who was the new descanter that had been superadded to the first. He dealt with the topmost part in the harmony; yet although he sang the highest part, his music did not constitute the " air," as it does at present. That belonged to the tenor, as it did indeed for centuries afterwards. The treble was merely a light accompaniment, thrown lightly and carelessly in, with great skill and dexterity, by the jongleur who was chosen to undertake this novel addition

to the concord.   But after a while the natural wayward-
ness of singers, who were encouraged by liberal applause
to astonish and amuse their audience by originality of
musical invention, and often by the perpetration of
musical licence—I say, this permission to trust to their
own extempore powers was frequently abused by the
jongleurs, and the liberties which they took with the
music in seeking to make originality of descant were in
defiance of good taste, and threatened to spoil rather than to
improve the effect of the harmony.   Indeed, when we think
of the position of two extempore singers, neither knowing
from moment to moment what note his fellow might take
and yet having to make allowance for such progression
by skilful calculation of probabilities, based on the progression of the tenor below,—I say, when we imagine the
position of the jongleurs, we cannot but acknowledge
that they were likely to be betrayed into frequent
musical errors, which would often escape the notice of
the mixed audience who listened to their songs, but on
that account were all the more pernicious because they
threatened to become habits with the jongleurs, and to
impair ultimately their sense of musical consonance.

To check the licences, then, and to amend the errors,
the troubadours began to arrange the parts beforehand,
and the descant, instead of being merely governed by the
whims of the jongleurs, was carefully written down and
rehearsed before performance.   The troubadours made
use of the same free intervals and the same bold combina-
tions, which the jongleurs in their extempore singing
employed.   And we have many beautiful examples of
descant written by the troubadours for the jongleurs in

three parts, of which we may quote the following as instances :— [1]

Treble.

in which we may notice that the discord of the second at 1 is resolved regularly by contrary motion ; but at 2 it is not so resolved, though the resolution is but suspended, and takes place at 3. Let us also observe the passing notes at 4; and other points of harmony throughout the song will be suggested by these. Here is a round, no less aptly harmonised than the preceding :— [2]

[1] MS. Bibliothèque Nationale, 5397.
[2] MS. Bibliothèque de Montpellier.

Treble.
Counter Tenor.

And the discords at 1 and 6, and the passing notes at 2,

3, 4, 5, will strike us, and also the apt alternation of harmonious intervals, so as to procure the most pleasing change and variety. In this way, from pure wit and delicate ear was the art of harmony slowly forged by the troubadours aided by the jongleurs. And such, as we have described it, was the final point of development which it reached under the troubadours.

Minstrels' Gallery in Exeter Cathedral.

CHAPTER XIII.

THE COURTS OF LOVE.

Discussion as to the Evidence for the Existence of the Courts of
Love—Allusions by the Troubadours to the Subject—Some
Descriptions of the Courts of Love—The Troubadours' Idea
of Love—Conventionality of the Troubadours—Their Idea
of Love Illustrated in Life — The Extravagancies of Barbesieu—The Follies of Pierre Vidal—The Courts of Love.

DISCUSSION AS TO THE EVIDENCE FOR THE EXISTENCE
OF THE COURTS OF LOVE.—The nature and even the existence of the Courts of Love, which played so congenial
a *rôle* in the life of the troubadours, have been made the
subject of considerable discussion and doubt. Some writers
have denied their existence ; others have affirmed it.   It
appears to us that there is, and ever will be, considerable
difficulty in exactly defining the precise scope, competence,
form, and jurisdiction of these tribunals ; in laying down,
in so many words, with complete accuracy the entire and
incontestable method of procedure adopted in them.   But
we are wholly inclined to follow the opinion of Raynouard and of Gabriel Azais, who maintain a *prima
facie* case of probability for the Courts of Love, owing
to their complete harmony and affinity with the ideas
and customs of the chivalrous epoch of the troubadours.[1]

---

[1] Balaguer, *Historia de los Trovadores*, I. 277.

When we proceed to cite the names of the writers on the subject who have strenuously upheld the existence of the Courts of Love, we can deploy a long list of weighty and trustworthy authorities, and can indicate, indeed, a wide consensus of opinion; while, on the other hand, we can enumerate a few clever opponents, such as Diez, and some merely superficial and frivolous objectors, such as F. Hueffer and others. In contradistinction to these latter we may set down the names of the following eminent writers, who have maintained, and in some cases elaborately demonstrated the existence of these courts: Raynouard, the author of the great collection of troubadour poetry; Don Victor Balaguer, the latest and perhaps the greatest historian of the troubadours, whose elaborate history was published a few years ago in Madrid, in eight volumes; Gabriel Azais, Papon, Bouche, Nostradamus, Gaufredy, Caseneuve the historian of the Juegos Florales; Chasteuil, Rolland, Guinguené, and Crescimbeni. With such a weight of authority on the side of the Courts of Love, we may proceed with reasonable security to discuss them as best we can from the materials at our disposal, and to ignore, not the existence of the Courts, but the existence of objections which are often the outcome, not of a sincere desire for truth, but of literary vanity.[1] The two main contemporary authorities for the history of the Courts of Love are Andrew the Chaplain, who lived probably about the

---

[1] Balaguer, *Historia de los Trovadores*, I. Discurso Preliminar.

end of the twelfth century,[1] and Martial d'Auvergne, who
lived in the fifteenth century, and spoke of the Courts of
Love · in his day. The work of Andrew the Chaplain is
to be found in manuscript in the Bibliothèque Nationale
at Paris,[2] and bears every evidence of the high antiquity
which Fabricius has assigned it. The work of Andrew
was one of the first which was issued by the print-
ing-press of Europe. Menckenius, in his *Miscellanea
Lipsiensia Nova*, mentions that he examined a copy
without date and without the name of the place of
impression, and found the book to be one of the earliest
of printed works extant.[3] The title of the book was
*Tractatus amoris et de amoris remedio Andreæ capellani
papæ Innocentii quarti.* The work has been known,
indeed, by different titles, but the most common name
under which it is quoted and referred to is *The Book of
the Art of Love (Livre de l'art d'aimer).* The information, which comes from Martial d'Auvergne, as
being of a later date, is not of so much value.

ALLUSIONS BY THE TROUBADOURS TO THE SUBJECT.—
The troubadours themselves, however, putting these two
authors aside, bear ample testimony in their poems to the
existence of these courts. Even so early as the time of
William of Poitou, the first troubadour whose works
have descended to our perusal, we find mention made of
the Courts of Love. " If you propose to me a game of

---

[1] Fabricius, *Bibliotheca Latina Medii Ævi.*

[2] MS. Bibliothèque Nationale, coté 8758.

[3] Menckenius, *Miscellanea Lipsiensia Nova.* Leipsic, 1751,
VIII., i., 545.

love," says the troubadour, "I am not so foolish but I shall choose the best side in the trial."[1] In a tenson or contention between the two troubadours Giraud and Peyronet, the first-named says, "I shall conquer you, provided that the *court* is loyal and honest. I send my tenson to Pierrefeu, where the beautiful lady holds a court of information." "And I," replies the troubadour Peyronet, "choose as my court of judgment the honourable castle of Signe,"[2] by which we must understand the ladies or gentlemen who constituted the court at that castle.

SOME DESCRIPTIONS OF THE COURTS OF LOVE.—Jean de Nostradamus is very explicit in his remarks, declaring that tensons were disputes on points of love between troubadours and ladies, who discussed together some beautiful and subtle question of love. "In this," he continues, "if they could not come to an agreement, they referred the matter for decision to the illustrious lady presidents who held open and plenary court at the Castle of Signe, and other places, and these gave judgments which were called the judgments of Love."[3] In these castles which have been mentioned, and in other castles, says Balaguer,[4] the most celebrated, accomplished, and beautiful ladies, to the number of ten, of twelve, of forty, and even of seventy, formed tribunals of judgment. They

---

[1] Guillaume de Poitiers. "E si m parletz."

[2] Giraud et Peyronet. "Peyronet d' una." Quoted in Balaguer. *Historia de los Trovadores,* "De las cortes y de los puys de amor,"

[3] Jean de Nostradamus, *Vies des plus célèbres*, p. 15.

[4] Balaguer, *Historia*, I. 279.

deliberated and passed sentence according to the usages of love, etc. Nostradamus declares that he saw the sentences of some of these tribunals written in magnificent books of vellum.

THE TROUBADOURS' IDEA OF LOVE.—By constantly musing on this one subject, Love, the troubadours exaggerated its importance beyond all limits. To them it was to be made to yield every sensation in life worth having. Although many of them doubtless composed their songs and harmonised their music in pure enthusiasm for the art, yet not even to themselves would they admit this as the efficient cause for their labours. "It is love that makes me sing," cries one. "For sweet love do I labour night and day in the improvement of my lays," exclaims another. "For love sing the birds, and for love sing I," cries a third, in ecstasy at the thought that he could so excellently compare his slow and artful progress to perfection with the spontaneous effusion of nature. In the main, these avowed pretensions were the real ones. A poet or a musician devoted to his art is apt to seek retirement from a world of distractions, in order that he may devote his enthusiasm to a mistress who is never unkind, and to a love which is commensurate with life, and may haply be renewed after death. But the troubadours seized every opportunity to court the distractions and follies of intrigue, and whether it were through the fashion of the times, or through their own inclinations, delighted to involve themselves in countless amatory adventures, to which their music and their minstrelsy served merely as the artistic introduction.

Many of them, after singing sweetly for awhile, suddenly, with a strange fatuity, laid down their lute, and perished miserably in the cause of some paltry amorous adventure : the truth being, that since they professed love as their creed, they were afraid, as a point of honour, to refuse an intrigue when one was offered them, and often perhaps against their will were led into the meshes of amours which, in a more sober age, would never have been spread to entangle their steps. The passion of love is idealised in their poems to the highest possible degree. It is of far more importance than life ; it stands on a pedestal as exalted as honour, perhaps even a trifle higher. It is more than religion, for it is itself a religion of a higher and a purer kind than that of dogma. As nothing is high enough or exalted enough to say about God, so nothing is high-flown enough or extravagant enough to predicate about love. Love must occupy a man's every thought; it must be complete mistress of his actions. If at one time it compels him to take up his lute and sing, it must with equal readiness force him to lay his instrument down again, and abandon music altogether. Several troubadours being so unfortunate as to lose their lady-love—the theme of all their songs, the inspiration of all their poetry—threw down their art and minstrelsy entirely, and vowed never to sing a song again while life in them lasted.

CONVENTIONALITY OF THE TROUBADOURS.—That there was something extremely conventional in all this exaltation of the tender passion, and in this self-devotion of every troubadour to a chosen dame, whose praises he vowed to sing and whose beauty to extol against all rivals, may well be judged from the fact that each and all of them celebrate one common type of beauty, which is as constant in their lays as are the long-drawn faces and figures in the paintings of Cimabue and his school. She is a lady, whose skin is white as milk, whiter than the driven snow, of peerless purity in whiteness. Her cheeks, on which vermilion hues alone appear, are like the rosebud in spring, when it has not yet opened to the full, but shows manifestly what a wealth of blushing red it could put forth if it liked. Her hair, which is nearly always bedecked and adorned with flowers, is invariably of the same shade—a shade, by-the-bye, which has excited the encomiums of poets from the most ancient times to the present—being the colour of flax, as soft as silk, and shimmering with a sheen of the finest gold. Wherever she moves, this paragon of goddesses, her presence, her aspect attract every eye in astonishment and admiration. She cannot enter the hall without the faces of every guest being uplifted in awe of her beauty. She cannot walk through the meadows without the birds, lost in ecstasy, singing of her charms, and the flowers winking at her as she passes. Often enough, a troubadour, who had been disappointed in his affection for a lady whom he long had celebrated, would transfer his devotion to another, and commence in turn to vaunt her loveliness with as much zeal as he extolled the old one. But his description of the personal appearance of his flame would not vary in the least degree, and the new lady-love would in like manner be eulogised for her flaxen hair, shining like gold, her cheeks roseate like the young rosebud, and her skin purer than the driven snow and white as milk or whiter.

THEIR IDEA OF LOVE ILLUSTRATED IN LIFE.—It seemed to be a point of honour among the troubadours to intoxicate themselves with their mistress's charms, and in this exalted state of spirit to begin to sing. Meanwhile, if such were their exaggerated notions of the passion in its literary or musical form, in ordinary life the extravagancies of many of them gave colour to the oft-repeated supposition, that love was to them more than heaven, and that they esteemed it far higher than religion or virtue or any other of the restraints of the spirit. To testify to the violence of the passion which inflamed them, a party of troubadours and of barons, their friends, determined to exhibit to mankind their sorrow for the heartlessness of their lady love, or their zeal for her favours; and nothing could suggest itself to them as a greater means of self-mortification than to imitate the penitential discipline of the monks, and subject their limbs to the rigorous vicissitudes of the weather. Accordingly they clothed themselves in the winter-time with gauze and gossamer material of the lightest texture, and wearing nothing more than these cobwebs on their naked skin, walked through the snow in pitiful pilgrimage about the country, half dead with cold, and shivering sufficiently to excite the compassion of the most obdurate lady, if she had only been there to see, or if they had desired to listen to her. When summer came, and the heat of the sun beat down in torrid rays upon the landscape, so that mankind at large threw off their heavy garments and went as lightly clad as custom permitted for their ease and comfort, these penitents of love exchanged their gauze and gossamer garments for thick furs and heavy woollen wraps, which they wound round their bodies in great quantities, until they were almost suffocated with the heat and melted with the oppression of the enormous coverings.[1]

THE EXTRAVAGANCIES OF BARBESIEU.—Richard de Barbesieu, who was a troubadour of Saintonge, in the English dominions, possessed an acknowledged genius for poetry and song, but was withal a man of very gloomy and taciturn disposition, who, when he attached himself finally to a lady, was likely to allow his passion to carry him to extremes. After a while his affection settled upon the Countess of Touai, who, unfortunately for the poet, was a woman of excessive vivacity and gaiety, who was never weary of society and brilliant conversation, as much as her ardent admirer seemed to avoid it. She encouraged the attachment of Barbesieu, however, because, like all the ladies of her time, it was necessary, as a point of amorous etiquette, to have a troubadour in her train, whose genius should be devoted to singing her praises. But with her encouragement of his talent her interest in him ceased, and she refused to give him the slightest testimony of love, or to offer any promise that in the future she would do so. Enraged at the

---

[1] *Middelalderens Elskovshaffer, Literatur historish-kritish Undersögolse*, p. 27 (Copenhagen, 1888).

Countess's obduracy, Barbesieu quitted her train and her company, and attached himself to the society of another lady, whom he began to extol with the same exaggerated adulation which he had formerly employed in the case of the Countess de Touai. "I like not such men as you," said his new charmer. "You have abandoned the loveliest lady in the world, and there is every probability that you will abandon me. Go! I will have none of you, and if you take my advice you will travel straight from me to the side of your former lady-love, and renew your allegiance to her, which ought never to have been broken." Barbesieu, following her advice, found the Countess bitterly incensed against him, and having now no mistress to turn to, resolved to make himself a hermit of love. Monks and friars for the love of Jesus Christ, or for devotion to a saint, were accustomed to spurn the world and live in sequestered solitude. Wherefore, then, should not he, who had as great a love for a lady, imitate their good example and seek in the indulgence of a solitary life that consolation in misery and reflection on the past, which they whom he would copy so originally enjoyed? Accordingly, filled with this idea, Barbesieu chose for the purpose of his hermitage a sequestered forest, where he built himself a little hut, in which he proclaimed that he was henceforth determined to pass his days, and would never show his face to the world again until he had been restored to the favour of the Countess de Touai. For two years the unfortunate troubadour endured the heats of summer and the colds of winter, the rain, the wind, and the discomfort which prevailed through the forest, and for two years the inexorable lady refused to receive him back into her good graces, to his despair and also to the unspeakable regret of all the lords and ladies of the district. These came in a large party at the end of his long period of probation, and exhorted him to leave his anchorite's cell, and once more to take his place in the world of men and women, pointing out to him that nothing was gained by thus indulging in a penitence which brought no return. Barbesieu, however, was firm in his resolution, and their well-meant efforts were destined to end in failure. The next move of these sympathetic friends was to go to the Countess de Touai herself, and entreat her to have compassion on her anchorite, who, they said, was truly and earnestly attached to her, and heartily sorry for aught he had done to offend her. To this request, the Countess replied by giving utterance to as singular a whim as ever entered the head of woman—a whim, in fact, as singular as was the resolution of her lover, which had brought all these incidents to pass. She said that if one hundred ladies and one hundred gentlemen, who were truly in love with one another, would come to her with their hands joined, and falling on their knees before her would thus solicit the pardon of the troubadour, she would grant it, but on no other terms. A diligent search was apparently not necessary to produce this large instalment of lovers, and after a few days, the required amorous company presented themselves before the haughty lady, and by their kind intercession Barbesieu was relieved from his life in the wood, and was

readmitted to the good graces of her whom he had so
mortally offended.[1]

THE FOLLIES OF PIERRE VIDAL.—Pierre Vidal, a troubadour who followed Richard Cœur de Lion in the third
crusade, carried to still greater extent these amatory
extravagancies. He attached himself to Louve de
Penautier as his lady-love, and not content with singing
her praises in the most high-flown and extravagant style,
he determined to give a convincing proof to the
world, which should strike all mankind, how entirely
he was devoted to her service. Remembering that her
name, Louve, which he had already celebrated in scores
of sonnets, meant "a she-wolf," he elected to celebrate
it in a still more signal way. He gave out that
henceforth he would be called "Loup," or "the he-wolf,"
and thus he and his lady-love would, in the thoughts of
all men, be eternally coupled together. After a while even
this demonstration of his immoderate affection was not
sufficient for Pierre Vidal, who has been well called "the
Quixote of the troubadours," and whose extravagancies
we merely here record in order that the reader may see in
a pronounced and excessive form the same zeal and sentiments which in a more modified degree actuated all
troubadours alike. Even this demonstration did not
satisfy Vidal, who, to convince men he was in earnest,
and possibly also to stamp upon the memory of those
around him the fact that he was henceforth to be called

---

[1] La Curne de Ste. Palaye, *Histoire littéraire*, Art. "Barbesieu."

"Loup," and by no other name, dressed himself in the skin of a wolf, and offered to be hunted on the mountains by the dogs in that eccentric guise. Accordingly, a pack of hounds was brought, huntsmen were prepared, and the extraordinary hunt began, Vidal flying in front in his wolf-skin, and making every effort possible to elude the velocity of the dogs behind him. But as was naturally to be expected, although the troubadour was fleet of foot, and nerved, moreover, by a desire to win the approbation of his lady, the dogs and the horses ultimately caught up with him, and then a scene began for which history or fiction can scarce find a parallel. The unfortunate troubadour, wrapped so artfully in his wolf's hide as to defy detection from the real animal, was seized by the jaws of the howling pack of hounds, and tossed from one to the other as they worried him, with barks and uproar. The huntsmen coming up, offered to drive off the dogs, but to Vidal the baiting and the worrying were the climax of his self-sacrifice. " I will not allow the dogs to be driven off," he exclaimed, in the midst of the canine mob. "I am submitting to their mangling teeth for the best of purposes." The unfortunate poet was almost killed by the ferocious animals who had seized him, and with his last breath—for he was supposed to be dying—demanded to be carried to the castle of his lady-love, whither he was brought to all appearance dead. His wounds afterwards healing and his health restored, he indulged in another eccentricity of a less perilous nature, which was to allow his hair and beard to grow until they reached his feet, and to compel his servants and jongleurs to do likewise. Attended by these latter as his retinue, he went through the country from castle to castle, exciting the commiseration, not unmixed with the ridicule, of all those who came into contact with him.[1]

THE COURTS OF LOVE.—To check such excesses as these, and likewise to regulate the conduct of ladies, whose harshness and severity brought their knights to such a pass, Courts of Love arose in various places, the object of which was to legislate on all questions of the affections, to arrange disputes between lovers, to pass sentence on any lover who was in the wrong, and generally to establish a system of jurisprudence, which should be useful in determining any vexed questions which might arise between lovers themselves, and so to render unnecessary any appeal to the courts, except as a last resource. Of these courts, the most celebrated were those of Queen Eleanor of England, of the ladies of Gascony, of the Viscountess of Narbonne, of the Countess of Champagne, and of the Countess of Flanders. Of these it will be seen that the first three, which were likewise the most celebrated, were in the English dominions, and exercising as they did a wide jurisdiction over the neighbouring district, to these would be submitted the disputes of the English troubadours and their lady-loves. There were also several courts in Provence, those of Pierrefeu, Signe, Romanin, and Avignon, being the most celebrated. History has preserved to us the names of the ladies who judged at these courts.

---

[1] La Curne de Ste. Palaye, *Vie de Pierre Vidal.*

CHAPTER XIV.

THE COURTS OF LOVE (*continued*).

Constitution of the Courts of Love—Method of Procedure—Example of a Trial—The Courts of Love: Traditions about them —The Tensons of the Troubadours referred to the Jewish Minstrelsy—The Laws of Love—The Theory of Love as Conceived by the Troubadours—Some Causes Célèbres—Another Judgment of Queen Eleanor's—Further Cases before the Courts—An Interesting Argument from Precedent—Various Causes Célèbres—The Jeux Partis and Puys d'Amour.

CONSTITUTION OF THE COURTS OF LOVE.—We said in the last chapter that the names of " the ladies who judged " at some of these courts have been preserved. This expression implies what seems to have been commonly the case, namely, that the judges, or if the term be preferred, the jury, were ladies.[1] The lists of the courts of Romanin, Avignon [2] and elsewhere disclose the fact that nearly all the ladies who acted as judges were married ladies. In the court of the ladies of Romanin [3] I find the name of one unmarried lady, Hugonne de Sabran, daughter of the Comte de Forcalquier, and in the court of the ladies of Pierrefeu perhaps one name may likewise be supposed to be that of a spinster.[4] But these are strik-

---

[1] Though the King of Navarre held a court of love. De La Rue, *Essais*, I. 221.

[2] Nostradamus, 217.

[3] *Id.*, 131.

[4] "Jausserande de Claustral." Nostradamus, p. 27.

ing exceptions to the general rule that all the ladies who composed the courts should be married, or widows, while further there was another principle of selection, namely, that they should belong to the *haute noblesse* of their district. To take the court of Pierrefeu, the last one mentioned, as an example, we find that the majority of the ladies were the wives or widows of feudal seigneurs, while a countess, a viscountess, and the daughter of a count were found in the ranks of the jurors. Similar was the composition of the other tribunals of like nature, which probably in considerable number, though only the names of a specified selection have been preserved to us, existed during the times of the troubadours to try and to legislate upon all questions concerned with that grand subject which was uppermost in every one's thought and mind—that treasury of culture, art, breeding and elegance—Love. Large numbers of ladies assembled to constitute the court. There does not appear to have been any exact regulation as to any specific number required. In the court of the Countess of Champagne we read of " a very large number of ladies assembled in court." "*Quam plurimarum dominarum consilio*,"[1] says André, speaking of this tribunal.

On one special occasion the enormous number of *sixty* ladies is mentioned as having met in full court to consider an important case connected with a lady's behaviour to a nobleman of rank. " Comitissa vero," says André, " *sexagenario* sibi accersito *numero dominarum*, rem tali

---

[1] André, *Livre de l'Art d'Aimer*, folio 56.

judicio definivit," [1]—" She summoned sixty ladies as jury or assessors, and then passed sentence." The court of the ladies of Signe was composed of ten ladies of rank, that of Pierrefeu likewise of ten, and that of Romanin of fourteen.

On a general estimate, we may suppose that the number of ladies in the court ranged from that of the smallest enumerated here, ten, to the largest, sixty, and was probably of an average midway between these numbers. We have said that the courts were nearly always composed of ladies. But not invariably so. The troubadour Guillaume de Bergedan has addressed a request for a trial to a gentleman.[2] And this gentleman, a seigneur of the district, considered the question submitted to him, and pronounced the decree necessary " with the advice of his council," who were probably gentlemen like himself. A dispute between the two troubadours Giraud Riquier and Guillaume de Mur was submitted to the arbitration of gentlemen, one of the arbiters being King Henry II. of England.[3]

METHOD OF PROCEDURE.—But such arbiters as these were exceptional, and the judges were as a rule the ladies of the district, meeting in such numbers as we have described, and acting under the superintendence of one of their number chosen to take that superior office. We are led to assume that one of the ladies was appointed the

---

[1] André, *Livre de l'Art d'Aimer*, folio 96.

[2] See his poem beginning " Amicx Senher."

[3] " E mo senher Enricx jutje ns en chantan Guillaume de Mur et Giraud Riquier."

president. Firstly, from the fact that many of the courts took their name from some leading lady, who, on that account alone, would seem to have been in superior authority to the others, as for instance the Court of Queen Eleanor of England, the Court of the Countess of Champagne, etc. Secondly, from such expressions as these in the judgments: "The Countess" (who had convened the court) "declared the following sentence."[1] But like the method in vogue with an English jury, the complete assent of all the ladies present was necessary to the legalisation of a verdict, for, says André, in relation to the verdict of the Court of Love in Gascony, "*Dominarum ergo curia in Vasconia congregata, de totius curiæ assensu*, perpetua fuit constitutione firmatum ut," etc. "When the court of the ladies of Gascony had assembled, it was resolved, *with the assent of the whole court*," etc. The method of procedure then, as we have thus far determined it, was for the leading lady of the district, or her who was acknowledged as the president of the court, to summon a sufficient number of ladies who we may presume were specially chosen for the function, and were the recognised members of the court; and meeting with them at some place appointed, to hear the complaint made and the cause pleaded in due form before them.

EXAMPLE OF A TRIAL.—We may take as an example the following:—

"A process between a young lady and a lover of hers. The complaint of the lady plaintiff was that once she

---

[1] André, *Livre de l'Art d'Aimer*, fol. 96.

remembered the defendant as gay and joyous as could be, neat in his attire, pleasant, gracious, and agreeable. That now all is changed. The defendant has become pensive, dreaming, and melancholy. He seems to be tired of life. If she speaks to him, he ponders a long time before giving a reply. If any one gives him a bouquet, he tears all the flowers to pieces. And directly he hears the jongleurs begin to play, tears fill his eyes and he can only gasp for breath. He is cold when it is hot, and hot when it is cold.

"On the part of the defendant it was urged, that in the service of love, pain and sorrow were necessities; that there was never a joy which was not purchased at the expense of a hundred griefs. The loyal lover, it was maintained, was always the most sorrowful. The defendant had fully resolved to abandon all love, and to recover and regain the time which he had lost and spent upon it. After much more to the same effect, the defendant begged the permission of the court to be allowed to depart from the service of love for evermore.

"The plaintiff, however, replied that the defendant ought not to have any such permission; that any other objects in life save love, such as money or the goods of this world, were of inferior consequence; for, indeed, if he lived and enjoyed good health, that was sufficient. She maintained further, that the foundation of all his sorrows was pure fantasy and should not be attended to.

"The defendant declared that he would as soon die as live. He declared further, that would to God he could become joyful! But no one could make him so. For when he remembered the joys and the follies of the past, there was no joy for him, but he could with difficulty restrain himself from weeping.

" The arguments on both sides having been heard, the court decided that the defendant should be sent to the country, and should remain a prisoner in beautiful gardens for the space of a month, in order that he might see the beautiful flowers and verdure, and enjoy their beauty. The court likewise ordained that the plaintiff should accompany him, and should remain with him during the whole of the said months, and indeed until he was quite cured." [1]

THE COURTS OF LOVE: TRADITIONS ABOUT THEM.— Plainly enough the original audiences of these sorts of disputes would be the lords and ladies of the castle at which the troubadours exhibited their musical and oratorical powers.[2] But in the punctilious etiquette of the age, which delighted to give the nicest form to everything—these matters being debated with profound seriousness—the chance and ordinary audience of a feudal castle was not considered sufficiently formal and ceremonious to give the necessary *éclat* to the contentions of the minstrels. And in this way the Courts of Love gradually grew up.[3]

---

[1] The 40th Trial in Martial d'Auvergne's *Arrests d'Amour*. The most ancient edition of this work is that of Lyons, of 1533, which is the first one that contains the commentary of Benedict le Court. *Arresta Amorum. Cum erudita Benedicti Curtii Symphoriani explanatione.*

[2] Söderhelm's *Anteckningar om Martial d'Auvergne*, p. 69. Helsingfors, 1889.)

[3] *Ibid.*, p. 14.

In order to give the support of tradition to these courts, and to authenticate the Laws of Love which were gradually formed as the basis of their jurisprudence, the most fantastic stories were set afloat as to their origin. If the Koran was believed to have been sent down from heaven, the Laws of Love were declared to owe their origin to witchery and enchantment. Fables of troubadours riding in forests, and finding scrolls attached by chains of gold to such and such a dragon's neck, or such a wild bird's perch, and how these scrolls contained the veritable statutes and regulations of the Court of Artus or the Court of Narbonne—such fables were set on foot and propagated in order to magnify the importance of the courts, to mystify the vulgar, and to give a prestige to an elaborate and ceremonious form of procedure which, without some halo of romance surrounding it, might have passed for trifling or folly. Let us briefly recount the fable respecting the presentation of the Laws of Love to the Court of Artus. Once on a time an English troubadour had plunged into a deep forest, with the object of arriving through its labyrinthine groves at the town of Artus. But going astray in the wood, he found, after some wandering, a maiden, who spoke to him as follows: " I know what you are searching for, but you will not find it without my assistance. You have wooed but not won an English lady, and she has demanded as a proof of your fidelity that you bring to her the celebrated falcon which sits on a perch before the palace of Artus. In order to obtain this falcon, there is an indispensable preliminary which has to be gone through. You must fight in combat with all or any of the knights of the palace, and demonstrate by your victory over them, that your lady-love is more beautiful than any of theirs." After many romantic adventures the troubadour ultimately found the falcon sitting on a golden perch at the entrance of the palace gates, and at once laid hold upon it. Suspended by a golden chain to the perch he found a scroll, which on examination proved to be a draft of a code of Laws of Love, which it henceforth became his duty to publish to the world. The story then goes on, how this code of laws was presented to the court, and at a full court, consisting not only of ladies, but of gentlemen, was accepted as the foundation of all their jurisprudence, and was ordained to be observed by all people at large in perpetuity, under pain of penalty most heavy.

THE TENSONS OF THE TROUBADOURS REFERRED TO THE JEWISH MINSTRELSY.—Before giving the code of thirty-one laws which were common to all the Courts of Love in the English, the French, and the Provençal dominions,[1] it will be interesting to notice from what far-off and unexpected beginnings this amatory jurisprudence, whose climax we are considering, originally and undoubtedly commenced. We have spoken of the tensons of the troubadours which were laid for decision before the Courts of Love, and to decide upon which the courts were perhaps originally convened. These tensons or contentions were entirely

---

[1] Von Aretin, *Beiträge zur Geschichte*, etc., III. 56. (Monaco, 1858.)

identical, and certainly derived from the similar feats of poetry and music which were a habitual and favourite form of art with the minstrels of Arabian Spain, who in their turn merely repeated in Europe a style of minstrelsy which is common to all Semitic nations. Not only did the Saracens and the pre-Islam Arabs delight in a form of music and song which required ready wit, effusiveness of style, and spontaneousness of tune, in which two musical combatants *answered* one another, but among the Hebrews of Biblical times " to answer " meant " to sing," and the whole of Bible poetry is built on this form of question and answer, which oriental scholars denote by the word " parallelism." The oldest poem in the world, as we remarked in a previous chapter, the Song of Lamech, is constructed in precisely the same way as the tenson of the troubadours. A colon stands in the middle of each verse, dividing it into two parts, exactly in accord in symmetry and sense. They might have been sung by two people, with improvement rather than with any prejudice to their meaning. Certainly in later ages of Hebrew minstrelsy, in the services of the Temple, in the singing of the psalms, the method of declamation by question and answer was almost universal. This was repeated in the contentions of the Semitic minstrels in Arabia, when two singers stood forward and extemporised verses in answer or in opposition to each other ; was by the Arabians carried over and popularised in Spain ; and now appeared in such strange and fantastic surroundings, from the lips of silk-bedizened troubadours, who applied their talents and the resources of this ancient form of art to a subject as far removed as conception could imagine from the themes thus treated among the Jews.

THE LAWS OF LOVE.—We have noticed in relation to these amatory tribunals, that one lady assumed the office of president, and with due formalities convened the court before whom the two troubadours were invited to plead. We have sketched, as far as we were able, the method of procedure adopted. It now remains, before we offer an account of some of the trials and the verdicts that were given, to enumerate the thirty-one Laws of Love, which were accepted by common consent among all the courts, and which were invariably quoted to the pleaders as impossible of contravention :—

THE LAWS OF LOVE.[1]

1. Marriage cannot be pleaded as an excuse for refusing to love.

2. A person who cannot keep a secret can never be a lover.

3. No one can really love two people at the same time.

4. Love never stands still; it always increases—or diminishes.

5. Favours which are yielded unwillingly are tasteless.

6. A person of the male sex cannot be considered a lover until he has passed out of boyhood.

7. If one of two lovers dies, love must be foresworn for two years by the survivor.

---

[1] André, *Livre de l'Art d'Aimer*, fol. 103.

8.   No one, when once a lover, can be deprived of his title without a very good reason indeed.

9.   No one can love, unless the soft persuasion of love itself compel him.

10.   Love is always an exile where avarice holds its dwelling.

11.   It is not becoming to love those ladies who only love with a view to marriage.

12.   A true lover never desires the favours of any one but his own lady-love, out of real affection.

13.   A love that has once been rendered common and commonplace never as a rule endures very long.

14.   Too easy possession renders love contemptible. But possession which is attended with difficulties makes love valuable and of great price.

15.   Every lover is accustomed to grow pale at the sight of his lady-love.

16.   At the sudden and unexpected prospect of his lady-love, the heart of the true lover invariably palpitates.

17.   A new love affair banishes the old one completely.

18.   It is only worth and excellence that make a man worthy to be loved by a lady.

19.   If love once begins to diminish, it quickly fades away as a rule, and rarely recovers itself.

20.   A real lover is always the prey of anxiety and *malaise*.

21.   The affection of love invariably increases under the influence of jealousy.

22.   When one of the lovers begins to entertain suspicion of the other, the jealousy and the love increase at once.

23. A person who is the prey of love eats little and sleeps little.

24. Every action of a lover terminates with the thought of the loved one.

25. A true lover thinks there is no happiness except in pleasing his beloved.

26. Love can deny nothing to love.

27. A lover can never be surfeited with the consolations which his beloved may offer him.

28. A moderate presumption is sufficient to justify one lover in entertaining grave suspicions of the other.

29. Too great prodigality of favours is not advisable, for a lover who is wearied with a superabundance of pleasure is generally as a rule disinclined to love.

30. A true lover is enthralled with the perpetual image of his lady-love, which never at any moment departs from his mind.

31. Nothing prevents one lady being loved by two gentlemen, or one gentleman by two ladies.[1]

THE THEORY OF LOVE AS CONCEIVED BY THE TROUBADOURS.—It will be seen by the above Laws of Love what the theory of love, as understood by the troubadours and their lady-loves, actually consisted in. It rested with the lover to show his devotion, and to convince the lady of his sincerity, by means of a number of conventional signs, and also by a course of behaviour reproachless so far as her love was concerned, and often branching out into extravagancies and affectations. This was his part of

---

[1] André, *Livre de l'Art d'Aimer*, fol. 103.

the compact; and when he had succeeded in demonstrating
that he was a genuine and immaculate lover according
to the laws of love, he might claim certain privileges
from her which she, on her part, was not permitted to
deny. A reference to the twenty-sixth law will show
very clearly the perilous element in this punctilious etiquette of love-making, which did not cease by any means
at symbols and idle declarations, but marched inflexibly
forward to the complete mastery of the science. It may
well be made a question how far the heart played its
share in these extravagant liaisons, and if, either on one
side or the other, there was real sincerity and depth of
affection. It may be inquired whether, if the gentleman
showed certain conventional and understood symptoms of
affection, and clearly demonstrated, by his behaviour and
circumspection, that no other contending object of affection reigned in his heart, whether possession and fruition
did not automatically follow, much in the same way that,
on the payment of the purchase money, there ensues the
possession of a house. These inquiries and doubts, we
say, may well suggest themselves to our minds; for it is
hard for us, who live in such a different amatory atmosphere, with whom love and its associations are the
subject of private contemplation and spontaneous impulse, to imagine any feeling of real passion and devotion
subjected to the rules of so artificial an etiquette, and
minutely analysed and legislated upon in the way that
we have already indicated and shall proceed further to
describe. I say, that such inquiries and suppositions will
very naturally present themselves to our minds. We

must beware, however, not to confound the spirit of the age we live in with that far-off and distant time, when punctilious etiquette was the very essence of all behaviour, and when romantic extravagancies were as common in life as they are rare at present. We must remember that the human heart can beat quite as warmly under the most fantastic surroundings as it can in the soberer and colder air of to-day or yesterday, and that there is nothing so contrary to reason or to true historical sympathy as to pass an adverse judgment on the actors in a drama because the dresses and the scenery are different from those to which we ourselves are accustomed.

SOME CAUSES CÉLÈBRES.—We will now give a selection of the causes tried in certain of the Courts of Love, with the judgments arrived at by the ladies constituting those tribunals. On the 29th of April, 1174, the following case was brought before the Court of Love presided over by the Countess of Champagne: "Can real love exist between married people?" The question was debated in the usual style, and, at the conclusion of the proceedings, the Countess of Champagne pronounced judgment as follows:—

"We declare and affirm, agreeably to the general opinion of those present, that love cannot exercise its powers on married people. The following reason is proof of the fact: Lovers grant everything, mutually and gratuitously, without being constrained by any motive of necessity. Married people, on the contrary, are compelled as a duty to submit to one another's wishes, and not to refuse anything to one another. For this reason it is evident that love cannot exercise its power on married people.

"Let this decision, which we have arrived at with great deliberation, and after taking counsel of a large number of ladies, be held henceforward as a confirmed and irrefragable truth."[1]

The following cause was tried before the Court of Love presided over by Queen Eleanor of England :—

"A lover to whom his lady-love had accorded the last favours in her power, requested from her the permission to bestow his homage on another mistress. She granted his request, and very soon he ceased to feel the usual transports of affection for his first and former flame. After a month he returned to his old love, and declared that he had never besought any indulgences or desired any favours of affection from the new mistress whom he had so obsequiously courted, and that his sole idea had been to put to the proof the constancy of his best beloved and first loved friend. She, however, on his coming to her with this tale, deprived him of her love, declaring that he had rendered himself unworthy of it by the mere act of soliciting and accepting permission to leave her."[2]

The question at issue seems to have been a knotty one, and, after due deliberation and debate, Queen Eleanor pronounced an unexpected verdict against the lady whose conduct was under consideration. Subjoined is the sentence of the Queen of England :—

"Such is the nature of love! Very frequently lovers

---

[1] André, *Livre de l'Art d'Aimer*, fol. 56.
[2] *Ibid.*, fol. 92.

pretend that they desire the affection of some one to
whom they are not really attached, simply in order to
assure themselves of the fidelity and constancy of their
beloved. It is an offence against all the laws of love and
rights of lovers to refuse, on such a pretext, any tender-
ness or favour to the lover who desires it again, unless
that lover can be clearly convicted of having broken faith
or proved disloyal to his duties." [1]

ANOTHER JUDGMENT OF QUEEN ELEANOR'S.—Another
cause célèbre tried before Queen Eleanor was as follows: "A lover entreated a lady for her love, but was
never able to overcome her reluctance to grant it to him.
In order to win her over to his wishes he sent a number
of beautiful presents, which the lady accepted with as
much good grace as delight. Nevertheless she did not
diminish in the slightest degree her accustomed severity
to the gentleman, and persistently refused, after receiving
all his presents, to display any kindness to him, or grant
him the slightest favour. He accordingly brought the
matter before the Court of Love, and pleaded that he had
been deceived by the false hope with which the lady had
inspired him, by accepting his presents." [2]

The judgment of Queen Eleanor on this issue was in
keeping with the sternness and abruptness which she
could sometimes so well assume :—

" A lady who is determined to be inflexible must either
refuse to receive any gifts which are sent with the object
of winning her love, or she must make compensation for

---

[1] André, fol. 92.   [2] *Ibid.*, fol. 97.

them, or she must be content to be classed as a courtesan." [1]

FURTHER CASES BEFORE THE COURTS.—Before the Court of Ermengarde, Viscountess of Narbonne, the following case was tried :—

"Can the greater affection, the more lively attachment, subsist between lovers or between married people?" The Viscountess pronounced the verdict of the court as follows, after a philosophic consideration of the case :— [2]

"The attachment of married people and the tender affection of lovers are sentiments both in form of nature and of morality completely different. There can therefore be no just comparison between objects which have not the slightest resemblance or relation to one another." [3]   Another case brought before the same court was this :—

" A lady who was attached to a gentleman by a recognised union of love, married. Has she the right to reject her former lover, and to refuse him the favours which he is accustomed to receive?" [4]   This important question was carefully weighed by the Viscountess and her ladies, and the following judgment was pronounced :—
"The addition of the marriage tie by no means annihilates the former love affair, unless the lady decides to bid good-bye to love for ever, and to love no one in the future."

---

[1] André.
[2] "Philosophica consideratione."
[3] André, *lib. cit.*, fol. 94.
[4] *Ibid.*, fol. 94.

AN INTERESTING ARGUMENT FROM PRECEDENT.—Queen Eleanor of England had the following curious case brought before her court:—

"A gentleman was deeply smitten with a lady who had given her affections to another. She, however, was so favourable to him, that she promised if ever a time should arrive when she should be deprived of her first lover, she would then give ear to his prayers and adopt him as the successor. A little time afterwards the lady and her first lover married. The gentleman immediately, pleading a decision of the Countess of Champagne's, demanded the love of the newly-married lady, for in that decision it was solemnly laid down that real love cannot exist between married people. The lady, however, resisted his application, declaring that she had not lost the love of her lover by marrying him."[1] After careful deliberation of the court, Queen Eleanor pronounced the decision as follows :—

"We are not inclined to controvert the decision of the Countess of Champagne, to the effect that true love cannot exist between married people. This, a solemn and deliberate decree of the afore-mentioned court, ought to hold good. Accordingly we order that the lady grant to her imploring lover the favours which he so earnestly entreats, and which she so faithfully has promised."[2]

VARIOUS CAUSES CÉLÈBRES.—The following decision will doubtless commend itself as an equitable one to most people. The case was, that a lady had imposed upon her

---

[1] André, fol. 96.　　　　[2] *Ibid.*

lover the condition of never praising her in public, no matter what might be said to her detriment. The gentleman performed his *rôle* of silence well, until one day, finding himself in company with a number of ladies and gentlemen, who with one consent began to speak ill of his lady-love, he could contain himself no longer, and burst out into her panegyric and defence, declaring himself desirous to avenge her honour, if need be *à l'outrance*.[1] The Countess of Champagne, on the question being brought before her, gave judgment as under :—

"The lady has been too severe in her commands. The condition, to begin with, was illegal; for it is not right nor possible to reproach a lover who yields to the necessity of rebutting calumnies and slanders hurled against his mistress."[2]

A complicated *cause célèbre*, which was the subject of a long and animated discussion before the tribunal of the Countess of Champagne, turned on the following moot points for decision :—

"The lover of a lady went away on a long journey beyond the sea. His absence was to last a considerable time. She herself had no hopes of his speedy return, and, indeed, she was in despair of ever seeing him again. Time wore on and she sought for herself a new lover. A trusty servant of the absent gentleman opposed the course the lady had taken, accused her of infidelity, and brought her before the Court of Love of the Countess of Champagne." The lady's defence was as follows :—

---

[1] André, fol. 91.　　　　[2] *Ibid.*, fol. 91.

" Since after two years' widowhood a lady is considered to have completed her term of mourning for a dead lover, and can then, with the full permission of the court, engage herself in a new attachment; far greater reason have I, after long years of waiting and watching, to search for a substitute for my absent lover, who neither by letter, nor message, has consoled me nor given me the slightest ground for hope or joy, although he has had plenty of opportunities for doing so." [1] Long debates we are told were held on this complicated question,[2] both plaintiff and defendant doing their best to prove or disprove their respective positions. At last a decision was arrived at, and the Countess pronounced judgment as follows :—

" A lady has no right to renounce her lover under the pretext that he has been for a long while absent from her, unless she has proof positive at the time that he has broken faith with her, or has failed in his duties. The absence of a lover on some errand of urgency and for an honourable cause, gives no excuse whatever for so doing. Nothing ought to flatter a lady more than to have tidings from far distant places that her lover is acquiring glory there, and is making for himself a name in the estimation of the great. The fact of his not having sent a letter or a message may be explained as the effect of extreme prudence : he might not wish to confide his secret to a stranger, or he might fear that if he sent letters without taking the messenger into his confidence, the mystery of

---

[1] André, fol. 95.
[2] " Cum longâ esset utrinque assertatione certatum."—*Ibid.*

love might be too easily revealed, either by the treachery of the messenger, or by the accident of his death in the course of the journey. Judgment therefore against the lady." [1]

The following smart sentence was pronounced by the Countess of Flanders against a gentleman who was brought before her court:—The case at issue was this gentleman's conduct in having sought the love and obtained the last of favours from a lady, although he was already the pledged and acknowledged lover of another mistress — a fact he had been careful to disguise. After having enjoyed the favours of his new flame for some time, he returned to his old lady-love, and tried to pick a quarrel with the lady he had left. The court was especially asked to inflict punishment on this man. " He is to be deprived," said the Countess in her decision, " of the love and affection and favours of both ladies. And, in future, no lady who deems herself an honourable woman will be permitted to grant him her love." [2] If we may employ a colloquialism, this was rather hard on the gentleman.

The Countess of Champagne decided the following peculiar case:—"A gentleman loved a lady, and not having much opportunity of speaking to her, he arranged that by the medium of his steward they should communicate with one another. By this means they contrived to conceal their love in perfect secrecy. The steward, however, forgetting his duty to his master, pleaded his

---

[1] André, *Livre de l'Art d'Aimer*, fol. 95.   [2] *Ibid.*, fol. 94.

own suit with the lady, and so effectually that she gave him her complete affection." Filled with just indignation, the gentleman denounced the love intrigue to the Countess of Champagne, and the Countess, having convoked the large court of sixty ladies, pronounced the following judgment :—

" Let the crafty knave, who has found a mate worthy of him, enjoy his stolen pleasures, since the lady has not had sufficient shame and modesty to keep her from such a crime. But we decree that both of them be excluded in the future from the love of everybody; that the lady be never invited to an assembly of ladies, nor the man be seen near an assembly of gentlemen, since he has broken all the laws of honour, and she has violated all the precepts of womanly modesty in stooping to the love of one so low." [1]

A decision unanimous and for perpetuity was pronounced by the court of the Ladies of Gascony, which held jurisdiction in the English dominions, in the following cause :—" A gentleman divulged the secrets of his most private moments with his lady-love, and was brought before the court by the unanimous voice of all lovers of the district, who demanded his exemplary punishment, for fear that the example might become contagious." Judgment was given as follows :—

" The criminal to be deprived in future of every hope of love. He is to be disowned in every assemblage of ladies and gentlemen, and if any lady has the audacity

---

[1] André, *lib. cit.*, fol. 96.

to violate this edict she is to be denied the friendship of every honourable woman."[1] With the following case we must conclude our list :—

"A troubadour had loved a lady from her earliest years. While she was yet a mere child he had been passionately devoted to her, and when she grew up to girlhood he felt emboldened to declare his love. She promised to grant him the privilege of kissing her whenever he came to see her. But when she became a woman, and he was anxious to take regular advantage of this permission, she refused to grant him the favour, declaring that when she made the promise she was too young to understand the consequences." Judgment given in favour of the troubadour.[2]

THE JEUX PARTIS AND PUYS D'AMOUR.—Not less interesting were the amorous suits or cases which we read of in the Romances of the Round Table, which date from the twelfth century.[3] They were known by the name of Les Jeux Partis, and were common among the Anglo-Normans.[4] The Puys d'Amour were incontestably of Anglo-Norman origin, says De La Rue,[5] and were Courts of Love of a different complexion from those which we have before alluded to. They were more democratic in their composition, and were held on St. Valentine's Day.[6] Poems on love were sung by minstrels and troubadours before the court, and the best piece was rewarded by a

---

[1] André, fol. 97.
[2] Guillaume de Bergedan. "De far un jutjamen."
[3] De La Rue, *Essais*, I. 220.   [4] *Ibid*.
[5] *Ibid*., III. 221-5.   [6] *Ibid*., I. 225.

crown being bestowed upon its author. They originated in Auvergne most probably, which belonged to the English dominions in the twelfth century, and as a curious relic of their place of origination the presiding functionary of the court was always called the Prince du Puy. The troubadour or minstrel who was so fortunate as to obtain the verdict of the court for his song, took the title of King, or added to his name "li couronné." Thus Adam le Bossu the troubadour calls himself Li Rois Adenès, and in the MSS. he is represented with a crown on his head. Rogeret the jongleur likewise dignifies himself with the title " king "; and Pierckuis de la Coupelle, the troubadour or jongleur, is depicted in a MS. crowned and playing on a violin.[1]

---

[1] De La Rue, *Essais*, I. 225 sq.

CHAPTER XV.

Geoffrey Rudel—William Cabestaing—Gaucelm Faidit—Giraud
de Borneil—Rambaud de Vaquciras.

GEOFFREY RUDEL.—In recounting some of the stories
of the troubadours, which we now propose to do, we
are compelled to pass away from England proper to
the English provinces in France mainly for our materials, in order that illustrations of manners and
customs, which are not so easily obtainable in the historical remains of our own land, may be exhibited with
greater prominence and minuteness of detail elsewhere.
With regard to these stories, which we are about to
recount, we may mention that they have been submitted to a certain examination and scrutiny, and have
been found to be in all their main facts true, extraordinary as some may appear. The most passionate tale
of devotion to a lady-love, under circumstances romantic
and extraordinary, is that of Geoffrey Rudel, who
was a prince of Blaye, a town near Bordeaux, in the
English dominions. This troubadour was of a highly
romantic and sentimental disposition. Although he had
the choice of many ladies of rank to whom he could have
dedicated his poetry and his devotion, none of those whom
he saw had any influence on his feelings. He affected

and ultimately was enslaved to the extraordinary notion of dedicating his life and his talents to the service of a lady whom he had never seen at all, and whom, by report and repute only he knew as a paragon of beauty and virtue. This was the Countess of Tripoli, in Palestine, a city which had been taken by the Christians during the first Crusade, and in order that it should serve as an outpost against the Turks, had been created into an earldom for Bertrand of Toulouse, the son of Count Raymond Gilles. The Countess of Tripoli's beauty and charms were the constant theme of every crusader and traveller who, having been to the Holy Land, had had the good fortune to behold so peerless a woman; and Geoffrey Rudel, after celebrating her praises for awhile on his lute at home, resolved at last to embark and throw himself at her feet, as the slave and admirer of her celestial loveliness. Whether it were that his health was naturally weak, or that, as he himself and his contemporaries believed, the effect of his passion was so great as to overwhelm his strength and annihilate his spirit, certain it is that an uncontrollable weakness and agitation showed itself in Geoffrey directly he arrived at Tripoli. When he hastened to disembark from the vessel, so great was his agitation that he fell down, to all appearance dead, and was carried by pitying bystanders into the nearest house on the shore, where he was left in charge of the occupants. Meanwhile his companions, knowing his sad and romantic story, went in search of the countess, and told her the history of the troubadour pilgrim who had just arrived in port, and had taken such a long

journey attracted only by her marvellous beauty. Deeply
touched at such devotion, the countess hastened to the
house where Geoffrey lay ; but death had been there before her, and when she arrived, Geoffrey was fast expiring.
The pleasure and the excitement of anticipation had been
too much for his weak frame ; but the sight of the countess
herself retarded for a few moments the catastrophe. He
was enabled, at the sight of the peerless lady whom he
had so ardently desired to behold, to raise himself from the
couch on which he lay, and to take her hand, murmuring
as he did so, "Most illustrious princess, I will not complain
of death. I have seen you, and have thus achieved the sole
object, the sole desire of my life." The countess, filled with
sorrow, embraced him, and Geoffrey, fixing his eyes upon
her face, and then lifting them up to heaven, expired in her
beloved arms, the happiest man, as it was said, in the
world. The countess had him magnificently buried
among the Knight Templars at Tripoli in a tomb of por-
phyry, and over the tomb she caused a number of Arabic
verses to be engraved, expressive of his constancy and
devotion to herself. So smitten was she with grief and
sympathy, that she found it impossible to live any longer
in the world of men, and from that day forth immured
herself in the cloister.[1] This story may strike a sceptical
reader as one of those instances where history has passed
into romance. Unfortunately for such a supposition, an
ancient and unimpeachable Provençal record says expressly : " The Viscount Geoffrey Rudel, in passing over

---

[1] La Curne de Ste. Palaye, *Histoire : Vie de Geoffroi Rudel.*

the seas to visit his lady, died a voluntary death because
of her." [1]   Petrarch, likewise, is not disposed to romance
without a cause, nor is he at all likely to quote as historical a fact which was notoriously untrue.   Yet he alludes
to the same incident in all good faith, as worthy of credit
in his time ; and doubt must be harder now, when so
many years have elapsed since the time of Petrarch.

WILLIAM CABESTAING.—William Cabestaing's adventures and extraordinary end are likewise confirmed by
several authorities, not only in ancient printed works, but
likewise in manuscripts, and we therefore with greater
confidence put forward a story which has not a parallel
that we know of in history or fiction since the times of
Thyestes.   This troubadour was a poor gentleman of
Roussillon, of noble birth, but of exceedingly reduced circumstances, so much so, that in his boyhood he was placed
by his parents in the household of Raymond of Castel-
Roussillon to act in the capacity of page.   Raymond was
a knight, and seigneur of the district from whence he
took his title, and his household was conspicuous for ease
and affluence.   The faithful page displayed such amiable
qualities of mind and character, that he soon became a
general favourite with the seigneur's household, and was
universally beloved of the family.   Lord Raymond himself took such a fancy to the youth that he made him
gentleman usher to his wife, imagining that no better or
more pleasing person could be found in his whole establishment, and none more likely to be acceptable to his spouse.

---

[1] In Cressimbeni.

This lady, whose name was Margherita, was enchanted with the youthful gentleman usher, whose voice, manners, and personal beauty were irresistible attractions, so that she speedily fell in love with him, and for a time concealed her passion successfully from his notice. She was always fain, however, that he should take her meaning if it could be done without her having to break the subject to him. But William, deterred by youthful bashfulness, and timorous likewise of the distance between himself and his mistress, obstinately refused to understand her indications. At last she resolved to reveal herself to him, and, taking advantage of a private moment when they were together, she said,—

"William, if a lady loved you, could you love her again?"

"Yes, certainly, madame," replied the young man, "if I believed her to be in earnest."

"That is well spoken, William," answered his mistress. "Now, tell me, can you not distinguish true love from that which is only counterfeit?"

These questions opened the young man's eyes, and it was not long before the vein of poetry and song which was already germinating within him, found vent in a beautiful poem to an anonymous lady, which, though her name was not mentioned, Margherita easily concluded to be herself. Full of happiness that his affection had turned towards her in the manner she so ardently desired, Margherita took another opportunity when they were alone together of plying the youthful troubadour with still further questions as to his state of mind.

" Hast thou found at last," she said, " that a lady can love thee? If so, dost thou find in me a true friend or a faithless one? "

" Since the happy hour," returned the young man, " when I first entered your service, I have been charmed with your goodness, and the truth and frankness of your behaviour to me."

" Then I swear to thee," replied Margherita, " that thou shalt never have cause to change thy opinion. Never, no never will I deceive thee." Whereupon, intoxicated with her passion for him, she threw her arms round his neck and embraced him in a transport. William Cabestaing poured out his passion thenceforth in poetry of the sweetest tune, and while doing his best to conceal the amour from the eyes of the world, succeeded only in awaking the strongest suspicions in the eyes of those around him. The courtiers and dependants of Lord Raymond were not slow to carry the rumour of the intrigue to his ears; in a short time the whole story became public property; while the two main actors in the drama were in blissful unconsciousness that any one knew the secret they so carefully guarded. Lord Raymond was a man of violent and jealous temper, and his unfortunate condition was complicated by the fact that he really had a great regard for his wife. Accordingly he resolved with all dispatch to come to the bottom of the matter. Having inquired, therefore, one day what was become of William Cabestaing, and learning that he was hawking, he immediately hid arms under his clothes, with the full intention of killing him, and took the road which led to where the troubadour was. The latter seeing the seigneur approach, advanced towards him, not without secret uneasiness, and asked him how it was that he thus rode alone.

"It is because I wish to talk with you," replied his lord. "I charge you to tell me by God and by your faith, if love really inspires the verses that you compose, and if a lady is indeed the object of them."

"Unless I loved," replied the troubadour, "how could I sing? Love, since you ask the question, has indeed complete possession of my soul."

"I would know, then, who is the lady?" replied the suspicious Raymond. To which Cabestaing made a neat rejoinder by quoting a poem of Bernard de Ventadour's, advising a gentleman to reveal everything to his lady-love, but nothing about her to those who asked him. This did not content the persistent baron, who pressed the troubadour for an answer, till at last the latter, in order to remove suspicion from Margherita, declared that his real lover was Lady Agnes, the sister of the baron's wife. The baron was taken in the snare. Transported with the declaration which removed his suspicions, he embraced the troubadour, promised him his good offices with the lady, and pointing towards the castle of Robert of Tarascon, the husband of Agnes, declared that they would both go there together. Thither, therefore, they accordingly went, and when they arrived, Raymond, after the usual civilities, addressed Agnes thus :—

"By the faith you owe me, my lovely sister, answer me. Have you a lover?"

" Yes, my lord," she said, " I have."

" I beseech you, tell me," said the baron, " who he is."

" That I will not," replied the lady. " Women are not bound to confess such things."

But in the meanwhile, while she was speaking, she had remarked great distress in the face of William Cabestaing, and knowing the truth of the affection which existed between him and her sister, and suspecting that this visit turned on its discovery, she with great readiness and presence of mind avowed her lover to be William Cabestaing. Everything thus appeared ended, to the delight of the baron and to the satisfaction of William Cabestaing, while the Lady Agnes was not long in taking her own husband into her confidence, to whom she disclosed the pardonable deceit. It would certainly have been better for the two lovers if matters had ended here, although they would not have won an unenviable notoriety as the victims of the tragedy which subsequently ensued. But blinded by their passion, and lulled by the supposition that the baron's suspicions had now completely evaporated, they began to carry on their *liaison* with greater openness than heretofore. Nay, to such an extent of audacity did the lady herself go, that she compelled the troubadour to compose a sonnet, in which he declared that he loved her and her alone. The sonnet was composed, and by a second violation of prudence was addressed and sent to be carried by a jongleur to Baron Raymond himself. Apropos of this, we may remark that, so easy were the morals of the time, that many of the troubadours' panegyrics on married ladies were conveyed by the jongleurs indifferently to the husbands and to the wives, on the supposition probably that the former would be delighted with the ladies' praises.[1]   Such, however, was not the case with the Baron of Castel-Roussillon.   Transported with rage at the temerity and insolence of the lovers, and at the knowledge of the guilty *liaison* which had been thus communicated to him, he became like one distraught, and brooded only over blood and vengeance.   On some pretext he invited Cabestaing outside the castle, into a secluded spot, where he stabbed him to death, and mutilated his body, cutting off his head and tearing out his heart.   The latter he took in derision to the cook of the castle and bade him dress it for my lady's dinner, as she had taken a fancy for heart that afternoon.   The cook, obviously unaware what heart it was he was dressing, and imagining, we are told, that it was venison, cooked it in his best style, and served it up as an appetising dish for Lady Margherita's repast.   The lady partook of the heart with relish, while her remorse-less husband gloated over the sight, until she had entirely allayed her hunger with the dainty.

"Do you know," he then said, "what you have been eating?"

"No," she replied; "but I found it delicious."

"This may perhaps enlighten you on the subject," exclaimed the baron, pulling out from under his cloak the head of William Cabestaing.   "Behold the head of the

---

[1] La Curne de Ste. Palaye, *Histoire : Vie de Guillaume Cabestain.*

man of whom you have just eaten the heart. It is right that you should have enjoyed it," he added; " for you loved him so passionately during life, small wonder that you should enjoy him so much when dead."

The lady, at this frightful sight, fell lifeless on the floor, but soon recovering her senses she screamed aloud. " Yes, barbarian, I have found that meat so delicate and beautiful, that for fear I may ever lose the taste of it I will eat no more as long as I live."

To be braved and taunted by the woman he had so injured, incensed the baron to a still greater pitch than before, and drawing his sword he rushed towards her with the intention of committing a double murder. Margherita fled from his approach, but finding escape impossible, rather than that he should enjoy the satisfaction of killing her, she precipitated herself from a balcony of the castle which happened to be at hand, and was killed by the fall. The report of this event was likely to impress the mind with sympathy and terror in an age when love ruled over the manners like a despotic sovereign, and was considered the soul of all chivalry and romance. And according to the Provençal historians, all the knights of Roussillon, Cerdagne, and Narbonnais, were accustomed ever afterwards to meet once a year, and to take part in a solemn service in memory of Margherita and of William Cabestaing; and all the lovers of both sexes came to pray for the repose of their souls.

GAUCELM FAIDIT.—But of all the troubadours who enjoyed the favour and the patronage of the troubadour king of England, one of the most remarkable for the

vicissitudes of his life and an adventurous career was
Gaucelm Faidit. Unlike those whom we have hitherto
mentioned in these chapters, he was lowly born, and
possessed no advantages of birth or connection to advance
him until King Richard, struck by his musical and
poetical gifts, took him by the hand and raised him in
the world. Gaucelm Faidit was the son of an artizan of
Uzerche, in the Limousin; and therefore, being a subject
of the English crown, was brought early into contact
with its brilliant young prince. Although not endowed
with the wealth of the great barons of his time, he
emulated their manners entirely by extravagancies and
follies without number when he was a youth, passing
most of his time in gaming and in dissipation. To complete the list of his offences against society, he espoused
a young woman of low birth and questionable morals, who
seemed likely to draw him still deeper into the slough of
despair. But, on the contrary, the girl being endowed
with a charming voice, and of a character exceedingly
artistic and refined, seems to have been the first to direct
his talents to their true goal. "She sang his songs,"
we read, "and he wrote them for her." After many
attempts and failures at making his mark as a minstrel,
he at last acquired the distinction of being acknowledged
a troubadour, chiefly through the interest of Richard I.,
who at that time had not succeeded to his father's throne.
Gaucelm Faidit, with a character at once adventurous
and audacious, having now acquired a position in the
social scale, in which he might give play to all his
ambitions and wishes to make a figure in the world,

attached himself very prominently to the celebrated
Marie de Ventadour, " the most esteemed lady," says the
old Provençal historian, " in the province of Limousin ;
the lady who prided herself most on doing whatever was
right and good, and who best preserved and defended
herself from all evil; who always shaped her conduct by
the rules of reason, and never at any time committed an
act of folly." Gaucelm Faidit addressed to her his vows
of love, and, as was usual among the ladies of that day,
who affected to consider themselves goddesses, to whose
shrine inferior man paid homage, and who made it a
point of honour to have as many worshippers as possible,
Marie de Ventadour did not repulse her ardent admirer.
But she required him, if he was to deserve her love and
expect to awaken affection fully in her, to show himself
as much a warrior as a poet, and to proceed to the Holy
Land as a crusading troubadour along with her husband,
who at that moment was setting out on the expedition.
Although the reverse of martial, Gaucelm Faidit consented to give this proof of his affection, and his name
figures in the roll of the Third Crusade. His time at that
enterprise seems to have been more taken up with send-
ing ballads to his lady-love about the exploits of the war
than in performing any himself; and as soon as he could
find a convenient excuse for quitting the ranks of holy
warriors and returning to his native land and the château
of Marie de Ventadour, he embraced the opportunity
ardently. The reception which the lady gave him after
all the dangers he had braved in her behalf, did not
satisfy his expectations. Accordingly, after several com-

plaints of her coldness towards him, so unmerited after all his enthusiasm for her wishes, he presented himself before her one day with an ultimatum. "Madame," he said, "you see a lover who is beside himself. He is overwhelmed by your rigorous treatment of him. If you will not put a stop to such ways, he is resolved never to see you again. Yes, I am resolved of that," he exclaimed. "Perhaps I shall find another lady who will despise me less." With that he flung out of the apartment and immediately quitted the château. Marie de Ventadour, left to herself, was afraid of his evil tongue if she suffered him to relinquish her love in this mood of mind, for he was noted for his sharp sayings and the bitter assertions and insinuations which he could shape into satirical verse. Accordingly she took counsel with a friend of hers, Madame de Malamort, and as a result of their deliberations the following stratagem was played off upon the troubadour. Madame de Malamort sent a message to him asking him which he preferred most, a little bird in the hand or a crane flying in the air. At the receipt of this message from the lady, the curiosity of the troubadour was aroused, and mounting his horse he rode to her château to ask her for fuller information as to her meaning.

"My meaning is briefly this," said Madame de Malamort: "I am the little bird whom you have in your hand, and Marie de Ventadour is the crane who flies over your head high up in the air." She then called his attention to her personal attractions, her charm of manner, and her social position and influence; none of which, perhaps, equalled those of Marie de Ventadour, but were, nevertheless, of considerable worth as the world went. Gaucelm Faidit could not refuse this plain proposal to exchange one lady-love for another, which was made with becoming modesty by the lady who offered the exchange; although there seems a difficulty in imagining, in our days, how the proposition could have been so urged without a sacrifice of womanly reserve. Nevertheless, it was so, and the proposed bargain was accepted unconditionally by the troubadour.

"Now then," said Madame de Malamort, "I wish you to bid your adieux to your late lover in a discreet and subdued style, and then you can go into ecstasies when you begin to celebrate me." The troubadour, who had fallen completely into the trap, did as he was requested, and took leave of Marie de Ventadour in a final chanson notable for its sobriety and self-restraint. But when he began to pay assiduous court to his new lover he found her demeanour suddenly changed to ice, and she gave him emphatic and unmistakable notice that his attentions were not required. Unable to attack her openly without showing to the world the trick of which he had been the victim, his indignation evaporated into general invectives against love and even against poetry and minstrelsy, which brought a man no fitting reward. He determined to renounce both for the future. But his resolutions, like those of so many men before or since him, were entirely transient, and ere long he had recovered completely from his chagrin, and was handling his lute with the same skill as ever. Several ladies in the meantime had done

T

their best to console him for his complaints against love
in general and poetry in particular. Among them was
Marguerite d'Aubusson, who, in her turn, very un-
generously played off a stratagem on him, more unkind,
and certainly more notorious than the former trick with
which Marie de Ventadour and her friend had duped him.
Marguerite loved him not, though she affected to interest
herself in him, and the chief reason of her interest was
that he might be induced to celebrate her charms in one
of his songs. As he delayed doing so, one day, when he
was about to take leave of her after a visit in the afternoon, she allowed him to kiss her neck, and this favour
at once inflamed the impressionable troubadour to the
necessary song. Marguerite had now achieved the satisfaction of her vanity; and having no affection for the
troubadour nor any further need to display any, she
employed him as the instrument for gratifying her
passion for a rival whom he hated with all the hate of a
vain and depreciated man. His rival was Hugh de Lusignan, the son of that Count of Marche who afterwards
married Queen Isabella of England. Marguerite had a
special wish to meet her lover, and could think of no
better place for doing so than Gaucelm Faidit's château,
whenever the latter happened to be away. She had easy
access to the place always by order of its master, who
was only too delighted when she paid him a visit, and the
nature of her relations with Faidit being well known to be
merely those of a friend, she could go there without fear of
compromising her reputation. Not so in the case of Hugh
de Lusignan, who was her lover avowed and real. Accord-

ingly, directly Gaucelm Faidit's back was turned on his château, the Lady Marguerite pranced thither on her palfrey, and not finding its lord at home (as she fully expected him not to be), waited complacently while Hugh de Lusignan effected an entrance at the window, or by the postern, or wherever else he contrived to steal in un-noticed. Then she held her assignation with her lover in the place where least of all it would be expected—in the castle of his deadliest rival. This pleasant trick was ultimately found out; but it made the world laugh, and was one more of the many woes and disappointments which afflicted Gaucelm Faidit in his later years. But the greatest of all the ills he had to suffer was the death of his munificent patron and friend, Richard I. of England, in whose honour he composed one of the most beautiful of his Planhs, or "Songs of Sorrow." [1]

GIRAUD DE BORNEIL.—Dante, who has placed several troubadours in his Inferno, has thought well to thrust to a considerably deep latitude in those regions the next troubadour to whom we shall allude. But as far as can be seen, the judgment of the Florentine poet is a partial and unfair one. This troubadour is the celebrated Giraud de Borneil, the panegyrist of the beautiful Fleur-de-lis, whose sweet songs are always delightful and in excellent taste. Giraud de Borneil's contemporaries and chroniclers certainly formed a very different estimate

---

[1] The life of Gaucelm Faidit is taken from the preceding authorities mentioned. His poems may be found in Raynouard's *Reculée*, *Le Parnasse Occitanien*, and Bartsch's *Chrestomathie Pro-vençale* (Elberfeld, 1830).

of him from that of the epic poet. They praise his sobriety, his industry, his study ; they declare that he set a pattern to his fellows by his abstention from extravagancies and unthrifty habits. Instead of indulging in profligate expenses—the common bane of all the race— we are told Giraud would frequent the schools, and would endeavour to apply the principles and lore which he acquired there to his poetry. He early laid it down that the matter and manner of the thought was of more importance in verse than the empty elaboration of the rhyme ; and when he went on his rounds of visits from castle to castle in the summer, accompanied always by two excellent jongleurs who sang his compositions to perfection, the interest manifested in his thoughtful productions was always great in the extreme.

RAMBAUD DE VAQUEIRAS.—Rambaud de Vaqueiras, the next troubadour in our list, was knighted by the Marquis of Montferrat, and attached himself as loyal lover and troubadour to Beatrix del Carat, the Marquis' sister, whom he has rendered famous in poetry and song by the name of the "Bel Cavalier." The following curious story gave the origin of the name. Like Bradamante, Beatrix was fond of martial exercises, was an excellent horsewoman, and would have made a most immaculate knight if she had belonged to the other sex. One day, when the Marquis returned from the chase, he paid his sister a visit, and by accident left his sword in her apartment. Delighted at the sight of the weapon, and seized with a strong desire to handle it, Beatrix took off her dress, and, standing in shorter and more convenient habiliments, buckled on the sword by a baldric round her waist, and respired deliciously in that state of freedom from conventional restraint, and in the feeling that in the privacy of her chamber she almost resembled a man. Thereupon she drew the sword from its scabbard, tossed it up in the air, caught it again most dexterously, and wheeled it glittering and bright with inconceivable rapidity from one side to the other. All the while, though she was in complete ignorance of the fact, her lover had been gazing in a state of ravishment through a crevice in the door, and had seen the whole performance from first to last, his face glued to the door, and his attention rivetted on the minutest detail. From that time forth he dubbed her " Le Bel Cavalier," and by this name, as we said, he has made Beatrix del Carat famous. Nothing neater or more graceful could be pictured than the manner in which the contract of love was first arranged between Rambaud and this charming Amazon.

" Vouchsafe, Madame," he said, " to give me your advice. I love a lady of superlative charms. I converse with her continually without letting her know the state of my feelings. Tell me, ought I to die of love, for fear of revealing myself to her ? "

" By no means," replied Beatrix. " I advise you to declare your love, and to request the lady to retain you as her lover and her troubadour. If she is wise, she will certainly not take it amiss, but on the contrary will think herself honoured by such a declaration, for believe me, you are so lovable and noble in yourself that there is no lady in the world who ought not freely to receive you as her knight."

"Then, Madame," said Rambaud, " you are the lady."

"Then, Rambaud," said Beatrix, "you are my knight."[1]

---

[1] Jean de Nostradamus, *Les vies des plus célèbres Troubadours.* Crescimbeni.   La Curne de Ste. Palaye.

CHAPTER XVI.

STORIES OF THE TROUBADOURS (*continued*).

The Monk of Puicibot—William de la Tour—Pierre Vidal—
Raymond de Miravals.

THE MONK OF PUICIBOT.—A curious history is that of
the Monk of Puicibot, who left his monastery to become a
troubadour, and returned thither again after he had
demonstrated the hollowness of troubadour life, which he
had been taught by his original vows to shun. "It was
love," says the Monk of Puicibot, "which seduced me
from my monastery." A lady who was nearly related to
him, and therefore was allowed the privilege of entering
the cloisters to see him, paid him many visits, and at last
by her reasoning, and still more by the eloquence of her
beauty, induced him to leave the convent and enter the
world. In order to do the latter in a proper and respectable style it was necessary to have found and procured
some reputable patron or protector, by whose kindness
and interest the aspirant to troubadour honours might be
raised through the degrees of knighthood, and be introduced to the courtly society of his neighbourhood. The
patron whom the monk chose was the gallant English
troubadour, Savari de Mauléon, the friend and adherent
of King John, whom that monarch had made governor of

all the English possessions in Gascony.   Savari supplied
the monk with horses, money, and habits, and with all
that was further necessary to enable him to " go through
the courts," that is to say, to proceed from castle to
castle in the way we have so often described.   While engaged in this artistic pilgrimage the monk, or as we must
now call him, the troubadour, Aubert de Puicibot, fell
in with a lady of great beauty, and became deeply
enamoured of her.   At this time, apparently, he had not
been raised to the full grade of knight bachelor, and the
lady refused to listen to his suit until that advance in his
rank had taken place.   Savari de Mauléon fulfilled his
wishes in this respect, and Aubert de Puicibot, probably owing to his incarceration in a convent, where the
married state was expressly forbidden, plunged immediately into matrimony with the lady of his choice, instead
of merely devoting himself to her as her troubadour and
her knight, in the usual method of his musical and poetical confrères.   Their wedded life was at first all smiles,
and Aubert was congratulating himself on his domestic
felicity, when business took him on a journey to Spain.
During his absence an English troubadour gained the
affection of his wife, and the pair eloped together.   In
those days bad news, such as that of an elopement, the
speed of which is at present like the lightning, did not
travel so fast as in modern times, and Aubert de Puicibot,
who must have lingered for a very considerable while in
Spain, at last determined to return, entirely ignorant all
the time of what had happened at home.   On his way
back from Spain he passed through a town, where he felt

inclined to indulge in the same profligate vices which had
been his constant pursuit during his absence from home,
and commissioned some one to find him a lady of venal
character, who would allow him complete access to her
charms in return for a sum of money. He was informed
after due search, that at a small house belonging to a
very poor woman there was a beautiful girl who gained a
scanty pittance by the sale of her beauty. Hither Aubert
de Puicibot betook himself, and discovered in the girl his
own wife. She had fled with the English troubadour and
lived with him for a while. But being abandoned by a
lover in whom she had placed too much reliance, she was
left without a penny in a strange city, without either the
means or the courage to return home. In this deplorable
condition she had sunk a step lower than before, and
it was thus her husband found her. With an access
of ungovernable anger he told her that she must prepare
for death, determining to cast her down an adjoining preci-
pice, and make her end an example to all erring women.
Touched, however, by her grief and supplications, he
adopted the more merciful castigation of shutting her up
in a nunnery, from whence he made her swear that she
would never seek to escape. He himself determined to
retire to a monastery again, and seek once more in the
contemplation of heavenly things that peace which he
could not obtain in the world at large. He accordingly
sold all his possessions, and entered the monastery of
Pignan, not the only troubadour who closed his life in so
unexpected a manner.[1]

---

[1] La Curne de Ste. Palaye, *Histoire*. Crescimbeni, etc.

WILLIAM DE LA TOUR.—The story of William de la Tour consists of facts considerably more extravagant than the preceding. This troubadour, the Baron of La Tour in the French provinces of the English crown, was from his earliest years of a sensitive and fantastic disposition. He eloped with a woman of humble rank, and intoxicated with her charms, devoted his whole thoughts and soul to her homage. Shortly after the elopement she died. The troubadour was thrown by this event into the wildest grief and distraction. Loving her with such exceeding love, he would not be persuaded that she was dead. Accordingly he gave orders that her tomb should be so constructed that it could be opened at pleasure, and that he could have access to the body. Every night, after she was interred, he opened the tomb, and in the midst of the solitude of midnight, drew out the dead body of his lady-love from the vault, gazed earnestly at her beloved features, embraced her, kissed her, and was even seen to speak and hold dialogues with her as if she were alive. He conjured her to tell him whether she were really dead. If so, he begged her describe to him her sufferings in purgatory, and how many masses she would wish to be said for her soul. If, on the contrary, she were alive, he implored her to return with him to their deserted home. This access of fatuity lasted ten days, and some of the poems of this troubadour that remain to us are concerned with the theme we have just alluded to. But not content with this exhibition of weakness, he carried his grief to extravagant excess likewise afterwards, being persuaded that his lady-love, though dead, would in-

fallibly rise again. Certain preliminary conditions had
to be complied with on his part, he believed, before this
desirable result could be achieved, the principal being
to recite the whole Psalter with five hundred Pater-
nosters and Aves every day for a whole year. We read
that he gallantly undertook this task, but we do not read
that the task had the desired effect.[1]

Pierre Vidal, who accompanied Richard Cœur de
Lion to the Holy Land, might justly be called the Don
Quixote of the troubadours. His adventures are of the
wildest, and his indiscretion constantly led him into pre-
dicaments and imbroglios, from which he extricated himself often with but indifferent success. He admired every
beautiful woman he saw; and with a presumption not
uncommon, believed himself as much the object of their
admiration. His behaviour to the highest nobility, even
to princes, was full of extravagance. Nevertheless, his
compositions announce a superior genius. The troubadour Giorgi, who is distinguished for his acumen and judgment, has remarked in one of his poems, that to consider
Vidal a fool is to be a fool one's self; since, if his actions
were those of a fool, his compositions show a great understanding. Perhaps we might assign Vidal a similar
position among the troubadours to that of Goldsmith in
literature, who " wrote like an angel, but talked like poor
poll." In the same way, while Vidal wrote and sang
divinely, his actions, and presumably his talk likewise,

---

[1] Accounts of this troubadour will be found in the works previously quoted.

were those of a foolish and conceited man. His career in the world of gallantry began with an unfortunate incident, so far as his talking was concerned. For having spoken lightly of the wife of a knight of his acquaintance, the knight revenged himself for the indiscretion by slitting Vidal's tongue.

But a more romantic, if equally infelicitous, connection with a lady awaited him in his next amour. Among those who conceived a friendship for the Quixotic troubadour was the Viscount of Baux. This nobleman became particularly attached to the erratic genius, whose talents he admired, though he may not easily have tolerated his eccentricities, and finding him an agreeable and lively companion, kept him as a constant guest at his castle. The viscount was the fortunate possessor of a charming wife, and as Vidal was notoriously the slave of every beautiful woman with whom he came in contact, he was not long before he fell desperately and irresistibly in love with the lovely Vicomtesse de Baux, and persistently addressed all his poems to her. The viscount, far from being jealous, granted the erratic troubadour the most familiar access to his wife, and to prove that the friendship which he had contracted with Vidal was not impaired in any way by the choice of a lady-love so nearly related to himself, entered upon a bond of brotherhood with the troubadour. To demonstrate their fraternity sincere, he presented Vidal with armour and costumes like his own, so that at a distance the two sworn comrades were scarcely distinguishable, and even from a nearer point of view there was frequent danger of confusing their persons. This extraordinary similarity of attire, joined with the fact that the troubadour and the viscount both loved the same lady, gave Vidal the idea how he might possess the favours of his beloved in a shorter and less arduous manner than by any lengthy and elaborate etiquette of courtship. This way was to introduce himself into the viscountess' bedchamber when that lady was asleep, and relying on the fact that even if she woke, her slumberous eyes would scarcely distinguish him from her spouse, to give her a kiss, and by this preliminary onset pave the way to a more vehement display of affection. He accordingly put his ingenious idea into execution, and kneeling down by the side of the sleeping lady, kissed her with un-controlled emotion. The viscountess awoke at the rude salute, but imagining at first that it was her husband, said nothing beyond giving vent to a complaint at the abrupt and inopportune occasion selected for a caress. When, however, Vidal began to urge his suit, and she saw what imposition had been practised on her, she began to scream with all her might, till her woman who slept in the next room ran in to her assistance, and the presumptuous trou-badour was glad to beat a precipitate retreat. The vis-countess, however, was so indignant at Vidal's conduct, that she could not rest until her husband had revenged himself upon the audacious bard. This the viscount, who was sincerely attached to Vidal, entirely refused to do, treating the matter as a joke, and advising his wife not to take too seriously a foolish prank of Pierre Vidal's, who everybody knew was a fantastic, extravagant fellow. The more he attempted to pacify the lady, the greater grew her indignation, until at last it was judged prudent for Vidal to leave that part of the country. With many fond adieux to his good friends, he left for Genoa, and determined to embark on the third Crusade under Richard Cœur de Lion. If high and haughty words could have been any substitute for prowess, then Vidal would assuredly have been the most courageous crusader in the expedition. "My enemies," he said, "tremble at my name. The earth shakes under my steps. All that oppose me I bruise and cut to pieces."

While Vidal was thus boasting of his prowess, a fatal trick was played him by the friends of Richard in Cyprus. They engaged him to marry a young Greek girl, who they solemnly declared was niece to the Emperor of the East, the heiress of untold wealth; and, in fact, as a result of this marriage the whole Eastern empire was to be transferred to the management of Vidal. They played their part in the hoax so well that Vidal was completely taken in, and performed the marriage ceremony in an imposing and elaborate manner with the spouse who was destined, he believed, to bring him so much fortune. Intoxicated with his great destiny, he caused himself to be entitled the Emperor of Constantinople and of the East, while his wife was flattered and ennobled by the title of Empress of the same dominions. The ermine and regalia of that illustrious line were scrupulously imitated in the attire of Vidal and his spouse, although we are compelled to suppose that both the fur and the gems were of an artificial or at least an inferior quality. A throne was carried in front of him on all occasions; and whatever money he could save from present ostentation, for the purpose of future display, was carefully husbanded by the eccentric troubadour, in order to dazzle the world all the more brilliantly when the time came at last for his ascending the imperial throne.[1] If we were to continue this account of the extravagancies of Vidal, we might fill the chapter with them alone. We think we cannot better conclude these anecdotes than by giving an illustration of one of those complicated and surprising intrigues so dear to the spirit of the time, in which the troubadour Raymond de Miravals played the chief part.

RAYMOND DE MIRAVALS.—He had a wife who possessed every qualification necessary to attract the affection of a husband, but whom he very capriciously rejected for the sake of a lady whose fascinations were so irresistible, that he promised to divorce his wife in order to form a union with her. The wife so soon to be divorced had consoled herself during the neglect with which her husband had treated her, by falling in love with a knight called Bremon; and when the troubadour Raymond threatened to dissolve the matrimonial tie, she was secretly delighted, because it offered her the prospect of an otherwise impossible union with Bremon. Accordingly, on hearing the intelligence from her husband, she affected a sorrowful air, and declared that she would not tolerate such usage at his hands as to be divorced for no sufficient reason by him, and that she would send for her

---

[1] La Curne de Ste. Palaye, *Histoire.* Balaguer, *Historia de los Trovadores.* Crescimbeni, et alibi.

parents and friends in order that they should see her righted. Meanwhile she sent immediate notice to Bremon, promising to marry him, and share his fortunes. Enchanted with the idea, Bremon came directly with a party of knights to the lady's castle, and dismounted at the gate. The lady being informed of his arrival, told her husband that her parents and friends had come to fetch her, and that she earnestly desired to go away with them at once. Raymond conducted her with all speed to the castle gate, being glad to have the affair so quietly ended. The lady, just ready to mount her horse, desired Raymond, since he chose to part with her, that he would give her in marriage to Bremon. He consented with all his heart. Her lover, advancing towards her, received her from the hand of Raymond, put the ring on her finger, and rode away with her along with his knights. The too confiding troubadour, who had just made away with an excellent wife, then rode off in haste to his lady-love, for whose sake he had consented so ruinously to break up his home. The lady-love in question was the vainest and most worthless of women, and could think of no better means of increasing her own reputation for supremacy over the hearts of men, than by showing how lightly she prized the affections of so celebrated a man as Raymond de Miravals, who had just made such a sacrifice for her. Accordingly, when he came and claimed her promise to espouse him, she replied, "It is well done, Raymond; you have sent away your wife to please me, and now you shall do something more for me. Go and prepare everything for a magnificent wedding, and return and fetch me when

I shall send you word." Raymond departed, and busied himself with preparations for gorgeous nuptials. Meanwhile, the lady for whose sake he took so much pains married another lover, one Oliver de Saissac, on the very day after she had dismissed him on his fool's errand ; and when the troubadour had completed his arrangements for the magnificent wedding, it was only to find that he had incurred all the expense and given himself unending trouble for a woman who already, before the preparations were well begun, was another man's wife.[1]

---

[1] Jean de Nostradamus, *Les vies des plus célèbres Troubadours.* Crescimbeni. La Curne de Ste. Palaye, etc.

CHAPTER XVII.

THE FALL OF THE TROUBADOURS.

Decline of the Jongleurs—The Jongleurs' Assumption of other
Occupations—Their Depravity and Lawlessness—Fall of the
Troubadours—The Connection of the Troubadours with the
Albigenses — Albigensian Propaganda — The Troubadours,
how Influenced by the Albigenses—Practical Results of the
Adoption of Albigensian Opinions by the Troubadours—
Religious Antagonism among the Troubadours—A Musical
War—Crusade against the Troubadours and Albigenses—
Incidents of the Crusade—Continuance of the Crusade and
Extinction of the Troubadours.

DECLINE OF THE JONGLEURS.—The race of troubadours
came to an end before that of the jongleurs. Different
causes co-operated to these two results. With the former
it was a sudden catastrophe which mainly helped to
produce so unfortunate a climax; with the latter it was
rather the gradual process of decay, or of absorption into
new phases of life. We may put the reign of Henry III.
as the last limit of the troubadours in history. In the
reigns of Henry V. and Henry VI. we still find jongleurs.

Let us briefly explain how the gradual process of decay
operated in the case of the jongleurs. In relation to the
romances and poems which it was their profession to
sing, they acted, if we may so express it, the same part
which is played by publishers at the present day. The
expression is not ours, but Petrarch's, who, in alluding

to the functious of the jongleur in one of his Letters
to Boccaccio, explicitly introduces this comparison.[1] He
deduces their similarity to publishers, and compares the
parallel condition of a work when it had been recited
by a jongleur to admiring crowds and when it had been
issued in print or manuscript by a publisher and sold
to admiring purchasers. Although printing was a late
growth, the multiplication of manuscripts was assiduously
carried on in early times; and even in the days of Robert
Wace, that is to say, the end of the twelfth century, the
practice of reading was growing into favour. " Et les
estoires lire as festes," says Wace. By the fourteenth
century it began to be commonly the custom to read the
romances aloud instead of singing them,[2] until we reach
the conversational style of reading in vogue in the age of
Chaucer, who, however, alludes to the old custom of
delivery as still possible even in his day—*e.g.* in his
poem of " Troilus," he says,

" And red wher so thow be, or elles songe."[3]

Directly such a practice became fully established, the
vocation of the jongleur was at once placed at a discount,
and the manners of an age of literary verse began to
oust the gay requirements of musical poetry. The extreme length of the poems of some of the English trouvères
also contributed directly to the same result, for no
ordinary memory was capable of retaining such enormous
and interminable lays.

[1] Petrarch, *Rerum Senilium*, V., Ep. 3, p. 793.
[2] Jusserand, *Wayfaring Life*, p. 190.
[3] *Troilus*, Book V., line 1,809.

THE JONGLEURS' ASSUMPTION OF OTHER OCCUPATIONS.—
Under such circumstances, the jongleurs found a more
profitable market for their talents by turning elsewhere
for employment. They justified their name of jongleurs,
or "jougleurs," by betaking themselves to juggling and
acrobatic tricks; they gained employment in towns as
waits or city bands;[1] and finally, they found occupation
by enlisting their talents of mimicry and mummery in
the service of the Mystery Plays.[2] In the first case they
became the forerunners or forefathers of our mountebanks
and conjurors; in the second case of our musicians; in
the third, of our actors. Mystery plays were first introduced into England by Geoffrey, Abbot of St. Albans, at
the beginning of the twelfth century, but did not gain
popularity till considerably later. Growing in favour,
however, each decade, they offered increasing scope of
employment to the jongleur.

THEIR DEPRAVITY AND LAWLESSNESS.—In this way
the jongleurs began to be absorbed into other fields of
activity. They became disorganised, degenerate, and
depraved. John of Salisbury, a monk of Canterbury,
denounces the jongleurs for their vices and wickedness
even at the beginning of the thirteenth century. At the
end of that century the Mystery Plays were bad enough
to be condemned by Wadington, and the jongleurs with
them. By the fifteenth century, the date of their extinction, synods of the Church were lifting their voice

---

[1] Supra, Chapter XI.
[2] De La Rue, *Essais*, I. 168 sq.

against the jongleurs. The Synod of Bayeux, for instance, anathematised them at that epoch as men not only unfit for all human fellowship, but even unfit that any lady should look upon their performances. It has been curiously remarked, that when the jongleurs became disorganised and lawless, they began to turn their attention to singing the deeds of the great outlaw, Robin Hood, and to elevating him into a national hero.[1] They sang his exploits, extolled his audacities into virtues, and multiplied or invented his adventures, until a Robin Hood cycle of ballads began to force its way on to the surface of English literature. These ballads, which have been carefully collected and collated by Ritson, may be studied in his admirable edition, published in London.

FALL OF THE TROUBADOURS.—We have said that the jongleurs were extinguished by slow decay, the troubadours by sudden catastrophe. The shock which the troubadours of other lands received by the cruel and merciless annihilation of their brethren in Provence, paved the way to the rapid extinction of their class; and the blow which fell on the sensitive centre of their race, fell more or less upon all. At the courts of Alphonso X., King of Castile, and of James I., King of Arragon, in the middle of the thirteenth century, and even at the court of Frederick, King of Sicily, at the end of that century, and at Venice and Genoa at the beginning of the fourteenth,[2] troubadours might still be found, but they

---

[1] Jusserand, *Wayfaring Life in England*, 209.
[2] Bartolommeo Giorgi and Bonifazio Calvo.

were the scattered and inconsiderable residue of a great race which had been well nigh extinguished in the ruin of Provence. A cataclysm descended upon that beautiful country and its smiling fields, and along with the land annihilated its art.

THE CONNECTION OF THE TROUBADOURS WITH THE ALBIGENSES.—We shall conclude, therefore, our history of the troubadours with a short account of that extraordinary event. A small sect of enthusiasts had appeared some time previous in Albigeois, whose religious tenets presented one of the strangest aggregations of truth and error which it has ever been the lot of creed to enjoy. The sectaries were known by the name of Albigenses, because of the place where they originally formulated and made famous their faith. But when they entered other lands, and especially Provence, where they rendered themselves more particularly notorious, they still retained their ancient and geographical name. As this had no allusion to their opinions, we had better offer some explanation of the latter before proceeding any further. The tenets of the Albigenses seem to have been a natural growth from the waifs and strays of those infidel opinions of Eastern mysticism, which had travelled to Europe through the medium of the crusades. They reposed on the Duality of Principles, a Good principle and an Evil one, which had first been revealed as an ultimate truth to the world by the religion of Zoroaster, and was destined at a later date to serve as the cardinal feature of Manichæism. The Duality of Principles, as a basis for religion, while satisfactory in many respects in its metaphysical aspect, presents serious dilemmas and unexpected weaknesses with regard to its relation to morality. For if Evil be as eternal and as inextinguishable as Good, and be every whit as justifiable in its existence and operation, then there is no virtue of which one can wholly approve, and no vice which we can entirely condemn. Everything becomes relative, and fixed principles of moral conduct have no foundation in nature. One may very easily see to what practical results in life at large such views on religion and morals unavoidably lead, and how nearly and unfortunately akin they were in their general effects upon practice to the life of love and pleasure which was being led by the troubadours and their lady-loves, as yet unconscious that the courts of love and the encouragements of amorous laxity were directly in accordance with the precepts of religion.

ALBIGENSIAN PROPAGANDA.—The troubadours and their lady-loves were indulging in all the pleasures of amour upon amour, uncontrolled by aught but social etiquette, and every decade increasing in a marked tendency towards immorality. Meanwhile, at a lower level in life, far beneath the courtly exponents of these dangerous theories, the Albigenses entered the land and began to propagate their doctrines with all the zeal of modern fanatics. They used to write the main tenets of their creed upon tracts, and when going through sequestered places in the country, where there was no fear their propaganda would be interfered with, would disperse them among the peasantry. At other times they would take a supply of these leaflets and drop them

on the wayside or on the mountains, in the hope that
poor people or shepherds might find them. It is curious,
in reading the accounts of the mission of the Albigenses
in Provence, to find exactly the same methods of propagan-
dism employed in the middle ages, which are usual among
ardent missionaries at the present day. The secret con-
venticles and houses of entertainment which they opened
for the benefit and information of any one who chose to
come, were not long in attracting several proselytes to
their creed. In these places they " ate and drank," to use
the words of Izarn, " to their heart's content ; they kept
themselves warm and comfortable though it was cold
without ; and they amused themselves with their he or
she cousins as they pleased, for they were able to give
themselves absolution when they wished, and there was
actually no sin which could not be cleared from their
consciences by the first deacon they met with." This
latter allusion refers to the two classes of ministers among
the Albigenses, who were entitled respectively Bishops
and Deacons. These functionaries were supposed by their
simple followers to be in direct communication with the
Holy Ghost, with whom at any moment they could
place themselves in personal contact. In order to do so,
they blew seven times into the mouths of the believers,
which action was supposed, in some mysterious manner,
to secure the presence of the Third Person of the Trinity
at their incantations. These, however, were but the
methods which the missionaries employed with the
vulgar. For among the propagandists were men of intelligence and culture, as we may easily gather from the fact

that ere long representatives of the sect found their way into the boudoirs of the ladies of Provence. The same elegant chambers which had not long before echoed to the sound of lutes and guitars, while troubadours sang of love and passion, now resounded with the words and whispers of religious controversialists, who harangued their fair auditors with the same earnestness, and were listened to with the same attention, which had previously been the case with the minstrels of love. Provence and its *élite* were plainly passing through a religious phase—though of a very peculiar kind—somewhat similar, though the religion was different, to that which has exercised the curiosity of the speculative, in the times of Louis XIV., when Madame de Maintenon led the fashion of religious contemplation. Wherever a company of fair ladies were assembled, says our principal authority for the Albigensian propaganda,[1] there sure enough was some preacher who would hold forth by the hour on the mysteries of the faith. Where the ladies Domerqua, Renaud, Bernard, Garsens, sat spinning at their distaffs—some spinning and others weaving—the new gospel is being carefully explained to them all the while by one of the ministers. " Was there ever such an assembly seen!" remarks our author.

The Troubadours how Influenced by the Albigenses.—The principles of the Albigenses as inculcated in the boudoirs of countesses and received by the attentive ears of courtly troubadours, were obviously conceived in a

---

[1] Izarn.

very different spirit from those which were poured into the duller ear of the vulgar. The troubadours and their friends found this system of morals and religion most congenial and agreeable to their own wishes about life and to the manner in which they spent their time. For if Evil be indestructible and everlasting, being indeed the great serpent that encompasses the universe and entangles all things in its folds, what need of virtue and of self-restraint and other hindrances to delight and pleasure, since to practise these is but to make a silly opposition to the principles of Eternal Nature, which approves of one form of life no less than another. These principles, heard in the boudoirs of châteaux, were caught up and repeated from mouth to mouth in those gay and happy assemblies of rank and fashion, which we have hitherto found but the recreation grounds of courtly ladies and silk-bedizened troubadours, who with lute and song proclaimed the empire of ideal love. Not only were the Albigensian doctrines extremely appropriate to the theory of life among the troubadours, but coming from the East, they found a congenial soil in Provence at large, which we noticed at the beginning of this work as possessing an elective affinity to Oriental culture and life, and as having frequently at various times in its history submitted to the influence of Oriental ideas and even dominion. The same inherited facility, which made Provence give so ready a welcome to the art and to the music of the East, made it likewise welcome this offshoot of Eastern religion, though its welcome was destined to be disastrous in its consequences.

Another reason for the affinity of the creed with Provence, and particularly with the musical society which so readily received it, was the fact that the Albigensian doctrines of the religion of two principles, and all the minor tenets hanging to this main one, contained, if in a much perverted and vulgarised form, the main elements of certain old religions, or perhaps we should rather call them speculations, of antiquity, in which music played a large part, and which were, in fact, fathered by two musicians, the one a theorist, the other a legendary executant. Whatever be the historic position of Orpheus himself, certain it is that the Orphic fragments have ever carried weight as curious specimens of religious philosophy, while the opinions of Pythagoras are purely historical, so far as their authenticity goes. Both these systems of thought reposed on the Duality of Principles, and maintained that matter, which was the Evil Principle, was eternal and indestructible, and that at first a seething chaos, it was by the infusion of Good, which is Harmony, attuned to symmetry and order,—along with other subordinate tenets to the effect that the mainstay of the universe is the musical octave, etc., etc. Such a general elective affinity of creed recommended itself insensibly to the appreciation of the troubadours, and numerous were the converts who professed themselves Albigenses without at all understanding into what a wilderness of perils such a profession would lead them.

PRACTICAL RESULTS OF THE ADOPTION OF ALBIGENSIAN OPINIONS BY THE TROUBADOURS.—So long as the acceptance and appreciation of the creed limited itself to a mere abstract assent to principles in themselves not innocuous, but from their pacific character not presenting any danger to the powers that be, the curious propaganda was suffered to run its course unchecked. But ere long the troubadours, growing completely enamoured of their new doctrines, began to compare their creed with that of Rome, very much to the disadvantage of the latter; and since to think was with them the invariable precursor to expression, they did not scruple to put their views into music and verse, and hurl them at the obnoxious persons and institutions which provoked their spleen.

"God confound thee, Rome!" sang William de Figueira. "Thou draggest all who trust in thee into the bottomless pit. Thou forgivest sins for money, and takest the offences of others on thy shoulders, too much charged as they are with guilt already."[1]

In a similar spirit Bertrand of Marseilles attacked the clergy, though in what respect the Albigensian bishops were superior he leaves unsaid. "Ah! false and wicked clergy," he sings, " traitors, liars, thieves and miscreants, your balance is gold, and your pardons must be sought by silver. Your portion is the portion of hypocrisy, and the world rings with your roguery."[2]

Elsewhere we hear of churches being called " the dens of thieves," the cross " the mark of the beast"; altars, holy water, pilgrimages, confessionals, all denounced and vilified. Plainly this sort of rebellion could not be allowed to go on for long, more especially by such a sensitive

[1] Raynouard, *Choix des Poésies.*
[2] *Ibid.*

court as that of Rome, and loud were the complaints sent daily to the Vatican of the excesses against orthodox belief and the injuries to the power of the Church which were committed by the troubadours. The musical knights seem to have flung themselves into the breach in this religious contention with the same gallantry and recklessness of consequences which they manifested in the tilt-yard or at the crusades. But in espousing this new Albigensian creed, they were many of them in ignorance of what it fully meant, and how nearly all its tenets were in the eyes of strict Christians complete and damnable heresies.

The denial of Christ Himself was one of the prime tenets of the creed, the Albigensians boldly explaining His personality into a phantom or shadow of Ahrimasdes, the Principle of Good. Next to this repudiation, the denial of the Virgin Mary, whose repute was fast increasing in Christendom, followed as an easy consequence. Baptism was rejected and vilified, transubstantiation was denied; and, more particularly, derision and abuse were poured on the clergy, whose easy and often dissolute lives offered an excellent target to the attacks of fanatics, who, whatever may have been the impiety and nefariousness of their doctrines, were at least in earnest about what they believed.

RELIGIOUS ANTAGONISM AMONG THE TROUBADOURS.— A new occupant at this time ascended the Papal Chair, whose temper was certainly not disposed to tolerate or connive at these impious and sacrilegious opinions which were fast honeycombing the land of Provence. Even if he had been inclined to pass over with a smile the religious crazes of musicians and the heresies of ladies, the reports and urgent appeals which reached him continually from Provence would not have allowed him to remain idle.   Antagonistic to the large majority of amateur religionists and courtly dreamers, were a small but violent party of orthodox churchmen, among whom a few troubadours, pronounced recreants by their brethren, were prominently to the fore.   It was estimated by the contemporary chroniclers that all the principal troubadours except two were on the side of the Albigenses, and these recreant two were the troubadours Izarn and Fulke, the troubadour bishop of Marseilles.   Izarn was a man of extreme narrowness and violence of opinion, the chief merit of whose poetry consists in an unlimited power of vehement abuse, and curious skill in misrepresenting and traducing the views and spirit of his opponents.   Fulke of Marseilles had been in his youth the gayest and loosest of the troubadours, and had astonished his contemporaries by the recklessness of his living and his outrages on social propriety.   After a misspent life, he became in his maturer years a harsh and sour ascetic, and endeavoured to make people forget by the austerities of his demeanour those offences against social propriety of which he had been so notoriously guilty in his youth. Both Fulke and Izarn still retained their power of music and minstrelsy, although they had thrown in their lot with those whom the troubadours not very elegantly called " the black-coated rabble of Satan."   And if music and minstrelsy were in the meanwhile to carry on the duel, Fulke and Izarn declared themselves fully prepared, if not with success at least with determination, to champion the orthodox side.

A MUSICAL WAR.—Most curious was the musical and poetical battle which ensued. The troubadours used to send their jongleurs into the market-places on market days and at fair times, to sing odes and pasquinades dealing with the main points of the Christian and Albigensian religions, and lampooning most severely their adversaries. The jongleurs despatched on this strange errand acquitted themselves but too well, and striking their lutes or touching up their violins they very soon attracted the sympathies of scores of listeners, while they sang their masters' invectives against the Church and the Christian faith.

" If the Holy Ghost, who took the form of man," sang one troubadour,[1] appealing to the great deity of the Albigenses, " listens in aught to my prayers, I will stop thy mouth, O Rome, in whom all the perfidy of the Greeks is revived. Thou dost exceed the bounds prescribed thee by heaven ; and, a blind leader of the blind, thou draggest them into the bottomless pit. Do not talk of the world lying in wickedness, for it is treacherous Rome that is the authoress of all carping and strife."

On the other side the exact opposite was maintained. " Rome, thy laws," says a troubadour of the opposite party,[2] " ought to be strictly adhered to for ever. I trust

---

[1] William de Figueira.
[2] Germonda, *Le Parnasse Occitanien.*

that thy power will triumph over all pride and over all heresy. Cursed be those heretics who dread no vice and believe no mystery! Viler than Saracens are those miserable heretics, the dearest of whose wishes is that the people of Avignon, instead of going to Paradise, should be doomed to the flames of hell."

"Thy throne, O Rome," sings a hostile troubadour again, "is established in the bottomless pit. Thou takest the crooked road, O Rome, and woe be unto him who follows in thy track! Thou art a glutton of men. Like an enraged beast, thou devourest both great and small. If the good Count Raymond only lives, he will make men repent that they have abandoned themselves to thy impostures. Thy crimes, O Rome, arise from thy cardinals. Their only aim is to sell God and the friends of God. But I comfort myself in the assurance that Rome and her power will speedily decay, and that she herself will ere long cease to exist."

With coarse violence and obloquy Izarn issues his fulminations against the erring troubadours :—

"In what school hast thou been taught, my friend, that the soul of man, when it has quitted his body, goes into that of an ox, an ass, a sheep, or a pig, or into the first animal it meets with after its separation from the body, until it returns again into the body of some man or some woman? This, however, thou declarest for a fact to those thou hast seduced; thou takest from God to give to the devil; and thus dost thou hope to get salvation."

"Dost thou believe," thunders the same recreant troubadour elsewhere, "in the seven sacraments? Dost thou believe in the change of the elements into the body and blood of Christ ? "

" Let us suppose for a moment that thou art right in these points "—it is thus they proceed, in loud and rancorous argument with one another—" yet I will overthrow thy doctrine by another argument."

" In eight points I have convicted thee, obstinate heretic, and ere thou art delivered to the flames, take this to comfort thee at thy burning."

CRUSADE AGAINST THE TROUBADOURS AND ALBIGENSES. —With such heat and animosity was the argument conducted, that it was evident to the most dispassionate observer that the present state of things could not last long. In due course Innocent III. authorised the organisation of a crusade against the heretics, and the merits and advantages of this holy war were preached from a thousand pulpits in Italy and France, as if the enemy to be attacked were Oriental infidels instead of knights and gentlemen of European renown, and crowds of unfortunate peasants who even yet in name were Christian. Fulke was foremost in the good work of exciting the animosity of his co-religionists against the hated " sons of Belial," as he delighted to call them, and the crusaders, assembling under the command of Simon de Montfort and the Papal Legate, Arnold of Citeaux, made preparations for entering the land of infidelity, which they were soon to convert into a blackened wilderness. Meanwhile, on the other side, the troubadours were arming, chevaliers and knights of high degree gathering their retainers and vassals, drilling their troops, and pouring forth in the enthusiasm of the moment martial songs and calls to arms innumerable. And there was putting of castles in defence throughout Provence, and concerting of plans of military operations. The leaders of the troubadours were the Counts of Toulouse and of Foix, the Counts of Béarn and of Comminges, the Vicomte de Beziers, Guy de Cavaillon, Guillaume de Montagnogont, Arnauld de Comminges, Raymond de Miravals, Guillaume Rainols d'Apt, Bertrand de Marseilles, and other troubadours of lesser note.

INCIDENTS OF THE CRUSADE.—It was against the Vicomte de Beziers that the fury of the crusaders first discharged itself. The enormity of the multitudes which had assembled under the banner of the cross to engage in this holy work of indiscriminate pillage, may be judged by the fact that nearly a quarter of a million of men are stated to have composed the army of the crusaders. We must be careful of accepting such a statement as a completely truthful account of the numbers. The main authority for an account of this crusade is an epic poem by an anonymous troubadour, entitled *Aisos es la Cansos de la Crozada contr els Ereges d'Albeges*, and epic poets have an excusable tendency to magnify numbers or to exaggerate events for poetical purposes. At the same time we must remember that to these crusades crowds of persons in unparalleled and enormous multitudes used to flock, led on by fanaticism and the hope of plunder; and if we were to use a well-worn expression in the social life of to-day, we might say that "the unemployed," ever in evidence in the world, swarmed *en masse* to the religious wars in the hope of improving their condition by what could be made out of peculation. The immense multitudes which crowded to the standards of Peter the Hermit and Walter the Penniless, consisting of people of all ages and of both sexes, were parallelled by the hordes which, if not enormous, were certainly swelling, and which attending at the summons of Innocent, accompanied Simon de Montfort and the Papal Legate to the war. We have said that the fury of the invaders was first wreaked on the Vicomte de Beziers. Hither against the town of Beziers, a host consisting of twenty thousand men-at-arms, and two hundred thousand combatants of lower rank, besides bishops and clergy countless in multitude (we give the census of the epic poet), marched in panoply and fury, carrying a large cross at the head of their host, and intoning psalms and litanies as they passed over the fruitful fields.

"God never made clerk or grammarian so learned," says the troubadour who has sung of the war, "that he could recount the names of the clergy and abbots in that host."[1] "And see," he continues, "in what spirit they came!" 'There shall not one stone be left on another,' said the Papal Legate in allusion to unfortunate Beziers, a town of comparatively small size, which had to endure the brunt of all this expedition.

"When the town was captured," continues the troubadour, "and the Papal Legate, Arnold of Citeaux, was asked by the general how the soldiers were to distinguish between Christians and Albigenses: 'Slay them all,' he said. 'The Lord knoweth them that are His.'"[1]

---

[1] *Aisos es la Cansos de la Crozada contr els Ereyes d'Albeyes.* [2] *Ibid.*

In pursuance of this sanguinary edict, which involved heretic and believer in like destruction, the entire population of Beziers were slaughtered like sheep, and the city of Beziers was set on fire. Next the crusaders marched to Carcassonne, where the Vicomte de Beziers, who had not been present at the sack of his city, commanded in person. The siege of the town was commenced by the operations of several large military engines, all of which were surmounted by huge crosses. At a short distance from the soldiers stood the clergy, the bishops, and the inquisitors, intoning antiphons and psalms, and exciting the crusaders to deeds of daring. Meanwhile inside the town was the music of guitars and violins, the jongleurs parading the streets, and singing to the desperate people their masters' songs, who themselves were on the bastions leading the defence against the foe. The same unfortunate fate which had overtaken Beziers was likewise the fortune of Carcassonne. The city was taken by storm, the hordes of invaders poured into the streets, the population were massacred wholesale, and four hundred of the more impious were chosen to be burnt at a public *auto-da-fé*, which was intended to strike terror into the heretics. And next against the Count of Toulouse the fury of the crusaders turned itself—but why should we pursue the details of an enterprise, which resulted in the ruin of Provençal poetry and song, and the extermination of those gallant troubadours who were its gay and artistic exponents? For after scores of such captures, and after repetitions of such massacres, in which the noblest and fairest fell victims to the zeal of the crusaders, at the very crisis of the crusade, Pedro, the troubadour King of Arragon, having but recently triumphed over the Moors of Spain in the battle of Navas de Tolosa, found himself at last at liberty to help his brother troubadours and kinsmen. Accordingly he sent a sirvente or war song to the camp of the crusaders, entrusting its delivery to one of his jongleurs, who was bidden to sing it to the assembled host as the message of the king. The jongleur proceeded in the performance of his task with due care, and was happy in his minstrelsy until he came to this phrase of his master's ditty: "For the love of my lady I am coming to drive ye out, barbarians, from that beautiful land that ye have ravaged and destroyed."

Hereupon one of the crusaders called out with ready wit, "So help me God! I do not fear a king who comes against God's cause for the sake of a harlot."[1] This brought the song to an untimely end.

CONTINUANCE OF THE CRUSADE AND EXTINCTION OF THE TROUBADOURS.—Pedro began to collect his army and set out on his march. Let us hear the troubadour who sings of the war describe his coming:—"The good king of Arragon," he sings, "on his good steed is come to Muret, and has raised his banners, and assembled round him many a rich vassal who owes allegiance to his crown. He has brought with him the flower of Catalonia, and great knights from Arragon. And yet all these valiant men and all their beautiful armour he must lose."[2] For

---

[1] *Aisos es la Cansos de la Crozada.*
[2] *Ibid.*

he came with all his host and was conquered in that battle of Muret. Himself was slain, and his gallant army either perished on the field, or were driven into the waters of the Garonne. Deprived of the expected aid from the king of Arragon, the unfortunate people were now abandoned as a prey to their enemies. The crusaders made a holocaust. Remorseless destruction was spread far and wide. Castle after castle was taken; town after town was razed to the ground; and at every place, at every capture, there was indiscriminate murder and cruel slaughter. When the crusaders captured La Minerve near Narbonne, they committed many enormities of more or less atrocious character, but specially signalized their conquest by selecting one hundred and forty of the Albigenses and burning them alive in a great bonfire, all being thrown in together. Simon de Montfort, the general of the crusaders, whose name is synonymous with chivalry and gallantry, was nevertheless hurried forward into the excesses of his companions, and did not scruple to torture to death one hundred innocent captives at the sack of another town. When once the passions of mankind have been excited by war there seems to be no limit to which cruelty and bloodshed will not go, while the cause of the contention is obliterated in the fury of the combatants. We might enumerate numerous incidents similar to the preceding. At Lavaur, for instance, eighty chevaliers, many of them troubadours, convicted of complicity with the heretics, were gibbeted. While the sister of Almeric, the troubadour commander, was charged with complicated incest, thrown down a deep well, and oppressed with stones. By the intervention of " a Frenchman courteous and gay," the other ladies of the town were spared, but four hundred of the most impious of the Albigenses, with their troubadour leaders, were burnt " with immense joy " by the crusaders. Wherever the pageant of monks, military and clergy, traversed the fertile land, they left desolation and ruin behind them; vineyards were blackened and destroyed, gardens and fields were trampled on and harried, towns and cities reduced to ruins, villages burnt, castles wrecked and razed.

Under such circumstances culture was fain to hide its head. All the stimulus to poetry and song was taken away by the annihilation of the bright and glittering society which had been minstrelsy's chief inspirer and genial patron. The gay reign of love and the troubadours was over for ever.

APPENDICES

A Note on the Geography of Minstrelsy.—At a certain period of history, it seems as if music and song are the chief modes of recreation among the people, and in song and story are told tales of the gods, of war, and of politics. Minstrelsy is widespread, and when it is not varied by religion, where also life anticipates some of the ease of later days, the minstrel's calling may be taken up even by the most noble. It spreads to whatever places chivalry is found in, and prepares the way for further literature.

The Minnesingers in Germany in the thirteenth century may well be compared in many important respects with the troubadours. The names of the more celebrated of them, Hartmann von der Aue, Walter von der Vogelweidt, Wolfram von Eschenbach, Gottfried von Strassburg and others, have attained an abiding renown in Germany, though not a European fame.

On the Information afforded by the Troubadours as to the Political and Social Life of the Time.—Politics played a great part in the sirventes of the troubadours. We may take as a striking example of this the sirvente of Richard Cœur-de-Lion against the Dauphin of Auvergne. The sirventes of Bertrand de Born, Richard's intimate friend, abound also in political allusions. The famous English troubadour, Savari de Mauléon, has furnished us likewise with many political allusions. While the sirventes are the main mine for political information, the entire corpus of troubadour poetry abounds with matters of remarkable interest on social topics, and it must be added that while the political information is generally concerned with the by-paths of history and forgotten intrigues between princes or barons, the social

information is broad and luminous, and sheds a flood of light
on the manners of the time. We have, for instance, in the
works of one of the troubadours [1] an entire code of etiquette
according to the ideas of the period, in which behaviour is
regulated down to the art of paring the nails and washing
the hands. Ladies are exhorted not to lace too tightly, from
which we may infer that a habit common among their fair
sisters of to-day was equally and recklessly indulged in by the
lady-loves of the troubadours.

ON THE PLACE OF THE TROUBADOURS IN THE HISTORY OF
LITERATURE AS A WHOLE.—To set down the poetry of the
troubadours and trouvères as the commencement of modern
literature, does not seem to be by any means a rash assumption or generalisation. There can be no doubt that although
the bulk of the English minstrelsy which has descended to
us from them, is written in a tongue different from the language spoken in our isles at present, the influence of it, as
propagated through not only translations, but through its
bilingual and cultivated hearers, must have been exceedingly
strong and permanent, and could not have perished in order
that a new English literature might begin. The large obligations which Chaucer is under to these forgotten pioneers
of our literature, both in style of thought and form of expression, will be apparent to all readers of that poet.

ON THE AUTHORITIES CITED AND EMPLOYED.—Most of the
writings of the troubadours are still in MS., and must be
studied at the Bibliothèque Nationale, Paris; the Bodleian
Library, Oxford; the British Museum, and elsewhere. Most
particularly is the first-named library rich in MSS. of this
nature, and with especial regard to the music of the troubadours, it is only here that satisfactory researches can be
made. MSS. of Chardry; Thomas de Bailleul; Denis
Pyramus; Benoît de Sainte-More; Adam de Ros; the Saxon
Trouvère; Adam le Clerc; Richard Annebaut; William de
Wadington; Peter Langtoft; Marie de France, and of the

---

[1] Amanieu des Escas.

romances of *King Horn*, *Sir Fierabras*, etc., etc., are in
the British Museum. The Bodleian Library at Oxford pos-
sesses likewise an excellent MS. of *King Horn*. The third
complete MS. of this romance is in the Cambridge University
Library. The MS. of *Generydes* is in the library of Trinity
College, Cambridge. The library of Corpus Christi College,
Cambridge, possesses a valuable MS. of the *Distiques* of
Hélie de Winchester. The best MSS. of *Sir Eglamour* and
Sir Degrevant are likewise at Cambridge.

LIST OF AUTHORITIES CITED IN THIS WORK

Abulfeda, *Annales.*—Aimericus de Pergrato.—*Aisos es la Cansos de la Crozada contr els Ereges d'Albeges.*—Albertus Canonicus Aquensis Ecclesiæ, *Historia Hierosolymitanæ Expeditionis.*—Ali of Ispahan, *Liber Cantilenarum.*—Al. Marrekoshi, *History of the Almohades.*—Ammianus Marcellinus.—Andreas Capellanus, *Tractatus Amoris et de Amoris Remedio, sive* André, *Livre de l'Art d'Aimer.*—Andres, *Dell' Origine e Stato Attuale d'Ogni Letteratura.* —*Anecdotes Arabes* (Paris, 1752).—Anna Comnena, *Alexias.*— Apchier, Garins d'.—*Archæologia.*—*Aucassin et Nicolette.*—*Aye d'Avignon.*—Bailleul, Thomas de.—Balaguer, *Historia de los Trovadores* (Madrid, 1888).—Barche, *Essai sur l'Histoire de Provins* (Marseilles).—Bartsch, *Chrestomathie Provençale.*—*Beowulf, The Deeds of,* edited by Earle.—Bertrand de Born.—Blanqui, *History of Political Economy.*—Blount, *Law Dictionary.*—Bourdillon, *Introduction to "Aucassin et Nicolette."*—Burney, *History of Music.*— Cabreira, Giraud de.—Cadenet.—Calanson, Giraud de.—Camden. —Capdeuil, Pons de.—Cardonne, *Histoire de l'Afrique et de l'Espagne.*—*Cartulaire de Bullington.*—Casiri, *Historia Arabe.*— *Chambre des Comptes, Depôt du Greffe.*—Chardry.—Chaucer, *Troilus.*—Child, *History of Women.*—Clerc, Adam le.—*Cotton MSS.*— Crescimbeni, *Vite de' Poeti Provenzali.*—*La Cronique de Normandie.* —*Les Croniques et Excellentz Faits des Ducs de Normandie.*— Cunningham, *Growth of English Industry and Commerce.*—*Cursor Mundi,* edited by G. R. Morris.—Daniel, Arnaud.—Dante, *De Vulgari Eloquio.*—D'Aretin, *Aussprüche der Minnegerichte* (Munich, 1803).—Le Dauphin d'Auvergne.—Davies' *Extracts from York Records.*—*De Cangé MSS.*—De la Rue, *Essais Historiques.*—Denis Pyramus.—*Les Deux Menestriers* (Bodleian MS.).—Diago, *Historia de los Victoriosissimos Condes de Barcelona.*—Diez, *Die Poesie der Troubadours.*—Diez, *Leben und Werke der Troubadours* (Zwickau, 1829).—Diodorus Siculus.- *Les Dits de Hue Archevesque.*—*Domesday Book.*—Donaldson, *Theatre of the Greeks.*—Ducange, *Glossarium.*

—Duchesne, *Normannorum Historia Scriptorum.*—Dugdale, *Monasticon.*—Eccleston, *Introduction to English Antiquities.*—*Eglamour of Artois, Sir.*—*English Guilds.*—Escas, Amanieu de.—Fabre, *Histoire de Marseille.*—Fabre, *Histoire de Provence.*—Fabricius, *Bibliotheca Latina Medii Ævi.*—Fauchet.—Fauriel, *Histoire de la Poésie Provençale.*—Fétis, *Histoire de la Musique.*—*Fierabras, Sir.*—Finlay, *History of Greece.*—*Flamenca.*—*Floire et Blanceflor.*—Fortunatus.—Fournier, *Le Royaume d'Arles et de Vienne.*—Fulcherius Carnotensis, *Gesta Peregrinantium Francorum.*—*Fundgraben des Orients.*—Gaufridi, *Histoire de Provence.*—Gauterius, *Bella Antiochena.*—*Sir Gawayne and the Green Knight.*—*Generydes.*—Geoffrey of Monmouth, *Historia Britonum.*—Gerbert, *Musica Antiqua.*—Ginguené, *Histoire Littéraire de France.*—Ginguené, *Histoire Littéraire d'Italie.*—Giraldus Cambrensis.—Grimm, *Rechtsalterthümer.*—Guibert, *Gesta Dei per Francos.*—Guy de Chalis.—*Guy of Warwick.*—*Harleian MSS.*—Hawkins, *History of Music.*—*Histoire de la Vie Privée.*—*Histoire Littéraire de la France.*—Hoveden, Roger de.—*Hugues Capet.*—*Huon of Bordeaux.*—Ibn Chaldun, in *Fundgraben des Orients.*—*Issue Roll of Thomas Brantingham.*—*Isumbras, Sir.*—Jorsen, *Notes to the Arabic Version of the " Thousand and One Nights."*—Jusserand, *Wayfaring Life.*—Justinus Lippiensis.—Kiesewetter, *La Musique des Arabes.*—*King Horn.*—La Borde, *Essai sur la Musique.*—La Grange, Marquis de, *Preface to " Hugues Capet."*—*Lais Inédits.*—Lambertus Ardensis.—Lane, *Arabians of the Middle Ages.*—*Le Bel Inconnu.*—Le Grand d'Aussy, *Fabliaux et Contes.*—Lenthéric, *La Provence Maritime.*—Lerberke, *Chronicon Comitum.*—Lewis, *Greek Tragedy.*—*London Restituta.*—Luc du Gast.—Madox, *History of the Exchequer.*—Marie de France.—Martial d'Auvergne, *Arrests d'Amour.*—Massieu, *Storia della Poesia Francese.*—Mattheson, *Critica Musica.*—Matthew Paris.—Mauléon, Savari de.—Menckenius, *Miscellanea Lipsiensia Nova.*—Michaud, *Histoire des Croisades.*—*Middelalderens Elskovshaffer* (Copenhagen, 1888).—Millot, *Histoire Littéraire des Troubadours.*—Moulton, *Ancient Classical Drama.*—MSS., many, as alluded to in notes, principally in the Bodleian Library, Oxford; the British Museum, London; the Bibliothèque Nationale, Paris; and the Bibliothèque de Montpellier.—Nostradamus, Jean de, *Les Vies des Plus Célèbres Troubadours.*—Orange, Rambaud d'.—*Le Parnasse Occitanien.*—*Partenopeus de Blois.*—Pelloutier, *Histoire des Celtes.*—*Perceval of Galles, Sir.*—Perron, *Femmes Arabes avant et depuis*

l'Islamisme (Algiers, 1858).—Petrarch, *Res Seniles.*—*Philoména.*—
Pluquet, *Notice sur la Vie de Geoffroy Gaimar.*—*Poésies du Roi de
Navarre.*—Poulson's *Beverlac.*—Power, *History of the Mussulmans
in Spain.*—Prætorius, *Syntagma Musicum.*—Prudentius.—Raynouard, *Choix des Poésies des Troubadours.*—Reissmann, *Musikalisches Conversations-Lexikon.*—*Reliquiæ Manuscriptorum Omnis Ævi.*
—*Revue Critique.*—Richard Cœur-de-Lion.—Ricobaldus Ferrariensis.—Riquier, Giraud.—Ritson, *Dissertation on Romance and Minstrelsy.*—Ritson, *Notes to " Ywaine and Gawin."*—Robertson, *Historical Essays.*—Robson, *Introduction to " Three Metrical Romances."*—
*Roll of Household Expenses of Richard de Swinfield, Bishop of Here-
ford.*—Rolland, *Recherches sur les Cours d'Amour.*—*Roman d'Alex-
andre.*—Ros, Adam de.—Rossillon, Giraud de.—*Li Roumans dou
Chastelain de Couci.*—Rowbotham, *History of Music.*—Rymer,
Fœdera.—St. Didier, William de.—Sainte-Palaye, La Curne de,
Histoire Littéraire des Troubadours.—Scheid, *Dissertatio de Jure in
Musicos.*—Schott, *Proverbia Græca.*—Silvester, Bernardus, *De Gu-
bernatione Rei Familiaris.*—Sismondi, *Histoire de la Littérature du
Midi de l'Europe.*—Söderhelm, *Anteckningar* (Helsingfors, 1889).—
Statuta Concilii Sarisburensis.—Stimmung, *Bertrand de Born.*—
Strabo.—Strutt, *Horda.*—Taine, *Histoire Littéraire de l'Angleterre.*
—Thornton, *Nottinghamshire.*—Tytler, *Lives of Scottish Worthies.*
—Vaqueiras, Rambaud de.—Ventadour, Bernard de.—Verelius,
Runografia.—Villedat, *Sur la Position Historique de Bertrand de
Born.*—Volstanus Diaconus.—Von Aretin, *Beiträge zur Geschichte*
(Monaco, 1888).—Wace, Robert, *Roman de Brut.*—Wace, Robert,
Roman de Rou.—Warton, *History of English Poetry.*—Welfitt,
Extracts from Canterbury Records.—William of Malmesbury.—
William of Poitou.—William of Tyre.—Winchester, Hélie de.—
Wright, *Domestic Manners and Sentiments.*—*York Plays.*—*Ywaine
and Gawin.*

INDEX

Butler & Tanner, The Selwood Printing Works, Frome, and London.

ATLANTIC OCEAN
NORTH SEA
Biscay
MEDITERRANEAN
BLACK SEA
ST PETERSBURG
HAMBURG
BERLIN
COLOGNE
COBLENG
VIENNA
PARIS
LYONS
GENOA
BARCELONA
ROME
NAPLES
SICILY
GIBRALTAR
CONSTANTINOPLE
CRIMEA
TAGANROG
TREBIZOND
ALEPPO
Long W of Greenwich
Long E of Greenwich